Alone, isolated from the vast resources of Guardian, Dixon Simmons reentered a world that had left him impossibly damaged as a child. He stepped back into that evil by choice. To protect all he'd come to love, he was willing to pay whatever price was demanded—even if the price was his soul.

She went by many names. Her true identity was as dead as her heart. Until him. The man was every bit as lethal as she was and deliciously sexy. Dixon Simmons piqued her interest, and what started as lust turned into another "L" word. She gave a "forever after" with him no hope. They'd have to stay alive for that to happen.

Caught in a violent abyss of ultimate malevolence and ominous threats, two damned souls find in each other a redemptive love that defies reason. However, redemption comes at a high cost. They must first save the world from a merciless force known only as Stratus.

DIXON

THE KINGS OF GUARDIAN - BOOK TWELVE

KRIS MICHAELS

❀ Created with Vellum

CHAPTER 1

ARUBA, eighteen months ago–

DIXON SIMMONS SAUNTERED INTO ONE OF THE upstairs rooms of Joseph King's palatial beachfront home in Aruba. The sound of the post-wedding festivities on the beach filtered through the open windows, accompanied by the ever-present sound of the Caribbean surf. Zane Reynolds and Jewell King had finally taken off enough time to say "I do" in front of a preacher. He was very happy for them. He was also very happy it was *them*, not him. He didn't see marriage happening for him—ever. "What did you need to see me about, boss man?"

Jason King, his boss, and CEO of Guardian Security dropped into a huge wingback chair and loosened his tie. The man dwarfed the chair, and Dixon was surprised the thing didn't shatter on impact.

"Take a seat, D." Jason pointed to the matching chair across from him.

A sense of foreboding soured his gut. Two things were wrong with this scenario. One, Drake wasn't here, so this wasn't a training complex issue, and two, the look in Jason's eyes told him shit was about to get serious.

He planted his ass in the chair. "What's up?"

"I'm not going to beat around the bush on this." Jason nodded his head as if he agreed with himself.

"Well, I appreciate that." Dixon had no stomach for bullshit. Never had.

"What do you know about Stratus?" Jason leaned forward and planted his elbows on his knees, staring straight at him.

Dixon chuckled. "You mean the folklore? They're some kind of ultra-badass bullshit organization bent on total domination of the world. Shades of James-fucking-Bond. Why?"

Jason took off his glasses and folded them

neatly before he set them precisely in the middle of a glass-topped, white wicker side table. He looked back at Dixon.

Fuck him standing. "No." His denial was out before his brain caught up.

Jason sighed and glanced at the door. "What I'm about to tell you doesn't leave this room."

"All right."

"No, I mean it is between you and me only. Drake is not part of this conversation, and he can never know what I'm about to say without my express consent."

Dixon narrowed his eyes and stared intently at his boss. The man had never prefaced any conversation with the demand he keep secrets from his twin. It was like asking the right hand to keep a secret from the left hand. "Why?"

"Because it involves your father."

Ice cold hatred crystalized in his veins, and each burr of frozen hate carried a lifetime of memories back from the obscurity where he'd pushed them. He ground out words through a clenched jaw, "What the fuck are you talking about?"

"Do I have your word that nothing I say leaves this room?"

Dixon jerked his head in a nod because talking right now was too fucking much to ask of him. "Within the last two years, nuggets of substance have emerged from some of the interrogations we have conducted. We've intercepted several coded messages—the likes of which we've never seen—glimpses of data, human intelligence, and other random incidents that have confirmed our suspicions." Jason steepled his fingers together. His focus drifted to his hands as he spoke. "Stratus is real, and it is global. From what we can determine, they have viable monetary resources, although we have yet to identify the source."

Dixon stood and ran his hands through his hair. "What does Stratus have to do with my fucking sperm donor?"

"The FBI asked for our help in an operation. Long story short, while several of our domestic operations investigators were working a case in New York, they stumbled across certain intelligence we were able to piece into the information we had already acquired. During the course of the subsequent investigation, we confirmed what we believe to be Stratus connections to the underbelly of crime in New York."

"And?" Dixon glared at Jason.

Jason lifted an eyebrow and restated his words, "Stratus exists and is linked to illegal activities in New York."

Dixon put his hands on his hips and glared at his boss. *He. Would. Not. Go. There.*

"Your father is our way into Stratus."

"Fuck. You." Dixon walked away from Jason so he wouldn't hit the man. Drake wasn't here to keep him from committing careeracide.

"The threat of this organization is global. It is real, and if we can get a fingerhold, just a fucking fingerhold, Dix, it could save us years of work and potentially thousands of lives."

"What the fuck are you talking about?" Dixon spun around.

"Intelligence we have indicates Stratus is building assets through organizations like your father's."

"But you don't know that son of a bitch is involved."

Jason lifted his eyes. "Your father is as dirty as they come. He hasn't been charged or prosecuted because he owns people. He's climbing the ladder, gaining power and influence, two of the things Stratus wants. Since he lost the city councilman seat, he's been maneuvering to find favor in his party's camp. He is the perfect candidate for Stratus. If they aren't involved with him, they are watching him."

"What do you think I can do? He knows I'm with Guardian. We haven't hidden that." Both he and Drake would flaunt it in the fucker's face if they could.

"We can craft an exit for you. Of the two of you, he'd take *you* back."

At Jason's words bile rolled and surged in his gut. His father would take him back because the sadistic bastard swore Dixon was just like him. He Was. Not. *He couldn't be.* He didn't know how to respond. The shit his father had made him do. The things he'd unknowingly done. "I..."

"You're not that damaged child anymore, Dixon. You've been working with Doctor Wheeler for years, and he thinks you can handle this." At the comment, his eyes leveled on Jason. The man continued, "Do you think

I'd ask you to go back there without full knowledge of your mental state?"

Dixon turned his back and walked to the window. White fairy lights illuminated the wood deck where his friends and family gathered to celebrate Jewell and Zane's wedding. "You don't know what you're asking."

"That's where you're wrong. I do know. I'm asking you to go back to the monster who forced you into impossible choices—choices no child should ever have to make. But I'm going to arm you with everything you need to take your vengeance on that motherfucker. In conjunction with the Council, we've worked up a list of coded targets within your father's realm of illegal businesses—all are sanctioned hits. He'll require proof of your allegiance. He'll demand you pay. The names are your way back in, should you need them. Until this mission is over, you are the only asset who will have access to those names."

"I'm not a Shadow."

"No, but if necessary, you will use the sanctioned list as a means of showing your loyalty to your father."

"What, exactly, do you need me to do?"

"Find us a way into Stratus."

"It could take...years."

"It could."

"What do I tell Drake? I have to give him an exceptional reason for my severing all contact. If I just disappear, he will leave Guardian and hunt me down. You *know* he will."

"He cannot go with you. He will kill the bastard for what he did to you."

That was the truth. "What makes you think I won't?"

"I don't doubt you would, but imagine the satisfaction in taking him down. Making his life's work, his ambition...void. Making him impotent before that happens. It's payback time, Dixon. Do you want in? Do you want to take back the life that bastard took from you, or do you want to continue allowing Drake to be your life support while his life passes him by?"

Dixon stifled the 'fuck you' on his lips. He watched his brother through the window as he mingled with their friends below.

"He's protected you since the day your uncle took you away from your father."

Which was true. He didn't know exactly

how it had happened, but it had. At first, it was just them. Drake had held him through the nightmares and the terror that followed. He held him when the darkness knocked him to his knees, and the memories made him vomit the contents of his stomach. It had always been his brother who'd pulled him out of those horrific times, and Dixon had hung on to Drake with all that was in him. Drake had saved him from drowning in evil, and he basked in the normalcy his brother literally forced into his life.

He hadn't realized until this moment he was still doing that—letting Drake sacrifice his life. Jason's words shined a spotlight onto an ugliness he'd chosen not to look at, but the truth was undeniable. There wasn't an instance he could recall where Drake hadn't left something he wanted to ensure whatever Dixon wanted was the priority. Hell, the man even shared women with him, and Dixon knew, deep down, a threesome wasn't his brother's thing. Did that make him a selfish bastard? Yeah, it did.

Drake's presence held the manic side that lived inside Dixon at bay. Dixon's large personality rolled over Drake's more quiet nature, but they had found a balance. The anger that burned deep inside of him wasn't the same as the anger Drake lived with. Drake's anger was for Dixon's sake, for what Dixon had gone through. Had Drake suffered? Yes, but Dixon knew his brother had worked through his shit with Doctor Wheeler.

Dixon's anger ran through his veins and lived inside him because of what *he'd* done, what *he'd* lived and what *he'd* witnessed. He and Drake had an understanding, and they had each other. Drake gave, and Dixon took. That was a constant. It worked, at least for him. He watched Drake laughing as he and Jacob headed to the poolside bar. "I'm one selfish son of a bitch."

"No, you're existing. Maybe it's time to take control of your life and start living." Jason stood, walked to the window, and stood beside him.

"This is going to hurt him." Dixon nodded at the gathering below them.

"He's already hurting, Dix. It's time to start the process of healing. For both of you."

"How long do I have?"

"For?"

"New York?"

"When you're ready."

Dixon nodded and headed toward the door.

"Dix?"

"Yeah?"

"I've got your back man. Whatever it takes."

Dixon nodded. He knew Jason wasn't blowing smoke up his ass, but the words he spoke in return almost choked him. "As long as it takes, Jace. As long as it fucking takes."

CHAPTER 2

PRESENT DAY:

"OPERATOR TWO-SEVEN-FOUR."

"Sunset clearance, zero operative."

"Standby, zero operative."

"Archangel."

"The asset is still doing grunt work. His talent is being wasted."

"Meaning?" Archangel's voice held an edge of irritation.

"Meaning he's spent the last two weeks collecting money from pimps, and roughing up a moron drug dealer that tried to skim money off the top. That one is lucky to be alive. The fool pulled a knife on him. Our asset has impressive skills."

"It has only been three months. We didn't think he'd be welcomed with open arms."

"Hmmm."

"Can you get closer?"

"Depends. Do you need me closer?"

"If the opportunity presents itself. Check in as scheduled unless something happens."

"Of course."

DIXON ROLLED HIS SHOULDERS AND CHECKED HIS anger at the door. It was a conscious decision, and an act that got harder to perform with each passing day. His hand lifted to the ornate gold knobs that opened the rich mahogany doors to his father's study. The bastard's opulent brownstone was built off the proceeds from the prostitution and drugs that built the man's empire. Of course, the bastard had invested in legitimate businesses, and they were the only items on the income sheet his potential constituents and business partners saw. A deadly viper in a mirage of respectability. His immoral hypocrisy oozed out of his pores, and the stench of it made Dixon's gut roll.

He'd stepped three feet inside the viper's den and the man snapped, "Well, did you get the money?"

"Yeah."

"What?" The word whipped forward like a rattler's strike.

Fuuuck... Dixon cleared his throat. "Yes, sir."

The man glared at him. Dead eyes. There was never any emotion in those eyes—just death.

"Sit."

Dixon unbuttoned his suit coat and sat down. The bespoke suit he wore was another layer of his father's propaganda. When he was on the streets kicking ass and collecting Daddy-dearest's blood money, he wore jeans, shitkickers, t-shirts and leather coats. But he wouldn't dare come to his father's house in anything but a suit.

"How long have you been back?"

Four months, three days and five hours, you motherfucker. "About four months."

His father spat, "Four months since you

showed up in my territory. Four months since you turned your back on your brother and his way of life. Four months."

"Four months of freedom. Of not being held down by those assholes anymore. Four months of showing you I can be what you wanted me to be. It took a hell of a long time for me to figure life out, but I am where I need to be." The lies tasted bitter on his tongue.

"So you say." His father examined him.

Dixon shrugged. It was all he could do. Either the man believed him, or he didn't. Only time would tell. Four months of kowtowing to the monster that had permanently scarred him and Drake. Yeah, the motherfucker had taken his ten pounds of flesh over the last four months, and Dixon had given him additional blood, sweat, and tears on top of what the fucker wanted, just to prove himself.

His father stood and turned around, pulling the picture behind his desk away from the wall. Dixon gave a mental chuff of laughter at the small safe located behind it. How very gangsterish of his old man. However, the retinal scanner on the damn thing was impressive. He wondered how long it would take Justin to break into something like that. Guardian's resident cat burglar had mad skills.

His father punched in a code after the scan that switched the light to green. Dixon didn't attempt to see what his father was doing. He knew the old man had the house wired. Every move he made when he was here was recorded. Jason had told him the system was on a closed loop, hardwired and inaccessible unless the hacker was on site. Dixon could do basic shit, but his forte wasn't hacking or coding, so he was careful to be exactly what he wanted his father to believe he was, no more, no less.

As Dixon watched him, it registered that this was the first time his father had turned his back on him since he'd returned. The gun in his shoulder holster heated his ribs like a branding iron. The bastard wasn't stupid, he knew what he was doing, and Dixon had no doubt it was a test of some sort. Everything the man had put him through since he'd showed up at his door had been a test. Dixon had spent four months doing shit a junior-rated thug would have found coma inducing.

His father turned with a folder in his hand. "Here." He handed it to Dixon before he sat down in his throne of a chair situated behind his massive desk. Dixon rose out of his seat to take the file and then dropped back down. He didn't look at it or open it. One of the very first lessons his father had taught him when he'd taken sole custody of him was *never* act without permission. He'd been beaten until he passed out on more than one occasion for doing so. Childhood memories of days spent with Dad. *Good times.*

"I want this problem eradicated." His father nodded at the folder on his lap. Dixon continued to stare at the man. His father relaxed back into the comfort of his throne and held Dixon's stare.

Eradicated. That was a term Dixon learned, too. So, he wanted whomever was in the folder dead. This was a step in the right direction…at least as far as Guardian was concerned.

"Take Mr. Smith with you."

Dixon cocked his head at his father. "You don't think I can do this by myself?"

His father crossed his fingers over a belly that was growing a bit soft in his old age. "Are you questioning me?"

"In this instance, yes. Witnesses are loose

ends, which means I'm going to die, or Mr. Smith is going to die."

An evil smile spread across his father's face. "You have a very good memory."

Oh, he remembered, and Dixon tried not to physically react to the violent memories. He remembered watching his father debate who to kill, and he remembered dropping to his knees in relief when his father murdered the teenage boy beside him instead of him. *His old man walked over to him and pushed the hot barrel against his temple and hissed, "Witnesses are loose ends. Loose ends will not be tolerated."* Yes, he remembered, and it was another notch on the fucked-up belt that tied him to his old man.

Dixon stared across the expanse of the mahogany desk. He waited. Volunteer nothing, give nothing, do nothing unless told to do it. A mantra to live by...at least while in his father's presence.

"Go alone. Don't disappoint me." The man leaned forward and pulled his laptop across the expanse of his desk.

Dixon lifted to his feet and opened the folder. A name and an address. Another test no doubt. Dixon read the information a second time. He closed the folder and dropped it on his father's desk and spun on his heel. Turning his back on his old man sent a cold chill up his spine every single time he did it, but he needed to show the bastard he wasn't the scared boy he used to be. The fucker's intimidation tactics wouldn't work any longer. Dixon was literally a killing machine. He'd learned from the best and had trained countless others. He slowly ambled out of the mausoleum of an office. The name in the file was one he already knew. It was one he'd memorized a little over four months ago. He stopped at the front door and retrieved his overcoat and cashmere scarf before donning both and heading out into the chill of autumn air.

The last four months had been hell on earth. The future didn't look any better, but he'd manage. His father was a peacock, and the fucker was ambitious. When he could, Dixon would encourage the man, provide him an opportunity to strut his imagined magnificence. *Dixon* was the stronger of the two of them. He knew that now. He'd made it through the hell his father had put him through, and he'd grown strong. His life was filled with examples of men who didn't need the affirmation of others or financial or political influence. Strength came from within. He'd survive any beating his old man would hand out—mental or physical.

It took fifteen minutes to walk to where he'd left his vehicle. It gave him time to leverage the lessons he'd learned from Dr. Jeremiah Wheeler. The man had been his therapist since he'd taken up residence at the ranch. Dixon wouldn't have been able to deal with the mental refuse his father dredged up if it weren't for Jeremiah's voice playing on repeat in his mind. He wasn't responsible for the atrocities his father committed. His father was the monster and his father, the man responsible for his welfare, had put him in impossible positions and forced him to make incomprehensible decisions. His father was the animal.

THE DOOR SHUT BEHIND HIS SON. HIS HEIR apparent. He leaned back in his chair. The boy had grown into an impressive physical manifestation of a man. He mourned what could have been. That whore was responsible for the events that had separated them. Her cunning and intelligence was the only redeeming quality she'd had.

He had needed time to clean up her fucking mess, so he let her half-witted brother take both the boys. The other one was useless. That one had taken after the whore of a broodmare he'd bred. That twin was weak.

He sighed and dropped his pen. What a useless waste of life. By the time he'd fixed the damage she'd done and put people and resources in place to ensure *he* was untouchable, Dixon had been in the military and untouchable. A wrinkle he had not foreseen. He needed an heir, a successor.

He stood and moved to the far side of the room. The bookcase unlatched and swung away from the wall. Behind were his pictures of his heirs. He examined each one. His boys didn't have any idea of the power they would inherit, but only if they learned from him. Dixon was once again where he deserved to be —at his right hand. Dixon had learned his lessons so well as a child. But of course, the time they'd together had been limited and not enough to completely enlighten him. He glanced from Dixon's picture to that of a ten-year-old boy holding his mother's hand. Another broodmare, but thankfully, one of higher quality. This boy hadn't been tested yet. He wasn't quite old enough. Soon he'd take control of the young one as he had Dixon. Soon...he glanced once again at the images of his oldest heir. They'd been snipped from old video feeds while the boy had been in training. The exhilaration he felt each time Dixon had internalized his corrections and advanced could not be contained. A young mind can be molded, transformed and shaped.

Of course, the training wasn't easy. Dixon had made mistakes. Children make mistakes. That is why *his* discipline had been so important. Now, Dixon was back, but his training was incomplete. It remained to be seen what weakness of character he needed to 'repair'. He glanced at the monitor at the top right corner of the wall. He'd completed the rooms where he'd implement any needed corrections. There would be no interruptions when he took on the younger one.

His brows furrowed for a moment. He'd

need to start assembling the props required for both Dixon's remedial and the young one's initial training. If he didn't utilize the pathetic lives he extracted from society for those purposes, there were always other uses for them. He sighed and shook his head. The burden of training his boys was a heavy mantle, but one he'd shoulder even more now that he'd aligned with a wielder of significant power.

He pushed the bookshelf back into place and wandered over to the fireplace. The flames licked the logs. He grabbed another piece of wood from the brass adorned rack beside the impressive marble façade. The organization that had approached him had proved valuable. He was cautiously optimistic that he could use the redundancy and layers of the organization to his benefit. The mirror over the fireplace reflected the image he'd cultivated. He smiled in satisfaction. His image was pristine. There were no flaws. No weaknesses.

CHAPTER 3

SIX HOURS. That was how long he'd waited. The middle-class neighborhood fell into slumber in a predictable fashion. Dogs were walked for the last time by people who huddled against the cold and waited for their animals to do their business so they could clean it up and head back into the warmth of their homes. Dixon watched from the dark recesses of an alleyway as the lights of the apartment buildings shuttered. The windows he'd fixated on had darkened over an hour ago. He wasn't in a hurry because even though the man was coded, he wasn't an assassin. Killing during an operation was one thing. Singling out a person, tracking them and taking them out wasn't something he'd ever pictured himself doing.

Well, check that. Being honest with himself —because, hey, he was the only one he could be honest with—he *had* pictured doing just that to his old man. Did he want to be the one to pull the trigger? He mentally shrugged. Sometimes. It had been a constant internal debate since he'd left his initial meeting with Jason. A part of him wondered if killing the old fucker would eliminate the apparitions of the past or if it would send him headfirst into the chasm of evil that had spawned him. He give himself a fifty-fifty chance of going either way. He wasn't at all certain he'd come out right side up after this.

He inched out of the alley and surveyed the rest of the block. Three apartments with lights still on in the next building over—nothing that set off warning bells. He returned his attention to the mark's building. He could see one light on in what appeared to be a kitchen window in that apartment building. It was dim...the light from a nightlight or small lamp. Distant sounds of vehicles on the main thoroughfare two blocks over provided a white noise that absorbed the sound of a garbage truck and a long lonely wail of a siren. Dixon walked across the street and turned the corner, heading toward the front entrance. He'd reconned the area throughout the evening, keeping to the shadows, avoiding any interaction with humanity. He used the cars parked on the street to hide from two CCTV systems he'd seen on his drive through the neighborhood. There was one further down the street, but the position of the camera made it impossible for him to be picked up on this particular approach. It took about thirty seconds to pick the lock on the front door, a typical hardware store lock that was only good for keeping honest people honest. Criminals and professionals in this business were only delayed momentarily by things like locks.

The ball cap on his head was pulled down over his brow in case there were any cameras in the common areas of the building. The chances of that were slim, but he'd be damned if he'd work for four fucking months shoveling the waste of his father's illicit activities to end up having a random two-hundred-dollar camera system from a big-box warehouse store blow his cover.

He glanced up the stairs. The apartment directly over his mark's was under renovation. There was a waste chute constructed from the back window and plastic draped over the windows with what appeared to be plaster splattered over the edges near the wall. Apparently, someone was texturizing the walls or spray painting. Dixon slipped down the hall and turned right. Apartment 1C at the back of the building and the end of the hall was his goal.

The door to the mark's apartment was cracked open. Every nerve in his body fired at once. Dixon pulled his pistol out and screwed on the suppressor. He wasn't planning on guests, but if there was someone else who'd broken in, he'd use that as a subterfuge for the kill. A home invasion gone bad, a story that had been told before and would be again. He listened for a moment before he slid into the apartment. A soft thud drew his attention. He visually swept the area around him quickly before he skirted the furniture and headed toward the location of the soft sound.

He rounded the corner and froze. His mark knelt facing him. Even in the muted light from the window, he could recognize the bastard from the files Jason had given him to memorize.

A figure in black, wearing a ski mask held a handful of the man's hair, exposing his throat. She looked up... *she*? Fuck, yes, the person behind his mark was a woman. The knife in her hand slid across the bastard's neck. The sound of cartilage snapping and wind escaping the mark's severed throat told him what he couldn't clearly see. The body dropped, and she followed the corpse forward, moving into a fighting stance.

Dixon smiled and edged into the room. He lifted his left hand, his gun still held firmly in his right. "Looks like you brought a knife to a gunfight." He caught the surprised jerk of her body at his words.

"I don't need a knife to beat you—gun or not."

Dixon let his smile grow. Fuck, that voice was sexy. Husky, a little breathy and damned if he didn't catch a hint of excitement.

"Think you can get out of here without using it?"

"You mean you'd let me walk?" she teased in a low murmur.

"Not a chance, baby, but I'll give you even odds. Still think you can get by me?"

"I know I can, hotshot. Okay…I'll put down my knife if you put down your gun."

An evil chuckle floated from him. "You'll lodge the damn thing in my heart."

"Oh, tempting, but I don't generally kill if there isn't a profit in it for me." She lowered her voice and purred, "Why don't you just let me walk out of here? No more bloodshed tonight.

"Put your knife down first." Dixon lifted his chin and motioned toward the desk, not more than a foot from her.

"And then you'd shoot me…I don't think so, Quick Draw." She casually wiped the blade of her knife against her tight black pants.

"At the same time?" He nodded toward the bookshelf next to where he stood.

"Why would you trust me?"

Her words stopped his thoughts. "Don't you

mean why would *you* trust *me?*" He pointed at her and then at himself.

She laughed and shook her head. "No, I meant why would *you* trust *me.* I already know I can't trust you. You are a murderer and all."

Dixon cocked his head and clicked his tongue. "Nah, that would be you. You killed him."

"Him? Yes, but you wouldn't be here, with a gun, at two in the morning if you weren't after the same thing."

"And so we are back at square one. I needed this kill. You do too. Who gets to claim it?"

The woman adjusted her footing slightly. "My kill. My money."

"My kill, personal reasons," Dixon replied.

"You mean to tell me you aren't getting paid to take this scum out?"

"Not a penny."

"All right my avenging angel, I'll play your game. You put your weapon on the bookcase, and I'll drop my knife on the desk."

"On the count of three?" Dixon's body tingled in anticipation. It had been forever since he'd fought with a worthy opponent, and he knew in his gut this woman would be phenomenal. He could tell by the way she moved the fight would be epic.

"*One.*" She spoke and slowly extended her weapon while watching him do the same.

"Winner owns bragging rights?" Dixon clarified.

"Agreed. I don't like to lose money. *Two.*" She dropped her arm again as did he.

"How much are you out when I win?" Dixon loved her low sexy chuckle. So confident and fierce.

"Only ten thousand." She laughed again. "I can make it up if you happen to be better than I give you credit for."

"Oh, I'm better," Dixon taunted her.

"We shall see. *Three.*"

They both dropped their weapons. Dixon couldn't have blinked in the time it took the woman to fly across the room. She swept at his legs, and he managed to jump up, just missing her crippling attempt at putting him on his ass. He punched forward, throwing himself into her, knocking them both back into the room. She twisted under him before he could gain purchase on anything but her arm. They both popped up. The woman spun and jumped up, using his clothing to hold him as she moved. He grabbed her shoulders as she arched back away from his grasp, which propelled her legs up into the air. She scissored them around his neck. She curled toward his neck a split second before she whipped herself backward pulling him down. He somersaulted through the open door, landing flat on his back with her hard as fucking iron thighs clamped around his throat.

Surprisingly, she had him in a choke hold, and he was already feeling the effects. There was only one thing he could think to do. It was the only way he'd been able to get Jade the fuck off him when they sparred, and she'd used this move. He extended his hands down the woman's leg, grasped for that portion of ribs just under her arms and dug his fingers in.

She jumped, just enough for him to push his fist between her legs and leverage them open with his forearm. He gasped in a lungful of air and rolled. Toward her, not away from her. His movement pinned her to her back. Her legs were fucking powerful, and he grunted against her strength. He managed to grab her shoulder and twist over her. One of her legs was pinned between his chest and hers, the other slammed down on his back. He grunted against the blow. He'd been kicked by a fucking mule, and it hurt less. She tried to twist under him, but he held her with the weight of his body. She brought her boot down on his back again.

"Fuck!" Dixon twisted just enough to grab her leg behind the knee. He pushed it forward, rolling her and pinning both shoulders. She had one leg pinned between them and the other held to her chest with his arm. She reached up with her hands to try to rake his eyes, but he tipped her leg further, throwing all his weight on both her legs so he could use his hands to capture hers. She struck fast, and a fist landed against his cheek. He turned just as a finger pushed into his eye. He jerked his face away and down, hiding the injury against her chest and blindly gathered her arms.

The second he had both her wrists in his hands, she hissed, "Motherfuckingsonofabitch!"

Fuck me, my thoughts exactly. The bitch had nearly blinded him. A stream of tears poured from his injured eye, and he repeatedly blinked while she squirmed under him. Frustrated, he tightened his grip. He couldn't see out of his damn eye. He closed it and drew a deep breath.

"Fine, you fucking win." The woman went slack underneath him.

Dixon didn't believe her submission for a fucking second. She groaned. "Get off, you're heavy."

Dixon lifted his head and glared at her with the one eye he could use. She was fucking beautiful—for a murderer. Dark hair. Delicate features. Fine porcelain skin. He blinked her back into focus. A small spattering of light freckles dusted her nose. Her eyes were dark brown and insanely sexy. She had to have some Asian influence in her heritage. Lucy Liu on her best day couldn't touch the beauty of this woman.

"What happened?" Her words plucked him from his dazed observation.

"You fucking tried to gouge out my eye."

She narrowed her eyes at him and lifted her head, staring at his eye. "Come down here."

Dixon lowered his head incrementally. Her gaze drifted from his injured eye to his lips. "Lower."

He blinked his injured eye and opened it.

Tears still ran down his cheek, but he was able to see. Barely.

"Fuck, dude." She stared at him. "That's going to leave a mark."

"You think?" Dixon still pinned her. He felt her flex under him but apparently, she was not trying to get away.

"Yeah. Want me to kiss it and make it better, Quick Draw?" She licked her lips and fuck him if he didn't follow the path of her tongue with his blurred vision.

"I'm afraid you'd kill me." Which, considering protests from his back and his blurred eye sight, wasn't an untrue statement. The woman was a fucking flurry of deadly aggression.

"I told you, I generally don't kill without being paid."

"Generally?"

"Hmmm...some people just deserve to be ended." She lifted her eyebrows a couple time in rapid succession. "Some people, I'd rather fuck. What do you say?"

"Am I in the dead category or the fuck category?" Dixon blinked again, trying to clear his vision.

"Oh, you are in the fuck category," She purred.

"I only fuck in the hard, vicious, pound you through the wall and fuck you until you scream for mercy type way." Dixon wasn't in the mood to play nice. He hadn't been for one hell of a long time.

Witnessing this hot-as-fuck contract killer take out that scum and then almost best him in a grappling match made his cock hard. Was that kinky as fuck? Probably. Did he give a shit? No. No, he did not. He'd been mucking through the fucking wasteland of his father's defecation for four months. He deserved a release.

"You better make it good then, Quick Draw, I don't like sex any other way."

Dixon lifted slightly and released her. He dropped down on her and ground his erection against her.

Her husky voice dropped a bit lower when she spoke, "Damn...fucking someone with a dead body next door gets you going, huh?"

"Only when the fucker deserves it, and a hot as fuck woman wants to be pounded through the wall." Dixon reached between them and yanked down her pants.

She gasped and pulled at his shirt, reaching under it to score her nails across his back. Her leather gloves prevented her from cutting his skin. He still hissed because there was no doubt, she'd left a fingertip path of bruises.

"Where's my 'through the wall' pounding?"

Dixon lifted onto his knees and unbuttoned his black cargo pants. He glanced up and across the room. In an instant, he was on his feet and lifting her up. She tripped as he pushed her backward toward the wall. Grabbing her, he yanked her up into his arms. Her legs dangled as he slammed her against the wall.

Their first kiss wasn't a mere press of flesh against flesh, no it was an explosion of teeth and hard, painful pressure. She growled and bit down on his lip. The biting taste of copper burst against his tongue. "Bitch."

"Bastard."

"Damn straight."

She kicked her legs, finally freeing her boot-covered foot from one of her pant legs. Both boots hit the small of his back, and the flap of fabric hanging from one leg swung forward between his legs. "Where's that cock of yours?"

Dixon reached between them and worked his dick out of his pants. "You better fucking not have any diseases." He pushed the underside of his cock against the wet heat of her core.

"I'll hunt you down and kill you if *you* give *me* something, you bastard." She gasped and shivered against him a second before she leaned forward and bit his shoulder hard.

"Dammit!" He slammed his hips forward and speared into her center with one thrust. He withdrew and slammed home again.

"Yes! Fuck, harder!"

Harder? Any harder and he'd split the woman in half. She wasn't bigger than a minute. Dixon grabbed hold of her ass and leaned her into the wall. The change of position was just enough for him to move his hips with a beat that a salsa dancer would envy. He jacked his cock into her with such force and speed her body bounced against the wall and the picture beside them suddenly tilted on its hanger. Dixon didn't fucking care if the motherfucker fell.

She arched her back, and he dropped his head to her shoulder. Sweat dripped from his hair, and her skin was slick with her own perspiration. He clawed at her legs. The leather gloves he wore had no traction against the wet skin. He managed to link his hands behind her, lifting her legs over his arms … *oh fuck, fuck, fuck…* The nuclear explosion at the base of his spine was going to happen way too soon. He lifted his head and found her ear, biting down on the lobe. Hard.

She arched off the wall almost, unbalancing him as she clamped her legs around his torso. The low raspy moan that followed would be a sound he would use as spank bank material for life because it fucking lit him up. He exploded, then imploded until he couldn't see, think, or even breathe. He went off like a massive brick of C4.

Hours later…maybe days…she unhooked her linked feet from behind him. Only then did he release his grip on her. He propped his hands on the wall and pushed back so he could look down at her. Fuck, she was tiny. Maybe five feet tall? He pushed away when she stepped to the side and set about trying to reconfigure her clothes. He carefully tucked his over sensitive cock back into his pants and refastened the buttons as he watched her do an acrobatic balancing act on one leg while trying to pull her pants back up over the tread of her boot. Well, no wonder his back felt like he'd been hit with a baseball bat. That thick rubber was at least two inches thick on the sole, and the boot had a four-inch heel if it was a millimeter. Five-foot if she was lucky.

"You won, Quick Draw. Your kill to claim." She hiked up her pants and buttoned them as she walked back into the room where the dead body lay. She returned with her knife and carefully lowered it into a scabbard that hung down her back. The small amount of hilt that may have shown above her neckline was covered by her thick hair.

"What's your name?" He wanted to know. Fuck him if he knew why.

"What do you think we're doing here? Dating?" She chuckled and walked straight up to him. "I don't date, and I don't do names. We fucked. Get over it."

Dixon crossed his arms looking down at her. A self-assured smirk spread across his face. "I fucked you through the wall and that orgasm I gave you damn near knocked your ass out."

She reached up and slapped his cheek softly. "Don't flatter yourself, Quick Draw." She turned on her heel and walked to the front door. She stopped and looked back over her shoulder, "On a scale of one to ten, I'd give you a six." She slipped out the door silently.

Oh, no she didn't. That was fucking hilarious. Dixon chuckled as he went into the other room and grabbed his weapon. He unfastened the silencer, pocketed it, and re-holstered his automatic. He checked the room over and left the way he'd come.

CHAPTER 4

"Turning our attention to New York. Have we made any progress with the junior Senator?"

"No. We've applied pressure, but he's the real deal. He believes he can change the world and we have yet to find a skeleton."

"Blackmail situations?"

"No, ma'am, the man isn't into drugs or prostitutes and has an uncanny way of avoiding any compromising pictures. Our contractor has sent what he's been able to stage, but so far it's nothing that the public wouldn't easily dismiss."

The woman at the head of the table pushed the folder away and leaned back into the comfort of her Italian leather, ergonomic, and obscenely overpriced, chair. She crossed her legs and admired her new Louboutin heels. The brilliant, unmarred red sole became her focal point as she assessed the situation.

The vote would happen early next year, and without the junior senator's vote in their favor, the win would be in grave jeopardy. Her assistant sat quietly while she debated the ramifications of losing the vote. Far-reaching economic goals were tied to winning. It was a linchpin that needed to be secured before another series of moves could be made in a delicate chess game where the pieces had been set to advance the organization's goals.

She uncrossed her legs and retrieved the folder. "The governor is firmly in our control." It was a statement, not a question. A puppet who thought he was going places, they told the politician what to do and when to do it. "There is sufficient time for an interim appointment due to a tragic accident."

"Yes, ma'am."

"Assuming that scenario, we need a candidate to fill the vacant seat." She lifted her tablet and tapped through several directory trees until she reached the personnel folders for the

New York interests. She scanned through the names and backgrounds. Her frown deepened. The candidates were abysmal, and only one would work.

"Pull up Simmons." She glanced at her assistant. He tapped at his keyboard and the screen split. The left side showed the man's image. Middle-aged. Blond hair, blue eyes, distinct and pleasant features. Physically, he was acceptable. Her eyes drifted to the right. Commercial business interests. Law degree, not practicing. He was tied to several other prominent politicians by past interactions as an elected city official and had even graduated law school with two of the people her organization currently directed. His finances were acceptable.

"Now the red background, please." The veneer of the man's public persona was stripped. She read the details and once again leaned back in her seat. This could be a tough nut to crack. Information was spotty, but she detected a distinct psychotic thread in his history. "Next." Her assistant displayed the next page. *Three sons. Ex-wife dead...ah...yes. Indeed.*

She reached over and picked up the phone,

activating the scrambler. She waited for the device to connect and secure.

A female voice responded. "Yes?"

"The operation we've been running on Guardian...I need one name removed from the kill list."

"Which one?"

"Dixon Simmons."

"We haven't located him. He's off the grid. The targeted Guardian personnel have been particularly difficult to pin down."

A rare laugh fell from her lips. "Knowing you, my dear, that is tantamount to orgasmic."

Her counterpart's low hum confirmed her suspicions. She glanced at the screen in front of her and relayed the information she had uncovered. "I've found Dixon Simmons, but he is embedded in a particularly sensitive economic operation and could be useful."

"He's Guardian."

She tapped her long red nails against the smoked glass of the conference room table. Her eyes swept the background on display. "I'm not sure that is still the case."

"Send me what you have."

"Indeed. Eliminate him from your mission."

"Already done."

"WHAT THE FUCK HAPPENED TO YOU?"

Dixon had braced himself for his father's reaction. The damage caused by his broken blood vessels had taken over the white area around his blue iris. He looked like a walking gore poster. His sunglasses had shielded him from any unwanted looks today as he went about his daily business.

"Next time you decide to off someone, you should probably check how many other people want him dead." He stared over the expanse of his father's desk at the man who gawked at him like he had three heads.

His father's eyes narrowed, and his nostrils flared as red traveled up his neck. "Be careful." The sound came out low and dangerous like the rattle at the end of a snake's tail.

Fuck. That. "Of what? Either you sent the contractor after the same man you told me to eradicate, or you are a step behind someone else."

"Your work is complete?"

"*Her* work is complete. I watched her do it." Dixon crossed his arms over his chest. "She has very impressive…talents."

"Of course, you eliminated her." His father sat down in his chair.

"No."

"She's a loose end."

"No. I witnessed her committing murder. She has nothing on me. There is no physical evidence, no video. If anything, it gives us an advantage." Dixon had thought long and hard on how to spin last night's encounter for his father's benefit.

His father sat forward in his chair, interested. Yes, Dixon had bait on the hook and chum in the water. "Explain yourself," his father demanded.

"You use Smith or me to do your house cleaning."

His father's jaw worked, and Dixon rather enjoyed watching the man prep himself to stroke out. He'd be damned if he'd allow the bastard to intimidate him any longer. Well, at least that was the intention. Since he'd returned to dear old dad, the nightmares he thought he'd left behind years ago had started haunting him again. He rocked back on his heels before he spoke, "You're overlooking a potential resource who could reach irritants in places neither Smith nor I can access, or during times we are unavailable. *She* has exceptional skills."

"Better than yours?" His father sneered at him.

"No. But close." He smirked in satisfaction.

His father studied him as if he was trying to read his thoughts. Once upon a time, Dixon believed the fucker could do just that. Not any longer. Dixon stared back, not flinching and not looking away first. That was a sign of weakness. Another lesson learned from the monster across the desk. This was a battle of wills he would not lose. Finally, without blinking, the sadistic bastard spoke, "You're sure she's a contractor?"

"Yes."

"How do you know this?"

Dixon lifted an eyebrow. "I have my ways."

"Which you will tell me."

"No."

"Then Smith will find her."

Dixon laughed. "Not if she doesn't want

him to find her, he won't." He dropped his hands and put them in his pockets. "She's a professional. Smith is a thug."

"Smith has been loyal and effective. I haven't had any problems."

"You send him to rough up pimps and drug dealers. What is his skill set for deactivating digital alarms? Can he locate camera systems and manage to avoid detection on approach? What if he needs to track his assignment? Can he blend in? I can. She can. Smith? His knuckles drag the ground. You cannot mistake him for anything other than hired muscle. Yeah, he can pound the shit out of worthless, inept thugs. Don't get me wrong, he has a presence on the street that works in your favor, but I assume you someday want to…elevate your game."

His father's head snapped up, and his eyes narrowed. "What have you heard?"

Dixon's disdain wasn't forced and slipped out easily. "Other than you're trying to gain a political foothold? Nothing but what the news is reporting. Knowing you the way I do, I assume your goals far exceed those being bandied about by the talking heads on the local news stations."

His old man relaxed into his chair. "Knowing me the way you do…" He lifted an eyebrow. "How well do you think you know me?"

Dixon snorted. "Everything you do advances your position at least one step closer to whatever your current objective is. You never move without considering the entire board and always outthink your opponent by four or five moves." Which was the truth. Unfortunately for his fucked-up sperm donor, the man had developed myopathy. If there was any sense of karma in the world, that would lead to his father's downfall. Dixon made certain he operated far outside his father's peripheral vision.

A smug smile appeared before his father boasted, "I'm better than that. I see the end of the game."

Dixon nodded. "As you know I'm fucking tired of playing inside the lines. When you finish the game, I want to be there to see them fall. It will be fucking spectacular."

His father laughed. "Oh, my boy, you have

no idea. The people I'm"—he lifted his fingers and made air quotes—"'working with' are short-sighted. They plod when they should be running."

Dixon kept his expression carefully blank. This was the first time his father had ever indicated his involvement with anyone. Four months and finally, *finally* a fucking breadcrumb. "Why work with them, then?"

"Ah, they have the leverage and underpinning I need to advance my agenda. As always, I will use them to get what I want and then move on." His father waved a hand at the door. "The idea of hiring this contractor is something I'll think about. You made a good point. A skilled soldier is always useful."

Dixon nodded and spun on his heel. His father's voice stopped him at the door. "Don't come back here until you look presentable. You look like shit, and your flaws taint me."

Dixon refused to let the verbal dagger his father thrust into his heart affect him, at least not in front of the bastard. He exited the study and drew the doors closed behind him. He didn't remember walking out of the residence, only feeling the cold air on his face as he turned and made his way toward where he'd parked. *Your flaws taint me.* It was what he'd said to Dixon before every beating, what his father had termed "lessons". The words chilled him to the deepest recesses of his soul. So much for not letting the bastard get to him.

CHAPTER 5

"Operator Two-seven-four."

"Sunset clearance, zero operative."

"Standby, zero operative."

"Archangel."

"He's not working."

"Explain."

"I can't. He hasn't checked in for over two weeks. He goes out and drinks at night. He's making inquiries about a certain contract killer."

"Has he made contact with the contractor?"

"Not yet."

"Find out what he's looking for but be cautious. The mark has claws deep inside our asset."

"How deep?"

"Deep enough to send you in to provide high cover."

"Valid point."

"Check in as scheduled unless something happens."

"Of course."

"Your usual?"

Dixon glanced up at the blonde. Her breasts pushed over the confines of the bustier she wore and threatened to spill over at any moment. Normally, Dixon would have chatted her up and fucked her senseless, several times. She was nice looking, definitely doable, and as she'd told him in more ways than he could count, she was available. But she wasn't the woman he was looking for.

"Thank you." Dixon watched the swing of her hips as she headed to the bar. Leggy and willing. Yeah, that woman would normally turn his crank. He chuckled to himself and shook his head as he pulled out his cigarettes and lighter. Drake wouldn't chase that skirt.

The man was a homebody and would probably read a book every single night if Dixon didn't drag his ass out. Their childhood had changed them both. Dixon was only comfortable around anonymous people. He loved being the life of the party because it meant he was fucking alive. Drake, well Drake put on a happy face and followed his lead. They were almost a whole person when they were together. Almost. Dixon was sure it was his deficiencies that held Drake back from finding real happiness. He was too busy holding Dixon together to worry about his own needs.

The blonde was back with his whiskey, a coaster, and an ashtray. Smoking wasn't allowed in the tavern...yeah right. His father owned and controlled the establishment, so whatever he wanted, he got. He lit up and stared down a woman at the bar who glared daggers at him. Whatever.

Dixon leaned back into the booth and took a sip of the whiskey as his eyes flitted from face to face. Several he recognized. Some were new, and the others were nameless entities that floated in and out like the tide on a beach. The ebb and flow of customers seemed to pulse like a live organism.

Fuck, what he wouldn't give for a long, nonsensical conversation with Drake. The verbal banter they exchanged was a coping tool. They used it to focus on things outside their own heads. They rarely had to talk when they were alone together. Some people found that eerie. Speech between them just wasn't necessary. They were that close. A minuscule lift of an eyebrow or the tilt of a chin a fraction of an inch communicated all that needed to be said. It weirded people out. Not that they gave a shit. There were times, though, when he couldn't stay inside his head. It was too fucking crowded. He'd start, or Drake would, depending on who needed to temporarily quiet the noise. He could use some relief from the mental din right about now.

He took a final drag on his cigarette and blew it out through his nose before stubbing it out. He immediately lit another. This waiting sucked. When his father had agreed to "add another soldier", he'd made inquiries of the people who had access to that sort of information. The woman he described was known in those circles simply as "Joy"—a misnomer if ever there was one. He put the word out he wanted a meeting. In order to make himself available to her, he pried his ass out of his apartment every night and sat in the back booth of his father's upscale tavern.

The door opened, and several people walked in. For a second, he thought one of them was Joy, but when the woman turned around, he deflated. Was he stupid for wanting to see her again? He took a long draw on his cigarette and blew the smoke out across the room. Yeah, but fuck self-preservation. He was stuck in this cesspool for God only knew how long. He deserved a diversion.

The broken blood vessels in his eye had almost cleared which meant he'd have to go back to that fucker's beck and call soon. Why hadn't his father assigned him to scraping scum for the last two weeks? It worried him. There were no directions called in, and Smith was absent, if he didn't count the few times he'd seen him here at the tavern. Not that they talked much. The guy would come in, slam two shots and leave, all while saying the absolute minimum to either Dixon or the wait staff.

He'd found out from the waitress that Smith was new to the tavern, having arrived in the area a couple months before Dixon. The man was still a mystery, but not one that required his time or attention.

As he'd worked jobs for his old man, Dixon had put casual questions to people. A picture of the snake's underbelly emerged. Through innocent questions asked of a host of people, he'd built a map of his father's enemies, his allies, and the oppressed few that managed to eke out a living either as a prostitute, pimp or drug dealer. For the most part, he'd learned how to navigate the landmines around that fucker.

Movement at the door caught his attention. *Bingo.* He lifted his drink and emptied the glass as she walked toward him. Tonight, she had her hair up in some kind of updo thing. Her hard as steel legs were displayed perfectly in sky-high heels and a tight black dress with a slit up the front of one leg. The soft dove-gray cape she wore flapped open and he could see the form of her thigh when she walked toward him. The high neckline wasn't his favorite, but the gunmetal colored fabric looked phenomenal on her. He stood as she approached. Elegantly, she turned her back to him. He lifted the cashmere cape from her shoulders and folded it over his arm. The back of her dress plunged open only to fold delicately and nestle just above her ass. So much for the high neckline. He wanted to run a fingertip down the length of all that exposed skin to see if it was as smooth as it looked. The time they'd spent had been about fucking, not about touching. Thankfully, her cape hid his obvious desire.

She smiled seductively and slid into the booth as he laid her cloak down and slid into his seat. "What do you want?"

Dixon smiled and lifted a finger toward the waitress. She swaggered over. "Another for me and…" He glanced at Joy…that name sooo did not fit.

"I'll have what he's having."

"Whiskey neat?" The blonde's eyebrows lifted in a dare.

Joy blinked and regarded the waitress. "Make it a double." Joy returned her gaze to Dixon, completely dismissing the waitress. The woman grumbled a reply as she passed him on the way to the bar.

"Enough of the niceties. What. Do. You. Want?" Joy's stare leveled on him.

"I have a business opportunity." Dixon reached into his suit jacket and handed her an envelope containing ten thousand dollars. "And, I believe I owe you this."

Joy lifted the flap of the envelope and closed it almost immediately. "You won. This isn't mine."

"I didn't claim the…" He stopped as the waitress came back and plopped both drinks down before flouncing away. Dixon glanced around him before he continued, "Prize. You lost out. My way of evening the score." She lifted her hand and pressed her index finger on the top of the envelope, pushing it slowly and decidedly toward him. When she could no longer push it because the table was wider than her reach, she lifted her finger and sat back. "We had an agreement. I lost. I am a woman of my word. *This* is an insult."

Dixon lifted his drink and took a sip. "It wasn't meant to be."

Joy lifted her drink and downed it. "Thanks for the drink." She moved to slide out of the booth.

"I have been asked to find out if you could be placed on retainer." He hadn't been, but there was no way she would know that.

"Retainer?" Her motion stilled, but she didn't relax.

"Mmmhmmm. We'd be working together." He swirled the amber liquid in his glass but watched her.

"Why would I want to change from free-lance to retainer?"

"Nothing says you couldn't take on free-lance contracts, but the retainer work would come first." Dixon took a sip of his whiskey. "Interested?"

She caught the waitress's attention and lifted her empty glass. "In the job or in working with you?"

"Both." She might have rated *his* last performance a six, but she was as close to a ten as he'd ever had.

She leaned back in the booth and crossed her arms as she stared at him. He'd made the offer. Keeping his mouth shut was the best approach.

The waitress did a drive-by, swapped her empty for a full and headed back to a group that had pulled two tables together in the center of the pub.

"What is the potential for exposure?" Joy lifted her glass to her lips and took a sip.

"Very little. The employer keeps himself well insulated. Of course, if you fuck up and leave evidence at a scene, that is on you." Dixon suppressed a chuckle when she gave an indignant snort.

"I'm a professional. My scenes are perfect."

He watched her face. The smugness came from confidence and experience, of that he was positive. She'd been around the block.

"There is no such thing as a perfect scene." He believed that. There was always something left behind to give away the killer.

"Bullshit." She leaned forward and lowered her voice. "I can name ten targets on the books as accidental death or death from unknown causes that were assassinations."

"Yeah, and how would I be able to validate they were contract hits?"

He laughed when she blinked at him and her mouth opened just to close again. She scowled and took another sip of her whiskey.

"I can't, can I?" The exact opposite was true

for the Shadows he'd met at the Complex. At times their coded and sanctioned hits needed to look like accident. History had revealed if you dug deep enough, there was usually hard evidence the death was "commissioned". Unless she was a Shadow or worked for the CIA or Mossad, he doubted she could substantiate her claims. No matter how hot she was, she was an independent, thus barely a player in his world.

"I'll think about it." She leaned forward and placed her chin on top of her laced fingers. "In the meantime, care to try to change that six to a seven?"

All body parts below his belt were onboard with that idea. "Six? Woman, I rocked your fucking world."

Her head lolled to the side as she pretended to think while her chin still rested on her clasped fingers. "Yeah…no, but you did get points for enthusiasm."

Dixon threw his head back and laughed. That husky voice of hers joined him. He raised a glass to her in a silent salute. He finished his drink and leaned forward. "I only do anony-mous hotel room fucks."

"That's good, Quick Draw, but I only do

anonymous hotel room fucks if I pay for the room." She ran her finger around the rim of her whiskey glass and then licked the tip before sucking it into her mouth.

Dixon groaned and didn't try to hide his interest. "Good thing I don't have a problem with women who pay to play."

Her eyes snapped to his. "Oh? What an interesting attitude. I really hope you achieve that seven tonight."

THE HOTEL ROOM DOOR SLAMMED OPEN, hitting the wall with enough force to bury the knob into the sheet rock. Dixon kicked it shut, their lips fused together while he backed her into the room. A quick glance told him they were heading in the right direction. He reached down to pick her up, but she spun out of his arms. Her cape came off with an elaborate twirl. "Be a good boy. Take off your clothes and get onto the bed. She pointed to the bathroom. "I'll be right back."

Dixon waited until she'd shut the bedroom door and palmed his cock. Fuck, he was hard, but that didn't stop him from scanning the hotel room. He checked for the obvious; cameras, recorders, or anything out of place. Since she had the keycard already, he figured she'd planned to fuck him, or someone else, tonight.

He checked under the bed, behind the tables, in the drawers and closet. It was clean. His coat landed on top of hers. The lightweight sweater came off next followed by his forty-five automatic. He placed the pistol on the nightstand before he unclipped the hard-plastic holster that attached to the back of his jeans. There was no fucking way a person with even a portion of functioning brain cells would stick a loaded gun inside his waistband without a holster. Ass meet bullet. He chuckled at the thought of trying to explain that injury.

His Italian leather boots and silk socks found their way next to his coat and sweater. He'd just unfastened his jeans when the door opened. He stood by his weapon, and that wasn't a happy accident. The woman was a contract killer after all.

She walked out of the bathroom, and if it were possible, he would have swallowed his tongue. The dress was gone. She was completely naked except for those fucking heels. She ran a hand from her hip to her neck. She dropped her head and her fingertip pulled her bottom lip down. "Mmm, what is this? You still have clothes on. As you can see," —she twirled— "no concealed weapons."

Dixon's brain rebooted after being shut down by the three-sixty view of her banging-hot, naked body. He shucked his jeans and boxers efficiently and started toward her, but she lifted her hand, stopping his forward movement.

"I believe you told me you didn't have a problem with a woman being in charge." She motioned toward the bed with a waggle of her fingers. "On your back."

Dixon glanced from her to the bed. "What if I don't want to be on my back? What if I prefer you with your legs in the air?"

"We can play that game later when you're paying. I want you with your cock straight up in the air and hands behind your head." She walked past him and landed a stinging slap on his ass. "Now."

Okay, while his male ego told him *that*

shouldn't have been hot, his cock violently disagreed. His balls drew up and a pearl of precum hung from the tip of his shaft.

Fuck it. He'd play, for a little bit at least. He rolled onto the bed and put his hands behind his head, but his eyes never left hers. She reached up and pulled two pins from her hair sending the black fall to her shoulders. She circled the bed, her eyes traveling over his body. "So many scars. You've led a violent life."

She had no idea. The scars she could see weren't anywhere as brutal as the scars he carried on the inside.

"Two gun wounds." She trailed her finger along his scars. "Knife." Her fingers traced the rippled skin along the base of his neck. "Fire?"

"Burning Sulphur."

"Military."

"Something like that." He wasn't interested in trading life histories; he wanted sex. With her. Now.

She kicked off her heels and leaned over, placing her knees onto the mattress. She inched forward until she could sit on her knees next to him. "Touch yourself." She reached for her bare breast and rolled her nipple between her fingers. He watched her pull while she pinched it. Her mouth fell open, and a low, sexy-as-fuck moan resonated straight into the base of his cock. She switched nipples and spread her legs before she ordered, "Show me what you like."

So she likes nipple play? Fuck him if he wasn't going to incorporate that the first time he got a chance. He reached down and grabbed the base of his cock, giving it a firm stroke to the crown. He twisted his wrist around the top before he lowered his thumb to the head and let the side of his thumbnail split the slit on the top, pushing just enough to give himself a bite of pain. He lowered his hand and repeated the process, all while watching Joy watch him.

She kept the nipple torture going. The way she rolled and tugged on those beautiful peaks was a violent act. Her free hand slid down her taut belly and fingered the top of her mound. She'd been waxed smooth, and her sex was prominent and swollen even before she split the folds of her skin and sandwiched her clit between her fingers. Dixon's hand sped up as he watched her pinch her swollen sex and then writhe under the sensation.

He reached down and rolled his balls with his free hand, pulling them away from his body. He could fucking come from just watching her pleasure herself, but that wasn't how he wanted to end things tonight. He'd rather bury his cock so far inside her he'd never find his way out.

"Hold your cock up straight for me. She stood up on the bed and walked up to his hip. She turned as she straddled him, her back to his chest. Slowly she folded down over him until she sat on the top of his legs. His cock was cradled in the crack of her ass. She leaned forward and pulled the bedspread up. He tensed and shot his arm out toward the night-stand. She laughed and held up a packet. "It's just lube, chill out." She tossed it back toward him and leaned forward over his legs. Her tongue danced over the inside of his knees as he ripped open the packet.

Anal sex wasn't something a person did with a hookup. It took trust and intimacy, or at least he fucking thought it did. He pushed up, so he was sitting, her perfect ass arched right there. He set the packet down and grabbed both globes of her pert cheeks in his hands and spread her open. He had experience at this, albeit a fucking long time ago, but he had game. She'd give him a ten tonight. That he would guarantee.

He grabbed her and repositioned her with a minimum of fuss. She looked back over her shoulder at him, and he smirked at her as he lowered his lips to the dimples at the top of her ass. His tongue traced those indentations as his hands spread her ass cheeks. He used his thumb to put pressure on the nerve endings surrounding her tight pucker. The slight jump of her body under him at first contact was perfect. She pushed back into the sensation of the pad of his thumb rubbing the opening. Dixon continued with his tongue's discovery of her, slowly easing his way down to where his thumb pushed in, not penetrating, just teasing. He added the movement of his tongue, and she mewled while pushing against his light pressure.

She moved and reached back, gripping a handful of his hair. "Fuck, yes!" She held him there—as if he was going to go anywhere. *Give me some fucking credit.* With his free hand, he started to trace her clit, teasing a flick against the nub while alternating his assault on her ass. He breached her with his thumb at the same time as he trapped her clit between two fingers. She damn near bucked out of his grip.

He played her like a fucking instrument. He kept her aroused as he stretched her to take him. He was hung. Not bragging. Just fact. Taking her ass could tear her apart if he didn't make sure to prep her. He reapplied the lube to his fingers for the last time. "I'm going to fuck you now."

"About time…ah…" She panted, her head hung between her arms while she rested on her chest with her ass in the air. He brought his palm down hard on her ass. Fuck if that didn't make her moan again. He squeezed the rest of the lube onto his cock and slicked up.

Dixon pushed into her and damn near gave up before the head of his cock forced through her resistance. He froze. Her body trembled between his hands and a fine sheen of perspiration broke out all over her body. He held her hips, willing himself not to move no matter how much the tight heat of her ass begged him to do so.

Finally, he heard the words he'd been

waiting to hear. "Move." *Thank fuck*. He dropped down over her back and pressed forward, taking clues from her body when to stop. When he was fully seated, he used the hand that he'd lubed his cock with and reached between her legs. He split her sex and stroked her clit. His free arm wrapped around her hips and snugged her against him before he dropped a kiss between her shoulder blades.

"Are you going to fuck me, or what?" her husky voice challenged, not that he needed much enticement.

He trusted her to know her own fucking body. He pulled out and slid back, in slow, measured strokes while his fingers continued to torment her clit.

He was close, so fucking close. She was fucking tight and hot. Sweat poured off him and squelched between them. As far as he was concerned, the best sex in the world was hot, sweaty and borderline violent.

She pushed up onto her hands and then started to meet his thrusts. "Yes, harder!"

Dixon grabbed her hips and pulled her back into him as he thrust forward. His orgasm was right there, a sharply defined line, and he was barreling toward it faster than the speed of sound. He leaned forward and wrapped his hand around her neck, pulling her up and back into his chest while drilling into her. He tightened his hand around her neck, not to choke her, but to let her know the power he held. He tipped her head and hissed, "I own you."

She shook her head, panting the word no, over and over. Dixon used the hand not holding her neck to grab one of her nipples. He squeezed and rolled it. She gasped.

He growled, "I own you. Go ahead and fight me. You want it that way and so do I."

He saw stars when she came. Her body clenched and milked him. He slammed through his orgasm and tried to control their burn as they melted into the bed.

He slid off her and gently removed his cock from her body. The slightest of whimpers escaped her. Dixon pretended not to hear. This woman would not want him to witness any weaknesses.

He pushed her damp hair off her shoulders. She rolled her face toward him and narrowed her eyes. He lifted his eyebrows in question. Instead of answering she rolled off the bed and headed for the bathroom. He grabbed a pillow that had somehow managed to fall onto the floor and propped his head up. He could hear the water in the bathroom running as she cleaned up. She emerged several minutes later with her dress on. She stepped into her heels and grabbed her cape from the chair, upending his stack of clothes. She headed toward the door.

"Joy," Dixon called, stopping her. She looked back at him. "How do I contact you?"

She turned fully and gazed at him. "Why?"

"Because what we have started here is something I want to continue."

Her brows drew together. "Why?"

Dixon blew out a breath of air while he considered whether or not to tell her the truth. Fuck it, what did he have to lose? "Because maybe we're both fucked up, but our fucked up works together."

She stood in the door for several long moments before she recited a string of numbers.

He smiled as she turned to leave. "I pegged that ten this time, didn't I?"

She glanced over her shoulder and made a

point of running her eyes over his body. "So fucking needy. Honestly, you barely reached a seven. Next time, you better bring your 'A' game."

His laughter followed her out the door.

CHAPTER 6

"Operator Two-seven-four."

"Sunset clearance, zero operative."

"Standby, zero operative."

"Archangel."

"He's back. Something has…changed. Less grunt work, more interaction with the other side of the operation."

"He's being brought on board."

"Perhaps.

"Has he made contact with the freelancer?"

"Once, but…"

"What is your concern?"

"I don't know. Something is wrong."

"Can you substantiate?"

"Negative."

There was an audible pause before Archangel cleared his voice and dropped his command, "Check in as scheduled unless something happens."

"Of course."

"Where have you been?" The old man snapped as soon as he entered the office.

Dixon straightened to his full height. "Doing what you asked." He strode forward with the signed documents. The legalese had nearly made his eyes bleed, but he'd reviewed the documentation and obtained the signatures from the very unwilling business owners. The packet of photos that he'd dropped on their desks had shut them up–quickly. His father had taken great pains to document shit that needed to be reported to the cops. His gut rolled at the contents of the envelope. The date and time stamps were what killed him. They were taken three days ago. He could have prevented it had he known what was being set up. He could have stopped those fucking predators. He heard Jeremiah's voice in his head. *It wasn't you that allowed it to happen. It was your father. You can't stop events you are unaware of.*

His father sighed and shook his head. "I can see through you. You can't hide anything from me."

Dixon stood motionless. He had no idea what his father was talking about, but that didn't mean jack-shit. The man could rave like a banshee or lash out with deadly intent at the drop of a hat.

"Your moralistic slip is showing. I thought I taught you this lesson before." His father opened his top desk drawer and pulled out two pictures. "Pick one."

Dixon glanced at the two photographs. "What do you mean?"

"Pick a motherfucking photograph!" his father screamed, spittle flying.

Dixon dropped his eyes to the two pictures. One showed a vibrant young woman holding a baby. She was smiling and happy. The other was a photograph of a handsome man in his mid-thirties in a snowsuit on skis—her husband? His head was thrown back, and he was captured in mid-laugh.

"Which one?"

Dixon shook his head. "No." He wasn't a child any longer. The sick fucker wasn't sucking him into this again.

His father jumped to his feet? "No? Did you tell me no?"

Dixon stood his ground and nodded. Once.

His father picked up both photos and carefully placed them back into the drawer. "Very well, you may go." The words were said in a polite congenial tone. The motherfucker was certifiable. Dixon left the study, went back to the small office he'd been given over two weeks ago and grabbed his keys, coat, and gloves.

"You should have picked a picture." Smith's form blocked his door. He was studying his shoes or the wood flooring, but one thing was certain, he wasn't looking at Dixon.

Dixon put on his coat and buttoned the front. "Yeah, and why is that?"

The man lifted his eyes to Dixon's, the sadness he let Dixon see was almost overwhelming. "Next time, choose." He turned slowly and walked down the hall.

Dixon turned off his light and headed out of The Residence. He'd wanted to text Joy or call her, but he assumed his telephone in the office was being monitored. The cell he carried was provided by his father. There was no way he'd enter that number or any number of importance into anything the bastard could track. Not when the son of a bitch allowed sick motherfuckers like the shit he dealt with today to walk free...all for the bargain basement price of a run-down building in a shit sector of the city.

He did the walkaround of his vehicle and ducked down to look under it. A pair of small high-heeled boots stopped at the passenger's side door. He rose and looked through the window. Joy cocked her head at him and then looked at the door lock. He hit the key fob, and they both opened the doors at the same time. His gun was drawn. She laughed and used the 'oh shit' bar and the hydraulic running boards to climb into the SUV, shutting the door behind her. Dixon glanced up and down the street before he holstered his weapon and slid into his seat. He punched the start button so he could crank the heat. It was fucking cold. Thanksgiving was in a couple weeks. There had been a deluge of snow that had melted into filthy grey clumps after being shoved along the curb.

"I need a date." She brushed an invisible piece of lint from her fur.

"I thought you didn't date." He slid his finger over the touchscreen, sending the heater into furnace mode.

"I don't." She turned in her seat. Long strands of diamonds hanging from her ears caught the fluorescent lighting from the street-lights. "I'm working. I need plausible deniability. Being single at this event would draw attention that I do not desire."

"How very romantic. Of course, I'd love to be your date for the evening." He stared at her, taking in the mink coat she wore and the diamonds that fell from her ears. "I'm assuming I need a tux?"

"Of course." She lifted her bag and slipped off her boots, pulling out a pair of incomprehensibly high heels. She glanced at him and then to the road. "Well hurry up, or we're going to be late."

Dixon chuckled gave her a two fingered salute. "Roger that, your wish is my command."

"See, everything goes so much smoother

with that attitude, Quick Draw. Keep it." She half stood up as he pulled away from the curb. With a quick shimmy of her hips, the length of her dress fell to her feet. The white material shimmered in the passing streetlights. "Watch the road."

Dixon snapped his eyes forward and corrected his steering to avoid the ass end of a car that hadn't been properly parallel parked. She sat down again and reached for her bag. "What do you know about art?"

"I know what I like. I favor realism. An abstract is okay if the colors are to my liking. I have a friend who collects art. I like most of it, but he could tell you the artist, the creative period they were in when they painted it and why it is valuable." He chuckled at the length Justin King could go on about an artist. "I could regurgitate that information if I needed to do so."

"Awesome. You do the talking if we have to interact. I think pictures in the bins at craft stores are art." She flipped the visor down and ran her finger along the bottom of her lip. "Oh, there is roadwork being done about a block from your apartment building. You might want to circle around to get into the parking lot. It would be easier than waiting for the flagmens to get off their asses and let us through."

Dixon swung his eyes to her and lifted a single eyebrow.

"What? Like I wouldn't follow you and check you out after you suggested we work together? What do you think I am? An amateur? That is hardly flattering." She settled back into the seat and lifted her chin regally.

"Did you happen to pull my tux out and send it to the cleaners for me?" The woman was bold, he'd give her that.

"No, but I did take it out of the garment bag and steam it for a bit. When was the last time you wore that?" She reached down and picked up the massive bag, again shoving it between them and dropping it to the floor in the second-row seating.

"Shit…a wedding almost five years ago." He hadn't worn it in Aruba. Everyone wore chinos and polos because that was what Zane and Jewell requested. So, yeah, five years ago when Doc and Keelee got married…fuck, he hoped that bastard still fit.

"Well it is Armani, so vintage isn't necessarily a bad thing." She waved dismissively. "Hopefully no one will notice."

They rode in silence until his apartment building came into view. Dixon pulled into his parking slot and put the vehicle into park. "Are you coming up or waiting here?"

"Waiting. You have ten minutes." She turned her head and blinked at him. "Well? Go!"

Dixon laughed and opened the door. There was never a dull moment around that woman. He shut the door and sprinted up the stairs to his apartment. Evidently, he had a date tonight.

DIXON PRESENTED THE GILDED INVITATION JOY had provided him and escorted her into the long white tunnel of the art gallery's entrance. Her mink and his cashmere top coat, scarf and gloves were spirited away in an instant. A passing waiter offered them champagne which they both accepted and neither drank. A prop for the evening. They strolled down the corridor, occasionally stopping to look at the art. Through his peripheral vision, he saw her studying people rather than the canvases. Her eyes bounced from person to person.

Dixon turned to move them further along. Her hand at the inside of his elbow guided him across the grand hallway to a smaller painting near a cluster of people. Dixon recognized several men and one woman immediately. The men were current New York senators, both had been prominent in the local news of late. The woman was a legendary television reporter. Joy spun so her back was to the group. Dixon put his arm over her shoulder and gazed at the painting while she obviously listened to the conversation. The current debate centered around the upcoming legislation in the spring session. Joy smiled up at him and started toward another painting. He fell into step with her and continued on. They traversed the exhibit, and Dixon lost count of the times she directed him away from or toward a certain painting. She asked his opinion and at times seemed enthralled by his responses. At other times he knew her attention was elsewhere. He could have told her he liked the purple and pink elephants in one landscape they were viewing, and she wouldn't have heard him. Her eyes darted around the room, searching.

"What are you looking for?" He turned her around when she applied pressure to the inside of his arm.

"Inconsistencies." She smiled up at him. "What are you looking for?"

Dixon winked at her. "A good time."

"And this isn't it?" She lifted her hand and made an elegant sweep toward the painting.

He took a sip of his champagne and grimaced. He flagged down a waiter as he passed. He took her glass from her and set both warm, flat, wine flutes on the silver tray. He took her hand and tucked it through his arm. "No, this doesn't do it for me."

"Such a shame, because I'm afraid I'm busy later." She gave him a delicate shrug of her shoulders. "But I'm free now."

"Now?" Dixon cast a glance around the gallery. There had to be at least two hundred of New York's elite in attendance. Movie stars, models, political leaders, and the uber-wealthy, mingled and talked about the three artists that comprised the showing. From the conversations, he'd heard there was a bidding war on several of the paintings.

"Come with me." She pulled him with her to a small door at the very end of the long hall. She glanced over her shoulder before she opened it and slipped in, tugging him after her.

"Getting busted for trespassing would be a bad thing," he whispered after the door shut.

She shushed him and lifted her gown before she took off at a fast clip down the corridor. Yeah, something told him he wasn't here to get lucky. He followed her as she wound her way through the maze of offices and warehouse space behind the gallery's storefront.

"Here." She motioned to the door. "Open this." She slipped him a set of lock picks, and he took them from her. He didn't have gloves on, and he'd be damned if he was leaving fingerprints or any trace evidence. He reached into his pocket and grabbed his linen handkerchief. Using it, he removed a hefty pick from the set, inserted it in the top portion of the lock barrel, and then used a more pliable pick to work through the tumblers. The bolt moved, and he rotated the handle of the door using the hanging portion of the handkerchief to cover his palm. She scooted through the door, and he followed. The office wasn't anything spectacular. He stood guard by the door and watched as she searched the drawers, finally pulling a thick folder from the bottom right-hand drawer.

She flipped through pages quickly before stopping and reading one. She shuffled through several more before plucking one out of the stack and folding it several times. She lifted her gown and stuck the paper into her garter belt on the inside of her thigh. After adjusting her skirt, she replaced the file and held out her hand, waggling her fingers at him. He narrowed his eyes and handed her his handkerchief.

She meticulously wiped the few surfaces she'd touched before handing it back to him. They slipped out of the room and headed back to the front of the gallery. Dixon heard the footsteps the same time she did. He spun her into the wall and slammed his lips onto hers as he grabbed at her skirt as if trying to lift it.

"Hey, you can't be back here." The shrill sound of a surprised woman broke them apart.

"Oh, sorry. The door wasn't locked, and we were just..." Joy didn't finish the sentence, rather she giggled like a teenager and hid her face behind her hand as if she was mortally embarrassed.

"Right, I get it, but seriously, this portion of the gallery isn't open to the public. You need to leave." The woman moved to the side of the corridor and pointed toward the door they'd entered several minutes ago.

Dixon lifted away from Joy and adjusted his coat, giving her time to smooth her jacked up gown. He nodded to the woman as they passed by. They meandered arm in arm through the display gallery and back to the main entrance. Their coats were exchanged for the tickets Dixon provided, and his SUV pulled up at the valet station as they walked out of the building.

Dixon swung his head to Joy after assisting her into the SUV. "Where to?"

"Head east. I'll tell you where to drop me off."

"Holy hell, you were serious?" His head snapped toward her. She was shimmying into a pair of pants.

"Well, yeah." She gathered the gown from the hem and pulled it off over her head. A plume of shimmery white material floated toward him. He swatted it back toward the passenger seat. He missed all but the briefest flash of breast as she pulled down a black t-shirt and tucked it into her black jeans. She dove between them and grabbed the huge purse she'd deposited there earlier. She pulled the boots out and plopped them onto the floorboard. The high heel shoes went in seconds before she started cramming the gown into the satchel.

"What is this? A scene from some type of grown-up, contract killer, *Mary Poppins* rip-off? Is that bag bottomless?" Dixon pushed the white fabric, that somehow had escaped her efforts to plunge it into the deepest recesses of the never-ending suitcase, off the center console towards her.

"Oh crap, I loved that movie. Julie Andrews was badass in that one. She didn't take shit from anyone, and she was connected, you know. Like she was my O.G., Original Gangsta." Joy spoke to the floorboard because she was bent in half putting her boots on.

"Only you would equate a British nanny to a gangster." Dixon slowed to wait for the light to change. He glanced at the dashboard. It wasn't even ten o'clock and fuck him if he didn't feel like he'd run a marathon today.

"Yeah? Really?" She popped up and blinked at him with a sincerity he didn't think she could fake.

He laughed. "Honestly. I kinda like the way your brain works."

Dixon was rewarded with a wide smile. "Well, Quick Draw, I kinda like the way your things operate, too." She pointed toward a building on the right. "Stop here."

Dixon pulled over as she gathered her purse and checked around her. "Ah ha!" She grabbed a folded piece of paper, which he assumed was what she'd taken from the gallery, and crammed it into the pocket of her pants.

"What were you working on tonight? A contract?" His words stalled her exit.

Her brows furrowed in that now familiar way, telling him he'd confused her. "Did I kill anyone?"

"Not that I'm aware of." He half laughed that comment.

She pulled the purse into her lap. "Then I obviously wasn't working a contract." She snapped her head up. "I have skills in other areas."

Something about her tone demanded he acknowledge her comment. That specific declaration seemed important to her. "I have no doubt. I'm sure I've only glimpsed half the skills you possess."

She kept their gazes locked and searched his expression as if looking for any indication he'd been less than serious. Finally, she nodded. "Okay." She opened the door and jumped out, throwing her mink over her shoulders. "See you." She shut the door and started down the street.

Dixon put the car into drive and moved forward, lowering a window and calling out, "Don't be a stranger."

She laughed and flipped him off. "I *am* a stranger. Keep driving, sexy. You ain't getting none of this tonight." She turned and walked the opposite direction, going back toward where they'd started.

Dixon shook his head and took his foot off the brake. His stomach growled in protest, reminding him he hadn't eaten since breakfast. The human refuse he'd dealt with at lunch had killed his appetite. He headed back to his neighborhood and called in a take-out order from his father's pub. The bartender delivered it curbside along with a bottle of Maker's Mark.

The Philly cheese steak smelled amazing. Dixon grabbed a handful of seasoned fries and munched on them on his way back to his apartment. He'd give anything to talk to Drake right about now. His mind was spinning. Between his fucked-up sperm donor, the work he'd done, the things he'd seen today, and his totally unexpected experiences with Joy this evening, his brain was pegged in the red zone. Checking the parking area, he grabbed another couple fries and popped them into his mouth. A couple argued as they passed by on the sidewalk. A car horn honked ahead of him and he watched as the animated couple made their way to the hybrid. His eyes followed them as they got in and pulled away.

What would it be like to have that...well, not necessarily *that*—although there was angry sex and make up sex to think about—but what would it be like to have a lover you could talk with, argue with...make up with. He'd been a serial dater. The only constants in his life were Drake and Guardian, and the latter had separated him from the former. Which sucked on par with the supermassive black hole at the center of the universe and *that* was a cosmic fuck-ton of suckage.

With one final glance around the area, he locked up his vehicle and headed back to his apartment. Dixon opened the lock and turned on the lights. He dropped the food and whiskey onto the high granite counter that divided the small kitchen area from the living room and grabbed the television remote. He lifted it, pointed it over his shoulder and while he pulled his sandwich out, he hit the power button. Dropping the remote, he pulled his automatic out of its holster at the small of his back, set it beside his sandwich and pulled out a stool. Swiveling so he could see the screen, he flicked through channels before he landed on the one where the local news would come on in...ten minutes.

He took his tux jacket off and draped it over the chair. Just as he'd done earlier, he walked his apartment and swept it to make sure Joy's little visit hadn't deposited any electronic devices. Once again, he found nothing.

He rolled up the sleeves of his dress shirt and sat down on the stool at the kitchen bar. Dixon took a huge bite of the cheesy steak goodness and reached out for his computer. He called up the sports page and several other pages before accessing the benign link at the side of the web page. He waited for the fantasy football app to queue up and pulled up his league. He glanced at the personal message board and watched as someone typed a message. Fuck, Guardian had been waiting for him to log on. He checked this emergency board once a night. His jaw froze, and he swallowed the bite before he read the words couched in sports vernacular for a second time.

>*Trade request: Drake for Fury vs Morales.*

The food he'd just swallowed threatened to come back up. He leaned forward and tried to suck air into his lungs. If he understood the message properly, Drake had been killed—as far as anyone other than Guardian knew. *Trade Drake for Fury versus Morales.* Some years ago, the assassin "Fury" had appeared to have died during an op gone bad. It allowed him to have his life back as Joseph King. If Guardian had "killed" his brother, there existed a direct, credible threat against Drake, but from whom? Guardian had removed a valuable asset from their arsenal. Whoever they were, Guardian considered them lethal and remorseless, and he wasn't there to watch Drake's six. The danger inherent to their job was always a reality; sometimes it was more real than others. His hand shook, making hitting the right letters on the electronic keyboard difficult.

>*Trade accepted.*

He typed the words before he carefully backspaced, removing all traces of his response. The message on the board disappeared before the blinking cursor typed a single word.

>*Fire.*

Dixon stared at the blinking cursor for several long minutes. No, he wasn't going to tuck tail and ask to be pulled out. Fuck, he was working in a vacuum here. He carefully tapped out the response.

Fight.

If he needed to be pulled out, he would have typed, "Fly". He deleted his response and watched the original message disappear.

<3

The image appeared briefly before being erased. *Jewell.* She was an amazing person, and he loved her like the sister she'd become to him. Still...what the fuck was going on?

He sat watching the message board for several minutes. When nothing else came up, he updated his fantasy team, replacing a defense that was on a bye week, and logged out. The forum was real. They had dummy bot accounts logging in and running the other teams. He futzed around with his team because the competitor in him didn't want to have a fucked up showing against a computer program. He closed out his browser and left the history intact.

Jewell had blessed the communication and routed herself through so many wickets she swore nobody could ever know it was her posting in the group. Dixon trusted her. She knew more about tech than almost anyone on the planet. The odds of her being right were always in his favor, so she was a safe bet.

His appetite suddenly gone, he rolled the sandwich up in the foil it came in and tossed it into the garbage. He grabbed his gun and the television remote and transferred his ass to the recliner in the front room. A flick of his finger muted the station and allowed him a brief respite from the overload of high-volume commercials.

So...Guardian would leak reports Drake was dead. Dixon steeled himself for the gut punch his fucking father would no doubt land. Though no one else could know, as long as *he* knew Drake was alive, his father's response didn't matter. He'd have to be fucking careful to craft his emotional response correctly. Too much or too little and his father's always hyper-active suspicion would destroy all the trust he'd tried to build in the last few months. How to react? He was supposed to be estranged from his brother, but they had had a lifetime of experiences.

The flash of a red 'breaking news' banner crossed the screen. He lifted the remote and unmuted the television.

"Initial reports say the westbound car crossed the median and drove straight into Senator Waxman's hired town car. The senator had reportedly just concluded a personal appearance on the Upper West Side. We have been informed the driver of the other vehicle was pronounced dead at the scene. However, hospital officials are not releasing any information about the driver of that car or occupants of the senator's vehicle at this time. Stay tuned as details develop."

Dixon stared at the smiling photograph of Senator Waxman that flashed up on the news backdrop. He'd stood not five feet from that man this evening. He leaned forward when the recorded video of the accident site filled the screen. The detritus of the wreck had shut down all traffic. His eyes scrutinized the vehicle that had taken out the senator's car. The mangled piece of metal had formerly been a small SUV. Police officers could be seen scouring the wreckage.

The anchor cleared for a commercial and Dixon hit the mute button. He dropped his head back on the soft suede of the recliner. His mind automatically tracked to Joy. He'd dropped her only a few blocks from the gallery and very near the crash site. He closed his eyes and reconstructed every detail of the wreckage in his mind. A breeze of dread swirled over him. She hadn't been scoping out a contract tonight. She'd been at the art gallery for whatever was on that paper. He leaned forward and dropped his head between his shoulders. She couldn't have been the driver of the SUV. Life couldn't be that fucking cruel. Didn't he deserve the small portion of lightness his private moments with Joy brought into the shitstorm that was currently his life? He lifted his eyes and looked at the television. Probably not.

CHAPTER 7

"What are our people telling us?"

"Massive trauma from the impact. He's brain-dead. His parents and his wife are at the hospital. Doctors are recommending life support be terminated." Her assistant clipped the report out at an efficient and professional pace as they walked through vacant, pristine halls.

"Our operative?" She glanced down at the shorter man as he walked beside her.

"She requested her family be taken care of."

"And?"

"It will be done."

"The Governor?"

"Will be appointing our man after a respectful period of time."

"We have reins on the new appointee?"

When there wasn't an immediate answer, she stopped walking and peered down at the man. His forehead scrunched, and his face looked as if he'd eaten something particularly distasteful.

"What is it?" She drawled. She'd done the background. She knew what a foul piece of putrid waste Simmons was, but he was a perfect veneer, and he had failsafe measures in place to ensure no one but the most aggressive could trace him to any criminal activity.

"Honestly, ma'am, I'm not sure. He is insulated. From the reports, he seems to fall in line, but…"

And this is why this little curmudgeon of a man had become her trusted assistant. "I agree, hence the stay of execution on his heir. We have almost two months to ensure our agenda is completed.

"And if that doesn't happen?"

She lifted a solitary eyebrow at him.

"My apologies, ma'am. In my zealousness to

protect our goals, I overstepped." He bowed slightly as he spoke to curtail her growing ire.

There was always an alternate route and an escape mechanism. Cutting losses in this instance, however, would set their agenda back years. The alternate route, while risky, might have benefits that complemented the expediency they desired.

She turned and continued down the Carrera marble floor toward her office as her assistant fell into step beside her. She had moved her pawn, and it was the world's turn to respond. They would observe, learn, evaluate and consider all information before the next move in this particular game would occur. Now that they'd recovered the wealth and position lost by the women who'd previously held their position, exhuming the multiple tentacles of Stratus from the faded past would serve them well. Witnessing the rebirth and growth of Stratus had become addictive.

"Operator Two-seven-four."

"Sunset clearance, zero operative."

"Standby, zero operative."

"Archangel."

"Asset is still in play."

"Have you made contact?"

"Briefly. I believe he is…managing."

"I may need to pull you. Another can fill in."

"I don't recommend that."

"Substantiate."

"Gut instinct. I'm here. You're not."

"…I'll juggle other assets to keep you there…for now."

"He's no longer on the street."

"Watch him closely. I don't need to tell you this is where shit could go south."

"No doubt. I'm lurking."

"Check in as scheduled unless something happens I need to know about."

"Of course."

"Did you see the news last night?"

Dixon glanced up at Smith, who stood in the doorway to his office at The Residence. For a big guy, he was awfully quiet. The bespoke suit he wore somehow hung wrong, as if his body was rejecting a transplant. "You mean the Senator's accident?"

Smith cocked his head as if confused.

"It was all over the media. They had special coverage. I turned it off at midnight. Why, what did I miss?" Dixon pushed his chair back and stood up, stretching his arms to the ceiling. His weapon gouged into his back, and he shifted to alleviate the pressure.

Smith leaned against the door and once again studied his shoes. "They're both dead."

Dixon snapped his eyes up to the big guy. "Who? The Senator?" At last report the man was in critical condition, so the news wasn't totally unexpected.

"No, the people in the photographs."

Dixon's knees went weak, and his ass planted into his chair. "What?" He didn't need to ask, he knew. He fucking knew his father had both people murdered because he wouldn't make a choice. He went cold.

"Choose one."

"That one, sir." Dixon pointed to one of the puppies his father had brought down to the place where he lived. His father called it his training

room. Dixon thought the windowless cell scary and lonely, but he'd never admit it.

"This one? Are you sure?" His father reached down and picked up the black furry puppy and stroked its head.

"Yes, sir. He's the one." He was so excited. A puppy. He could play with it and teach it to do tricks and love it. He wouldn't be lonely anymore.

The echoes of the puppy's last whimper, as his father broke its neck, rang like a solemn knell through his memory. *How could I have forgotten?* Jeremiah said blocking memories was a defense mechanism. Defense mechanism...as if there was any defense against the engulfing evil of his father.

He glanced up at Smith. "Because of me."

Smith glanced up at the camera in the corner of the room without responding. He stepped backward and glanced down the hall. "He wants to see you." The man turned on his heel and headed out of The Residence.

Dixon dropped his head into his hands and gulped air, pulling himself together, quickly. He was the stronger man; he knew it, and soon enough that motherfucker would know it too. He needed out. Out of the house. Out of his thoughts before he lost it and put a gun to that bastard's head. He stood and grabbed his jacket, fastening the middle button.

He stopped at the closed set of double doors and rolled his shoulders, trying to cloak his rage with normalcy. He knocked and waited for his father to bid him, "Come in."

"You wanted to see me?" He fucking tried to hide his anger, but of course, his father sensed his emotional turmoil.

"Your weaknesses will not taint me."

Dixon didn't even flinch at the words, and his father laughed. "You've forgotten so many lessons, but I'm feeling lenient today. I've received two pieces of excellent news, and I'm debating how to inform you of my joyous tidings..." His father chuckled and shook his head.

Dixon kept his mouth shut. Asking a question was beyond him at the moment. He needed out of this office before he drew his weapon and put the barrel to the motherfucker's head and pulled the trigger. He was hanging on to his pledge to Jason King by his bloodied fingernails.

"To hell with it, I'm in such a good mood,

I'll just tell you. Your waste of a twin was killed two days ago. DNA has been confirmed."

Dixon blinked back his rage. His hands tightened at his sides, folding into shaking fists. "How did he die?"

"Ha, get this, someone blew his ass up along with some whore." His father threw back his head and laughed.

"Where?" Dixon swallowed hard, the deaths of the two people in the photograph still fresh in his mind.

"Fuck if I know, some uncivilized place in the middle of the country. Why? Plan on going out to avenge your brother's death?"

Dixon shook his head. "No, sir."

"Hearing that weak son of a bitch was dead was the cherry on top of an extraordinary day. Your old man is moving up in this world. Come the new year, you and the rest of the world will witness just how important I am." He clapped his hands together and rubbed them with a gleeful expression on his face. "Once I'm in office, I will wield the power and the people who graciously arranged for my ascent will be forced to take note of my agenda." He stood up and smiled. "I'm taking the rest of the day off to celebrate." He walked by and clasped Dixon on the shoulder. "What a fabulous fucking day."

Dixon barely heard the words the man vomited. He waited until his father left his office before he returned to his own. He meticulously shut down his computer, organized his desk, gathered his keys and coat, and departed The Residence. He passed his vehicle, his head down and his eyes fixed on the icy sidewalk.

He counted his steps. *One, two, three, four, five.* Over and over. Screaming the numbers through his mind to push back everything else. He walked on, the bitter cold doing nothing to numb the rage in his soul. On autopilot, he crossed streets and moved forward. *One, two, three, four, five.* Snow mixed with rain and fell, wet and heavy, melting on his overcoat and drenching his hair and shoulders. The cold wind picked up when he rounded the corner and headed west.

He pushed open the door to the gym he'd joined several months ago. *One, two, three, four, five.* The old man behind the desk grunted at him when he signed in. His hands were so fucking cold he could barely hold the pen that dangled off the cheap ass chain.

Manipulating the plastic spinning lock on the metal locker he'd been assigned took several attempts. *One, two, three, four, five.* As his body started to warm, shivers overcame him. Finally, he managed to open the small compartment. He pulled out his workout gear, piled up his clothes and stuffed his gun and wet leather shoes into the bottom of his locker.

The beds of his nails were purple when he wrapped his hands. It didn't matter. The only thing that mattered was getting into the gym. He counted his wraps as he wound the tape. *One, two, three, four, five.* The numbers spun through his mind on autopilot. He couldn't stop counting, not yet.

He strode out of the locker room without acknowledging anyone. *One, two, three, four, five.* The heavy bag at the back of the gym beckoned. *One, two, three, four, five.* He stood in front of it and took a deep breath as he lifted his hands and stopped counting. Like a stop-motion movie, his mind replayed images, sounds, words, and memories. He lashed out at the bag, a scream of rage tearing from the incomprehensible pain that flowed through him.

Time was inconsequential as he purged his system. Hit after hit he drove his hatred, bitterness, regrets and pain into the canvas bag. Unrelenting, he pounded down the volume of his mental anguish with each reverberating impact into the bag in front of him. The miasma of swirling thoughts slowly receded as rational thought blinked in and out of the fury and grief-induced static that had seized control of his mind.

The burning in his hands, shoulders, and back registered first. The acknowledgment of exhaustion, dehydration, and emptiness followed. He stopped. His hands up as far as he could lift them, he stared at the bag. There was a red hue on the canvas. He glanced at his hands. The tape gapped in places and blood seeped from the abrasions the canvas had worn through his skin.

"Drink this."

A bottle of water appeared in front of him. Dixon turned his head and looked at her.

"Bad day at the office, dear?" She twisted the top off the bottle and waggled the water in front of him. Dixon grabbed it and downed the damn thing, although it was all he could do to lift his arm above his head to drain it.

"That was fucking impressive, by the way. I've never seen anyone go that long with the heavy bag. I think maybe you scared some of the regulars away." She leaned against the wall and folded her arms.

He had nothing. Had no idea what to say to her, hell, he didn't have a clue how to move. He was wiped.

She nodded toward the locker room. "One foot in front of the other, Quick Draw. Go take a shower."

Dixon blinked at her. *Had he spoken aloud?* No? Maybe? Who the fuck cared. He swung his head toward the locker room and put one foot in front of the other, just like she said. Out of habit, he unwrapped the tape from his fists as he walked and chucked it in the trash can just outside the locker room. He moved around a man standing in his way and stripped off his sweat-sodden shirt. It landed with a splat on the wooden bench in front of his locker. After toeing off his shoes, he pushed down his shorts and jock before he pulled off his wet socks.

"Shower."

Dixon swung his head as Joy walked into the men's locker room as if she fucking owned it.

Some naked guy behind him in the locker room bellowed, "Hey! You're not supposed to be in here!"

Dixon chuckled. *As if she didn't know that.*

Joy put her hands on her hips and gave the man a once over. "I'm giving you five seconds to leave before you lose that." She nodded toward the man's flaccid cock.

He scoffed at her and grabbed for his t-shirt. "Whatever. Crazy bitch."

Dixon tipped his head to the side, too exhausted to warn the man that he'd just tickled death, and death wasn't currently exhibiting her unique sense of humor.

Joy snorted and reached behind her neck. Dixon heard the sound of the knife leaving its sheath. She pulled it in front of her and examined it before she glanced at the man. "Go. Now."

The man grabbed his shit and damn near sprinted, half-naked, into the main gym. Joy turned toward him. "You. Shower." She pointed the tip of that long thin knife at him.

Dixon shook his head. "You're going to get arrested."

"Who me? I'm an angel. Besides, I paid off Jordy. We have the gym to ourselves. It's closed for 'maintenance'." She made little air quotes as she walked past him into the shower room. He heard her turn on the water.

"Come on. You stink." Joy's voice beckoned him.

Dixon couldn't move. He was utterly exhausted. The sound of water, however, lured him toward the shower. He turned the corner and stopped. Her jeans, t-shirt, thick-heeled shit-kickers, and leather jacket were folded neatly at the far side of the shower. The knife was lying balanced on the ledge that normally held soap. She tipped her hair back, plastering the thick fall onto her shoulders and back. She opened her eyes and sighed before she marched forward, grabbed his forearm and proceeded to drag him under the shower's spray.

The hot water peeled the last vestige of fog

away from his exhausted mind. He tipped his head back and closed his eyes.

Her voice floated to him past the wall of water falling over him, "We all have those days. I'm particularly unimpressed that you lowered your guard. Anyone could have capped your ass. I'm not sure why, but that is pissing me off."

Dixon dropped his head and looked down at her. She'd acquired soap from someplace and was lathering her hands. She slid the soap into his cupped hand and reached up to wash his shoulders and pecs. "Don't do that again. Call me. I'll watch your six until you work through it."

She grabbed the soap out of his hand, spun him and lathered up his back. Her fingers dug into his used-up muscles. He leaned his head against the tile wall and groaned. "I can't risk it."

"What the fuck are you talking about?" Her hands worked his back muscles, and he closed his eyes.

"I'm not giving that bastard a way to find you." He braced both arms against the wall as her hands moved down to his lower back.

"The same bastard that wants to put me on retainer?"

Dixon snorted. "I suggest you forget that conversation."

"Huh."

Dixon smiled under the fall of water. That "huh" could have meant anything from "okay," to "fuck you," to "you don't say".

"What happened?" She lowered her soapy hands to the inside of his thighs. His cock had already been mildly interested. The brush of her fingers against his balls woke the fucker right up.

"There is no way to explain it." How could he ever explain his father, explain the fear he carried and the life he and his brother had built. Now that life was threatened. Obviously, there had been a major threat to Drake and a woman. Was it Jade? He knew Jewell was safe... maybe Jasmine? No, she was out of Guardian and had been for a while. Fuck...his head snapped up, and he blinked to focus through the fall of water. Miss Amanda?

"Whoa, big boy. What just happened?"

Dixon shook his head. No way in hell he'd

tell a living soul about his brother, the Kings or Frank and Amanda. "Nothing."

"Bullshit. Something just sent an alert through your body. Your tension went from hammock slack to suspension bridge tight in less than a second." She stood behind him and swatted him on his ass.

"What was that for?" He turned his head and stared down at her.

"Listen, I get that you can't talk about shit that's going on. I'm not a Chatty Cathy myself, but you can tell me when you're losing it. I will watch your six, and I'd like to think you'd have mine, if for no other reason than…professional courtesy."

He lifted his hands and made a fist, looking at the damage he'd inflicted on his knuckles. She stepped into him, and he dropped his hands on her shoulders. The hot water poured on his back, sending a light sheen of mist around them.

He gazed down at her. "How do I know you don't work for him?" The question was one that surprised him but had come into focus as he worked the heavy bag. His desire to have an ally had blinded him to the possibility. He dropped his hands from her shoulders and took a step back and then another.

"I choose what assignments I take very carefully. I've investigated the creep you work for. He's...well, hell, I don't know what he is, but he sets off a warning siren so fucking loud in my skull that I'd be a fool to ignore it." She turned off the water and grabbed the knife from the soap dish.

"Yet you continue to show up."

"I do." She walked past him into the locker room.

He watched her grab two towels from the stack on the table and toss him one. He caught it but didn't move from where he stood. Joy bit the blade of her knife and bent over, towel drying her hair. She whipped her hair back away from her face and grabbed the hilt. "I'm not your enemy."

"And I'm supposed to take you at your word?"

"You should."

"And yet I don't."

She toweled off quickly and started to get dressed. Dixon wrapped the towel around his waist and walked to his locker.

"Then you're smart on top of being sexy as fuck. Heads up. You didn't secure your locker before you headed to your 'beat your hands to hell' therapy session. I locked it. Weapon safety and all that. It's on the bottom underneath your clothes." She dropped down on the bench across from him and pulled on her socks.

Dixon sat down on the bench. "Why are you here?"

"Why? Because I want to be. Personally, I'm not sure what to make of that. You're not my normal type of guy." She pulled on a boot and bent to lace it up.

"What is your normal?"

She snorted. "Not you."

"Okay, change of topic. Who sent you to kill that mark?"

"Meh...actually that was an adlib on my part." She tucked her long laces into the top of her boots and pulled her jeans down over the leather.

"An adlib? Killing someone is an adlib for you?"

Joy pulled on her other boot and sent him a dazzling smile before she laughed. "Kinda fucked up, huh?"

"Just a bit. You still haven't answered my question."

She glanced at him as she laced her other boot and shrugged. "Your question was who sent me to kill the mark. I answered you."

"So you weren't under contract?"

"Well, with myself…"

"You were going to pay yourself ten thousand dollars?"

"Hell yeah, bonus for taking out the bastard after stalking him forever."

"Why kill him?" He opened his locker and pulled his stack of clothes out. His automatic was exactly where she'd said it would be.

"Because he was a son of a bitch that preyed on young girls. He was part of a bigger organization that crashed and burned a couple years ago, but the fucker had set up shop around here doing the same shit on a smaller level."

Dixon dropped his towel and pulled on his pants. He'd worked the operation to take down those sons of bitches. "How did you find out about him?"

"See that's the deal. I kinda worked for this guy who ran an influential business, and I heard some things. Bits and pieces. So, I took it upon myself to find out the information I didn't have. I broke into that guy's house." She laughed again and shook her head. "Talk about a close shave. I spent almost the entire night in the dude's office closet because he and his partner were having a marathon sex session in the office. Damn those guys were hotter than hell and let me tell you, they had sta-min-a. Anyway, when they finally hauled their asses to the shower, I found the information I was looking for. It wasn't much more than I knew originally, but it gave me a start, and I've been working my way toward getting that monster for seven months now. Just so happened to be the day you showed up. Call it a happy coincidence." She pushed her jeans over her boots and stood up as she put on her coat. Joy grabbed her wet hair and pulled it out from the back of her coat and let it fall against the leather. Moving directly in front of him, she put her hands on her hips.

Dixon stood. The action put her within inches of his torso. She tipped her head back and looked up at him. "Fuck you are industrial sized, aren't you?"

The absurdity of the question forced a laugh from him. "No, you're just travel sized."

She flashed a smile at him. "Yeah, I am."

Dixon held out his hand. "Dixon Simmons."

The woman looked at his hand and then back up at him. Her eyebrows furrowed together again in that peculiar way they did when he confused or surprised her. Slowly she lifted her hand and slid it into his. "Your parents hate you or something? Dick-son? Is your father a dick?"

Dixon threw back his head and laughed. "The largest dick on the planet."

"Huh. What do people call you other than Dick's son?"

"D."

"Okay. Get your clothes on. I'm hungry. Watching you kill that canvas bag gave me an appetite for food and sex. Interested to see if you can raise that subpar rating of yours."

"I thought you didn't date?" Dixon put on his shirt.

"I don't. Eating is fuel for a fuck fest. So we are basically trying to ensure your rating doesn't decrease over the course of the night." She pushed his hands away from the buttons.

His knuckles and fingers were swollen and maneuvering the small buttons through the holes was almost impossible. While she'd been talking, he'd fumbled two in the middle. It took her seconds to finish the task.

She moved back and stuck her hands in her pockets as if embarrassed by her almost intimate actions. Dixon got it. They had established boundaries, so he put them back into their comfort zone. "So not a date, but a ratings prep. That's cool because I only do fuel-stoked fuck fests." He slid on his wet shoes before he holstered his automatic. He grabbed his suit jacket and wet coat. "Is your car close or should we call an Uber?"

She grunted. The nonverbal noise told him he didn't need to call anyone. He'd taken lessons at deciphering grunts from the best, but he'd give credit where credit was due, the woman was almost as fluent in Grunt as Frank.

DIXON DROPPED THE TAKE-OUT CONTAINERS ON the counter and watched as Joy went straight to his silverware drawer. "Seriously, just how much time have you spent in my apartment?"

She laughed and grabbed a couple of forks and then swiped some paper towels off a roll on the counter. "Don't get pissy. Silverware is usually in one of the drawers. You've got three, and I got lucky picking the right drawer on the first pull."

She pulled out one of the stools and used the bottom rung to step up far enough to slide onto it. She pulled one container out of the bag and popped the lid. "Chicken. That's you."

Dixon turned to the fridge. "Beer or water."

"Definitely beer, but you should have more water. You were like a man possessed at the gym."

He grabbed two beers and another bottle of water—because she was right. "Possessed... that's probably accurate."

"You know you can share. I mean leave out the in-the-weeds type deets, but dude, something is eating you alive." She pointed at him with her fork before she stabbed a forkful of tofu and veggies.

Dixon opened his water and drank half of it before he shook his head. "Just a fucked-up day compounded by a mistake I made. One that others paid for." He picked at his food.

"Huh."

Dixon glanced up at her. "Care to decipher that?"

She shrugged. "Is tearing yourself apart going to change what happened?"

Dixon pushed away his food and grabbed his beer. "No." He couldn't resurrect the dead no matter how much he wanted to.

"Huh, okay so did you know when you made this mistake others were going to pay?"

"No, but I should have."

"Oh, okay. So, you're what a clairvoyant? Or is it a fortune teller?" She pushed his food container in his direction with her fork and pointed at it. "You. Eat."

He pulled the container back toward him. "I'm neither."

"As you know, when you are in the business we are in, there are no absolutes. Variables change our circumstances. They say killers have no morals, but that's bullshit. I have standards, some would call them morals. I don't violate my guidelines. Did you?"

"Did I what? Violate my standards?"

"Yeah, when you made the decision that cost those people, did you violate the standards you set for yourself?" Joy tapped his takeout container again. "Chew on that question while you chew on your food."

Dixon took another drink of his beer. Did he violate what he set out to do when Jason asked him to take on this mission? No. His father had shown a brief flash of his hand today. He was involved with someone he was using to advance his own agenda. Something 'good' happened besides Drake's supposed death. His father mentioned something about "when he was in office" when he was talking today. What office that was, Dixon couldn't be sure, but after the recent events he could make a good guess. The old man was starting to open up, and that facilitated what he was here to do. To find a way to get Guardian a toehold in Stratus.

Dixon stabbed a piece of sweet and sour chicken. He tumbled her question around as he ate his dinner. The answer came out the same no matter how he phrased it. Did that make him feel any better about the two people who were dead? No. Would he have been able to save one of them? With his father, who the fuck actually knew? The man was insane, rabid, an animal without conscience. He'd need to be put down, soon, but not until Dixon got the information he needed. He took the final swallow of his beer before he spoke again. "No."

Joy jumped down from her stool and took her takeout container to the trash can. "Then what happened to them was collateral damage. It happens in war. Sometimes we can mitigate it and sometimes we can't."

"War." Dixon clicked on that term. That was what he was doing. He was fighting a one-man war against an evil force. The word shifted something inside him and like a lens slipping into place, he could see more than just his past, more than the hatred, and more than the guilt.

Joy threw away his empty container and walked past him as she took off her shirt. "You owe me, Quick Draw"

"Joy."

She turned at the name. It wasn't a bad name. She'd used it several times as an alias.

"Thank you." His words confused her sometimes.

"For what?" *Seriously, what had she done?*

"For having my back today. For knowing..." His words faded as if he didn't quite know how to finish the sentence.

She spun on her heel and marched back to him. "Let's get something straight, right here and right now. This between us, it is reciprocal. Someday you *will* pay me back. This isn't a favor or a friendship. This is two people who don't have anyone else, using each other to stay sane. Don't put a hashtag on it and call it social. It isn't. We're surviving."

He stared down at her. Damn those blue eyes. When he stared at her like that, she could swear he could see through every fucking layer of protection she'd built. He couldn't because she'd never allow it, but if she ever did let anyone in? It could be the man behind those eyes.

"Survivors. I can deal with that." He winked at her.

She reached behind her back, popped her

bra clasp, and shrugged out of it. His eyes tracked her movements. "I believe you have a reputation to enhance. Maybe you'll even get to a seven-point five today.

He chuckled and ran one of those big fingers across her collarbone. Her body shivered in anticipation. The man instinctively knew how to make her fly. She'd never ask for what he gave her. Never admit she wanted to be controlled during sex, to not have to make a decision, but to be...free from it all, if only for the duration of the sexual event. He got it. He let her set the parameters, but he was in charge inside those lines. After they'd fucked the first time, she'd realized that he understood. Any future sexual partners would have a very large cock to fill. She laughed at the mental image and spun on her heel to dash into the bedroom.

"I'm locking up." He called after her and then he laughed.

Laughter was good. She wasn't sure what the fuck had happened to send him off the deep end today, but for a while at the gym, she wasn't sure he'd surface again. She watched him beat his demons to death for over an hour. He hadn't known she was there. She'd slipped the day manager five grand to close the gym until she could get him out of there. The fuckwad in the locker room was the last to respond to the manager's notice to leave.

Why did she do it? Fuck if she knew. Seriously, one minute she was watching him walk out of The Residence where he worked and the next, she was emptying her emergency cash stash and moving people out of the gym.

She took off the sheath with her knife and laid her favorite weapon on the bedside table. Her boots and jeans were off before she heard his tread in the hallway. She crab-walked back into the middle of his king-sized bed and dropped down on the pillows.

Speaking from a strictly physical standpoint, Dixon was magnificent. The various scars and burns that disfigured his hard muscles told her he'd been through some fires. She appreciated that. Her own scars didn't mark her skin, as much as they were grafted onto her soul and mind. After today, she was one hundred percent positive the man taking off his shirt at the foot of the bed hid similar damage.

His muscles rippled under that pale skin of

his. She liked the fact he didn't have a hairy chest, and that his arms were as big as her thighs. He was massive, and he could fuck like a machine with that long, thick cock.

A sudden hunger struck her. Not for food, but for the taste of him. She'd never tasted him, and she deserved a diversion. Hell, she'd been Joan-of-fucking-Arc today. She should get a treat, right?

She got up and started crawling toward the end of the bed. His pants were unzipped and hanging from his hips. He was commando, and the thick patch of reddish-blond hair at the base of his cock beckoned to her.

She crawled straight to his crotch and nuzzled his confined shaft, kissing it through the fabric of his suit pants. His hand found her hair, and he grabbed it. "Yes, harder," she murmured. She loved her hair pulled, loved to feel the grip of a man's hand, the sting and the bite and the burn of a cock buried in her throat.

He gathered her hair and wrapped it around his hand. The zing of excitement pooled at her core. He pushed his slacks down with his free hand and held his cock, denying her what she sought. "Suck my balls." His growl resonated deep inside her.

She moaned when he pushed her down. She loved being able to let go, to let her sexual partner lead, but that had happened only a handful of times. She took charge because she couldn't trust the men she was with. This one...this one was different. He didn't judge her; didn't assume he knew her, or ask her what she wanted. On some instinctual level, he just...nailed it.

She laved his balls before sucking one and then the other into her mouth, rolling her tongue along the bottom of his sac. His hand clenched harder in her hair, and a growl rumbled from deep in his gut.

He pulled her off and pulled her hair back, forcing her to look up at him. "Stick out your tongue."

She did, and he slid his cock head along it, teasing her and perhaps himself. "You want this?" Her eyes shot to him. She wouldn't beg. Never would she cross that line and by the look, she got in return he understood it. Instead, he admitted, "I want it. I want your lips around my cock. Suck me."

He was big, and she struggled to take him, but he was insistent, forceful, and took away her choice, which was exactly what she wanted, or if she was honest, needed. He thrust into her mouth again, tightening the hold on her hair, using his grip to move her toward him. "Give me what we both want."

She lifted her eyes to him and was immediately struck by the storm in the blue eyes that looked down at her. He pulled her away. "Breathe."

Fuck, yes. She took a deep breath, and he pushed her toward his cock. She closed her eyes and took him as far as she could. He pulled out and pushed in again, breaching her throat.

"Yes. God, yes." He groaned, pulled out, and immediately thrust in again.

The girth of his cock made the back of her throat expand. She gagged, but he didn't immediately pull her off. *Yes, perfect. Please don't stop.*

He pulled her off his cock. "Tease your clit while I fuck this beautiful mouth."

Her fingers flew to her sex as he pulled to him again. Euphoria flowed through her. She was almost there, so fucking close. Dixon let her breathe. Not as much as she needed and only enough to keep her completely at his mercy.

He pulled her away again. "Deep breath. I'm going to cum. I'm going to own you." His strained voice deepened.

She opened her mouth to deny it, but he filled her mouth. "Don't come. Not until I let you." His thrusts were fast and deep. She grabbed his hips with both hands, her own need forgotten but not because he directed it.

Her eyes watered, and she gagged when he thrust into her throat. He roared, and his hand pulled at her hair. He pulled out. She closed her eyes as he painted her face and neck with his release. "Beautiful." His words fell in a whisper around her.

He released his cock, dropped to his knees and grabbed her legs, upending her onto her back. He tugged her to the edge of the bed and lowered his mouth to her sex. His hands found her nipples, and he twisted them sharply as he took her over the edge. She bucked against his face, her hands finding his hair and keeping him at her sex as her orgasm twisted through her.

Her hands dropped away from him of their own accord. She could have pushed him away, but right now, she was content, and honestly, she didn't want to fucking move. He turned his head and kissed the inside of her thigh, igniting a full body shudder.

His laughter against her leg forced her to move. She cuffed the back of his head. "Asshole."

"An asshole who made you scream."

"I did not."

"Beg to differ."

"No recording, no proof."

"Sex tapes? Kinky."

She laughed and then groaned. "I need another shower."

"I have one of those."

"Yeah? How totally civilized of you." She kinda liked his shower. It had a rain-head and messaging jets, although she'd probably need him to block the top one, otherwise, it might take out her eye. She'd been through his apartment with a fine-tooth comb. There wasn't any monitoring or listening devices that she'd found, and she was up to date on the latest tech. It was necessary in her profession.

"Totally civilized, because I'm a ten. Tens are like that." He rose up on his knees and leaned over her. His silent challenge was written on the confident smirk that spread across his face.

"Meh...almost an eight." She sat up pushing him back, so he was standing on his knees, and her legs were on either side of his thighs. "But the night is still young." She leaned in and bit his lip before he wrapped his arms around her and pulled her into him. His hands cupped her ass, and she wrapped her legs around his waist as he stood. Fuck, the man was magnificent. A twenty on a scale of one to ten, but she'd never tell him that.

He slapped her bare ass and laughed when she gasped. "I'll just have to do better, won't I?"

CHAPTER 8

"Mr. Simmons, I'm pleased you could make time to meet with me."

"Governor Charles, my time is yours." He hated fucking kowtowing to the weak son of a bitch in front of him, but from his dealings with Stratus, he knew there was a hierarchy within that organization, and he was unsure where the man in front of him fell. If he had his way, that man and many others would fall at his feet.

"Excellent. I'm sure you're aware of the horrific accident that recently befell one of our own."

"Senator Waxman? Yes, tragic. I feel for his parents. I, too, lost one of my sons. Although we were estranged..." He closed his eyes and cleared his throat.

"I'm so sorry for your loss. Was it recent?"

He cast his eyes to his hands and spoke quietly, "Yes, a few days before Senator Waxman's accident, I believe. His twin brother is with me, and he is my solace in this difficult time."

"You have a younger son, too. Is that correct?"

"Yes, out of wedlock, but I support both him and his mother financially. I've never denied I'm his father. He was a pleasant surprise although I never loved his mother." *The fucking broodmare.* "Why do you ask?"

"Let me first say, I'm sorry the timing of this meeting is so soon after your loss, but as you may know, I have been looking for a suitable person to appoint to Senator Waxman's vacant seat."

He gave the man his best blank stare. "I'm sorry, I don't understand how this pertains to me." But he did understand. This was it.

The governor's façade slipped, and a glimpse of confusion crossed his face. *Unacceptable. This man's weaknesses cannot taint me.*

He'd make sure whoever he was dealing with in Stratus knew of the man's inadequacies. He sat passively while the governor recovered. "I would like to appoint you, Mr. Simmons, to fill his seat."

He closed his eyes for a moment. All of his work culminated in this moment. His words were practiced, humble and precise, "If you feel I am worthy, I accept." A thrill of triumph catapulted through him. Finally. The fulfillment of his dreams. He'd reached the pinnacle of what he'd been building toward for as long as he could remember.

HER ASSISTANT CONTINUED HIS BRIEFING. "THE official announcement will be released on the date you selected. A press conference and widest affiliate distribution is scheduled. Our polls are telling us the death of his estranged son will play well with public opinion."

"Indeed. And the remaining son. What have we learned?"

"From Guardian itself, nothing. But our information arm has been digging. According to what we can piece together through our limited access to reports from other law enforcement agencies, the separation had been coming for some time. There is a series of disciplinary issues dating back years. The remaining son apparently doesn't like to follow the law to get his job done. Finally, Guardian cut ties. The reports we can gain access to are spotty because Guardian's tech team covers their tracks well when dealing with other law enforcement agencies. The majority of what we can find, or access, is masked or coded, but we believe his twin was the one that reported him and caused the organization to boot him.

So probably no love lost between the two, although the death of a twin had unique psychological implications she would need to research. With a mental note to do so, she turned to her assistant. "And while he's been working for his father?"

"He is good. Damn good. His carefulness seems to be innate, not paranoid. He is a cautious man. We assume he performed low-level tasks for his father's unofficial revenue stream, but that cannot be validated. Lately, our source says he's been working from The Residence."

She leaned back in her chair. That meant that Simmons had pulled the wayward son closer. Was it to watch him or to use him? Regardless, the Guardian reject was close to the elder Simmons. Proximity had its advantages. "I'm interested in the son. You said we have a contact. Therefore, we have a way in?" She glanced at her assistant.

He bent his head and swiped the screen of his tablet repeatedly. "We do."

"Be cautious. If there is any loyalty to figures in his past, or to his father, I want to know."

"Of course, ma'am. I'll issue your instructions and gather that information for you."

"Double check on the elder Simmons' separation from his unofficial revenue stream. I don't want any ties between the two. We control the major networks so there won't be a problem from the national level or in any of the major markets. I don't want any small-town, moralistic journalist to find even a breadcrumb. Understood?"

"Absolutely, ma'am."

"Operator Two-seven-four."

"Sunset clearance, zero operative."

"Standby, zero operative."

"Archangel."

"No change."

"Understood. Continue to monitor."

Dixon leaned over the cool granite of the kitchen counter and gazed out the small window onto the street below, alive with people. He lifted his coffee to his lips but smiled before he could take a sip. He enjoyed the soft padding sounds of her footfall coming down the hall—probably more than he should given she was a hired murderer; they didn't date–they fucked–and there was zero potential for this dynamic to transition into anything but what it was. Sex.

This was the sixth time in the past two weeks that she'd been in his apartment when he'd arrived home. She had a toothbrush in his bathroom. Which was...well, it was what it was.

He turned around and leaned against the counter. She had on his t-shirt. The damn thing hit her mid-thigh. He'd admit she rocked the hell out of it. She made a beeline for him and grabbed the coffee cup out of his hand. She took a sip and moaned. "Thank God, at least you make good coffee."

Dixon pulled the coffee from her hands and set it aside. "I do other things pretty damn well. At least that was the message I got last night when you rode me, then again when I bent you over the bathroom vanity, and let's not forget about me slamming you up against the wall."

"Oh, yeah, sorry about the mirror, by the way. I hope you're not superstitious." She twisted away from him just far enough to grab the coffee and pulled it to her again.

"Seven years bad luck? Woman, I have that market cornered, another seven years doesn't mean shit." He leaned down and nuzzled her neck.

"Stop, I'm going to spill my coffee."

He continued to nip at her neck, just below her ear. "My coffee," he reminded her.

"Stop, or I'll burn both of us." She leaned back, trusting him to keep her upright, and took a sip of his coffee. "Why are you up so early?"

"It isn't early." He glanced at the clock on the stove. "It's almost ten."

"Oh." She took another sip. "Why did we sleep so late?"

"Because I don't have to work today, and as far as I know, you don't work."

Her brow furrowed. "Not true. I work, just not when I'm with you."

"Well, that's good because I prefer you not kill anyone when we're fucking."

She tipped her head back and laughed. "Right? That would be awkward."

"Extremely. I'm heading out soon. I need to pick up a few things." He wanted an old cell phone with a sim card. He knew of several bodegas that still had them encased in plastic, dangling on hooks, covered in dust.

"Huh. I hate 'things', so I'll tap out." She moved in his arms, standing on her own instead of letting him hold her. He dropped his hold, and she spun, taking his coffee with her.

"Then I'll see you when you're *not* working."

Dixon raised his voice as she strode down the hallway. Her laughter was his only response.

At the moment he was happy they didn't have a conventional relationship because he needed to check in with Drake. It had been too fucking long, and the fantasy football message boards had been silent. Using a public computer at a hotel business center where his father had had a business meeting, he'd finally checked his dead drop email. Other than a message sent months ago letting him know there was a new threat, there was nothing. He spent ten minutes making a new account and dropped everything he knew or assumed into the draft email.

Today his sperm donor was in the state capital, a trip he was particularly happy to take, and according to snippets of conversation Dixon had heard, the fucker was meeting with the governor, again. With his father's political aspirations, there was little doubt as to why the meetings were occurring. It was the question of who was forcing the appointment that interested Dixon. He was getting closer. The badly blurred endgame he'd encountered when he'd first started this assignment seemed to sharpen and clear, at least in his mind.

"I'm out of here." Joy waved at him as she crossed the living room and headed to the front door. He lifted a hand in response. Theirs was a weird fucking relationship. Dixon laughed out loud at his choice of words as it was, literally, a fucking relationship. Not a friendship, although he'd be lying if he said he didn't enjoy her company. They talked about the most random shit, and she pulled him out of his own mind. Most of the time. But not today. He stretched long and hard, feeling the strain of his muscles. He had things to do.

HE SAT ON A LOW CEMENT EMBANKMENT AT THE edge of one of the many Christmas exhibits at Rockefeller Center. A mass of humanity crushed past him. He pulled out the phone he'd purchased that morning. He'd charged it while he'd made his purchases and mentally prepared for his first offensive strike against his father. He slid the back open and pulled the tiny sim card out of his pocket and inserted it back into its slot. It would take several minutes for the phone to acquire a signal. His eyes traveled almost sightlessly over the people who milled around. Fuck, he was melancholy today. He wanted to be back at the ranch, to laugh with Drake, and to tease Miss Amanda or joke around with Doc. He wanted to be there Christmas morning. Everyone he cared about would be at the ranch.

Dixon's eyes caught on a flash of long black hair, and he shifted, thinking for a moment he'd seen Joy. His gaze worked its way through the crowd, but there was no one in sight who looked like her. He shook his head and glanced down at the phone. Maybe not everyone he cared about was at the ranch. Joy was becoming important to him. He'd admit he liked her, and sex with her was otherworldly... but she'd never consent to a relationship. She kept him at arm's length, and she'd never deviated from what she wanted. Their relationship was quid pro quo. He didn't have the right to suggest anything else.

He sighed and stared at the phone. After all the women he'd fucked and left, he probably deserved her attitude. Karma, it seemed, had smacked him on the ass with a metal-studded paddle. The one woman he could actually fall for only wanted him for sex. Yeah, karma filled a shoe labeled 'serves you right, you callous bastard' and it fit just a bit too well.

He glanced around the area again before he punched out the number he knew by heart.

"Go."

Relief washed over him. No matter how many times he told himself that Drake was okay, hearing his brother's voice was the confirmation he needed. "Hey. Glad you're not dead."

"Me, too. You okay?" He heard the immediate concern in his twin's voice.

He smiled and for the first time in months told the absolute truth. "I am, for now. Out of the fucker's grasp for the moment, and I needed a sanity check. How're things at the ranch?"

"Fuck, everything is good here. Dix, there is a new threat."

Dixon sighed, "Stratus. I know." He'd known since Jewell's wedding. Not telling Drake had been almost impossible.

"How?"

Wow, there was not enough time left in the year to explain how or reply to the thousand questions he knew Drake would have. Instead, he deflected, "Look, I don't have time to go into it. I couldn't respond to the dead drop. They watch me, monitor me all the time, but I was able to buy this burner cell. I accessed the internet, and I've opened a new email account. Tell Jewell it is under our mom's maiden name. She'll find it. The information I could validate is in the draft message folder. I'm destroying this phone as soon as we finish talking so there will be no way for them to trace that action. Are you okay?" He had to get Guardian the information he'd heard and the assumptions he'd made. The fantasy football board was for extreme emergencies only. Like the supposed death of your twin brother.

"I am. Lying low after a minor run-in with some goons put into motion by the Russian Mafia and backed by Stratus." Dixon snorted at the *minor* run-in bullshit. The man on record as dead. That spelled major in every fucking book he'd ever read. His brother continued, "When are you coming home?"

Fuck, get me a jet, and I'll be there in time for

dinner. "I don't know. There have been... complications. I'm working on it." Complications—maybe that was the wrong word. Incremental glimpses of possible information on Stratus.

"What *are* you working on?" There was a determination in his brother's voice that he knew well, and that didn't bode well for Jason.

"I can't say, and you wouldn't understand. Besides, you knowing what I'm doing wouldn't help." Dixon wasn't going to pick that scab. No way in hell he'd make his brother bleed.

Drake released a defeated sighed into the phone, "I...fuck, Dix. I miss you."

"I miss you more." His brother had no idea how true that statement was.

"Ha. Semantics."

Dixon smiled at the verbal challenge and accepted it immediately. "Bullshit. There are no semantics. What you're doing is shading your own reality. Our own truth." He knew he was smiling like a crazy person, so he dropped his head, trying not to draw attention.

"I miss you. Period and full stop." Drake's smile came through the connection. Dixon could picture it.

"Still shades of your truth." Dixon countered, egging his brother on.

"Define truth," Drake responded.

"That for which there is no alternative but to believe as an absolute," Dixon threw the definition out there without delay.

"Is there such a thing for us?" Drake's voice took on a serious tone.

"Yeah." Dixon glanced up and watched a husband and wife smiling as they swung a child between them in that weird step-pull-swing thing happy families did. "I think love is the absolute truth."

"Love for your family?" Drake asked.

"That is one type," Dixon admitted. He found himself acknowledging another.

"You've met someone?"

Drake got him. Man, it was so fucking good to talk to his brother. He admitted what he knew, "I'm not sure, but...it's complicated."

"Grab onto it, Dix. Hold on tight." Drake pleaded with his brother.

If only it was that simple. He sat up and swept the crowd with his eyes. "What about you?"

"I've found someone, Dix. She's amazing

and...just, fuck...take care of yourself and simplify those complications. Without you here, I'm as happy as I can be. I miss the fuck out of you."

Drake found someone. Dammit, it *was* him that had been keeping his brother from his destiny, wasn't it? He caught a glimpse of that fall of hair again and stood up, responding to his brother as he searched the crowd. "I'm happy for you, D. Take your own advice and grab onto that reality." He moved to the right and watched Joy wrap her arms around another man's neck. The man spun her around and kissed her firmly on the lips. Dixon spoke to himself, "It won't last. Good things never do."

"Dix, what are you trying to tell me?"

Fuck, he'd said that out loud. He spun and started walking away from where he'd been standing. "I...nothing, man. It's just fucked up here. Nothing is solid. Everything is so mired in lies, half-truths, and innuendo I can't trust anyone. Hell, half the time I'm not even sure what I feel is real." Wasn't that the fucking truth?

"Trust your gut. Don't take any chances."

His brother's warning echoed in his ears and wasn't it fucking appropriate? He barked out a bitter laugh. "Yeah, making a leap of faith could get me killed. Better to put my head down and do what I need to do, right?"

"Walk away, Dixon. Get the fuck out, now."

"I can't." He couldn't. Guardian needed information, and he was now poised to get it. He was too fucking close to turn tail and run. He had a strategy in play, and he'd given too much to this mission to tuck tail and run.

"Dix..."

He interrupted his brother before he could get going. "Yeah man, I know. Listen, I need to go. I'm safe, for now, and I'm being maudlin. Feeling fucking homesick, maybe. Keep your head down and protect what's yours."

"I will. Take care of yourself. I love you."

He choked up at that. "And I love you. Later, D."

"When? When's later, Dixon?"

He had no fucking clue. "Got to go. Merry Christmas, Drake. Whatever it takes."

"As long as it takes, Dix. Merry Christmas, little brother."

Dixon ended the call and then broke protocol. He knew his brother. He knew sure as shit what Drake would do, and he needed the big guns to sideline him. His phone call with Jason was short and to the point. *Stay out until called in.* It took fifteen seconds. There was no way anyone would trace that call. Dixon popped the back off the phone and lifted the sim card. He dropped the phone in a trashcan and bent the sim card as he walked. When it cracked between his fingers, he dropped the first piece in a pile of snow and walked over it before crossing the street with sixty or seventy other people. The second piece landed somewhere in the middle of the road.

CHAPTER 9

"YOUR FATHER WANTS TO SEE YOU." Smith's voice pulled Dixon's attention from the stack of documents his father had buried him under this morning. He wasn't a fucking lawyer, nor was he a secretary, and yet his father had determined that Dixon needed to read and understand all the supporting documentation for the legitimate businesses under Simmons Scepter, Inc. Such a pretentious name for the fucking company, but hey, that fit his old man's crazy like cream filling in an Oreo. Perfectly.

"Thank you." Dixon stood and reached for his coat. Smith didn't leave, standing firmly in his doorway. "Did you need something?"

Smith cast his eyes down the long hallway.

"Be careful." The man's words were barely audible from the distance he stood.

Dixon continued to put on his jacket. He fixed his collar and buttoned his suit jacket before he stepped around the desk and approached Smith. He stared the man in the eyes. "I am extremely careful, Mr. Smith. I am a survivor," he said just as quietly. He held the man's eyes until the guy nodded and backed away from the door, allowing Dixon into the hall.

It took thirty-seven steps to reach his father's office. He knocked on the door and waited for permission to enter. When he received it, he opened it and walked in. The fire in the fireplace blazed. His father was sitting in one of the large chairs facing the fire. There was a crystal decanter and two glasses on the table between the chairs. "Dixon, please come in and sit down."

Dixon's eyes swept the room before he complied. This was a new dynamic, and fuck him if it didn't set his nerves on edge. He unbuttoned his suit jacket and sat down in the chair. "You asked to see me?"

"I did. I wanted to share some news. I'll be

going to the state capital again. You will go with me."

"Yes, sir." The response was immediate. He was rather proud and disgusted by how eager the words sounded.

His father poured a portion of the dark amber liquid into both glasses before handing one to Dixon. "After the holidays, the governor is announcing my appointment to the vacant Senate seat."

Dixon blinked in surprise. He hoped he nailed it. He had no doubt his father had been salivating over the open seat. He raised his glass and spoke, "It's about time. Congratulations, sir, you deserve nothing less."

Dixon waited until his father took a sip. He let the liquid touch his lips but didn't drink a damn bit of it. There was no way he'd ever allow himself to relax around this fucker.

"Indeed. I'm sure you're aware that the media will require access to you and will, unfortunately, dig into your brother's tragic death." His father's eyes latched onto him and were evaluating his smallest reactions.

"I'm sure you'll provide me the information I need to be successful in promoting the correct image to enhance your appointment." Dixon relaxed into the chair where he was sitting, and his gaze drifted toward the fire and lingered there. His father's gaze drilled holes into him, and the weight of his stare was a tangible thing.

"I will not allow any flaws to taint me. As my most likely heir, you are not in a position to make even the smallest mistake." The warmth had faded from the man's voice.

His father had discarded the pretense of respectability he wore like a second skin, and the real nature of the psychopath was bared and ready to strike. But all of that was suddenly of secondary importance. His gaze whipped from the fire to his father. Dixon leaned forward. *Most likely heir.* If his sadistic father had another child, he would take down anyone or anything to make sure that child never lived through the hell he and Drake had been through. "Most likely heir? Drake is dead. Who else is there?"

A single eyebrow rose as his father stared at him. "Why? Would you kill to keep your birthright?"

"I've killed for less." Bile rose in his throat,

and he choked it down. There was no doubt he'd burn in hell for the things his father had forced him to do.

His father's head cocked as if he was considering the comments Dixon had flung back at him. Dixon lifted his glass and took a drink simply because the residue of bile was burning the back of his throat.

"A fortuitous choice of words." His father turned and stared into the fire as he spoke, "As an act of loyalty, I will require you to perform a service for me."

His subconscious demanded him to ask what type of service. He wanted to know what type of sick test would be next, but the questions never fell from his lips. He would be killing someone to prove his allegiance to his father. Guardian knew the bastard well. Dixon took another sip of his single malt which tasted like battery acid. Instead of demanding answers, or swinging his fist into the fucker's jaw, he stared and considered the fire as he spoke. "You know I'll do whatever it takes." *For as long as it takes, you motherfucker. I'll see you burn in hell.*

"We shall see, my son. We shall see." His

father responded almost as if he'd read Dixon's thoughts. "I will also need you to move into The Residence with me."

Dixon placed his drink on the table. He stood up and went to the fire. He withdrew the poker and opened the decorative screen with the tool. His mind was scrambling for the correct way to handle the demand. He nodded and bent to roll a particularly large log. As he split his attention from his father to the fire, he said, "I can do that tonight if you'd like, but may I ask if you've taken into consideration how having your grown son living in your residence would look to the public? The whole 'failure to launch' scenario has played out poorly for numerous politicians recently. Add the fact that I work for you, and having me under your roof may be a liability in the public's opinion." Dixon added another log to the fire and used the poker to shut the screen before replacing the tool and looking over at his father. "What does your PR management team say?"

"I don't have a PR management team."

"You should consider it, sir. People who do nothing but look out for your best interests and ensure you're only seen in only the best light." Dixon sat down in his chair and once again picked up the crystal glass.

"The people I'm working with are taking care of that portion of my nomination. They want to meet with you. I'll arrange it after I've reminded you of your allegiances. Let's call it remedial training. Your weaknesses will not taint me."

Fuck, he never assumed shit would fall apart so quickly. He needed time, but it was obvious psycho-dad had other ideas. One thing he knew for sure, he couldn't endure another of his father's 'training sessions'. If the man got him into one of those rooms, his father wouldn't come out alive—of that he was positive. No, he would not be tortured again. So, he did what he'd been trained to do, he looked for an advantage and kept the bastard talking. "Why remedial training?"

His father's gaze swept in his direction. "Because, Dixon, I don't trust you farther than I can throw you. You waltz back into my life and assume I will open my arms and return you to the fold." The man lifted his glass to his lips and took a drink.

"What have I done that hasn't been in complete alignment with your wishes and desires?"

His father chuckled. "You're good. I'll give you that."

"I'm sorry?"

Dead eyes turned to him. "Yes, you are, and you're flawed." His father stood and walked toward the fire, his back to Dixon.

Dixon's eyes swept the room again. The blinking red camera in the corner of the room caught his attention. It had never been on when he was in the office, and yet the camera tracked...*his father*. Not him? Who would have eyes on his father other than...*Stratus*.

"I'm not flawed," Dixon responded and stood before almost reaching for the weapon behind his back, freezing his hands on his hips out of gut instinct.

His father spun around the poker in his hand. "You think I can't see through the lies? The feelings you had for your brother betray you."

"Have. The feelings I have for my brother." Dixon watched the vein on the fucker's forehead bulge and pulse in response to the way he was talking back to the man.

His father's voice lowered to a cold, deadly hiss, "Loving the dead is a weakness."

"I have many weaknesses. Loving the dead isn't one of them."

"Don't lie to me. You loved your brother."

"I'll admit it. He was one of the people I cared about." His mind flitted to Joy and dismissed her mental image immediately. He hadn't seen or heard from her in over a week. The new fuck she'd found was obviously doing it for her.

His father suddenly moved to his right. Dixon took a step back just as the poker in the man's hand stabbed through the air. There wasn't much that needed to be done. Dixon thwarted the man's violence with a simple block and swat move.

The older man had made a fatal mistake. He assumed Dixon would roll over and take the punishment. He'd forgotten the training Dixon had been through, the skills he had that were honed to a razor's edge. No, he wasn't that scared boy who would do anything to stop his father's punishments and lessons. Not this time. Dixon twisted the iron bar out of his father's hand. He spun and used the poker to crack a hard blow against his father's knees. With a scream of agony, the man's legs buckled under him. Dixon threw the poker across the room and stepped behind the old man. He grabbed a handful of the meticulously styled blond hair. "When and where do I meet with Stratus?"

"Fuck. You. Smith will be here in seconds." Spittle flew from his father's mouth.

"Smith left. There is no one here." Dixon pulled his weapon and placed the barrel against his father's temple.

Even on his knees and with a gun to his head the man laughed. "Go ahead. Kill me. Kill me like you killed the cow that gave birth to you. Go ahead! Do it! Step off that ledge and be the man we both know you are!" His father's screamed demands were silenced when Dixon pulled the hammer back. The metallic echo of the weapon only competed against the snapping of the wood in the fireplace and his father's breathless pants.

Dixon twisted his father's face to the camera tucked away in the corner of the ceiling. "Look up, you stupid motherfucker." Dixon leaned down holding his father so the camera could see both of them and whoever was on the other side could hear his words. His father's eyes widened in surprise and then narrowed. A low growl came from his father's chest. The sound wasn't quite sane or human.

"They've been watching you. You thought you were impervious to Stratus? You're only a pawn in their end game. A pawn that can, and has been, sacrificed. Do you think you are the only play for them? The only one willing to do anything to satisfy a personal agenda? Look at the camera, you stupid fuck. What do you think they see? A mentally ill, deranged old man who would be impossible to control. They don't want you. They want *me*. I'm the perfect appointment. I've served honorably in the military. I worked for the most respected private security firm in the world, and both my brother and father have tragically died—my brother in a tragic explosion and my father, unable to deal with the grief and suffering of never reconciling their estrangement, kills himself."

Dixon's anger had died. The old man on his

knees was nothing more than a sadistic murderer. A cold-hearted mental case that hurt, humiliated, used, directed and killed to suit his mood and purpose. His father was a monster without a conscience. Dixon knew Stratus had to be aware of what this man had done. His words to his father crystalized his next play. He closed his eyes and called the sanctioned list to mind. His father's bleats of helplessness became white noise. The top of the list Jason had given him, the very first name on the sanctioned kill list, was Harvey J. Simmons, but Jason had trusted him to use discretion and make the man's death serve a purpose. Dixon turned his gaze to the camera. "You heard me. If this is your next play, turn off that fucking camera and send me someone that can speak for you."

He knew his father watched the blinking light. Dixon watched it, too. His father's laughter started as a low rumble. "They see your weakness."

"No, you old fool, they're getting permission." Dixon knew it. The person watching wouldn't have the clearance to authorize the hit, but...

The red light on the camera blinked red and went dark. Dixon closed his eyes and said a prayer, not for his father's soul, but for his own. He prayed the blackness he was plunging himself into wouldn't consume him.

A single gunshot echoed...

CHAPTER 10

"Do you need anything else?" Smith hovered at the door. For the first time, he didn't drop his eyes to the floor when speaking to him.

"Where is the control room for the camera system?" He couldn't afford to stop and think about what had transpired less than two hours ago. The man cocked his head. The mannerism reminded Dixon of a puppy trying to understand what he's seeing. "Do you know where the control room is located?"

Smith shrugged. "It isn't upstairs."

Not in the mood to play games, he snapped, "Is there a downstairs?"

Smith's eyes widened momentarily as if taken by surprise at his outburst. Dixon sighed and dropped into his father's chair. "Look, I can't play twenty questions with you. I'm racing against time here. You made your call on your loyalty when you helped me get rid of the damn body, so stop being stingy with information. What do you know?"

"He has redone the entire downstairs. I don't have access. It has the same retinal scan as his safe. I believe that is where the control room is located."

"Can we break down the door?"

"No. Reinforced steel. It is the lock or C4."

Dixon blew out a lungful of air. "Don't fucking tempt me."

"Do you want me to make some calls?" Smith crossed his arms over his chest. "I know some guys."

Dixon chuckled and wiped his hand over his face. "That sounded very *Godfather* of you, man."

Smith chuckled and rocked forward on the balls of his feet. "Well, your old man is swimming with the fishes, and it is about time. The man was an abomination."

"He was." Dixon agreed. He leaned forward and ran his fingers through his hair for the hundredth time since the trigger was pulled. "We need two cans of black spray paint, and I need five burner phones. Go to the neighborhood bodegas and pull the oldest pay-as-you-go cells they have from the back of the shelves. I want the type with SIM cards."

"Yes, sir."

As he turned to leave, Dixon stopped him. He pulled out his wallet and handed the man five one-hundred-dollar bills. "Pay for the damn phones." The man was his father's enforcer and as such, simply took what he wanted. The owners of the bodegas, mostly new immigrants, couldn't afford the continuing loss.

Smith stopped and came back for the money. "Times, they are a-changin', hey boss?"

"Like you said, it's about time." He listened as Smith exited the house.

Dixon flopped back into his chair. The last moments of his father's life spun through his mind on rewind. Stratus had turned off the camera. He'd made his play. His plan was to tie up his father, stick him in a closet and contact Guardian. His old man would be interrogated, and Dixon knew he'd crack. Once he'd been given the latest designer drugs, his father would tell Guardian whatever they wanted to know. Did he want his father dead? Fuck yes.

His father's sudden burst of strength was surprising, but not uncontrollable. He pushed the man forward, and his father had twisted with Dixon's weight landing on his chest. The scramble for the gun was quick, and Dixon was in control. When his father grabbed at the gun, Dixon removed his finger from the trigger and pushed his knee into the man's throat. The bastard was choking and damn near unconscious when he managed to thread his finger through the guard. He snarled at Dixon as he pulled the trigger and blew his brains all over the office wall.

Dixon ran his fingers through his hair. Fuck, the bastard took himself out, and now Dixon had *nothing* to give Guardian. He was literally starting the fuck over.

Dixon had vaulted to the camera in the office and had thrown his suit jacket over it before he'd recalled Smith with the office phone. As his father bled out on the Brazilian cherry floors, Dixon went from room to room and draped or covered every camera. When Smith arrived, the man glanced from his father to Dixon. Dixon still held the gun in his hand. He had no idea what loyalty Smith had to his fucking father, and he wasn't going to find out while unarmed. The man crossed his arms over his chest and asked if Dixon had called the clean-up crew yet. When Dixon admitted he hadn't, he offered to help remove his father's lifeless body. Even if Stratus wanted to record the movement with cameras in the local area, they wouldn't be able to do so. Smith was smarter than he looked, and he covered their tracks. A black van with blacked out windows had pulled up to the back alley of The Residence.

Smith said he'd called the removal crew that Dixon's father had used. The driver of the van took them to the local mortuary his father owned—a legitimate business with obvious side benefits.

He and Smith rode with the driver of the van in utter silence. The driver backed the vehicle into the loading bay and waited until they unloaded the body, which was wrapped in a body bag Smith had produced. Dixon wasn't going to ask why a body bag had been so readily available.

They watched the van depart and then entered the facility using keys that Dixon had pulled from the desk drawer on Smith's direction. "You trust him." It was an observation, not a question.

"With my life. He is a logistician. He works for people who are not to be seen. He is known and trusted by all. We have used him before. Too many times."

Dixon followed Smith has he pushed the gurney to the freight elevator. They traveled to the basement, into the crematorium and watched as the gas flames ignited. "Do you want to say any words?" Smith motioned to his father's lifeless body.

Dixon thought of the horror the man had brought into his and Drake's lives. He thought of the senselessness of his cruelty and the pain he'd inflicted to gain even the slightest advantage in whatever scheme he was working at the time. No, there was nothing he could say about the man. Nothing he would say. When a person left this life, they left a void in their loved one's hearts, a sense of loss and of sadness. This man left nothing. No one would mourn him. Dixon shook his head slowly and stepped aside. Smith dragged the body bag to the conveyor belt and lifted his hand to start the process. Dixon stopped him. He walked over to the bag and unzipped it so he could see the bastard's face. He nodded to Smith and walked *beside his father until the heat of the crematorium became too much. His eyes followed the body, never taking his gaze off it. He wanted to make sure the motherfucker was gone. Forever. The door opened, his father's body entered and then the door closed.*

"Do you want to wait?" Smith stood beside him. They both stared into the flames.

"When will the door open?"

"Only after the process is complete. There will be nothing left of him. Maybe bone fragments." Smith put his hand on Dixon's shoulder. "He isn't coming back."

Dixon's huff of air was one of disbelief. "That bastard has haunted me my entire life. If there is a way for the motherfucker to come back, he will do it."

Smith chuckled. "Never had one rehydrate and come back to life. Your worries...at least about him, are over."

Dixon stood and walked around his father's office. There was nothing in it that would lead a person to believe he was a monster. Nothing. But Dixon knew. He glanced at the hardwood floor. Smith's people had come in and cleaned the splatter of blood and brain that had hit the floor, wall and bookcase.

Dixon examined the work carefully. He saw a small speck of blood on the shelf and another on the book above it. The clothes he'd worn had been stuffed in the bottom of the old man's body bag and were now ashes. Dixon went to the kitchen and got a bleach-based cleaner and a paper towel. He returned to the office and swiped the tiny spots of blood that had escaped the cleaning crew's attention.

Because it was something to do until Smith returned, he inspected the bookcase, going over every spine of every book to ensure nothing of that bastard remained. He moved to the side where the bookcase fit against the wall. The crack next to the molding wasn't anything that would normally draw his attention until he noticed that it fused at the base of the shelf where the shelves stopped and a built-in credenza started. He ran his fingers over the crack and followed the trail with the bleach-soaked paper towel he'd been cleaning with. Dixon glanced at the backing of the shelving unit and grasped the framing at the side and pulled.

The shelves moved effortlessly. He pulled and moved out of the shelving's way. Dixon's gut dropped. The bastard. He saw pictures of him as a boy. The fucker had filmed the torture-slash-training sessions. He moved closer and inspected the photos. So many damn photos. His body froze, and only his eyes moved. There were photos of him in Louisville. When he was in college. Pictures where Drake was with him, and the bastard had cut Drake out or taken a black marker and blotted him out. There were pictures of him doing a flight inspection of a small aircraft they'd learned to fly. He swept over the pictures. The fucker had never stopped tracking him, at least not until he'd gone into the military. He turned his attention to the other photos. These were of a small boy...maybe eight or nine. Dixon had the distinct feeling this little one was unhappy. Not one of the pictures were of the boy smiling or playing. He pulled down a picture of the boy and who he suspected was his mother. There was a cityscape in the background. He didn't recognize it, but he knew Jewell's programs would be able to find the city and hopefully the boy and his mother. He needed to find the boy and make sure he was safe. He pushed the shelving unit back into place.

He built a fire in the fireplace before he sat down and started to go through his father's desk. He knew what he'd find. Legitimate business documents, the trappings of normalcy that the man had used as a mirage of respectability.

The phone rang on the desk. Dixon reached over and picked up the receiver.

"I believe we should meet." The woman's voice on the other end of the line was smooth and congenial.

"I wouldn't know why." Dixon glanced up when he noticed movement at the door. Smith stood with two white shopping bags dangling from his big meaty paws. He motioned to Smith to come in and pointed to the chair in front of the desk.

"It seems the governor is once again in need of a viable interim Senate appointee. From our research, you meet the criteria. We'd like to put you in the vacancy. We are assuming you've made plans to explain the sudden disappearance of your beloved father?"

"My father died of a massive clot to the brain. Tragic, really. I'm sure the masses will mourn his passing as he was such a benevolent man." Dixon lifted his brow at Smith who snorted.

"We can make the correct records appear in the correct hands, should you agree to work with us."

"And if I don't?"

"Then we'll leave you to your own devices, Mr. Simmons. I'm assuming you have old contacts in a certain security agency that would be able to help you out of this...predicament."

Dixon scoffed, "When hell freezes over. What is the cost of my appointment, and what is in it for me? If it's just legitimizing my father's disappearance, I've got that covered."

"Direct, aren't you?" There was laughter in the woman's voice.

Dixon was winging this shit. He grabbed at straws and tapped danced faster than he thought possible. "I am direct. What you see is what you get." *As if.* "I'm divesting the secondary holding company of my father's illegal activities as of this moment. His legitimate businesses were mismanaged, and he bled them to present an ostentatious display of wealth." That much Dixon knew from the time

he'd worked at The Residence. "A hard working, upper middle class man with prior military
experience and former employment in the
nation's security industry is very marketable as
an up and coming politician. Having my
fingers tied to the underbelly of this city is a
liability—for both of us. If you wish to enjoy a
mutually beneficial relationship with me, you
will replace the income I would have received
from the illegal activities with payments made
through shell companies to an offshore
account."

"Why would we agree to this?"

"Because there are several key votes coming
up when the Senate resumes its session.
Senator Waxman was a junior senator, but he
was active in three subcommittees and was the
swing vote on at least three bills."

"You have done your homework."

"I'm a certified genius, but then I guess you
knew that."

"We did."

"Then you won't be surprised when I tell
you working with my father has devalued you
in my eyes. The man was psychotic. To have
considered an association with him, you are

either desperate, or you are rash. I am neither."

There was a long pause at the other end of the connection. Dixon sighed. "Go, talk to your handlers. Next time have someone who can make decisions contact me." He hung up the phone and caught the surprise in Smith's expression.

"Who was that?"

Dixon held out his hand for the bags, prompting Smith into motion. Dixon pulled out the burner phones and the two cans of spray paint. He shook a can and popped off the lid. "I believe the woman on the other end was a flunky answering to my new business partners. Thank you for this." He took out his key ring and tossed them to Smith. "If you could go over to my apartment and gather my things. I'll be staying here." There was no reason to go back to the apartment. Joy was a thing of the past. She'd been gone without a word for over a week. She'd moved on. He wished it didn't eat at him, but at the same time, he wasn't surprised. All that shit about covering each other's asses was just her blowing smoke up his.

Smith caught the keys and bounced them in his hand. "You really a genius?" The man pegged him with a questioning stare.

"I am." Dixon spread his hands and smiled. "A word of advice? Be careful with whom you align yourself, Smith. You don't let on how intelligent you are, and that is smart of you. I will need someone like you, and I will not underutilize you or treat you like he did. The pay will make your service to me worth your time." Dixon dropped his hands to his hips and stared at the big guy. "But make no mistake about it; I'm going places. Come with me, or get out of my way. Make a decision. You'll regret standing still." There was a threat in his words, and the look on Smith's face told him the threat had registered.

Smith rubbed his nose and glanced at the camera in the corner of the room. "You'll get all the cameras shut off?"

"I will."

"And the tapes, the ones he has in that room. What will you do with them?"

"Any tapes in particular?"

"Maybe."

"You'll have access to them. If they need to disappear, then make them disappear."

"Just that simple?"

"Why complicate it?"

"You could blackmail a lot of people with what you'll find in there."

"I have zero interest in blackmail, Mr. Smith. My goals are much, much higher."

"Do you think you'll be able to attain those goals?"

"With loyal people at my side? Yes." Dixon watched the man as he thought.

Smith finally nodded to himself before he spoke. "Do what you said about the videos and I'll stand with you. No matter what."

Dixon extended his hand. The motion startled Smith. Dixon waited until the big guy extended his hand. "Don't disappoint me, Mr. Smith."

The man smiled. "The name is Smithson Young. Nobody knows that, and I'd like to keep it that way."

"Nice to meet you, Smithson. Your secret is safe with me. Please get my clothing from my apartment. I have cameras to black out." Dixon nodded toward the suit jacket draped over the camera in the corner of the room.

Smith nodded his head and then chuckled, "Yes, sir."

He watched the man leave before he turned to the corner of the room and eyed the burner phones. He could hear Drake in his mind. *"Keep your friends close and your enemies off balance and ready to fucking fall."* He wasn't sure what Smithson Young was, friend or foe, but, first things first. The phones had to be charged, and he needed the cameras blacked out. He'd already swept for listening devices. Then he'd take a moment with a new burner phone. He had a few calls to make.

CHAPTER 11

WATCHING the big man move through Dixon's apartment and pack his belongings into two large suitcases sent an inner chill through Joy. That and the fact that she was fucking freezing her ass off on his fire escape, tucked into the corner closest to the building trying to avoid detection. Her teeth knocked against each other. The subzero temps cut through her long-sleeved t-shirt and cargo pants. She tucked her hair into her collar trying to keep the wind off the back of her neck. She'd made it back from her latest job about an hour ago and promptly let herself into Dixon's apartment. It was fortuitous that she was in the bedroom when the big man entered the apartment. He'd made it into the bedroom before she could shut the window all the way when she fled to the fire escape. *Fuck, fuck, fuck.*

She glanced in and groaned. *Damn it, her coat.* Smith lifted it from the hanger and looked at it before he folded it and placed it in the suitcase with the rest of Dixon's clothes. The down-filled black nylon was obviously too small for a man of Dixon's stature. She watched as he checked every drawer in the bedroom and rechecked the closet. He approached the window, and she pressed against the brick, blending in with the late-night shadows. He spent several long moments looking out the window. She could see his shadow cast by the light in the room behind him. She listened as the man slipped the sash down and slid the lock back into its anchor. The light changed as he moved away from the window. She lowered and made herself small on the grating before peeking in when the man started turning off lights before he exited the apartment.

She waited until a split second after the front room light went off before she slipped her knife into the groove and slid the latch open. She was in the apartment and heading for the front door within five seconds. She listened before disengaging the lock the man had secured. Carefully, she opened the door and slipped out. The man had removed Dixon's belongings. That meant Dixon was unable to come get them himself. She shrank down and watched the man load both suitcases into a large black van. The driver pulled away from the curb as soon as the man had shut the door. She sprinted to her car while pulling her keys from her cargos. Pumping the gas three times, she hit the ignition, threw the machine into drive and pulled out into the street, damn near getting broadsided in the process. She waved at whoever was screaming obscenities at her and floored it. The black van turned right. She let it go and traveled two streets up, *thank you very much for fucking one-way streets*, and paralleled the van, making sure to keep her car behind another. It took her six miles to realize where the van was going. Oh fuck, this was not good. She floored the gas pedal and shot through an intersection after the light had turned red. The urgency running through her veins didn't make sense, but it was there nonetheless. She parked within a block of Dixon's employer, and she used that term loosely. The bastard was a large viper at the bottom of a disgusting and deadly pit.

She rubbed her arms as she worked her way around to the back of the brownstone. The lights in the house were out except for two on the east side of the building. She pushed back into the shadows of the neighbor's house when the back door opened.

She immediately relaxed. Dixon set a small step stool down and climbed up on it. What was he...well, shit. He sent a blast of spray paint at something. Probably the camera system. That was odd...why didn't he just deactivate it?

He was down the stool and back in the house before she could approach him. She picked her way through the shadows, moved toward the house, and up the stairs to the back door. The lock took thirty seconds to pick because she was fucking freezing, and her hands wouldn't stop shaking. She slipped in and dropped her picks back into her pocket. At the sound of male voices, she pulled up and moved to the side of the hall, making herself as small as possible.

"Your bedroom window was unlocked, and

the window was up about six inches." That wasn't Dixon's voice. There was a long pause before she heard the laugh she'd come to look forward to.

"I have a stray that comes around sometimes. I feed it, and pay it some attention, but the damn thing doesn't want a home. Did you check to see if there was a cat on the fire escape before you shut the window?"

"The fire escape was empty. No snow so I couldn't tell if I scared it away." The man chuckled. "I think, perhaps working for you will be much better than working for the other. He would have had me kill the cat."

Dixon walked past the hall where she had crouched behind an antique table. The hall light illuminated his strawberry blonde hair. "Cats have nine lives. I'm sure the one that has been hanging around my apartment found some other sucker to give it what it wants."

"Is there anything else you require, sir?"

Joy's eyelids popped wide and then she rolled her eyes. *Sir? Really? Was this guy for reals?*

"No, other than to thank you for your work today. I'm glad you were available to assist me."

"I hope you won't be offended when I say the pleasure was all mine."

She heard a low, menacing rumble of a laugh and the sound of a door opening and closing. Hearing Dixon step away from the hall cleared her to lift away from the wall. She carefully moved toward the hallway and...

The muzzle of an automatic was trained directly at her head. "Why are you here? Answer me quickly. You won't be the first person to die in this house today."

"What, I can't come visit you in your new digs...*sir*?" She mimicked the other man's inflection as best she could and then snorted before she attempted to push away the gun. He slammed her into the wall and lodged the muzzle of the weapon against her forehead. *Okay, well...she hadn't expected the hostility.* And damn it if the thrill of his anger didn't turn her on. Yeah, the rougher the better, baby. She winced, well, maybe not tonight.

"Why. Are. You. Here?" His jaw clenched as he spoke.

Daaammmmnnn, her heart raced, and it wasn't in fear. "Oh, Quick Draw, are you fishing?" She chuckled and leaned into the muzzle of the gun. "Kill me if you want, because I'm ready for that. I'm sure I'm already living on borrowed time. But to answer your question, I'm here because I saw your goon packing your belongings, and fuck me if I wasn't curious." And worried, but there was no way in hell she'd tell him that.

His eyes narrowed, but the pressure of the muzzle against her skin did not let up. "What happened to your face?"

Oh. Joy shrugged as well as she could being pinned to the wall. "My latest job decided he didn't want to die." The bastard had almost killed her–the black and blue marks on her body a testament.

His eyes flitted over the bruise under her eye. It was black and red and a long way from turning yellow around the edges, but the blood had started to mottle. Dixon narrowed his eyes. "The bruises are a couple days old."

"Well yeah, it takes two days to get back from Asia even if you fly nonstop." Which she had, and no, thank you very much, she wasn't going to examine why she pushed it to make it back to the man who had the muzzle of a forty-five automatic pressed against her head.

"When did you go?" he snapped. The weapon still drilled into her.

"The day you had 'things' to do. I met my contact at Rockefeller Center. I was in the air by three that afternoon." She waited for him to decide what he was going to do. Something had happened that altered the way he interacted with her and that was...concerning, but not detrimental. Through their time together she'd learned the man that currently held her life at the tips of his fingers was deadly, but he wasn't a cold-blooded killer. That was her forte, and she had no problem recognizing her traits in others. Dixon Simmons would kill if needed, but it wasn't his default setting. She was getting kinda tired of the barrel of the weapon smashed against her forehead. "Why are you in this place? Why did you have him bring your things here?"

"Remember that retainer position?" His finger rode the hammer of his weapon back into place, and he retracted the barrel of the weapon.

"Told you I wouldn't work for that bastard." She'd reached out to people she knew and found out far more than she'd ever wanted to know about the man who called himself Dixon Simmons' father. It had been an act of true self-discipline not to slice the fucker's throat.

"The bastard is dead. I'm in charge now." His forearm across her chest still pinned her to the wall. His eyes traveled down her neck and his brows furrowed before he lifted his arm, tucked a finger in her turtleneck collar, and pulled it down. "Fuck. Tell me whoever did this to you is dead."

"I'm here, aren't I?" What did he think she was? Weak? If she was alive, her last job wasn't. It was just that simple sometimes. Interesting that his father was dead. With an effort not to show it hurt, she rolled her shoulder and pulled away, adjusting her collar. She didn't want sympathy for her mistakes and underestimating that bastard had been a mistake. She'd taken a fucking beating and running around in the freezing temperatures hadn't helped the stiffness that permeated her entire body.

She spun and started walking, although she had no idea where she was going. "How did your...predecessor die?" She wasn't sure if she should let it slip that she knew the man was his father or not. The people she was linked to had been very thorough with Dixon's background.

"Take the next door to the right." He spoke as he followed her.

She glanced back at him and smirked. "Know what I'm looking for?"

"No clue, but I need a drink. It has been one motherfucker of a day." He waited for her to move and followed her into a luxurious and impressive office.

The roaring fire in the huge marble-detailed fireplace drew her like iron to a super-charged magnet. She extended her hands to the fire while keeping an eye on him in her peripheral vision. "You didn't answer me."

He walked over to her and handed her a tumbler filled with dark amber liquid before taking a seat in one of the large chairs positioned in front of the fire. His shoulders slumped slightly, and he shook his head before taking a long hit off the alcohol in his glass. She turned to watch him.

"Did you know he was my father?" The question was low and quiet.

"My contacts alluded to the fact." She took a drink rather than keep eye contact with him.

He was extremely good at reading her, and this was something she didn't want him to see. Knowing his father was more animal than human, well, it felt as if she were betraying the trust they'd been building. Granted, it was a fucked-up trust, but it seemed to work for them.

He lifted his glass and examined the contents, but she knew he wasn't thinking about the alcohol. He glanced up at her. "About that retainer."

"Give me your wallet." She extended her hand.

He narrowed his eyes at her before he lifted out of the chair. He went behind the large desk and pulled his wallet out of the suit jacket slung over the back of the chair. He tossed it to her as he walked back to the bar and refilled his tumbler.

She waited until he sat down again before opening it and pulling a single dollar bill from the hand-tooled leather. She tossed the wallet back to him and pocketed the dollar. "I'm on retainer. You have me until you release me."

He stared at her, his expression impossible to read. "I require exclusivity, in *all* things."

In all things. Well, one wasn't going to be a problem, she hadn't had sex with anyone but him since the night they'd run into each other at her...job site. Hell, if she was honest, and why not be honest? So far, the new trend was working for her. She hadn't had any desire for sex for months before that. "We've been exclusive since we met." His eyes flicked to hers as if he doubted her. She cocked her head and scrunched her brows together trying to read his expression. "You don't believe me."

"I was at Rockefeller that afternoon. I saw you with him."

She blinked back her confusion and then realized what he'd seen. *Oh!* "My contact kissed me to slip me my paperwork. We walked. I left him and took a taxi to the airport. I did not fuck him."

Dixon took another long drink of his alcohol before he looked up at her. He made a motion with his finger circling the entire room. "It has been a day."

Huh, so not acknowledging what she said? Okay, she'd take that as acceptance until she found out otherwise.

So, his father died. God, she hoped it was by

lead poisoning. By his comments, however the bastard died, it had happened today. That would fit with the blackout job on the camera system. She set her glass down on the mantle and crossed her arms in front of her. "It would seem you've taken care of the video." She glanced around the office. The blacked-out camera in the corner matched the one at the back porch. "I'm assuming audio is not a factor?"

He shook his head. "Swept the house before I played Picasso. Three units in this office, one in the master bedroom, one each in the guest rooms and two in the offices down the hall, a couple on the outside facade. All have been destroyed. We are clear."

"The control room to the cameras?" She would assume he'd be able to stop the recording, pull the plug or whatever the techy people of the world did.

"Secured behind a retinal scanner."

"How you going to get to it?" Sooner or later he'd need to take control of whatever was in that room.

"I'm working on it." He smirked.

"Are you done with what you need to do for

the day?" She walked forward until she was standing between his legs. He glanced up at her, and his eyes made a visual track around the bruises on her face. She watched him lower his eyes to the bruises at her neck.

He downed his drink and nodded. "Why, do you have plans?"

"I do." She glanced out the double doors of the office. "Does this place have a bedroom?"

Dixon reached up and grabbed the waistband of her black jeans. "Since when do you need a bedroom?" He sat forward and lifted the bottom of her shirt. She closed her eyes and waited.

A soft pull of air was the only indication he'd seen it. He lifted the shirt farther and spread his warm hand against her stomach. "Holy hell."

She ran her fingers through his hair. "It looks worse than it is."

"It looks like someone beat the shit out of you."

"Yeah, okay, maybe it looks a lot like what it is." She laughed. "I feel like that heavy bag you beat to fuck that day." He pushed her back about a foot and stood up. She tilted her head way back to see him. "Damn, how do I forget how big you are?"

"The same way I forget how tiny you are." He leaned down and placed a kiss on her lips. "Come on."

She grabbed his hand and followed him out the door and to the left. "Where are we going?"

"I need a shower. A long, hot shower and by the looks of you, a few minutes in hot water won't go astray." He headed up the stairs, and she kept pace with him.

A shower actually sounded amazing. "Good, because I only do steamy, hot and recently washed sex." She glanced up at him and saw a small smile pull at the corner of his mouth.

The bedroom they entered wasn't the master, it was too small and not ornate enough based on what she'd seen of the rest of the house, but she could understand why Dixon wouldn't want to have sex on the same bed his father had slept in last night.

He led her through the room and into the bathroom. He pulled his button-down off over his head and flung it to the corner of the bathroom, stripping out of his shoes, socks, slacks, and boxers in no time. His body rippled when he moved. Joy leaned back against the door jamb and watched him. She'd never been much into foreplay. It tended to get in the way of orgasms. But she found herself wanting to climb his big body and use it as her own personal playground. There was very little she wouldn't allow this man to do to her...actually, she trusted him implicitly and if he wanted her blindfolded and tied to a St. Andrew's cross, she'd do it. A twinge from her ribs reminded her healing would be a better option; yet she trusted him, and she knew he wouldn't take it beyond what she wanted.

He moved to the walk-in shower and started the stream of water. He turned his head and gave her a once over and then raised a single eyebrow. Sexy. As. Fuck. She crouched down–carefully–and untied her boots. A hand appeared in front of her when she tried to lift up. She growled at the proffered hand and heard his laugh in response.

"Take my hand."

She grabbed it and used it to help her rise from her crouched position. Toeing off her boots, she narrowed her eyes at him. Her fingers swirled telling him to turn around. Oh, the man did not want to do it. He wanted to be all growly and possessive about the condition of her body, but that wasn't what this thing they had going was supposed to be about. She put her hands on her hips and waited. Not that the naked semi-erect vision in front of her was a hardship to look at, but seriously, he needed to give her a minute to get out of her clothes without wincing in front of him. It was just common courtesy.

He finally turned and entered the shower, shutting the frosted glass door behind him. She carefully tugged her t-shirt off and reached behind her to unsnap her bra. The movement hurt about as much as bending over and kicking out of her jeans after she pushed them down her hips. She glanced down at the bruises that covered her right side and the discoloration from her hip to her breast.

Had the man she'd been sent to kill not been hopped up on cocaine, she might not have been able to escape. Her skills were not the right ones to take on the bastard, but who was she to turn down a job? Now? Now she was exclusive, and that gave her the right to turn down anything else that flowed her way. Didn't it?

She opened the shower door and braced herself for his reaction. Dixon turned around and opened his eyes. Water trailed over his lashes, dripping across the brilliant blue orbs as he stared at the marks that the bastard had left on her. The last marks of a dead man.

He extended his hand and brought her under the warm water. Joy closed her eyes and dropped her head back between her shoulders and let the water pour over her. She gasped when his hands circled her waist. She snapped her head forward and realized he'd dropped to his knees in front of her. His fingertips snaked up the vivid divide of her unblemished skin and the deep purple and black bruises that littered the rest of her body.

He leaned forward and kissed the bruise closest to her breast. She let her fingers wind through his wet hair. His lips traced the mottled color, carefully laying down gentle sweeps of his lips against her skin. She closed her eyes. A lifetime ago, she'd dreamt of a knight in shining armor who would save her. She'd longed to have someone who would treat her with the reverence Dixon was giving her. She'd thought that hope had passed. She wasn't that innocent, wide-eyed girl that had trusted completely. That life ended many, many years ago when that bastard had killed her sister and ripped her innocence from her.

But here and now, she let herself remember those dreams, although Dixon's careful touches scared her. As his fingers drifted over her skin and his lips brushed over her bruises, her tired, wounded body voraciously consumed his gentle kindness. Dixon Simmons terrified her because she wanted this–with him. Her only goal when she'd escaped death at the hands of a drug-fueled maniac and had fled the penthouse apartment in Tokyo was getting back to this man.

As he worshipped her body, telling her with his soft, tender touches what neither one of them would ever admit aloud, she wanted to run. She trembled with the desire to escape, to flee the emotions and thoughts the man on his knees before her had resurrected, only she had nowhere else to go. Her emotions warred against each other. This moment, this man, and this feeling was why she'd fought so hard to come back; and yet this moment, this man, and this feeling held a power over her she shouldn't allow. Because of those emotions, the risks she took to do what she was paid to do no longer made sense.

Every time she took a job, she'd reconciled herself to the fact she might die. Hell, at times she'd hoped for it–the end of her existence. She drew her fingers through Dixon's hair as he kissed her ribs. Not anymore. The emptiness inside her had shrunk. Void of feeling, her life hadn't meant much. She pushed the envelope and sought out dangerous situations just to be able to *feel* something, anything. What she felt when she was with this man? Well, it mattered. At least to her.

He wrapped his arms around her and leaned into her while still on his knees. She wrapped her arms around him and held him. The weight of his presence sank into her and warmed cold, empty places. A past lover had accused her of not having a heart. That wasn't true, she had one, but it had been shattered into a million pieces and was so broken she'd swept the tiny shards that remained into a vault and locked them away.

Dixon leaned back and pushed her wet hair away from her face. "How bad was it?"

Joy held back the canned brush off that sprang to mind. She threaded her fingers through his hair and spoke the truth, "He was better than me, but he was strung out. If he hadn't been, I don't know if I would have been able to make the kill. He bled out as he was choking me." She bit her bottom lip before she spoke and gave herself permission to show him her vulnerability, "I didn't think I'd see you again."

He stood and gathered her into his arms. "You are mine, now. Exclusively." He turned off the water and made quick work of wrapping her in a towel before he swiped the water off himself.

He led her into the bedroom and folded them under the thick blankets of the bed after placing his gun and her knife on opposite nightstands. He pulled her close, tucking her into him, her back against his chest. Joy glanced over her shoulder at him. "Don't you want—"

He kissed her softly, stopping her question. "What I want right now is to hold you. I need to know something good exists in my life. Everything I've ever known has been tainted by that bastard...except you. I want to go to sleep with you in my arms, and I want to wake up with you here beside me." He kissed her again. "Go to sleep."

She turned her face toward the window. A shiver ran through her, and he tightened his hold. The shiver wasn't because she was cold. Being held, being wanted just because of who she was? She closed her eyes. Maybe sometimes, little girl dreams did come true.

CHAPTER 12

DIXON WOKE IMMEDIATELY. His eyes dropped to the woman asleep beside him. The horrid bruising on her body had sent a jolt of reality into his life. On his knees in that shower last night, he realized how important he'd let her become. The hot, casual fuck he thought he'd found had morphed into someone that mattered. Joy was the one thing his father hadn't been able to violate, and for that he was thankful.

He turned onto his side so he could watch her sleep. She was beautiful and so damn delicate. That thought brought a smile to his face. Delicate looking, but the woman had a strength that would rival a blend of tungsten, titanium and chromium. The woman was a force of nature. A diminutive one, sure, but he'd fought against her. If she'd been trying to kill him when they'd collided, he had no doubt he'd have been a pin cushion for that knife of hers. Would he have been dead after they met? It was a toss-up. She had skills, but so did he. The bastard that put the bruises on her was lucky he was dead. Dixon wanted to stalk off to whatever country she'd left his corpse in and resurrect the motherfucker just so he could kill him again. Yeah, that was kinda fucked up, but he was feeling protective even though she didn't need protecting. Hell, he'd put her on retainer so she'd be near him. Again...fucked up. He could hear Drake's voice in his head. *What the fuck, Dix? You hired a killer to keep her safe?*

Dixon chuckled softly at the thought of what else his brother would say. Yeah, he did hire her to keep her safe, but she'd never know that. Shit was about to get real. He'd need someone in his corner, and while he used Smith yesterday, he didn't necessarily trust him. He didn't know the man or his past. Those videos Smith wanted? He'd make sure he'd have a copy of what was on them before he released them. Knowledge was power, especially now. He'd thrown the gauntlet down with the Stratus underling. He wanted someone higher up. He needed a way to get Guardian in the door, and a minion that had no authority to make a decision wasn't going to cut it.

Joy's eyelids fluttered open. "Hi."

"Hi, yourself." Dixon pulled her into him. He enjoyed the soft sigh and the way she snuggled against him. His dick liked it too. She rolled her hips against him, and he groaned.

"You should have taken me up on my offer last night." Her hand snaked around his cock and stroked him.

"We were both exhausted. I only do wide awake sex." He rolled her onto her back and gazed down at her.

She smirked at him and reached up with both arms, snaking them around his neck. "Good thing I like wide awake sex."

He lowered and slanted his lips across hers. Her kisses were addictive. When he first realized that she wanted him to control their sex, it had been a powerful rush. His dominance of her was exciting, thrilling and euphoric. Making her let go, if only for the time it took to reach orgasm, was a privilege.

Today wasn't about conquering her, but making her let go. His hands explored her body as they lost themselves in each other's taste. He could kiss her forever and never get enough. His cock was dripping by the time he allowed himself to finger her sex. She gasped into his mouth and rolled her hips, looking for more.

He pulled away and rolled onto his left side, bringing her back to his chest and lifting her leg. Her right side was a battlefield of bruises that he wouldn't aggravate. He kept his hand behind her right knee and lifted it up, careful not to push her leg against her torso. He pushed his hips forward and grunted when her hand found him and guided him into her hot, waiting core. He slid forward and closed his eyes at the feel of her silky heat wrapping around his shaft. Her fingers pressed against the root of his cock as he hilted. He watched her stroking her clit as he withdrew and then thrust forward.

Dixon lowered his lips to her shoulder. Her

right hand traveled up and grabbed his hair, keeping him there. He licked and nipped the area he could reach as he listened to her quiet sounds fill the room. The woman hummed in appreciation, moaned when he thrust harder, and muttered words of encouragement when his hand left her leg to reach between them. She never let go of him, her hands tangled in his hair. He wanted to believe it was because she needed the connection as much as he did. He needed to believe that, and for the moment at least, he allowed himself to hope it was true. He worked her body until he felt her tighten and then snap against the rhythm of his hips. Thrusting into her while she rode out her orgasm, he chased his own release.

She turned her head and pulled him down, bringing them together in a sloppy, desperate kiss. "Take what you need from me. I'm here. I'm yours."

Dixon's back arched, and he lost it. Bright red spots formed behind his clenched eyelids. They blurred into blackness as he remembered to breathe. He dropped his head to her shoulder. and brushed a breathless kiss against her shoulder. "And I'm yours." His murmur dropped into the stillness. Her only response was a soft sigh. It was enough.

"Did you kill your father?"

Dixon sighed. "Yes and no. I put the gun to his head and took everything he'd worked for away from him. He pulled the trigger and killed himself."

She rolled over onto her back and narrowed her eyes at him. "So...no, you didn't kill him."

"I didn't pull the trigger."

"So...no, you didn't kill him." She turned, so she was facing him. "What did you do with the body?"

"Smith took me to the mortuary owned by my father. We used the crematorium."

"Any video of the event?"

"No."

"Are you sure?"

He nodded. "I want you at my side. I think it's best Smith doesn't know who you are other than my...woman."

Her eyebrow arched, and a small smirk ticked up the corner of her mouth. "You're sure you want to saddle yourself with me?"

Dixon laughed, "Oh, yeah, baby, ride me."

She slugged his arm and laughed, "You're like, thirteen, aren't you?"

"Most of the time." He pulled her on top of him and stroked her hair when she laid her head down on his chest. This felt so damn right.

"What's the play?" She asked in a sleepy, dreamy voice.

He continued to run his fingers through her hair as he spoke. "Play?"

"Yeah, what's the endgame? Your old man is dead. We are playing house, and you don't trust Smith. What's the endgame here?" She lifted her head and cupped her hands on his chest before she lowered her chin and looked at him expectantly.

"There is a vacant Senate seat that I believe I'll be nominated to fill." He watched her closely as she digested the news.

She opened her mouth, closed it, started to speak again and then snapped it shut. She pushed up and straddled him, naked and obviously confused. "Why the fuck would you want me around if you are going to be a senator?"

"Is there anything connected to you that

could come back to me?" He ran his hands up and down her thighs.

"Like a criminal record?"

"Exactly like that."

"Nah. I'm dead...I mean the person I was born as is buried. So, there is nothing there, but I mean...there is nothing there. Your idea to have me hang around as your woman would do nothing but complicate matters."

Dixon narrowed his eyes at her. "What about the name you use to get in and out of the country?"

"That changes with the job. Documentation like passports and such are easy to get with enough money." She pulled the blanket that had dropped when she sat up back over her shoulders. "But a simple passport wouldn't be enough to withstand the scrutiny of a zealous background scrub. I think it's best if I stay in the background."

"If I'm correct in my assumptions, you won't be subject to any scrutiny. We'll get you a new passport and driver's license. I have a feeling the less information that can be found about you, the better." Dixon flicked her a quick smile.

"Ah... say what, now?" She flipped the blanket over her head and clutched it under her chin.

He pulled her down on top of him and wrapped his arms around her. "Get the documents. I'll pay for them. I want you beside me."

"It won't work. Someone is going to ask questions."

"Maybe not if you have dual citizenship. Two passports, we can work the background in another country and use it."

"Smoke and mirrors?"

"Something like that. I have friends overseas that can help." Dixon ran through his available options; friends of friends he and Drake had made while working overseas; people who owed them and would be willing to do a favor or two. It could work. He just needed to be able to reach out. Now that the brownstone was his, he could do what he needed to do without the fear of being monitored.

She tapped his forehead. "I see the squirrels moving around up here, but I'm not sure I like where they're going."

"We won't make the relationship public until you are satisfied I've been able to produce a viable cover for you. Deal?" She narrowed her eyes and cocked her head at him again. He laughed, "How did I confuse you?"

"Why is it important that I be beside you through this?"

"Because I have zero allies that I can access. My gut tells me I can trust you. Hell, you haven't killed me yet, so I'm assuming my instincts are correct."

She scrunched up her nose at him and let out a huge sigh before she moved up on her elbows. He flinched and moved her weight off his ribs, tossing her onto the mattress. She landed with a wince. "Oh, fuck, I'm sorry." He gently palmed her bruised side with his hand.

"I'm fine. I'm a helluva lot tougher than I look." She rolled back toward him and pulled up the blankets to ward off the chill in the bedroom. "I'll give you the time you need, and you can count on me to be here for you." She dropped her eyes as if embarrassed by the comment. "What about that control room? How are you going to get into it?"

Dixon lifted his head and glanced at the bedside clock. It was just after five in the morning. He dropped his head. "It's unlocked."

She bounced up and slapped her knife into her hand. Her wince of pain at the movement vanished as she flew out of the room. Naked.

Dixon got up and put on his pants before he grabbed his gun and a blanket. He descended the stairs and headed to the back of the house. She stood at the top of the stairs. She spun and pointed at the door. "It was locked last night."

"It was."

"How?"

"I contracted the services of an information extraction specialist."

"A what?"

"A thief."

"Why didn't you just say that?"

"Long story."

"What if he stole something that can be used against you?" She darted down the stairs...still naked as the day she was born. Dixon shook his head and threw the blanket over his shoulder as he walked down the stairs.

"What. The. Actual. Fuck?" Her words fell in a confused heap. She turned around and blinked at him. She indicated a room whose door stood open. "What the hell was he going to use this for?"

Dixon grabbed the blanket and wrapped it around her shoulders. He glanced into the torture chamber his father no doubt called a training room. It wasn't the same room he'd used with him. His father had probably thought it an improvement from the hole he'd been trained in. Dixon waited, expecting to feel something more. He waited for the panic, fear, and anxiety to surface, but the only thing he felt was disgust for the man who'd given him life.

He draped his arm around her shoulder and nodded to the end of the hall. "The control room." The door stood ajar even though there was an alarm panel outside the door. The front of the panel was removed, and there were wires pulled from the interior. He opened the door and turned on the light. The monitors were all active but showed only splotchy light through the paint covering the lenses.

Dixon wrapped his hand around the cluster of wires leading to the computer system and yanked, pulling all the ends from the back of monitors. He moved Joy to the side, sat down at the desk and wiggled the mouse. The computer wasn't even password protected. He clicked on the folders located on the desktop. The folders were listed by date, going back for seven...no, eight years. Probably the date the system was installed.

"Man, nothing like putting all your shit in one bucket. Anyone could access those files."

Dixon shook his head. "No, see here? This is a receptacle. The cameras dumped the feed into this computer at exactly six thirty every evening and started a new recording. If someone was to access the camera system, like they did yesterday, the system dumped the recording the second the line was breached. The hacker would only have a live feed of what was happening at that exact moment. There was no way the people who hacked in could access any history." He called up the C prompt and sent a command to the DOS function of the system. "If anyone accessed this storage space via a tunnel, Trojan, or internet connection, it would be wiped."

Joy plopped her ass on the desk and wrapped the blanket around her. "How did you know that?"

"I talked to a friend of mine yesterday when I called in a favor from the thief that opened the doors. I asked them to try to get in using my father's computer upstairs. They couldn't and explained what was probably going on."

"Huh."

Dixon looked up at her. "What?"

"Who do you know that smart?"

"Lots of people."

"Huh."

He tipped his head and waited.

"Why do you need me again? I thought you said you had no allies."

"I said I had no allies I could access. The people I reached out to yesterday cannot be touched again. It was an emergency situation as my fucking sperm donor offed himself with my gun. Believe me, I have burned every favor and every bridge owed or promised to me from those people."

"What are you going to do with those?" She nodded to the computer. Dixon reached under the top desk drawer and smiled. He yanked the small thumb drive from the tape holding it in place. "I'm making an insurance policy."

He lifted the thumb drive and inserted it into the computer system following the detailed instructions he received yesterday. He watched as the system moved small packets of information to the removable device.

"And then?"

Dixon glanced over at her and smiled. "Then I'm going to go to work. Daddy dearest's death has forced not only my hand, but also those who had planned on using him. We buckle up, hold on, and hope like hell this ride ends with both of us alive."

The blinding smile his comments brought surprised him. She jumped off the desk and grimaced a bit before she collected her knife and headed out of the small office. "That's cool, 'cause I was afraid for a minute things were going to get boring." She padded down the hall and shouted over her shoulder, "It's cold in this house, dude. Could you turn up the heat?"

Dixon glanced at the desktop monitor and smiled as he pulled the thumb drive from the system. He entered the command Jewell had made him repeat back to her and hit enter before he darted down the hall. When Joy saw him coming, she laughed that damn sexy, throaty laugh and dropped the blanket, running for the stairs at full speed. He'd let her win the race to the bedroom. This time.

CHAPTER 13

"Operator Two-seven-four."

"Sunset clearance, zero operative."

"Standby, zero operative."

"Archangel."

"He's in position."

"You're positive?"

"Yes."

"He cannot reach out to us again. We won't answer. The success of the mission depends on him having no contact with us."

There was no sound on the line.

"Are you there?" Archangel's voice snapped across the connection.

"So, you'd rather he what...dies?"

"Watch yourself."

"Or what?"

Archangel sighed. "You are there to ensure he doesn't pay that price."

"Of course."

"Your attitude has been noted."

"And I care...why?"

"Do your job. Keep him alive. Check in as scheduled unless something happens."

The line disengaged without acknowledgment.

"PLAY THE VIDEO AND AUDIO UP TO THE POINT where our new associate was stupid enough to cut the feed."

Her assistant hit the play button, and she watched the events unfold. The video stopped. "Play the audio after that point."

She listened and directed her assistant to play it again after enhancing the volume. She leaned back into her seat and stared across the table at her sister. "What say you?"

"I concur. It is an insurance policy should he decide to rebel." Her sister slid her eyes to the third woman at the table. Collectively they were The Fates, the women who decided the world's trajectory. In the ten years since they'd assumed control from the elders, they had resurrected Stratus and recovered some of the economic, political and military might the elders had lost.

Third sent a blank stare back to her. Third was hard to read, even after all these years. "The legislation you want to be passed will do what, exactly?"

"There are two bills of paramount importance. The first is an economic aid package that will funnel directly into our coffers and allow the continued buildup of our infrastructure. The government will never miss the money as they believe it is going to aid the people of third world countries. We will, of course, ensure reports validating the aid is delivered. While we have good people in position; I want the best. The influx of money will help us attract and keep them."

"The threat of losing their life should keep them." Third replied immediately.

"True," Second added.

"Of course, as you know, I have no problem getting rid of problems, as my elimination of

Senator Waxman proves." First lifted an eyebrow and dared her sisters to challenge her.

"Back to this..." Second looked up at the monitor. "Simmons. Does he have the qualifications to take the seat?"

"With minor tweaks to his records, yes. He is a legal resident of New York. The press will have a field day with the lack of tax returns, but his association with Guardian will make him solid."

"He is guilty of tax evasion?" The second asked.

"No. Guardian personnel file masked reports as per their agreement with Congress. No personal information is divulged, and the Guardian employee base pays at a forty percent tax table to keep the nation happy. It is a similar agreement the CIA uses for their deep cover agents."

"I'm concerned about his ties to Guardian." Third motioned to her assistant and Dixon Simmons' photo flashed across the screen. "The information we have is spotty at best."

"We have validated that his twin *is* dead." Second smiled as she spoke. "He led me on a merry chase. The bastard." She leaned back and spread her hands. "We still do not have the location on the others that we've identified."

"You let one of them slip through your fingers." Third pinned Second with a glare.

"He was injured. Some believe mortally," Second defended her mission.

"Is there a body?" Third demanded in a sharp retort.

"No." Second acknowledged.

"May I direct the conversation back to the matter at hand?" First was always the peacemaker of the group. Both Second and Third possessed anger that needed to be harnessed and directed. "I believe we need to bring this to a vote."

"Concur." Second agreed.

Third tipped her head, acknowledging First.

"A majority carries the vote, as always. No dissent after the vote, and all energies are directed to the success of the majority's directive." First repeated the mantra they'd adopted to stop the infighting that had led to the inability of the elders to function as a unit.

"Agree." Third replied.

"Agreed." Second echoed.

"The motion is as follows: In regard to the realignment of the United States government: Dixon Simmons, a former Guardian, will be appointed to the vacant New York Senate seat. Failure to approve this motion will result in the immediate termination of Dixon Simmons by our asset on the scene." She shifted her eyes from the monitor in front of her. "All those in favor of approving this motion, please signify by raising your hand."

The First raised her hand and glanced from Second to Third. "Very well." She caught the eye of her assistant. "Log the vote and send word to our assets in New York." The curmudgeon nodded and tapped away at his station. First returned her attention to her sisters. "Now, on to the next order of business. This concerns our assets in Russia. Second, you have a report on the status of the oil reserves that have been diverted?"

DIXON GLANCED AT THE CLOCK ON THE WALL and leaned back in the large chair that faced the fire. He swirled his drink and watched the flames consuming the logs. It had been two weeks since his father had died. In that time, he had obtained a reasonably well-made cover story for Joy, who was now Joy Nguyen. According to her papers, she held a dual French/American citizenship. The fact that she spoke no French wasn't concerning, and they'd talked through a cover story should that topic arise.

She'd taken up residence with him, after a fashion. That she normally ghosted in after Smith left and rarely made an appearance when the man was present wasn't lost on him. Smith's concern for the sudden appearance of someone else was palpable. The man's eyes tracked Joy with a suspicion he couldn't, or didn't want to, hide. Dixon had taken pains to ensure the thumb drive with the files was safe before he allowed Smith access to the computer system and the files Smith wanted erased. So now he sat in the home owned by his dead father and tended his legitimate businesses while he waited for Stratus to move. The illegitimate businesses had been dropped. The ensuing chaos on the streets marked others scrambling to fill the void. Dixon didn't

give a shit. He had shed the illegitimate businesses to capture the attention of Stratus. Now
that he had it, he could keep it without
breaking the law.

He heard the door open and Smith speak.
The man appeared at the open office door
where he waited for Dixon to acknowledge
him. "Who is it?"

"A Ms. Samantha Banner to see you, sir."
Smith stood stoically at the door like a hybrid
butler-slash-hitman.

"Thank you, is the limo here yet?"

"Yes. Parked out front."

"Excellent. Did Ms. Banner give you a topic
of conversation?"

"Layers, sir."

"Layers?" Dixon's eyes swung to Smith's.

"Yes, sir. No further explanation. Shall I
show her in?" Smith waited without moving.

"Give me a couple minutes then bring her
back." Dixon waited for Smith to shut the door
before he withdrew his automatic and checked
the magazine. He slipped the clip back in and
chambered a round. He slipped the weapon
back into his holster and slid his jacket on. He
topped off his drink and then sat behind his

father's desk. When the knock at the door sounded, Dixon bid Smith in.

"Sir, Ms. Samantha Banner." Smith stepped aside and revealed a striking woman. Dixon did an immediate once over. She was short, perhaps five-foot-five-inches tall, middle eastern descent, and had very intelligent dark brown eyes that assessed him in return. Dixon waited until the woman entered and Smith backed out and shut the door.

"Ms. Banner. To what do I owe this visit?"

"I believe you requested it."

"Indeed? When was that?"

"I believe your exact words were, *'If this is your next play, turn off that fucking camera and send me someone that can speak for you.'* I would be that person," she sneered.

"Please, have a seat. May I offer you a drink?" Dixon wasn't about to move or turn his back on the woman.

"I regretfully decline. I drove and would never operate machinery after imbibing spirits." The woman unbuttoned her expensive suit jacket and sat down. She crossed her legs and stared at him.

Dixon waited. He wasn't going to start the

conversation, and he could out-stare just about anyone...except Drake...and maybe Frank. This one? Child's play. He crossed his hands over his abdomen, picked a point on the woman's face and waited.

Not more than a minute later she flinched before she cleared her throat and announced, "You have been saved."

Dixon snorted and chuckled before he asked, "Really? From what?"

"Perhaps your own faulty belief that you can negotiate with us." A sneer reappeared on her face.

"I don't want to negotiate with you, Ms. Banner. You're nothing. If I had to guess, you're not even mid-level management. Tell me, what benefit would it be to me to deal with minions?" Dixon leaned forward. "Your superiors want me in that Senate seat. They want me to vote a particular way. That is a done deal. I don't give a flying fuck about the bills that are up for consideration, but I want something in return."

The woman's dark olive complexion flushed red. Dixon knew he'd nailed Ms. Banner's position in the organization. He had tied the fly to the hook, and he was getting ready to make his cast. The woman cleared her throat and drew several deep breaths before she ground through her teeth, "What?"

"Listen very closely to my words, Ms. Banner. I won't repeat them. Go tell your handlers I will vote any way they tell me to *after* the money I require is deposited into my offshore accounts. It is the base price of doing business with me. However, there is more. I want them to take out several prominent players within Guardian, people who set me up and cast me out. I have information and a way in your people could never access. The information I have is segmented and protected should you unwisely decide to extract that information by force. I'm a certified genius, Ms. Banner. Your lack of intelligence requires remedial explanations that I find tedious. I won't deal with the likes of you. Now, be a good little pawn. Get up. Turn around and go report to your handlers. I'll be waiting."

"You will regret this," Banner spat from the chair.

"No, I don't think I will. You, on the other hand, will not fare well if you don't repeat my words verbatim. What would they do to you if they found out you denied them access to Guardian's heart?" Dixon chuckled and waved toward the door. "Leave. Now."

He watched the woman stand, button her jacket and jerk it down. She stared at Dixon the entire time. Ms. Banner probably believed she was intimidating. She spun on her heel and left the office. The woman was impotent at best. Dixon listened as the front door opened and then shut. Smith appeared at his office door moments later.

"Do you need anything else, sir?"

"No, I'm waiting for my date, then we'll be leaving for dinner. You may leave for the day."

Smith nodded but lingered in the door. Dixon glanced up. "Speak your mind, Smith."

The man glanced at him. "Thank you for allowing me access to those tapes."

Dixon nodded. "What did my father have on you?"

Smith stood stock-still before he cleared his throat and spoke, "There was a young lady. She found me attractive, which should have been my first warning. We dated. One thing led to another, and we slept together." Smith cleared his throat. "Here, in the room I used to have upstairs."

"He blackmailed you with...sex tapes?"

"No. The woman told me she was twenty-three. She wasn't." Smith rubbed the back of his neck. "She was fifteen." He lifted his eyes and shook his head. "I didn't know. I never would have touched her..." Smith cleared his throat. "I hadn't been here long...a month, maybe a little longer. Right before you came back. He used the tape to ensure my obedience."

"To make you kill for him?"

"No, sir. He only had to pay me to do what he needed to be done on the street."

"Then what was he forcing you to do?"

"Watch both you and the boy. He needed me to use my resources on the street to spy on both of you. Report back to him on what you were doing. The boy was easy. The mother is predictable and has a routine. The little guy seems like a good kid, but quiet. I did what he asked, but my primary focus was on you. Who you talked to, what you did outside of the time you spent here, working for him." Smith chuckled. "But I'll give you credit. You usually lost the people I sent to follow you, so I reported on what I could find out. Like what you ate and drank. What you wore. He was obsessed with knowing everything about you."

"Why would he need to blackmail you to do that?"

"I think it was because I saw the pictures. I told him I wouldn't have anything to do with crimes against children. He was a vindictive motherfucker."

"So, he needed to ensure your silence and compliance?"

"Yes, and he knew I would go to jail for life if the girl reported me. It would have been my third strike." He nodded toward the bookshelf. "She showed up the day after I saw those photos. You can't tell me it was a coincidence."

Dixon's eyes swung toward the built in. "He was a sick bastard."

"I wouldn't have let him put that boy downstairs." Smith shifted on his big feet and clenched his hands. "Adults, they are responsible for their actions. They make decisions and take chances that come back to bite them. Kids, they don't. That girl, she probably did what he said she had to do. I never would have touched her if I'd known how young she was.

That little boy, he needs to stay a kid for as long as he can. I wouldn't have let him touch that boy."

The big guy seemed legitimately upset. "What happened to the girl?"

"I don't know." Smith shook his head. "I'm hoping she is alive. I don't think he'd kill her in case he needed her to testify." Smith dropped his eyes. "I didn't know. I swear she looked older. Acted older. I trusted her, and that was a huge misjudgment."

Hurting kids was Smith's hard limit, and somehow his fucking father had known that. He glanced up at Smith. "I'm relieved to hear that, and I thank you for watching out for the boy." Dixon's gut rolled at the idea of what his father had planned for that child.

"Why did you come back?"

Dixon leaned back in his chair and shook his head. "I had no other option."

"There is always—" Smith's eyes shot to the hall, and he straightened. "Ms. Nguyen is here." He spun on his heel and left as Joy strode into the office.

The woman was draped in mink. Her heels were impossibly tall, but fuck they made her legs look a mile long. Dixon smiled and lifted out of the chair. "Did you have a good day?" Dixon asked as she dropped her purse into one of the chairs and walked over to him.

"Not really."

He tensed at her words. "Why?"

"Because I hate shopping and spending money on frivolousness. For me, it is the equivalent of pulling teeth without Novocaine. Why are there so many people in the stores this time of year? Why are we going to this thing again?" She cocked her head at him.

"You're whining?" That was surprising and unexpected from her.

She put her hands on her hips and her brow furrowed. "Fuck...I *am* whining. Dammit. I hate people, and I hate shopping. Answer my question."

"I'm sorry, which one?"

"Why are we going to this thing again?"

"Because it is expected that I am seen and that you be well turned-out." He leaned down for a kiss. She stretched up and met his lips.

As soon as his lips left hers, she let him have it. "Fuck you very much for that. Well turned-out. Is that the same as being a fucking bimbo arm candy?" She lifted up on her toes and bit his lip before she let go of him. "Besides, they haven't given you any indication they want you to actually take that seat, have they? It's fucking taking forever." She unfastened the clip of her mink and dropped the coat revealing a dark, jade-green dress that showed her body to perfection.

Dixon ran a hand down her side and cupped her tiny waist. "A man once told me the hardest part about fishing was the wait."

Her eyebrow rose a split second before she laughed with an inelegant snort. "Oh my God, you sound like a freaking fortune cookie."

"Good. You can eat me later. Right now, we need to head downtown, or we won't get to enjoy dinner before the ballet starts. We can talk over our meal."

"Oh, I'll devour you later." She waggled her eyebrows and laughed at the balls deep groan the thought of her mouth around his cock evoked. "Are you sure we have to do this?" Joy stood perfectly still and adopted a haughty expression before she spun on her toe, raising her hand in the air, almost tripping over the low table between the chairs in the process.

Dixon snaked out a hand to steady her. She grabbed onto his outstretched arm and used him as a prop to hold herself steady as she lifted her heel and adjusted the back strap. "Shit...seriously, ballet like totally sucks. Dude, you realize I'm going to be snoring about ten minutes after the lights go out, right?"

"Think of it as a job. Imagine you have to watch the prima ballerina because she's your target for later tonight." Dixon steadied her until she put her foot down and reached for her coat. "By the way, you look amazing tonight."

"What? You mean I don't look amazing every night?" She swatted him with her purse after she grabbed it off the chair. The damn thing was heavy, which told him she probably had a gun in it. He glanced at her dress and wondered where she'd put her knife because it was almost a guarantee that she had it on her. Although with the way that dress fit, perhaps the gun was her only weapon tonight.

"You point out this prima chick, okay? That's a sneaky-ass suggestion by the way, but a great idea to keep me interested." She fanned her hand out and put it on her chest as she blinked her long lashes at him. "It's as if you know me." She threw back her head and laughed.

Dixon grabbed his cashmere overcoat and followed her into the hall before he locked up the house and engaged the new security system he'd had installed. Smith could turn it off and on, but Dixon would know when he entered or left just in case the man decided he needed to do some snooping around on his own. The thing fed directly to Dixon's cell phone. It wasn't a perfect system, but it would let him know if someone tried to tamper with anything in the house.

He helped her into the waiting limo after waving the driver back into the cab of the vehicle. He waited until the car pulled away from the curb before he glanced over at her. "You know I don't know you. Not in any way that matters."

"Sex doesn't matter?"

"Other than sex," he conceded. "You said before, in the office, it was as if I knew you. I don't. Not really."

She turned in her seat. The familiar brow furrow was directed his way again "Ah...well in my line of business..." Her words trailed off before she shrugged her shoulder. "Ask me."

"Ask you what?" Dixon glanced out the window when the driver slowed to stop at a light.

"Questions, dork. Ask me questions." She reached for the seat warmer controls and cranked hers up.

Dixon chuckled, "Who is thirteen now?"

She flipped him off and fiddled with the sound system controls. He felt the car accelerate slowly. Ice coated the street in a thick layer with a small amount of fresh snow covering the asphalt.

"What is your favorite color?"

"Ummm...black."

"That's not a color. That is the absence of color." It was an automatic reply.

She turned and looked at him. "Okay, so, this is *not* how getting to know each other works. You ask a question; I answer it. You cannot tell me my answer is wrong. It's my answer."

"Sorry."

"Damn straight." She straightened in her seat. "What's yours?"

"Favorite color?"

"Ah...yeah?" She gave him an exasperated look.

"Tonight, it is jade green." He waggled his eyebrows at her.

"Good recovery, but not the answer I'm looking for."

"Blue. The shade the sky is in the summer when the sun is at its peak. I like it because it is vibrant and alive."

"Wow...that was really...I like black because it hides me." She stroked the fur she was wearing, not looking at him.

"You should never be hidden." Dixon reached over and took her hand in his. She glanced up and flashed him a sad smile.

"Favorite food?" She popped the question out.

He followed the topic change without missing a beat. "Fried chicken, mashed potatoes, gravy, biscuits and corn on the cob."

"How very southern of you."

"Actually, midwestern." His mind flashed to the dining room in Frank and Amanda's house, and he imagined Sunday night dinner with his family. It was the meal Miss Amanda made for him and Drake. Fuck, he missed them. The holidays were hollow without his family. He cleared his throat and smiled at her, forcing himself not to give in to that particular train of thought. "What's yours?"

"Any kind of vegetable."

"I've noticed you don't eat meat. Is there a reason you're a vegetarian? Or are you vegan?"

She snorted and shook her head. "Labels are for assholes. I don't eat meat anymore because I don't want anything that bleeds on my plate. It kinda grosses me out, you know?"

His head whipped her direction expecting her to be laughing, but she wasn't. Her gaze was focused out the side window.

"Because blood makes you remember," he whispered.

She turned and stared at him. "Yeah. For the most part, I can compartmentalize my life." She shrugged and cleared her throat. "Except when I see blood." She gave a self-deprecating laugh. "Fucked up, huh?"

"No. Not at all." He assured her as they passed a slower vehicle. "Favorite movie of all times?"

She snorted and slapped her hand over her

nose which made her laugh harder. "You do not want to know."

"Sure, I do." He laughed at her. "I'll go first. My favorite movie of all times is *The Hunt for Red October.* Sean Connery was fucking amazing in that movie. The science and engineering wasn't right, and it wasn't as good as the book, but as far as movies go, there is just something about it that stuck with me."

"Yeah, okay, I get that." She cleared her throat. "You have to swear not to laugh at me when I tell you what my favorite movie is."

"I cross my heart." Dixon swiped his fingers across his chest.

"Okay, well it was a movie I watched with my older sister when we were little. And that is why it was so special, so no laughing."

Dixon reached out again and squeezed her hand. "I promise."

"*Paint Your Wagon.*"

His mind flashed through all the films he'd ever watched, and he couldn't for the life of him come up with anything with that title. "I've never heard of it."

She looked out the window and spoke to

the darkness, "It's a comedy musical, with some crazy singing."

"You like musicals? How did I not know that?" Dixon interjected trying for some levity.

"Ha, yeah, well my employers weren't exactly doing a *Mary Poppins* imitation. I liked that movie, by the way. She was one badass nanny. Besides, it was the songs in this movie that we liked the best."

"You and your sister?"

"Yeah, she was older than me by five years. She was my best friend. We didn't have anyone else."

"Was?"

Dixon glanced at her, and she nodded. "She died trying to protect me from the man who was supposed to be taking care of us until our parents made it to this country."

"I'm sorry."

Her head whipped toward him, and she stared at him with that confused look again. "For what?"

"I'm sorry that you had to lose your sister to a monster, for what happened after she died, because I'm assuming it was horrific, and I'm sorry someone you trusted abused you." He knew only too well the scars that scenario could leave on a person.

They sat in silence for most of the remainder of the ride. Finally, she cleared her throat. "No one has ever said that. No one."

"Said what?"

"That they were sorry for what happened to me. I think you're the first person." Her voice was so soft he barely heard it.

He reached out and took her hand. "I had a similar experience growing up. That bastard did things to me that I will never speak of...to anyone. I was young and vulnerable, and he abused the trust a father is supposed to hold sacred. My twin brother went through hell, too...but our mother was the one that abused him. We struck out in the moral character gene pool." He exhaled a lungful of air because he needed to breathe, not because it was funny. "I was fucked up for a long time. My brother pulled me out of that hell. I know what I went through made me what I am today, and I'm not really sure if that's a good thing."

She swiped her fingers under her eye, catching a stray tear, and nodded. "I swore if I got away from him, I'd spend my life making bastards like him pay." She looked up at him and straightened her shoulders. "I'm not a bad person."

"Oh, fuck..." Dixon pulled her onto his lap. She came willingly and snuggled into him, which was so out of character for the woman that he realized she had exposed a very raw part of herself to him.

He kissed her forehead and closed his eyes as he spoke the truth he'd discovered through his own journey. "Sometimes because of circumstances beyond their control, people are forced to become someone or something they'd never otherwise become. Sometimes those circumstances lead to a desire for justice, or the need to avenge a wrong. For some of us, doing the unthinkable to protect the innocent is the only option, and each time we chose to defend, we build another barrier. It is like we each live in a cage of our own making. The bars are built and strengthened with each act and decision we make."

"A cage. God, I get that," she sighed the words into his chest.

"Hmmm... thing I learned is that the bars on our cage don't block us from escaping. They are simply devices we use to make us think we can't change our lives. Every time you make a decision that is different from the past, those bars weaken. You let me in and gave me a glimpse of your life. That bar on your cage is gone. You told me about your past, that bar no longer constrains you. With each decision, we can strengthen grip our pasts have on us, or we can weaken the power we've given it."

Her eyes glittered like diamonds as she stared at him. He had no idea what she'd do with the information, but he could see her desire to believe what he'd just told her. Whether or not she did depended on her. There was no way he could reconcile her past for her. Hell, he was having a hard time doing that with his own baggage, but he prayed for her sake that she'd believe him and start letting herself out of the cage she'd locked herself in. He dropped a soft kiss to her upturned mouth.

She dipped her head, breaking contact. "Have you removed the bars from your cage?"

"I guess you could say that is a work in progress." He ran his thumb across her cheek. "It's a slow process, but I'm making them weaker one decision at a time." He lifted her chin and slanted his mouth over hers.

She sighed and relaxed into his kiss, but he kept it light and comforting. When he broke their contact, she reached up and ran a finger along his jaw. "A fortune cookie philosopher. What other talents do you have, Mr. Simmons?"

He chuckled softly. "So many. Did you know I'm a pilot?"

She pushed away from him. "Really?"

"Yup."

"Take me flying?"

"I can do that."

"Excellent." She arched her back and did an *almost* graceful slide back to her side of the car. She braced her feet on the floorboards and her shoulders against the back of the seat to shimmy her dress back down into position. Dixon got an eyeful of leg and a glimpse of her pert little ass. "What other talents do you have?" She relaxed back into her seat. Apparently, she was done talking about herself.

"I'm a mechanical engineer. I've got a really awkward obsession with explosives. For most of my life I've been a serial womanizer..."

"Wait, what's that?"

"A mechanical engineer?" He got a punch on his arm for teasing her. "Oh, you mean a serial womanizer?"

She narrowed her eyes at him playfully. "Yeah, that one."

He shrugged. "I guess it means that I don't usually date. I fuck, and I move on."

"Huh, so that would make me a serial...manizer?" She screwed up her face for second before she lifted her hand..."No, a serial man-eater!"

He groaned at her wicked comment. "Why do I not want to hear that?"

"Oh, dude, don't feel bad. You're the only man I'm interested in eating, at the moment." She reached over and cupped her hand over his cock. Damned if he didn't push up into her grip and cover her hand with his.

"Exclusively mine. Remember?" He linked his fingers with hers and lifted them to his lips, depriving his cock of the stimulation that would lead to an embarrassing exit from the car in about three blocks.

She squeezed his hand, and he glanced over at her. "Exclusively mine." She echoed. She stared at him waiting for him to acknowledge her.

"Exclusively each other's." He winked at her after he said it, giving her a way out or to make a joke if she wanted.

"That works for me."

"So, tell me, Ms. Nguyen, what would you do if you could do anything in the world?"

"Besides you?"

Dixon laughed and nodded, "Yes, besides me."

"Hmmm...anything?"

"Yup. If you had a magic wand and could only use it to grant yourself one wish, what would it be?"

She was quiet until they pulled up to the valet. Dixon exited the car quickly and trotted over to where the door had been opened for Joy. He leaned forward and extended his hand, helping her out of the vehicle.

"Oh, this is beautiful!"

The outdoor gardens were lush and full, a stark contrast to the gloomy winter weather outside the enclosed courtyard. There were several bars and high-top tables with seating for those who were early or waiting on their reservation time. Dixon wrapped Joy's hand through his arm and slowly led her to the hostess stand.

"Reservation for Simmons."

The hostess checked her computer and smiled. "Yes sir, one moment please."

A man wearing a tux appeared beside them. "Sir, my name is Amos. If you would follow me?"

Dixon allowed Joy to precede him while taking a moment to survey the people already seated. Several sets of appreciative eyes followed Joy's progress through the seating area. Dixon ceased his observations and made eye contact with a woman who was staring at him. She held his gaze and then let her eyes roll past him, dismissively.

After they were seated Joy leaned over to him, "Who's the brunette?"

Dixon picked up her hand and kissed her fingers as he spoke, "The one in the black dress at my eight o'clock?"

"That would be the one."

"I have no idea, why?"

"If looks could kill, I'd be six feet under and

decomposing." Joy blinked her eyelashes at him and gave him a saccharine smile.

His gut told him there was something off about the woman too. Joy grabbed her purse and turned to him, speaking in a hushed tone, "I'm going to go to the can. If the bitch follows me, I'll find out who she is. If she comes here, you'll have about five minutes before I come back to figure out what the fuck her problem is."

"And if she just has a pole shoved up her ass and doesn't approach either of us?"

"Then I'll picture *her* as the prima ballerina tonight." She winked at him, leaned over, brushed a kiss across his lips, and stood. Dixon stood with her and moved her chair for her before he took his seat again. He ordered a bottle of wine when the sommelier approached and pulled out his phone.

"May I take a moment of your time?" The woman's European accent caught his ear.

Dixon rose. "I'm sorry, do we know each other?"

The woman looked at the chair Joy had been sitting in and then at Dixon. "Offer me a seat, Mr. Simmons."

Dixon narrowed his eyes before he pulled the chair out for her. He slid the chair in after she sat down and took a seat. "I believe you have me at a disadvantage."

"I believe I do, and that is the way we prefer it." The woman crossed her arms and leaned back in the chair. "You will be offered the Senate seat tomorrow. You will accept it. You will vote as we require, and then and only then will we consider the information you have on Guardian. If what you say is accurate, we will proceed at our pace and with our own players. You will not be involved."

"Thank you for your time." Dixon stood up and moved behind the woman. He leaned down and whispered in her ear as he grasped the chair. "Find another lackey to push your vote through and don't contact me again." He stood and pulled the chair out, jolting the woman into action.

She stood and spun on her heel to stare at him. "You will regret this decision."

"No, you tell your bosses that they just pissed away their one and only chance to put a boulder-sized hole in Guardian Security. If they decide to take me out for not agreeing to take the seat, ask yourself what I know and what have I done with that information. Now, if you'll excuse me, I believe my date would like her seat." Dixon nodded toward Joy, who was approaching. "I didn't think The Fates specialized in stupidity. My mistake."

Dixon watched unadulterated fear flash across the woman's features. Jason had cautioned him to use the name of who they believed was behind Stratus only if absolutely necessary. To him, getting this whole ordeal over as quickly as possible *was* absolutely necessary. He felt like he'd been dangling from a hook for far too long.

The woman glanced from Joy, who was now standing behind her, to Dixon. He smiled politely. "Do have a good evening and thank you for stopping by."

The woman, visibly pale and shaken, moved away from them. He offered Joy his hand, helped her to be seated, and pushed her chair in for her. She cast a glance in the direction of the rapidly disappearing brunette. "Sooo..." Joy looked at him. "Whatcha know, Quick Draw?"

"She was higher on the food chain than the one who came this afternoon."

Joy snapped straight in her seat. Glancing around to make sure there were no ears within hearing distance she crooked her finger at him and when he closed in, she whispered, "You holding out on me? You never told me there was a visitor this afternoon."

"I was saving it for table conversation. Do you remember I told you we'd talk tonight?" Dixon retorted in the same hushed tone. "Besides, you distracted me with that dress and all the talk about devouring me."

Joy laughed at that, turning several heads. Her sexy, throaty laugh would turn his head if he heard it too. She laid a hand on his and leaned back in, "I did do that, didn't I?"

"You did." He saw the sommelier heading his way and nodded toward him, giving Joy a heads up.

She glanced over at the man and smiled back at Dixon. He waited until their wine was approved and poured before he leaned in to speak with her. "A middle management mouthpiece came by the office not more than five or ten minutes before you came back to The Residence. The lady-in-black's visit tonight tells us two things."

Joy took a sip of the wine and leaned into him to whisper, "They are desperate to put you in that seat, and they knew where you would be tonight, but not necessarily that I would be accompanying you."

Dixon leaned in, so there was barely any space between them. He traced his finger along her shoulder and watched her skin tighten when a shiver ran through her. He whispered, "What an observant assassin you are, Ms. Nguyen."

She closed the distance between them and murmured against his lips, "I'm better than you know."

Dixon smiled as she kissed him. He didn't doubt Joy thought herself to be at the top of her profession, but he knew there were those above her—the elite who worked as Shadows. She was good, but she wasn't elite.

CHAPTER 14

"HE'S A BRAZEN ASSHOLE. Why are we pursuing him? We can find someone else." Third all but flopped back in her chair and crossed her arms.

"The Governor has already set the press conference to announce his appointment. We don't have anyone else that we can use without a longer delay." First reiterated the information she'd already stated.

Second snorted, "And a longer delay means there will be no vote in our favor."

"Correct. So, my position is that we contact him again and have the Governor offer him the seat." First spoke as she looked out her window.

"Concur." Second agreed.

"I don't like it, but I'll go along with the majority. You have him under surveillance, I assume?" Third asked.

"It wasn't necessary prior to tonight. Our agent has been more than adequate in providing information. Or so I believed." First responded.

"Do we have the ability to sway Simmons? Is there a connection between him and our asset?" Third mused out loud.

First leaned forward and glanced at the information she had on her desk. "I think there is a level of trust. I don't know if we can levy any pressure."

"Then we contact him. Tell him we are authorizing him to be the lead on the Guardian operation. What he believes and what happens are two different things. I have plans for Mr. Simmons. Plans that he will not like." Third sounded decidedly happy with herself.

"What are you thinking?" Second had obviously heard the tone of her voice, too.

"I'm going to show Mr. Simmons why he does not want to play with the big girls." Third leaned in toward the camera on the top of her computer making her bigger in First's screen.

She could see the fire in Third's eyes. Fire she hadn't seen in a long time—not since they overthrew the elders who were decimating the vision their sisterhood had been pursuing since it was formed under Mary Tudor. Bloody Mary had devised and empowered her three most trusted ladies in waiting, known as The Fates, to ensure her sister did not come into power. Unfortunately, with her untimely death, The Fates were too new and weak to prevent Queen Elizabeth's ascension, but they did not disband. They formed a triad and a legacy that had since changed the course of world events on numerous occasions. Today, The Fates were powerful, invisible, well-funded and perched on the verge of several worldwide events that would make them the most powerful entity on Earth, and no one knew they existed.

First smiled and leaned forward, not wanting to miss a single word of Third's brainchild. Her sister sneered at the camera as she spoke, "We use him. Install him as the senator to get the votes and intelligence we want. We let him spoon-feed us the information about Guardian, but we set the date and time of the event. We keep him busy with the left hand and with the might of our right hand we will take out Guardian as we simultaneously slay the acting senator. Mr. Simmons dies. No *man* will ever dictate our actions. We wreak havoc on Guardian. That agency is our largest security concern. The other international agencies are too mired in governmental red tape to be more than a lumbering threat on the horizon. I want Guardian destroyed."

"If we don't strike a death blow, they'll come after us." Second replied.

"They have no idea we exist. Who are they going to come after?" Third growled.

"True." Second added.

"We are a rumor. There is nothing that can be linked to us." Third scoffed.

"That Simmons knew *of* us is concerning though," First mused. "He could have been making an educated guess. Putting rumors together."

"What?"

"We've been compromised?" Second asked over the top of Third who shot out the same question.

First hadn't wanted to worry her sisters, but they needed to know. "Not our identities, but

Simmons named us as our collective." First flicked her perfectly manicured middle fingernail with her thumbnail. The wrinkle in the situation regarding her strategic movement within the American government was unforeseen, and if she'd let herself admit it, concerning. She'd sent Ten to meet with the man and to dictate his future course of action. She glanced back at the screen and added, "He further alluded that should we decide to remove him from the equation, any information he has about us would be released."

There was a hiss of air. That came from Third. "He has to have a weakness."

"His family is gone. Our agent hasn't indicated anyone close enough to be used as leverage." First flicked her eyes over the documents she knew by heart, still looking for any indication of weakness. She found none.

"So where does that leave us?" Second asked.

First drew a deep breath. "There is no change to the plan.

"We use him and then we eliminate him. We get him into the Senate seat, get the votes you require, and then we delay as much as we can on the Guardian situation. Should we find he has usable intelligence, we move on it. Use him as the face of the operation. If it goes bad, he is the one who falls on his sword. No ties to us. No witnesses to any further meetings. Move Ten to another country and move her tonight. It would be a shame to have the man identify her and lose her as an asset." Third deftly summarized First's own thoughts.

"Simmons will need a point of contact," Second added.

"Phone calls only. Synthesizers used to mask voices, the calls can be made by voice over IP and bounced a million times. We cut off the communication before it can be traced or spiked," Third retorted.

"That it can be done isn't the issue. My concern is...should it be?" First sighed heavily. "We can walk away."

"Hundreds of millions of dollars left on the table? Power to leverage the United States to our way of thinking in the other vote? No, I say we continue. We have essential operations that need that funding," Second said in a dismissive tone. "The man, Simmons, is smart, but he also has a grudge against Guardian. People seeking revenge make mistakes. I agree with Third. We use him, and if profitable for us, go after Guardian. But he is the only one that is exposed, the only one to take a risk until we eliminate him. That organization has cost us dearly because of their involvement in my operations in Colombia. Time, money, and trained people up in smoke because of them."

"We can't forget about our losses when the Bratva was taken down. Thankfully we'd just started our association. The money we invested into the hacker they'd groomed is starting to be realized. Our technicians are just now beginning to pull information off the cloned hard drives he sent us as a failsafe." First was hopeful the time and energy involved in breaking past the man's firewalls would be worth the investment. They'd been working on it for years and progress had only been reported within the last few months.

"The Bratva initiative was all a waste. Time and money that saw no profits, thanks to Guardian. Putting a bullet in Guardian's brain would eliminate many problems." Third spit out the words like they left a rancid taste in her mouth.

"The tech team has shown some advancement," First reminded her. Third's eyes rolled, and she shook her head. It was a common source of disagreement with them.

"Then it's decided. I'll brief Four. She will make the calls and keep us informed. Mr. Simmons will vote for us, provide us with information, and then die."

"Concur." Second stated.

"I will be the one to develop the operation to take him out." Third gave a deep throaty laugh. "Eliminating pestilence is my specialty."

"You know dancing on your toes all night has got to suck." Joy lifted her four-inch heel and extended her toe. Dixon's eyes traveled the length of her leg. The flash of streetlights let her see his desire. She was so going to get fucked the way she liked tonight. She twisted toward Dixon. "That prima chick was strong as fuck. Did you see the muscles in her legs?" She lifted her leg higher and turned her foot to look at her calf. "Maybe I should work out more."

Dixon chuckled, drawing her attention from her leg to the man admiring it. "I think your legs are perfect just the way they are."

"Yeah?" She turned her ankle this way and that and considered the musculature of her leg. "I don't know. Don't suppose you'd know someone I could wrap them around to prove how strong they are?" She'd never had a regular gym routine, and sparring partners were few and far between. She practiced her skills alone or against real opponents.

"I do." He reached for her just as his cell phone's ringtone peeled through the back of the limo. "Hold that thought," he cautioned her, waggling his eyebrows as he reached inside his coat to retrieve the device.

"Simmons." His eyes darted over to her as the voice on the other end of the connection spoke. She could hear the voice. Deep...and mechanical?

Dixon turned his head toward the window. "I accept. I assume you are making phone contact because your minions have failed. Send me a schedule of events I am required to attend and the way you want me to vote." He paused for a moment before he laughed, "No, you'll send it via messenger. I won't have a digital trail of this arrangement out there to be used against me." He listened and a satisfied smile crossed his face before he ended the call.

"Why are you doing this?"

"Making things right." He shrugged and pretended to get busy putting his phone away, but she saw through that bullshit.

She cocked her head and furrowed her brow at him. The man was so damn confusing sometimes. "Making it right with whom?"

He leaned back in his seat and closed his eyes. "With myself. When I'm done here, there won't be any bars on that fucking cage that I can't break down." His eyes opened and swung to meet hers. "Or I'll be dead, and I won't have to worry about it any longer."

Joy slid her hand into his and looked forward when he did. His last comment was a sentiment she'd always believed for herself. No one cared if she lived or died. It didn't matter if she came back from a mission. Or at least it hadn't.

She threw the man beside her a sideways glance. Getting back to him two weeks ago had kept her going. Hell, it had been the reason she'd fought as hard as she had against that coked-out bastard. Reading into that revelation was dangerous, and it was stupid to try to second guess someone else's emotions. But it was also the truth, and she'd learned the truth was an inconvenience that always needed to be acknowledged. Dixon squeezed her hand as if reading her thoughts. She flashed another look at him, but he still studied the neighborhood they were passing through, lost in his own thoughts.

They arrived at The Residence, Dixon tipped the driver, and the car pulled away from the curb. They turned to go in when she caught movement coming out of the shadows down the street. She halted the same time Dixon did. To say she was curious as to why Mr. Smith was walking down the sidewalk toward them at this hour of night was an understatement. Joy threw Dixon a cautious look and let him step forward to meet the man. She opened her purse and palmed her automatic. The man was a bull, but a .45 through the brain would stop anything, no matter how large.

"Smith? What are you doing here so late?" Dixon's question was calm and professional.

"What do you mean? You sent me a text?" Smith reached into his jacket to retrieve his phone.

A flash from the inside of The Residence caught her eye. Joy screamed, "Down!" and pulled on Dixon's hand. Dixon grabbed Smith's arm and yanked.

"What the—" Dixon's words were lost in the percussion of the explosion. She felt the heat an instant before Dixon's body covered hers and drove her into the sidewalk. The sounds of bricks, wood, and glass catapulting through the air were lost on her, but she knew it was happening. Joy felt a sharp pain tear through her thigh and tucked her legs closer to her body. Her lungs burned as she tried to inhale against Dixon's full weight. She blinked open her eyes, trying to focus through the smoke and shroud of dust that was falling around them. Her ears were so screwed. She could only hear muffled sounds. Alarms from vehicles parked along the curb sounded like they were submerged underwater. Dixon rolled off her onto his back. Joy gasped and lifted to her hands and knees and searched for Smith. He lay face down, halfway in the street. Dixon coughed, or she assumed so because his hand rose to his mouth and his shoulders shook. He dropped his hand and gazed at the debris surrounding them.

Joy glanced at the stone facade of the house and grabbed his coat. The front of the second story hung precariously, swaying above them. "Move. We have to move, now."

"What?" She didn't hear his reply but read his lips as he likewise tried to understand her. She pointed up. He blinked and shifted his gaze to where she pointed. His eyes widened in alarm. He rolled onto his hands and knees and glanced at Smith. He pointed at her and then across the street. Jolting forward, he grabbed Smith, rolled him onto his back and grabbed his arms before he stood and started to drag the man out of the way. Out of training and perhaps bolstered by habit, Joy grabbed the purse that held her weapon. Two steps farther toward safety she saw a cell phone. She reached down to pick it up. Pain tore through her leg, and she almost went down. She glanced at the back of her thigh and grimaced. A piece of glass was embedded in the side of her leg. Not large, but the motherfucker hurt like hell.

She limped beside Dixon as he dragged the huge man across the asphalt and realized, somehow, she was missing a shoe. Joy carefully placed her bare foot trying not to step on glass or sharp shards of the building material that littered the street. Her hand was buried in her purse, finger on the trigger of her weapon. She scanned the street, and she saw Dixon doing the same as he tugged the three hundred pounds of dead weight across the debris-laden street.

People started appearing from the surrounding buildings. Joy slipped her purse strap over her shoulder, withdrew her hand and closed the snap when two men in different states of dress raced forward to help Dixon get Smith to safety. A woman wearing pajamas and a robe reached Joy and insisted she sit down on the curb. She still couldn't hear shit, but she didn't need to hear to know someone had tried to kill all of them. She extended her leg and examined the glass in her thigh. Dammit. Stitches. Dixon dropped onto the curb with her as police cars pulled onto the scene.

"Smith?" She shout-talked at Dixon.

He glanced at the man who was being

tended to by a police officer. "Alive." His words were almost understandable between the ringing in her ears and the sirens that kept getting louder.

"What the fuck happened?" She leaned toward him and looked at the brownstone. The front of the building was gone. Chunks of brick, wood, and pieces of furniture littered the street. The area where they'd stood moments earlier had received little debris as the force of the explosion seemed to have gone up and out rather than just out. She'd worked with an explosives expert on several occasions and had learned enough to know whoever set the bomb didn't mean to kill them...unless they expected them to be in the house...but why not wait until later when there would be no doubt? But he would have been in the house if Smith hadn't strolled up to the front of The Residence. Was that by chance or was it planned?

"I'm not sure."

Joy started at his response and had to fight to remember what she'd asked. *Oh, right. What happened?* She swung her head toward him. "Why was Smith here?"

"I don't know." Dixon nudged her and

nodded towards the cops who were talking with a neighbor. One of the uniformed officers headed over to the curb when the neighbor pointed toward them.

"Mr. Simmons? I'm Officer Reyes. Is this your home?"

"Sir?" Dixon started to get up, but the man put a hand on his shoulder and squatted down, so he was on the same level as they were. A considerate cop. Huh...

"Was anyone else home?" The police officer asked him in a manner that led her to believe they'd found a body...or portions of a body...

"What?" Dixon shook his head staring at the building.

"Your father?"

"Dad?" He glanced at Joy. "I don't understand."

"We have found the remains of a body in the house." The police officer offered the information.

Dixon shook his head and clamped hold of her hand. Joy had to give him credit, the man could act. She almost thought Dixon believed the fucker had come back to life and may have been rambling around the house they'd been living in.

"What?" Dixon stared at the shell of the house. Fire hoses snaked into the back of The Residence, and smoke poured heavenward from the openings.

Joy carefully reached down and grabbed the glass lodged in her thigh. She closed her eyes as she pulled it out. Blood started to flow and drip down her leg. "Sir?" Joy made herself look up at the officer. "I think he got hit in the head, and I need stitches." She lifted her blood-soaked hand.

"Shit! Shackley, get the paramedics over here!" The other cop that had been talking with the neighbor turned and yelled through the sounds of the first responders.

Officer Reyes turned to look for the paramedics. Dixon took the opportunity and glanced at her, winked, and then turned toward the building and settled into a blanked-out stare. Okay, so the man *was* acting. He needed time. Probably. There were a lot of questions that the cops would want answered. How he was going to answer them was beyond her, but the man was resourceful. Her answers would be legit. She went out to dinner with Dixon tonight and saw the ballet. They came back to his place for a good time. She knew nothing about his father and had no idea why someone would want to kill anyone. The interesting part of the evening would be to see what Smith and Dixon were going to say.

She glanced over at Smith, who was now sitting up. The man's eyes drifted over to Dixon and then to Joy before they returned to Dixon, where they lingered. She lost sight of him when the paramedics sprinted across the distance that separated them. Shit was about to get interesting.

DIXON LET THE EMERGENCY ROOM PHYSICIAN examine him. He had been hit in the head by something, and the bump was plausible deniability.

"Well, Mr. Simmons, all things considered, you've been extremely lucky. I'd like to keep you overnight to ensure there are no complications." The old doctor reached for his tablet and swiped across the surface.

"No thank you, sir. I'll be fine." It would be a frostbitten day in hell before he'd stay in a building that anyone could enter and where security was a joke.

The man dropped his hand from the small device and narrowed his stare at Dixon. "Do you have someone at home that can look after you? There is a protocol for concussions."

"My friend, Joy. She was brought in with me. Stitches?" He glanced past the doctor to the other curtained off area where Joy had been wheeled. He'd heard her swear once or twice, so she was obviously fine.

"I will be able to look after him, too." Smith's voice came from the other direction. Dixon glanced over at the man and winced at the black eye and cut that ran down the side of his face. It was closed with butterfly bandages.

The doctor pointed at Smith in disbelief. "You need someone to look after you."

"Joy." Both Dixon and Smith responded at the same time.

"The woman over there?" The doctor pointed to the curtain. Dixon nodded his head and wanted to chuckle. The doctor had dismissed Joy. Big. Fucking. Mistake. "She needs bed rest–"

"Mr. Simmons?" Officer Reyes exited Joy's curtained off area.

Dixon looked at the man and blinked as if he'd never seen him before. "Yes?"

The man stopped awkwardly and cleared his throat. "Sir, I was on scene and introduced myself."

"I'm sorry, Officer...I'm really fuzzy on what happened. I remember being in the limo and then..." He glanced at the nurse that was walking down the hallway between curtains. "I was here?"

"I'm excusing myself now, Mr. Simmons. I meant what I said about needing someone with you tonight if you decide to leave against medical orders."

Dixon nodded at the doctor and looked over at the cop. "What happened?"

"Well, sir, there was an explosion at your residence."

"Yes, the doctor told me. But what happened? Was it a gas leak or something?"

"I'm not sure, sir. The fire inspector is on

scene now. However, we did find a victim in The Residence."

"A victim?" He sent a surprised glance to Smith who frowned back at him.

"Yes, sir. A male. Was your father home?"

"He wasn't supposed to be." Dixon glanced at Smith. "Mr. Smith is his assistant. Was Dad supposed to be home?"

"No sir, he is in Albany for the next two days. Some sort of political function at the state capital." It was the response they'd worked out if anyone turned up looking for his father. Dixon still hadn't found a way to permanently explain his father's disappearance. If only he could reach out to Guardian. Fuck him, he missed his organization's support.

"Is there any chance he could have come home early?"

"I don't think so. Smith, could you call him?" Dixon asked.

Smith nodded and palmed the phone from his pocket. He hit send and...all eyes turned to the curtained off area where Joy had been taken. She stood barefoot at the curtain's partition wearing a pair of dingy blue scrubs that were rolled up several times, leaving a wide cuff at the bottom of her pant legs. The scrub top almost reached her knees. She held her hand out and looked at the phone that was ringing. "I found this on the sidewalk after the explosion. I thought it was Smith's because he was reaching for his when..."

"Ma'am, I'll need to take that from you." The cop whipped a plastic evidence bag out of his cargo pocket and had Joy drop the phone into it.

"Why would my father's phone be at the house?" Dixon glanced at Smith who looked just as shocked as he felt. They'd destroyed the phone his father was carrying. The number Smith had called should have rung through to nothing.

"Do you think..." Smith reached for the stool beside the cop and plunked his ass down. "Could he have come back?"

"Would he have driven or would he..."

"Limo service." Both Smith and Dixon answered at the same time. Joy hobbled up to the side of his bed and grabbed the rail. To the casual observer she looked tiny and trauma-tized. Dixon knew better.

"Which one?"

Smith gave him the name of the limo service Dixon had used tonight. His thoughts raced. Could this be Guardian giving him an alibi? It had to be. The dead body, trace evidence...shit, was Jason still giving him high cover?

"Sir?"

Dixon flicked his eyes up to the officer. He'd zoned out. Fuck. He wiped his face with his hand. "Sorry officer, I was... What did you say?"

"Where will you be going, in case we need to contact you?" Officer Reyes repeated the question for him.

"I have an apartment." He rattled off the address and covered Joy's hand with his. "We will be there. Smith?"

"I'll be with them, or I'll be at my apartment." The man rattled off another address.

"One more question, why did you go to your father's residence tonight?" Reyes' eyes cut to him, sharp and intense.

"He was out of town, and my apartment isn't as close to downtown. I use the upstairs bedroom most nights. He doesn't have a problem with it." Because the motherfucker was dead.

"He?"

"Sorry, my father," Dixon answered.

"And you, sir?" He turned his gaze to Smith.

"I forgot that Mr. Simmons, the senior, wanted me to go through some documents before his morning meeting. He asked me to confirm the numbers he was given...I was returning to do that."

"Do you think it was him?" Dixon looked at the officer. He whispered the question in hopes of making the man believe he gave a shit.

"We don't know, sir. We shouldn't speculate, and you need rest. The three of you are very lucky the explosion didn't kill you, too. Our detectives will be in contact. The district is stretched thin. I'll give them this initial information while they work the scene. You can expect a visit from them. I'm sure they will have questions." He closed his small spiral notebook, sealed the baggie with the phone in it, pocketed both and nodded as he left.

Dixon watched the cop leave and waited impatiently as the doctor was found to fill out his and Smith's discharge paperwork, against medical orders, and waited while the nurse ran Joy through the concussion protocol. Smith sat stoically through the process, although his face had gone ashen, and he looked like hell. They hobbled out of the emergency room together.

"Where to?" Joy asked when she turned to him. Her mink was filthy, but it would keep her warm against the winter night. She'd shoved her feet into sneakers that were three sizes too big. A nurse had pulled them from the lost and found for her. Dixon didn't even want to think where they may have come from.

"My apartment. Smith, I think for tonight it would behoove all of us to stay together." Dixon glanced at the Uber app on his phone. Their car was almost to the emergency room entrance.

"Strength in numbers," Smith muttered.

"Something like that," Dixon confirmed. The explosion, the dead man in the house, a phone that wasn't his fathers but was? Either Guardian was watching out for him, or someone was setting him up. He had no way of confirming either hypothesis. He trusted one person unconditionally, and he didn't have access to him.

They got into the SUV that picked them up. Smith in the front and Joy in the back with him. She leaned against him, and he tucked her under his arm. The driver confirmed his apartment address, and they took off. Dixon stared out the backseat window. Smith was his father's employee. He didn't know squat about the man, but it was apparent someone wanted him at the house. He hadn't sent that text, and he hadn't actually *seen* the text to validate that Smith was telling the truth. He didn't know how they masked it with his number, but he'd find out.

If they'd gone into the house, they would all be dead. As it was, they were extremely lucky Smith had shown up, just preventing them from going inside. Dixon glanced down at Joy. Her head rested on his chest, and her eyes were closed. Her long dark lashes rested on her cheeks. He wanted to believe she wasn't involved with the events of the night. His gut told him she wasn't, just like it was telling him Smith had no idea what was happening.

The strands of the deadly web that surrounded him flashed as each strand connected to the other. He was standing at the center of those silk strings. He could feel the spider's weight as it approached. The fabric around him moved with each circumstance that presented itself, but he couldn't see where the damn spider was coming from, and that was a major concern.

They exited the vehicle and made their way to his small apartment. "Joy, you use the shower first, then Smith. I'll order food." There was nothing in the place except for the dishes in the cupboard. Joy dropped her mink on the chair and headed back to his only bathroom. She flicked the heat on as she passed the thermostat.

"She's been here before." Smith sat down on a stool at the counter in the kitchen.

"Many times."

"Is she...important to you?" Smith's head rested against his fist. His eyes were closed, and it looked as if he was struggling to stay awake.

"She's...interesting to me. You know as well as I do that getting close to anyone is risky." Dixon saw the man's eyes open and slide to where he stood. The pain reflected there was almost palpable.

"I've never had anyone. If she could be important, you need to make sure she stays safe. Send her away from this shit." The man rolled his shoulders and blinked at the over-sized recliner. "Mind if I relax in that?"

"Go ahead. Do you want me to wake you for food?" Dixon glanced at the clock. It was nearly four in the morning. Thank God for a city that never slept and had food delivery around the clock.

"Yeah, sure, as long as it is after ten or so." He got up and dropped his overcoat onto the stool he was sitting on. "I don't have double vision or nausea. The concussion isn't bad. I just need to sleep it off."

"You got it." Dixon watched the man sink into the recliner, kick the footrest out and lean back. Dixon did his rounds and inspected the small apartment for any unwanted electronics. He checked all the logical locations and a few where *he'd* place a device if he was setting up the joint. Nothing. Smith's heavy breathing sounded from the front room as he inspected everywhere but the bathroom. If someone bugged that room, they were stupid, but he'd check it before he showered. He shuffled through the flyers in the drawer and pulled two, one was from the corner bodega that stayed open all night. He'd place a grocery order. God only knew how long they'd be here. The shower turned off while he was on the phone finalizing his delivery. Joy walked out a couple minutes later. Her wet hair hung past her shoulders and was tossed from a towel drying. She had wrapped herself in a pale-yellow fleece blanket that had been tucked in the hall closet the day he moved in. It swaddled her and dragged on the floor, trailing behind her.

"I seem to be out of clothes, and I don't have a comb. You wouldn't happen to have one, would you?" She gathered the blanket and wiggled up onto the stool across from him.

"Afraid not. Do you have a place? I'm assuming you have one where you keep clothes and such." *Weapons, knives, telephones.* Dixon mentally ticked off the list of things he'd have in an apartment, at least if he had one his father or enemies wouldn't search.

"Yeah. I'll go there in a little bit." She glanced over at Smith. He was asleep, and there was no faking it. The man's mouth hung open, and he was snoring. "We should probably talk."

"Where do you want to start?"

"Did you sweep the apartment?" Joy countered.

"Everywhere but the bathroom."

"I did that. Nothing that I could find." She wrapped a length of the blanket around her shoulders as Dixon took a stool beside her. They both stared at Smith. "Did you see the text he said he received?" Joy lowered her voice even though there didn't appear to be any need.

Dixon glanced at the man's coat. He lifted it by the collar and patted the pockets down until he found the phone. The screen was locked, but it took less than a minute for him to bypass the safeguard.

"Impressive, Mr. Simmons."

"Child's play, Ms. Nguyen." Dixon sent Smith a long look before he hit the text icon. There were two threads on the phone. The identifier labeled one contact as *The Boss*. There was only one text and it read

< carry on as directed>

with no reply from Smith. It was dated the day Dixon's sperm donor died. He glanced at the time. About three hours before the event. The second was from his phone. It simply read,

<meet me at the residence, now.>

"Is that actually your number?" Joy asked, and Dixon hit the info button to check. It wasn't his number, yet his name was attached to it. He glanced over at Smith. The man pretended he wasn't the sharpest tool in the box, but he was savvy. He had street smarts, and he'd been able to exist around his old man for as long as Dixon had, so the wrong number on *his* phone labeled with his name was confusing and concerning. Dixon reached across the counter, grabbed his phone and sent a text to Smith's phone. It went through, and *his* name was also displayed. He toggled back to the first text message and showed the screen to Joy. "There's a space between the D and the I in my name which allowed someone to send a text that Smith believed was from me."

"Well, that would do it. They couldn't have sent the text to him from your phone because you had it with you, so somehow they manipulated his phone without him knowing about it and sent a text."

"Could be." Dixon placed Smith's phone on the counter along with his. "Or it could be he's in on the plan to kill me."

"Us." Joy interjected.

"Maybe." Dixon glanced at her when she whipped her head around to meet his gaze.

"Say what now?"

"We have a dead body in the remains of the house. Cops believe it is my old man."

"But it's not."

"Obviously, but I want to see what the cops say. If the people who I'm working with are behind the event, and they want to frame me, the cops will show up here and arrest me."

"If not?"

"Then they're giving me legitimacy. The old man dies in a tragic accident, and I garner the sympathy of the city."

"Ingenious."

"That it is."

"Which do you think it is?"

"My gut is telling me it is the latter. Not sure who would benefit from them framing me. The seat would go vacant, and the vote they want won't happen."

"Vote?"

Dixon smiled down at her and nodded. "Many, many threads being weaved, my dear."

"But what could the motive be?" Joy bit her bottom lip a second. "Is there some sort of reason you'd kill your old man? I mean a will that named you heir or something?"

"Not that I'm aware of and now with the house up in smoke, I'll probably never know." He'd searched the bastard's safes. There wasn't a will at the house. Justin had opened the safes the same day as the downstairs security system had been disabled, and they'd gained access to the basement. All he had to do was turn the handle, and the doors swung unobstructed. He'd never give Justin shit again as long as he lived. The man was a genius.

"I admit I'm confused. I keep thinking if they wanted us dead, why not wait a couple hours? We would have been in the house. We'd be toast. And why send Smith?" She dropped her elbows to the counter behind her and leaned back still watching Smith sleep.

"Too many questions and not enough answers." Dixon agreed.

Joy sighed and shook her head. "Go shower. I'll stand watch over the bear in the chair and answer the door if the delivery people show up."

Dixon glanced over at her. "In that?"

"Shit, dude, this is New York. I'm sure these

delivery guys working the late shift have seen it all." She pointed to the bathroom. "Go. I got us covered."

Dixon stood and felt every muscle complain. "Sorry about the sudden end to our date."

Her eyes lifted to his. "Date? Quick Draw, we don't date. Remember?"

Dixon chuckled and leaned down to place a soft kiss on her lips. "Seems my rules have changed." He winked at her as he lifted away and headed toward the bathroom. The shell-shocked look he got was not the expression he was hoping for. He stepped into the bathroom as he heard her call his name in a whisper. He backed out so he could see her.

"That's good because I'd only consider dating guys that showed me an explosive time."

Dixon laughed as he entered the bathroom. Hot water, soap, and white noise. Exactly what he needed to sort through the mess inside his head.

CHAPTER 15

JOY HELD onto the laugh and smile Dixon had flashed her before he entered the bathroom. She slid off the stool and worked her way through the house, meticulously searching the small apartment for any type of monitoring device. She'd already cleared the bathroom. The questions that spun through her mind were the same ones she'd voiced to Dixon but the thoughts she wouldn't express tumbled around with them.

She finished her sweep and perched herself back on the stool. In her line of work, she needed to know who the enemy was. Her eyes slid to Smith. Dixon had hired her. She trusted him in a way she'd never trusted another man. But Smith? No, she didn't know him, and if at all possible, she'd purposefully arrived and left without Smith knowing it. She had numerous reasons for not wanting to be seen or heard. None of them she cared to examine too closely, but Smith was on her scope in a minor way. Now? Her eyes narrowed, and she slid off the stool. She shuffled into the kitchen and withdrew a butcher knife from the wooden block on the counter. Her gun, the only weapon she had tonight, was hastily stashed in a storm drain before she was transported to the hospital, so using that to get answers wasn't an option. But hey...necessity was the mother of invention.

She walked over to Smith and sat gently on the arm of the recliner. She placed the tip of the knife on the strong, throbbing vein in his neck and pressed. The man's eyes popped open immediately. Joy smiled. "Hi. We are going to play fifty questions, and you are going to answer each one. If you lie, I'll kill you. If you tell the truth, you'll live. Got the rules?"

The man gave her the tiniest of head nods. "Who do you work for?"

"Simmons," Smith whispered just as softly as she was talking.

"Okay, I'll give you a pass on that one. Who *else* do you work for?" She twisted the knife slightly, putting pressure on the very tip of the long, triangular knife.

"I don't know..."

"The answer to that question isn't a lie, Mr. Smith..." Joy let the tip of the knife pierce his skin.

Sweat popped out on the man's brow. He started to speak again, and she shushed him. "Now I do happen to work for Mr. Simmons. He put me on retainer. Do you know what I do, Mr. Smith?"

The man swallowed hard, the motion pushed his throat against her knife. A dribble of dark, red blood trailed down his neck. The slightest shake of his head answered her question.

"Oh no? Really? Well, let's just keep this between us, okay? You see, I do what you do, but in an elegant, connected, defined, expensive, and lethal fashion. I'm very, very good at killing my targets and I have never been caught, because I'm smart, and I don't align myself with stupid men. And you? Well, you see, Mr. Smith, I don't think you're as dumb as you let on. But something you should be aware of is that your employers, whoever they are, think that *you* are expendable. My sources don't have much information about you, but that man in there saved your ass tonight. If he hadn't pulled you down and then dragged your ass across the street, you'd be dead. You owe him your life. Now we are going to have a little talk. If you lie, you die. Got it?"

"I work for him." The man's eyes drifted toward the bathroom. "Only him."

"How did you come to work for his old man?" Joy watched the man's facial features. From what she could see, the big guy believed what he was telling her. Whether or not it was the truth was another story.

"Referred by an associate that I did time with. I was told he needed muscle."

Joy leaned forward. "Tell me everything that happened tonight. And believe me, I'll know if you're lying."

Smith swallowed hard and started talking.

Dixon wiped down the mirror and glanced at his face. The dark circles under his eyes weren't unexpected. He had several cuts on his face from debris and his neck hurt like a motherfucker, even after the shower. He was fucking lucky the percussion of the explosion hadn't snapped his spine. He wrapped a towel around his waist and kicked his ruined clothes into the corner of the room.

He opened the door and froze when he didn't see Smith in the recliner. Dixon carefully padded out of the hall, his automatic in his hand, a round chambered, and the weapon's safety clicked off. He breathed a small sigh of relief when he saw the man in the kitchen putting away groceries. His eyes darted around the apartment. "Where's Joy?"

The man's eyes flicked to his for a nanosecond. He bent his head to the task at hand as he answered, "She went to get clothes for all of us."

"All of us?" Dixon dropped onto the stool at the counter. "Where the hell is she going to get clothes for me?" Smith had clothes at his apartment and Joy had an apartment somewhere, but Dixon was literally down to his towel.

"I didn't ask." Smith pulled a six-pack out of the grocery bag and handed one to Dixon before opening one for himself and downing half of it in one gulp. "Is it true? Did you pull me across the street?"

Dixon frowned at the bottle of beer in his hand before he gazed at Smith. "Yeah, of course, I did. The damn building was going to fall down on top of you if I didn't." He stared at Smith, who lowered his eyes and shook his head. "Why?"

The man shrugged. "Nobody's ever put themselves out for me before." He lifted the beer bottle and saluted Dixon. "Appreciate it."

"What happened to your neck?" Dixon motioned to the front of his throat.

Smith swiped at his neck and frowned. "Must have been from the explosion. I could have reopened it when I was putting away the groceries." The man turned around and placed the rest of the six pack into the fridge. "I'm going to go take a shower. Ms. Nguyen should be back shortly. She said within the hour." Smith glanced up at the clock mounted over the kitchen sink.

"Hold on for just a minute." Dixon wanted some answers first. "I left your phone on the counter. It's gone, so you know that I know what happened."

Smith turned and faced him. "I don't know how they faked the text. It was after midnight; the text woke me. I read it, rolled out of bed, got dressed, and came to The Residence."

"You didn't give your phone to anyone or leave it where it could be tampered with?"

"No, sir. Unless..." Smith's eyes snapped to his.

"What is it?"

"When Ms. Banner came yesterday. I left my phone on the desk when I came to your office to announce her arrival."

"That was the only time?"

Smith nodded.

Dixon leaned forward and spun his beer bottle between his fingers. So, it was Stratus who wanted Smith at The Residence last night. But why? Fuck, again there were too many questions and zero fucking answers.

If he went on the assumption that The Fates had planted a body in the house and were trying to pin him for a murder, they had to have worked fast. The ballet had lasted about two hours, including the intermission. They'd spent another hour and a half at the restaurant prior to going to the ballet and then thirty-five minutes on the return trip home. He hadn't received any indication that anyone had been in The Residence, so the entire alarm system had been compromised.

"I don't understand what is going on. I said as much to Ms. Nguyen before she left. There is no reason for anyone to fake your father's death." Smith folded the grocery bag he'd emptied and dropped it on the counter.

Dixon sighed, "Four entities know my father is dead. You, me, Joy and the people who heard it happen." He took a sip of his beer. It had warmed to the point of tasting like piss water. "Joy was with me. You?" Dixon looked at Smith and chose his words carefully. "I know you are a hired killer Smith, but I don't think you'd blindly walk into an explosion with the hopes of escaping unharmed, so I believe you didn't know the house was going to blow." He finished his beer and grimaced at the luke-warm brew. "That leaves me with the theory that whoever heard what happened is trying to manipulate me into prison or will be using this event to blackmail me."

"What are you going to do?" Smith crossed his arms over his chest as if warding off the cold.

Dixon shrugged, "The ball is in their court. I have no idea who did this, but when I figure it out, you can damn well guarantee that I'm going to go after them with everything I have." He was close to getting to the top of Stratus. He needed one fucking tie to the top tier. Fucking middle management was buried under so many layers Guardian wouldn't be able to find the top. That was one of the main purposes of this operation. Find a way into Stratus. Well, he'd pulled an audible and had changed the play. A way in wasn't what they needed. They needed fucking GPS directions to the top and Dixon had put his life on hold, faced his past, and witnessed too fucking much to stop now. Jason King would have to deal with his change of direction. He just prayed he wouldn't get killed in the process. He wanted to see his brother again.

Smith leaned against the counter. "Dixon,

you need to be careful. There are forces out there that can manipulate a person to do things that they never believed they were capable of doing. Your father was a monster, but you have to know there are others just like him or worse, who will stop at nothing to get their way." The man stared at him and then shook his head. "Just be careful."

"Spit it out, Smith. What are you trying tell me?" Dixon couldn't decipher the meaning between the lines of the man's warning. Of course, he was going to be careful, but what *prompted* the warning?

Smith lifted his arms off the counter and rubbed the back of his neck. He closed his eyes and shook his head. "Don't trust anyone." He opened his eyes and pinned him with a stare. "Anyone, do you hear me?"

"I hear you. Now let me ask you a question. Why are you still here? Other than the pay, which I admit is good, why are you still with me? You have your files. You could walk away." He'd discussed and agreed on a generous salary with Smith the day he'd given him access to the files, but Dixon suspected Smith had another reason for staying with him.

The big man shoved his hands in his pockets, and he stared at the floor for a solid thirty seconds before he spoke, "I..." He lifted his head, swallowed hard and pursed his lips. "I have no one else..." He dropped his head again and sighed before he headed toward the bathroom.

Dixon narrowed his eyes as he tracked the man. *Don't trust anyone*. Not. A. Problem.

"OPERATOR TWO-SEVEN-FOUR."

"Sunset clearance, zero operative."

"Standby, zero operative."

"Archangel."

"What the actual fuck happened?"

"We are working on that. What is your status?"

"My status? Damn near splattered all over a New York street. Thank you for asking. The asset is alive. There was another involved. The one I sent a request for information on. I need your geeks to scrub that information and look deeper. Shit isn't adding up."

"Noted. What happened prior to the incident?"

"Fuck...Ahh...Contact was made. You are aware there was a body found in the explosion?"

"We are. We are monitoring law enforcement and the coroner's input."

"Good to know, not that it does shit for me."

"I assume you can do the job I assigned you?"

"Yeah, but it would be easier if I'm allowed to break my cover."

"No. He can't know. It may change the way he approaches the mission. We can't have the slightest hint of ties with Guardian."

"It's limiting what I can do to help him."

"Watch over him. Things will move fast now. The explosion will undoubtedly set a myriad of things in motion."

"Right. He's survived the gauntlet of that fucking bastard father, now he faces the execution squad. Tell me again, why is he doing this for us?"

"For reasons far above your pay grade. He is facing the executioners, not the execution itself. He'll make it. You're there to ensure he does."

"It would help if he knew he had backup."

"It could also get him killed."

"He could die either way."

"You are there to ensure he does not."

"Noted."

CHAPTER 16

Joy stood in the alley across from Dixon's apartment and watched the street. A precaution, but she'd been distracted, and someone could have slipped in on her six. It wasn't in her nature to drop her guard like this. Fuck she was a sap. She leaned against the brick wall, in the dark and watched for anything out of the ordinary. Her nerves had been on edge all week, with damn good reason.

They'd spent the last seven days answering the same questions, phrased differently, from just about every agency in New York. The medical examiner had confirmed the body in the house was Dixon's father, *which was fucking impossible*, but they'd cremated that body and posted an obituary in the paper. She watched as Dixon and Smith handled the arrangements, insurance companies, the press, and a myriad of other administrative things that needed to be accomplished. Since her little detente with Smith, she'd determined two things. First, the man was devoted to Dixon and second, he was hiding shit. He wasn't stupid, in fact, he was pretty fucking impressive with the admin whirlwind. Glimpses of the man filtered through the mask he wore. She hadn't killed him, but he knew she could have and would if she felt he was a threat to the man who retained her services. That night she'd also determined that Smith may have killed, but he wasn't a killer. It would have been easy to sever his carotid artery. She and Dixon could have dumped the body and placed the blame of the explosion on Smith. Spun it to the authorities that the man had a grudge against the older Simmons and one of the man's less than savory colleagues had taken retribution. It would have exposed the older Simmons in a way she wasn't willing to allow...just yet. She'd had all those plans figured out within five seconds of pulling the knife from the butcher's block. Killing him would have been easy, but she wanted to watch the man...and she had.

Smith had no life. None. He worked for Dixon, went home, got himself ready for work the next day, did an impressive at-home workout and then showered. He turned on the tiny television in his apartment, ate two, microwaved, frozen dinners while sitting in front of the damn thing and then went to bed. She'd put listening devices in his apartment the day she'd retrieved his clothes. He hadn't checked his apartment for the devices, so *maybe* he wasn't part of her community, or maybe he wanted her to believe he wasn't. Fuck, he was still a mystery, and she hated mysteries. The miasma that was Smith deepened when she reviewed the recordings from his apartment. He'd said a total of three words since she'd been recording. If she deciphered the recording correctly, he could have been having a nightmare. She didn't know if he was awake or asleep when he spoke, but the words, *I'm so sorry*, were clear as a bell. Alive he was perplexing. Dead he was useless, so she let him live. For now.

She shifted her weight from one leg to the

other and watched the street from a new angle. The mild winter weather today meant people were out, which meant clearing her way into the apartment became a little more difficult. She waited another hour before she made her way across the street, around the corner and into the back entrance to Dixon's apartment building. She put her key in the apartment door and edged it open holding the ugliest, scrawniest, smallest Christmas tree she'd ever seen. Dixon lowered his automatic and lifted an eyebrow at her.

"Hey, it's Christmas Eve." She pushed her way in the apartment and offered the words as an explanation for the tree.

"Ah, and here I thought it was Arbor Day." Dixon returned his weapon to the shoulder holster he'd started wearing the day after the explosion.

"Smart-fucking-ass. I'm trying here." She held the tree out with one hand and looked at it. "There wasn't much selection left." Her free gloved hand went inside her down-filled coat and pulled out a small white plastic bag. "Lights and a star."

"You thought of everything." Dixon kneed

the recliner away from the corner of the room and waved a hand. She plopped the sad thing in the corner and handed him the bag. "Of course, I did. I only do Christmas Eve on a budget and at the last minute."

He laughed and pulled out the string of lights and yellow plastic star that she'd bought at the dollar store. She dropped her coat in the recliner and helped him twist a single strand of multi-color LED lights around the tree. He put the star on top, and she plugged in the lights. Dixon turned off the overhead apartment lights, and Joy sat back on her heels. Her vision blurred a bit. It was the first Christmas tree she'd ever had–at least the first she remembered. Buying the tree and lights tonight was an impulse. She'd never wanted to celebrate a season of hope...before Dixon.

His hand on her shoulder broke through her thoughts. She sniffed and wiped her nose on the back of her hand. "Stupid to get all mushy over a stick and twinkle lights."

Dixon sat on the floor beside her and pulled her into his lap. "What is your favorite Christmas memory?"

The bitter laugh that escaped her added

a few more tears to her eyes. She looked up at the star and sniffed again. "This is. I don't have any others." She leaned back against his hard chest and shrugged. "Pathetic, huh?"

He tightened his arms around her and shook his head. His five o'clock shadow scraped her temple. "Not at all. I'm glad I'm part of your first Christmas memory." He replaced his whiskers with his lips and kissed her.

She sniffed again and wiped at the tears that pooled on her bottom lashes. "What is your favorite Christmas memory?"

Dixon took a deep breath. "Wow...I don't know...probably pretty pathetic, too." He cleared his throat, "My brother and I had a Christmas recently, and we were with a family. A big family. There was a huge tree, and everyone was happy and laughing. Kids were running around hyped up on sugar and the thought of Santa coming. It was mayhem, and it was perfect."

"Your twin brother is dead, right?" Joy got nothing but a tightened jaw in response. She understood, the death of a sibling was personal. "I'm sorry. I know what it's like to lose someone you love."

"The last time I saw him, I lied to him. He knew I wasn't telling him the truth about what was happening in my life. What I wouldn't give to hug him and tell him I'm sorry."

"You two were close?"

"As close as you can get." He smiled. "You know, finishing sentences for each other and we have...*had* a way of knowing what each other were thinking." He chuckled. "That freaked out quite a few people."

They sat in silence for a while before Joy spoke, "My sister, she was everything. I don't remember much about my parents. They are like this foggy background, but Tess, she tried to protect me. Hell, she made sure I had food. The man who had us, well to put it nicely, he was cruel. Food was a privilege."

"Tess was your sister's name?"

She shook her head. "No, it was the American name she took from that movie I was telling you about. Her real name was Sung-mi. But we were kids, and we played, so she took the name, Tess, because there was this song, it was beautiful and lonely, and it told about the elements like rain and fire and about the wind. Tess was the name they gave the rain in the song. She loved the rain." Joy sat quietly thinking of the music and how much they loved it. They'd sung the song over and over.

"She liked the name Tess?" He prompted her pulling her from her memories.

"Yeah, and...well, anyway as you can guess, I wasn't a very cooperative kid. So, I rarely got to eat. She'd give me her food." Joy shifted gears, avoiding the painful subject and shut the door on those memories. She'd survived, her sister hadn't.

"You? Not cooperative? Say it isn't so." Dixon's chest vibrated against her back when he laughed softly.

Thank God he'd understood and followed her lead. "Right? Who would have thought it?" She grabbed his hands and laced their fingers together. "You asked me once what I would do if I could change anything in the world. Remember?"

"I do. In the car on the way to the restaurant." Dixon squeezed their joined hands.

She stared at the tree and then lowered her gaze to the hands that held hers. Closing her eyes, she whispered, "I wouldn't change anything tonight."

The quiet in the room reverberated so loudly she had to open her eyes. She steadily gazed at the lights flashing on and off. He finally moved and pulled her against him, kissing the top of her head. She let out a breath she hadn't realized she'd been holding and reveled in the warmth and security she felt sitting in the dark with Dixon.

He unlinked their hands and repositioned her like she weighed nothing. She straddled his lap, and in the light of the Christmas tree, she gazed into his beautiful blue eyes. The eyes of the man she'd let herself fall in love with.

"Neither would I." He lifted his hand and ran a finger down her jaw, stopping under her chin. "Merry Christmas, Joy."

His lips found hers, and she fell into the soft, emotion-filled kiss. The feelings between them had changed. This wasn't them fucking. His hands caressed her sides and back as his tongue danced with hers. This, what was happening tonight, was the end result of the long road to this moment. She wouldn't paint it as anything but what it was, at least on her part. Tonight, she was making love to Dixon, and for the first time, she didn't care if the man she was with knew how she felt. This man was different.

"What have you done to me?" She breathed before his lips fell on hers again. Her hands threaded through his deliciously thick strawberry-blond hair.

He lifted from the kiss when she was breathless with desire. "Nothing. It's all Christmas magic."

He lifted her off his lap and stood to extend his hand down to her. She stood and tilted her head back to look up at him. "Magic isn't real."

He wrapped his arms around her, reached down, cupped her ass and lifted her up. "What we have is."

She snaked her arms around his neck and wrapped her legs around his waist before she met his stare. "And *that* scares me. I mean, it's fucking terrifying."

"I'll protect you." He pecked her nose with a small kiss.

She lifted an eyebrow in a direct dare. "You know I don't need anyone to protect me."

"Then *let* me take care of you. I promise

your heart will be safe with me." He turned around with her in his arms and headed into the bedroom.

"Don't you dare fuck this up, Simmons." She slipped from his grasp and stood by the bed with her arms trailing from his neck to his chest. "There isn't much of my heart left."

"We'll make it whole again."

"Don't make promises you can't keep, Quick Draw."

"I won't break your heart."

She held his gaze. *No, he wouldn't break it, he'd shatter it into a billion shards of dust. His love could be the death of her.*

His kiss morphed, one turning into the next. Their clothes were disposed of before he laid her back onto the bed. He knelt between her legs and stared at her. "You are so fucking beautiful."

His fingers trailed over the healing wound where just seven short days ago, broken glass had slashed her thigh. He glanced down at his hand and moved slowly to kiss the raised skin. His lips continued down the outside of her leg to her ankle. He lifted her foot, giving his wide shoulders room, as he trailed kisses up the inside of both legs. Her hands clenched at the bedspread, his hair, his shoulder–whatever she could reach. His slow, tortuous worship of her body bypassed *any* of the parts that fucking *needed* him to touch them.

Finally, she groaned, "Simmons, if you don't put that fucking cannon in me soon, I'm going to reconsider not killing you."

He laughed and made a point of looking at the clock. It read 12:01. "Now it is official. Merry Christmas." He stopped and poured attention on her nipples. She arched up into his mouth, longing for the bite of his teeth. A quick flash of delicious pain coruscated through her, pooling between her legs. His muscles bunched under her hands. She scratched his back with her nails. "My little tigress." He chuckled the words against her throat.

"Want me to prove it?" She wasn't above threatening violence; her body was on the edge of an explosive orgasm, and she desperately wanted to feel him filling her before that happened. The thought of his hard, hot cock sent her hands lower. She cupped his balls with one hand and stroked his thick, long shaft with the other. The feel of that soft skin over the hard core of his cock was thrilling. Fuck, he was magnificent.

Dixon nudged her thigh with his knee and waited for her to lift her legs and release him before he dropped to his elbows, positioning himself over her. His hands tangled in her hair as he stared at her. "Merry Christmas."

"Merry Christmas." She whispered as she pulled him down and kissed him while his cock entered her. She arched her back into the bed and lifted her hips to meet his thrusts. When he lifted away from their kiss, she bit at his bottom lip. He stared at her. The look between them was naked and bare of all pretense but overflowing with their truth. It was too much for her. Her feelings were too much, and mixed with his tenderness, the moment was overwhelming. She felt him lower his head to the crook of her neck while he made love to her. She stroked and touched the muscles of his back and arms, his neck, his hair, anywhere she could reach. Tears fell from her eyes, but she didn't care. Not now. Not tonight. Dixon Simmons was a present she never expected to receive and, for tonight, he was hers. Tomorrow and the dictates of her mission be damned. Her orgasm shattered her thoughts, sending them into the universe.

Dixon lifted off the bed. Joy roused enough to turn her head. "Where you going?" She muttered and blinked up at him.

"Bathroom." He watched her flop back down onto the pillow with a groan. He smiled at the sight of her black hair spreading like a halo across the pillow.

He used the facilities and pulled on a pair of sweatpants he'd snagged as he left the bedroom. Joy's steady even breathing gave him the leeway to do something he probably shouldn't. He grabbed the new laptop that he'd purchased after the explosion and sat down in the recliner. The lights on the tree twinkled as his computer went through the boot-up process. He propped his elbow on the arm of the chair and dropped his chin into his hand. The Governor's announcement that he was being appointed to Senator Waxman's vacant seat was happening on the 27th. The mechanical voice hadn't contacted him again. He was flying in uncharted territory and damn him if he didn't feel like he was careening out of a cloud bank into the side of a mountain. His gut told him to tread carefully, but he had no idea where the threat lurked.

He had an overall plan that he'd been tweaking, and he'd set the bait for Stratus. They wanted Guardian. They'd proved that by going after Drake and the others. Holding the bait out, a chance to gut Guardian, should solidify his usefulness and his appointment. After that, well, that was where things were going to get dicey. Dixon smiled. Then the fuckers would know what it was like to feel the wrath of Guardian. Fuck with one of his Guardian brethren, and you sentenced yourself to hell on earth. Fuck with *his* family, and he'd personally deliver hell to your doorstep, wrapped in a fucking bow.

The distinct sound of a small snore wandered from his room, and he smiled. Joy had been burning the candle at both ends this past week. She was flying high cover as he and Smith worked through the needs of the day. He had no idea what she was doing until the early morning when she'd drag herself into bed for a couple hours sleep, but he knew it was for him. He was paying her far more than the dollar retainer for which they'd started the relationship.

The week had sucked in more ways than one. The high profile of his father had brought every agency known to man out of the woodwork. They'd answered questions for hours on end, and that is when Dixon confirmed Smithson Young was more than the knuckle-dragging thug he'd pretended to be. Over the last week, cracks had formed in that façade and had made it perfectly clear that Smith was something other than a hired killer. In fact, Dixon was reluctant to believe Smith would kill for money. Maybe if he was forced, but what would force him to follow his father's commands? Again, another unanswered question. He was getting sick and fucking tired of that particular brand of inquiry.

He pulled up the fantasy football site and logged in. There were three games on Christmas Day, checking his lineup was perfectly logical. He clicked on the message boards and typed. *Merry Christmas.*

Are you all right? The line disappeared as soon as it was typed.

He deleted his original message and responded. *Missing family.* He held down the backspace key.

He wants to come to you. The words were quickly eaten by the cursor.

Stop him. It isn't time. He cleared his words and sent a quick glance toward the bedroom where Joy slept.

Trying.

Need a favor. Smithson Young. He tapped out the words and waited two seconds before he deleted the message.

Dropbox when done. Will take a while unless you need me to let others in. The words appeared and disappeared as quickly.

Whenever is fine. He tapped out the words and hit the backspace just as quickly.

Another message flashed across the board before being sent into nothingness.

Be careful. <3

Dixon watched the words disappear. He closed the message board and tweaked his team before he shut the computer off. He missed his entire family, and those emotions were exposed to daylight because of the woman sleeping in his bed. What he felt for her was out of the boundaries of this assignment. Hell, they were as mismatched as two people could be other than sexually.

Joy'd never fit into his world. The idea of her living in his world was comical...unless he could convince her to stop the murder for hire gig. And that wouldn't happen. She did what she did because of what happened to her sister. He got that, and he'd never presume he'd have any sway over her actions. He rubbed the stubble on his jaw as he considered how okay he was with that idea. Part of the initial attraction he felt for her was her strength and independence. Who the fuck was he kidding? Ninety percent of that first night's desire was driven by the fact that she could fight like a hellcat and was a stone-cold killer. The fact she was deadly, dangerous, and sexy as fuck was a major turn on. That was something that surprised him. He'd never imagined deadly would be something that would crank his shaft, but damn, seeing her in action really did it for him.

Dixon leaned back in his chair and smiled.

Maybe it wasn't so surprising. Jade in full kick-ass mode was impressive, but he and Drake considered her a sister. A no-go zone if you will, and even though there could have been an attraction to the woman, he and Drake would never hit on one of the Skipper's sisters. Besides, the woman found her soul mate in Nic DeMarco. So, actually, no it wasn't a surprise that Joy turned him the fuck on. The woman was impressive. What he also needed to remember was she was a hired killer. The finite portion of his brain that reminded him of what she did for a living was never too far away. No, he'd never underestimate her.

Drake's voice piped through his mind *"But you might overestimate her."* Dixon clenched his jaw. The feelings he had for Joy had flown past lust and left desire in the dust. It would rip his fucking heart out of his chest if he'd misjudged her. The woman had become important. No, that wasn't the word. Essential. She was essential to his sanity, and as she'd admitted tonight, that scared her. Hell, the emotion behind that thought scared the fuck out of him, too.

Dixon's eyes followed the blinking lights on the tree as he allowed that thought to settle deep inside his bones. Whatever they had going on was deeper than either one of them ever meant it to become. He could now imagine a future with Joy.

A sudden, almost silent chuckle escaped him when an image of her and Frank meeting flashed across his mind's eye. Holy hell, that shit was funny. The woman was a live wire, arching and snapping with energy. Frank was a grounding force. He wondered if either would ever be the same after meeting, but that was a pipe dream. The chances of him finishing this mission, getting Guardian the inside track needed against Stratus, and convincing Joy to come back to the middle of fucking nowhere with him? Well, he figured those odds were less than five percent, and if there was one thing he knew, it was math. He could do the calculations in his head, and his brain told him what he didn't want to hear. Even if he survived this mission, his heart wouldn't.

CHAPTER 17

"IF YOU DON'T NEED me anymore, I'll head out."
Smith stood in the doorway of the new offices
Dixon had rented just off Park Avenue on East
48th Street. The corner office went for a
premium price, but since his appointment was
announced, he needed a place where the press
and his constituents could contact him.

Over the last three weeks, Smith had hired
a receptionist and secretary for the office and
Dixon had been interviewing the displaced
staff of Senator Waxman–either in person or
over the phone. He'd hired Waxman's Chief of
Staff, Constituent Services Representative,
Chief Counsel, State Scheduler and Legislative
Director. Smith was his acting Executive

Assistant, although that wasn't made public. All the other positions needed such as Administrative Director, Scheduler, and Systems Administrator were being farmed out between the staff he had on hand. Using Waxman's staff had saved Dixon a metric shit-ton of ass pain.

This afternoon he'd made his way back from D.C. where he'd voted on the first bill the newly convened Senate had in front of them. It was one Stratus had demanded he vote for. Dixon had voted against it.

He'd voted against Stratus and against the legislation. In doing so, he'd declared war. It was time. He was in position, and he was done. Done waiting.

Dixon leaned back in his chair and regarded the man for a moment before he nodded. "I think I have all I need." He glanced at the clock. It was earlier than usual for Smith to knock off. Hell, it was only four in the afternoon "Do you have a date?" Dixon smiled as he asked.

Smith's eyes dropped to the floor. "No, sir."

"Are you all right?" There was something off about the man. More so than normal.

"Yes, sir." Smith lifted his gaze, but he

focused beyond Dixon to the cityscape behind him.

Dixon wished like hell he'd been able to access his dead drop and read any information Jewell had been able to dig up about Smithson Young, but with the nomination came more work than he'd been able to keep up with, along with zero privacy.

"Alright. Have a good night." He watched as Smith turned and walked quietly out of the offices. The sound of low voices and phones ringing faded into the background. He pulled his phone, not his work phone, but his personal one, from his pocket and tapped out a text.

>*Track Smith*

>>*Boring.*

>*He just left for the day.*

>>*??? That's new.*

>*As I was saying...*

>>*Can't tonight. I have this Senator who pissed off the world today*

>*He can manage to stay out of trouble for one night :)*

>> *Have you met him?*

> *Yes, and you work for him*

>>*Point taken. It's a good thing I only do spur of the moment surveillance*

> *I'll make it worth your while*

>> *You always do*

Dixon chuckled to himself and pocketed his phone.

"Sir, the Senate Majority Leader is on line one. You have a meeting with Lester in twenty minutes. He has the brief on the next bill that is up for vote," Avery Robin, his newly minted secretary, spoke as she walked into his office. "I need to see you for about thirty minutes before business hours are up. There are several conflicting meetings on your agenda." She lifted an eyebrow at him. The State Scheduler he'd hired from Waxman's staff was on Avery's shit list. The man felt he had veto power over appointments she'd set up and Dixon had blessed.

"I'll talk to him again, and we can firm up the schedule after I meet with Lester." His legislative director was a mouse of a man but could abridge the entirety of a bill in five hundred words or less. He was very careful to ensure the party lines were represented, but not overpowering when the briefs were given.

Dixon hated to tell the man that he didn't give a rat's ass about the benefits of the legislation. If Stratus wanted it, he was going to vote against it. End. Of. Story.

He reached for the phone when Avery turned on her heel and headed out of the office. The call from the Majority Leader was probably a 'welcome to the fold' call. He'd voted against his party in order to vote against the legislation. The Minority Leader had caught up with him while he was in D.C. That was a 'get your ass in line' ass chewing. Dixon listened, thanked the woman and walked away. That was a ballsy move by him, but it was calculated to stir the waters.

JOY GLANCED AT THE REARVIEW MIRROR OF THE Fiat 500 she was driving. She'd been ducking and diving between the light traffic following Smith. She'd almost lost the guy at the airport but had found him and trailed him to the rental counter. The drive out of DC had been dicey, and she'd had to take calculated risks to keep up with him, but it was pretty fucking clear he was heading towards Virginia. The question was why?

She tapped the steering wheel as traffic became lighter. The small city of Charlottesville was easy enough to navigate through as she followed the little green car that Smith had folded himself into. She decelerated and let another car slip in between them. The road wound between some pretty impressive hills. As she topped a hill, she noticed his car was no longer in front of the two vehicles she'd put between them. There were three roads where he could have turned off. Joy glanced at her rearview mirror, slowed, and pulled into the first place Smith could have turned off the highway. She followed the drive through a tree-lined approach. At the end of the drive, a house sat on top of the ridge. It had all the signs of being constructed in the seventies, but it was beautiful. A small white dog bounced off the porch and barked excitedly. She quickly surveyed the area. The car Smith was driving was nowhere in sight. She whipped the Fiat around and left before the owners decided to investigate the dog's alarmed bark.

She pulled back onto the road and eyed the

second drive before she tucked the Fiat off the road and stared down the access point. There was no way the small car Smith had driven had gone down that road. The ruts were deep, and it looked like a logging road rather than a drive. She waited for another car to pass before pulling back out onto the road. She turned down the next drive and slowly made her way up the drive. Stopping just before the crest of the hill, she pulled the Fiat off the road and left it. Smith's actions were completely out of norm for the big guy. She didn't like the feeling of this unexpected road trip. She glanced down at her clothes. She'd worn a pant suit because she needed to blend in. Dammit, she should have changed, but she'd deal. A smile slipped into place. She'd wanted to try out these shoes for over a year. An old lover had given them to her as a joke, but they were pretty fucking amazing.

She tiptoed over the frozen ground and made her way through the trees. Her feet were damn near frostbitten, but she wasn't cold enough to abort the mission. She'd zeroed in on Smith's little green car. It was parked beside an outbuilding. Joy's eyes scanned the regal colonial home that sat atop another ridge. There was a limo parked out front and several men loitering about the car. One was smoking a cigarette; the others were leaning against the car. The chauffeur and perhaps a bodyguard or assistant?

A faint sound drew her attention to the outbuilding where Smith's car was parked. She watched the men in front of the house as she edged closer.

"You don't understand." Smith's voice carried through the open door to the building. Joy moved directly across from the building.

"What we understand is you didn't do your fucking job."

"I did! I told you everything. I–"

Joy winced at the sound of a fist hitting Smith. From the resulting grunt and moan, she could picture the act shutting him up. So, Smith was what? A snitch? For who? Stratus? What was he supposed to tell these people? She crept closer after casting a furtive glance at the men in front of the home to make sure they hadn't moved. Joy crept to the building and plastered herself against the brick.

"The fucking senator has a whore."

"No, he doesn't!" Smith's denial met with more blows.

"You didn't tell us about her. They could use knowledge like that. You failed to do your job. You know what that means?"

"She isn't a whore. She's a lady. I–" Smith's statement halted again. Joy closed her eyes. A lady. Fuck, she'd threatened to slice his throat. A lady was something she definitely was not. But why had he not told these people about her? And who were they? The wealth was obvious. She glanced over the estate again. She shook her head and sprinted into the woods. She raced back to her car, started it and pulled onto the drive. Smith hadn't told them about her because he was protecting her or Dixon. Either way, he was going to be killed because *he* was protecting *them*. Hopefully, those fuckers wouldn't extract too much from Smith before she got there. She had a much better chance of surviving this situation. The ideal would be if she could work it so Smith was acquitted of not telling the bastards about her.

She pulled right up to the building, got out and strode into the shelter where Smith was being held. Joy ignored the men running across the massive lawn toward her and walked through the open door as she called out, "Mr. Smith? Why did you want me to come all the way out here? Mr. Smith? I'm here, but why am I here?"

Smith's face was bloody. She watched him as he recognized her. He shook his head. She stopped him before he could speak, "You know I'm supposed to pick up Senator Simmons tonight. I don't understand..." She stopped and raised her hand to her chest. "Oh, my! Mr. Smith! What's going on?"

Joy spun around. The three men from the front of the house flew through the door behind her. She spun on her heel and pointed at Smith. "You set me up? Why? What have I ever done to you?"

She waited until one of the men behind her laid his hand on her before she moved. She needed to make sure the fucker's attention was fully on her. "Smith? Why? Why would you do this to me?" She called out again before she spun and punched the fucker holding her. He dropped like a lead weight. She dropped into her ready position and blinked at the other men as they circled. She counted ten. Fuck. She probably wasn't getting out of this, but hopefully, Smith would. Fuck, she hoped she read the man correctly.

DIXON RAN HIS FINGER THROUGH THE SILK OF his tie after he soundlessly shut and locked the door behind him. His new suite at the W was plush and afforded every comfort the small apartment they'd used immediately after the bombing hadn't. The one thing it didn't offer was a security system. He had hired security in the hall. Security he hadn't vetted.

Dixon leaned over and reached under the large table in the hall, pulling his weapon from the Velcro that secured it out of everyone's vision. The rooms were dark and quiet, but after the explosion, he took his time clearing each room.

It was almost ten at night, and he was exhausted. What he wanted was to take a shower and fall into a week-long sleep, but without Joy or Smith in the suite, he had a rare, private moment.

Dixon poured himself a drink and took a

sip of the whiskey before he set it on the bar and grabbed an ottoman to retrieve his computer from the top of the closet shelf where he'd hidden it. Paranoid, maybe, but he didn't care. He carried the footrest to the closet and used it to step on so he could make sure the thread he'd laid on the top right-hand corner was exactly where he left it. Old school, but effective in telling him if someone had moved the equipment.

He hit the flashlight on his phone, illuminating the upper portion of the shelf. It was gone. The thread was missing. With his cellphone's light, he examined the far corner of the closet where he'd stashed the laptop. There were fingerprints in the dust, smeared prints. From them, he could only determine the size of the fingers that made the marks. It looked as if someone short had placed their hand in several positions on the shelf before they located his computer. Whoever the woman was hadn't banked on the small thread. It was nowhere to be found.

That meant two scenarios were in play, neither of which he relished. One, someone with access to the rooms, a cleaning lady or management, had searched and found his computer. Or two, someone from Stratus had searched his rooms and found his computer.

No matter how he played it, the computer had to be considered compromised. Installing a program to monitor all his keystrokes would take only a couple minutes, and it would have been almost impossible for him to detect had he not had the software designed by Jewell that was installed on all Guardian computers. Fuck him, he should have downloaded the damn thing onto a CD before he flew out. Hindsight was always 20/20. He couldn't risk using the laptop without it being cleared first.

His computer system at the new Senate office was secure, but again, with so many new people and given the fact the computers were hosted on a shared server, he couldn't risk using those systems for anything other than legit Senate business.

Dixon stared at the laptop for a moment before he grabbed it and took it out of the bedroom into the large living area. He opened the refrigerator and put the laptop on the shelf and grabbed another unopened mini-bottle of scotch from the display by the fridge as he shut the door. If someone had enabled the mic or the camera, he wasn't going to risk having them learn anything but his drinking habits, because that was all they would see tonight.

He cracked the seal on the travel-sized bottle of Johnnie and tipped the bottle into the tumbler he'd used earlier. Fuck ice. Waiting for Stratus to reach out now that he'd thumbed his nose at them wasn't his idea of a good time. The way Smithson left this afternoon was concerning, but what really had him upset was the fact that Joy hadn't checked in. He glanced at his watch again. Dammit. He shrugged out of his suit jacket and flopped into a modern and very uncomfortable piece of designer furniture.

Tapping out a staccato beat on the arm of the chair, he weighed his options. Shit was going to happen, and it was going to happen soon. He removed the burner phone he'd been using with Joy and unlocked it.

His eyes bore a hole into the face before he pulled up the text program. Still nothing from Joy. He punched in a phone number and scrubbed his face. Dixon stood and paced the distance of the living area. He stopped at the window and stared out into the city. Fuck it. He tapped out the text and pushed send.

Dixon dropped the phone on the low bureau that held a seventy-inch television. He pushed his hands into his trouser pockets and stared unseeingly out the glass. New York was a beautiful contradiction. It boasted the elite of the world, cuisine, art, finance, diplomacy, engineering, architecture, and all points in between. From where he stood, it could be easy to convince himself that the city was something it wasn't. It wasn't home. No matter how well he fit in, no matter what he could do with the Senate seat, this city would never be his home. The phone beside him vibrated. He glanced at it and smiled. Finally.

"Senator, you have a call on line one, it's Mr. Smith." Avery's voice pulled Dixon from a mountain of paperwork.

He picked up the phone and punched the button. "Are you all right?"

"Yes sir, but you aren't." Smith's voice was

off, and the warning resonated as quickly as the man's tone.

"Excuse me?" Dixon snapped his eyes to the empty doorway, immediately alert.

"You failed to vote the way you were instructed." Smith's words shattered his hope the man wasn't connected to Stratus. Everything fell into line. The reason Smithson helped him dispose of the body and coordinated his Senate office, the text message from Stratus where he 'happened' to appear at the right moment to keep them from being killed.

Smithson Young was part of Stratus. Dixon leaned back in his chair. "I voted the way I wanted."

"There was a night when your father was alive, I told you that you should have chosen. Do you remember it?" Smith's calm voice filtered over the connection.

"I do." How could he forget? He didn't choose, and both people died.

"Don't make that mistake here. You need to make a decision now. Vote the way you are instructed, or Ms. Nguyen will die."

Dixon bolted to his feet before he took a

purpose-filled breath and tried to relax so he could think. "You're lying. You don't have her."

"I have never lied to you, sir."

"I'll need proof of life." And proof they were cagey enough to surprise and apprehend Joy. If he knew that woman, and he did, she'd fight like hell or even die before she'd be taken.

"That can be arranged. This phone line. Three minutes." The line went dead. Dixon glanced at his watch. Less than a minute had transpired since the beginning of the call. Even if he could get a trace on the conversation, it appeared Mr. Smith knew to disconnect before the source could be narrowed. *Fuck!* Dixon grabbed the phone and hit the intercom. As soon as Avery picked up, he was speaking. "I'll personally answer the next incoming call on this line. I need you to ensure no one comes into my office."

"Ahh...sure, I mean, yes sir." The woman's confusion was clear, but Dixon didn't have time to be diplomatic.

He waited for the phone to ring with his eyes fixed on the second hand of his Breitling. Exactly two minutes and fifty-five seconds after Smith hung up the phone, it rang again.

Dixon snatched it out of its cradle and punched the button.

"Joy?"

A disembodied mechanical voice answered, "No. You are required to vote for the bill which is being tendered for a vote to the Senate tomorrow. You will vote yea. If you don't, Ms. Nguyen will die."

"I won't vote for the bill if I don't know for an absolute fact that she is alive and will remain that way once I vote." Dixon's voice carried confidence he didn't feel. He was literally playing with Joy's life—that was if the bastards hadn't already killed her.

There was a low chuckle, "You do not get to make demands, Senator."

Dixon channeled Joseph and let loose with his own low, malicious laugh. "That is where you are absolutely wrong. Communicate this to your superiors. I will vote yea only if the minute before I cast my vote, I get a call on my cell from her telling me she is safe. If you don't, I'll vote nay, and both of your precious bills will fail." Dixon listened to the silence. "Obviously you failed to think this through to a logical conclusion. If Ms. Nguyen is not free, you don't get my vote."

"If you do not vote the way we dictate, we will release evidence that you killed your father."

Dixon rolled his eyes responding with scathing insult, "Of course, you would. I saw your next move like it was written in crayons on the wall and have taken steps to insulate myself. Yours is an empty threat. This is our deal. Ms. Nguyen for my vote." He maintained his confrontational attitude. Immediately flipping to a submissive 'yes man' would send an earthquake of tremors through Stratus.

"We will watch the proceedings. When the vote is taken, we will comply. But please note, Mr. Simmons, if you do not vote in our favor, we will find her, and we will kill her. Additionally, your father's death will be levied on your head, and we have an eyewitness that will testify as to how you killed him."

"Smithson Young."

"Not very smart for a genius, are you senator? Depending on a thug."

Even with the synthesized voice, Dixon could discern the mocking tone. Oh, he was smart, and he had the bastards playing into his hands.

"You have two minutes to get Joy on the line." Dixon dropped the phone into the cradle. He'd offer his left nut on a plate if it meant he'd get to speak to Joy. Smithson Young had sealed his fate. He didn't know what Smithson's deal was, but he was not a thug. His education and intelligence had become evident over the last month. Dixon's hand dropped to his keys and the fob that held the hidden thumb drive with all the files Smith deleted. He had the dates, and he would find out what Stratus had on the big guy.

The phone rang, and Dixon pounced on it. "Go."

"Hey, Quick Draw." Joy's low, husky voice slid across the line.

A chill ran down Dixon's back. Fuck, they had her. A small part of him held out the hope that the son of a bitch was fronting. He grappled for words, "Screwed up and got yourself into a jam, didn't you?"

She made a disgusted sound and replied, "No. Not really." He listened hard, and he could tell she was struggling to speak. Fuck, if they'd beaten her...

He envied her calmness because knowing those motherfuckers had probably hurt her had lit a fuse in him that nothing was going to extinguish. "Are you okay?"

He heard a low moan and a whoosh of breath before she sighed, "Been worse. You know that song I was telling you about?"

Dixon's mind did the ping-pong thing. The question was so far away from what they were dealing with it took him a second to connect the dots. "The one from the movie you and your sister like, the one about the rain?"

"Yeah, listen to it." She grunted in pain. Those motherfuckers were handling her roughly. They'd pay, and they'd pay dearly.

"Okay, I will. But Joy, I'm going to get you out of this. I'll vote the way they want me to vote." He needed the mother fuckers to hear and believe that fact.

She gave a low chuckle and then with more venom than he could imagine coming from her, she hissed, "Well that's awesome, because I only do death on my terms." Her grunt of pain was the last thing he heard.

When he realized it was disconnected, Dixon dropped the phone to the cradle. He had no idea how long he stared at the desk blotter. His mind reeled, seeing nothing but the next series of moves he needed to make.

"Sir?"

He blinked up and focused on Avery. "Sorry, what?"

"Your three-thirty is waiting, and you have a new meeting scheduled at five. Not my doing, by the way." She raised her eyebrow, obviously pissed at the scheduler again.

Dixon stood up and grabbed his suit jacket. "Cancel my three-thirty, give whoever it is my sincere apologies, cancel the five o'clock meeting," he glanced at her and winked, "with emphasis."

A huge smile spread across her face. "Most definitely, sir."

"I need you to change my travel plans. I'm heading to D.C. now."

"Now, sir?"

"Yes, now. I'm heading to the airport, make the arrangements. Oh, and Avery?"

"Sir?"

"I need your cell."

"My...*my* phone, sir?"

"Yes, I promise to take good care of it and compensate you for the time I have it."

"Ummm...okaaay..." She strung the word out as she grabbed the phone from her top right-hand drawer.

He glanced at the locked face. "What's the code?"

"One-two-one-two," she parroted.

Easy enough to remember. Dixon punched in the code and thanked her. The glittering pink case slipped into his pocket. "You, phone, travel, now." He pointed to the phone on her desk and spun on his heel.

"Sir what about the rest of your party?" She shouted down the hall after him.

Dixon turned in the elevator and pushed the button to the lobby. "They can join me tomorrow morning as planned." He watched her until the door closed. As soon as it did, he unlocked the phone and sent a text. An immediate reply later and he dropped the blinged-out phone into his coat again. He closed his eyes and breathed, "Hang on. I'm on my way."

346

CHAPTER 18

DIXON WAITED for the uniformed man to open his limo's door at the hotel. He pulled his cashmere coat collar up and nodded his thanks. The doorman frowned. "I'm sorry sir, I didn't see you leave earlier." The man looked at the limo and his frown deepened. "This isn't one of our cars."

Dixon smiled and winked at the confused doorman. "I must have snuck out when you were helping someone else. I had to pick up some luggage that was lost."

"Senator Simmons, someone from the hotel could have done that for you, sir. The concierge and manager would be extremely upset if he knew you were chasing misplaced luggage."

Dixon laughed off the comment. "Well I will let him help me now. It seems I have lost my key to my room."

The doorman beamed. "That won't be a problem, sir." He lifted a hand and the man at the concierge desk flew across the ornate foyer. "Senator Simmons needs assistance getting into his suite."

At the doorman's words, the young man's face lit up. "Of course! I'll accompany you up, sir." He waited for Dixon to palm the doorman a tip and give him instructions for the delivery of his luggage. Dixon pulled out his work phone and stared at the screen as if the face held the answers to the universe. The concierge hit the button for the floor his suite was on. Dixon glanced at the number and went back to staring at the phone. When the doors opened, he followed the young man down the hall and waited for him to open the door. "I'll have a new key sent up immediately, Senator Simmons."

Dixon finally moved his attention from his

phone, smiled and palmed the young man a hefty tip. "Thank you. I appreciate your professionalism."

"It is our pleasure, sir."

Dixon waited until the man departed before he slid the deadbolt and threw the privacy bar that would prohibit even those with a key to enter. He turned and breathed in the opulence of the room. White furniture, dark woods with gold trim and dark blue curtains made the sitting room more fitting for the White House than a hotel room.

"About fucking time."

Dixon swiveled and smiled. "Drake."

"I missed the fuck out of you." Drake stalked across the room and pulled him into a rib-crushing hug.

"No more than I missed you." He pushed his brother away and held him at arm's length. "You're okay?"

"Fit as a fiddle." Drake quipped.

Dixon laughed, "What the fuck does that even mean?"

"I have no idea, but we can look it up." They laughed and hugged again.

Dixon finally pulled away. "Look at you, all dressed up in Savile Row." Drake wore a black suit, crisp white shirt, and red power tie. The man looked every inch a senator.

"Well, you know my brother has been appointed a Senator of New York, and could you please explain the fuck out of that, because I'm lost?" Drake took off his jacket and tossed it over the back of a white, suede leather, wing-back chair.

Dixon shrugged out of his coat and tossed it over the matching chair. "It is a long story. You swept the suite?"

Drake pulled up short. "Of course I fucking swept the room. What did you think happened while you were gone, that I'd lost my mind?"

Dixon smiled at his brother's banter as he dropped into a chair. "Who knows what you've been up to while I've been working."

"Right. Like I've been sitting on my ass doing nothing."

"See, at least you admit it."

"Fuck you."

"Nah, I'd just lie there."

"Ass."

"Jerk."

A matching smile spread across Drake's face. "So, tell me what the fuck is going on."

Dixon unbuttoned his suit jacket and leaned forward. "Our sperm donor is dead." He watched for any reaction from Drake. The man blinked and then looked away before he nodded. "How?"

"Officially he was blown up in a tragic accident when a gas line blew."

Drake lifted an eyebrow. "Unofficially?"

"The fucker put a bullet through his brain when he was confronted with the fact that I was going to destroy his grand plans." Dixon leaned back in the seat and shook his head. His brother's stare locked on him, demanding information without him speaking a word. "He fucked up every plan Jason and I had to infiltrate Stratus. We wanted to be able to get in and work our way through the organization. Hell, at least *that* was the original plan. I've been flying by the seat of my pants without any aid from Guardian for so long, I lost sight of the original goal."

"Which means?" Drake's query was so like

his brother. Logical, step-by-step. He was always the steadying factor on every occasion. Unlike himself.

Dixon shrugged. "I've managed to get to the top of Stratus, perhaps even to The Fates."

"Excuse me?" Drake leaned forward.

Dixon sighed and scrubbed his face. "The Fates are an organization that has been a rumor and innuendo for as long as—"

"Stratus." Drake finished his sentence for him.

Dixon nodded. "Originally the intent was to find a way in using Daddy dearest as a vehicle to examine New York's underbelly for a path into the organization."

Drake loosened his tie and sat back. "Go on."

"He was already in bed with half the criminals in New York. While dealing with his..." Dixon closed his eyes as images of what he'd recently lived through flashed through his mind, "...antics, he led me to believe he had a business partner."

"Stratus?"

"That's what I assumed. I mean who else

would have the guts to try to put a collar on a rabid dog?" Dixon motioned to the bar. "Pour us one?"

"Or twenty?" Drake lifted out of the chair and headed to the stocked bar.

"One for now. We have a fuck-ton of work to do."

Drake turned and looked over his shoulder. "I'm listening."

Dixon nodded, almost to himself. "Anyway, I did his bidding and was finally pulled into the legit business, or so I thought." He cleared his throat and accepted the three fingers of dark liquor from his brother. He took a sip of the bourbon and waited for Drake to sit down again.

"How fucked up did it get?" Drake's quiet question held a litany of unused words. Words Dixon didn't need to hear to know the true meaning of the inquiry.

His hands were shaking, and he didn't try to hide it from his brother. It wouldn't do any good. Drake could read him like a printed page. The large print edition. Dixon swallowed past the lump in his throat. "He'd only gotten worse,

D. I cut ties with all his illegal businesses the day he died. It was a feeding frenzy on the street. He was a sick motherfucker." Dixon closed his eyes. "We have a half brother. He's maybe ten years old, and the bastard was going to 'groom' him if I didn't work out."

Drake blinked at him as Dixon's words registered. "Tell me the kid's safe."

"Yeah, the mom is good to him." At least that is what Smith and Joy had told him. Smith had volunteered the information, and he'd asked Joy to confirm it. "The bastard's will that was locked in a bank downtown provided for her and the kid. I didn't contact them. I couldn't give Stratus that target."

"That means you *did* give them a target."

"I offered in a roundabout way. I felt I needed to sweeten the pot, so I offered up Guardian, but before they could ask for the information, I pushed the envelope." Dixon took another sip of his drink and watched the micromovements of his brother's expression as he digested the words.

"What happened?" Drake asked after a moment.

"They wanted my vote on a bill."

"And of course, you voted opposite the way they wanted you to vote."

Dixon flicked his eyes to his brother.

"You contrary asshole." Drake laughed and shook his head. "They flipped their fucking lid, didn't they?"

"You could say that. They had a plant. Smithson Young. He worked for them and for dear old Dad. I kept him on. I had an idea he could be involved, but fuck, I was hoping he wasn't."

"Hindsight. Always 20/20. What happened? Did he threaten you?" Drake took a sip of his drink at the same time Dixon did, mirroring his actions almost exactly. They both smiled when their glasses lowered. This...this is what he missed so damn much. His brother was the other half of who he was.

"Yes. I'd sent Joy to track him–"

"Who?"

"Joy. She's a hired killer who I crossed paths with as soon as the old man pulled me into the thick of his shit. He sent me to kill this guy, and she was already there." Dixon stared over his brother's shoulder and relived seeing her for the first time.

"Joy is..." Drake prompted.

Dixon swung his eyes to his brother. "Essential." The single word conveyed a myriad of thoughts and emotions.

Drake blinked and nodded, "Noted. Continue."

"Stratus has her."

"You spoke with her?"

"Yes, and I arranged a swap. Her life for my vote."

"Do you believe she's alive now?"

"I do. I spoke with her..." Dixon glanced down at his watch, "...four hours ago."

"Did she sound okay?"

"She actually sounded pissed off. Other than telling me to listen to a song, she sounded normal."

Drake lifted an eyebrow. "Normal is pissed off?"

"For her? Yeah." Dixon would laugh at his brother's expression, but none of this was funny.

Drake nodded. "Explain the not normal part then."

"The song? It was from this movie, *Paint*

Your Wagon. Some damn song about rain being called Tess."

"Why would she want you to listen to that?"

"Beats the fuck out of me. But she was specific that I needed to listen to it."

"I brought the clean computer you wanted. We can log on, it has Guardian's security protocols. Nobody is going to track it. We can find it online." Drake shrugged and shook his head before he took another sip of his liquor.

Dixon mimicked his movements and then asked, "The movie or the song?"

"Both?" Drake offered.

"Let's do it."

A knock at the door jarred Dixon before he remembered the concierge was going to bring him another key. Drake stood quickly and slipped into the bedroom as he went to open the door.

They say reaction is a conditioned response to repeated stimuli. That was bullshit. His reaction was fueled by immediate hatred and anger. His right fist found Smith's jaw in an uppercut a split second before his left hit a hooked punch to the man's ribs. He grabbed the bastard's collar and threw him into the suite before he slammed the door shut. The click of a weapon at his right didn't stop him from dropping down and placing both hands around the bastard's neck. He squeezed. "You motherfucking son of a bitch." Spittle flew out of his mouth as Smithson pawed at his arms.

Smith sputtered something unintelligible, then gasped out,"...where she is..."

"D, I think he's trying to tell you he knows where she is." Drake's voice, calm and reassuring, said from somewhere over his shoulder.

"No, he works for Stratus, I don't trust him."

"Noted. So, how about we hear what he has to say and then we kill him." Drake's relaxed, casual remark drew Smithson's eyes away from Dixon and over his shoulder. If it was possible, when he saw Drake, the man's eyes bugged out even further. Dixon released the man and was off him in a second, not giving the bastard time to recover and strike at him. He'd been in too many fights to trust anyone was as incapacitated as they appeared.

Drake leveled his weapon at the man and smiled. "We are going to do this nice and easy. You are going to crawl to the middle of that empty space, and then you are going to sit on your ass and put your hands on top of your head. Any deviation from that plan and you get a bullet through the brain. Understand?"

Smith coughed and gasped for air but nodded his head as he rolled to all fours. He slowly made his way to the middle of the empty space and ass-planted. He immediately lifted his hands to his head and linked his fingers together.

Dixon pulled his eyes from the bastard and noticed Drake had his computer in one hand and his weapon leveled on the bastard with the other.

"Talk or die." Dixon barked the command. He was done. The bastard was the vehicle they used to trap Joy, and by the sound of their conversation earlier, they'd hurt her too. For that, Smithson Young would pay and pay dearly.

"I had no choice."

"Bullshit! We all have choices, just because you don't like the options doesn't give you the right to put another human being's life on the line!" Dixon damn near screamed the words at the man.

"D, dude, bring it down a decibel or two or

let me do the talking. We don't need security up here." Drake handed him the computer and walked in front of Smith.

"Now, between the two of us," Drake motioned between Dixon and himself, "I'm usually considered the calmer one. But you see, I haven't seen my brother in months, and that has really pissed me off." He placed the barrel of the weapon against Smith's forehead. "I suggest you talk and say the words that will salvage your sorry ass. 'I had no choice' isn't among any of those words. Got it?"

The man nodded, and Drake smiled, tapping his forehead with the gun. "Speak."

"They were going to kill me. They called me and told me I needed to come to them, or they'd hurt you. I did. I left right after I talked to you. I took a cab to the airport and rented a car. I drove to Virginia, following the directions they sent to my phone. When I arrived at the warehouse, they jumped me. They...they'd found out I hadn't told them about Ms. Nguyen and the fact that you and she are together. They wouldn't listen to me, I tried to talk to them, but that's when Ms. Nguyen came through the warehouse door." Smithson shook his head. "She acted like I'd asked her to come. She fought, hard. Sir, she is hell on wheels. She took on six men before one of them hit her with a shovel. She still didn't go down. I think they hurt her after that. They forgot about me and took her. I could hear her fighting."

"She tried to get you out of there?"

"Yes, sir. She didn't have to do that. They released me. They believed that I'd tricked her into following me. They told me to come back and keep an eye on you after I made the call earlier."

"And they assumed I wouldn't kill you?"

"I think they assumed I wouldn't make contact." Smithson lowered his eyes. "Or they assumed I'd go back to New York and hide."

Drake lifted his eyes to Dixon for a second before Dixon asked, "Why did you make contact with me?" It would have been simple to disappear.

"They know about the kid."

"The kid?" Drake asked.

Smithson lifted his eyes and looked up at Dixon. "Your brother."

"Right. How would they know about him?"

"I don't know, I only heard bits and pieces. They are pissed that you aren't compliant."

"Obviously." Drake drawled and cut his eyes to Dixon.

He met his brother's gaze and cocked his head a fraction of an inch. *Really?*

The smallest tug of the corner of Drake's lip said. *Yes really, dickhead.* He could hear the words as clearly as if the man had spoken them.

Smithson dropped his eyes again. "The boy is innocent. They can't hurt him."

Dixon returned his attention to Smithson. "Why would I believe you?"

"You and Ms. Nguyen are the only ones who have ever given me a chance. My entire life, people have treated me like shit because I look...like this. Stupid. I didn't lie to you."

"Yes, you did, each and every minute you didn't tell me Stratus had their hooks in you." Dixon sighed, "What was on the tapes you deleted? You deleted two nights, yet you only slept with her once. What else did you delete?" Dixon crossed his arms and watched the man.

Smithson licked his lips. "There was a woman. She came to me the next day. She had pictures and audio recordings. She told me that your father had given them the tapes in exchange for three hundred thousand dollars. She kept her back to the cameras and whispered. But sir, she turned quickly and left when your father came back unexpectedly. I know the camera caught her face on video. So did she. In exchange for the destruction of the file with her face on it, they promised they would leave me alone."

"Only they didn't."

"No."

Drake asked, "Did you make a copy of the files?"

"No, sir."

"And you assumed they would just what...behave like humans?" Drake prompted.

Smithson glanced at the man before he dropped his eyes and nodded.

All the facets of Smithson Young fell into place. The man was intelligent, and he genuinely trusted people until they proved they couldn't be. His father and the women from Stratus who'd abused his trust were probably just the top of the list of the people who'd treated this man like shit.

"Where are they holding her?" His twin wasn't going to let up.

"A warehouse in Virginia. The woman I talked to that day at your father's? She was there. I saw her when I was supposed to be leaving. She was getting out of a limo and going into the house." Smithson glanced over at Dixon. "There were two limos there. A third passed me when I was leaving. I can take you there."

"I'm afraid not, big guy. You can give us directions to the warehouse, but you're not going to be there." Drake glanced at Dixon confirming they were on the same page. Of course they were. That was a given. But what to do with Smithson was another story. A series of ideas clicked in his mind.

"I've got an idea on a way forward. I need your directions." Dixon still wasn't sure how involved in Stratus Smith actually was. He'd wait and talk to Drake after they took care of the man.

"On my phone." Smithson nodded to his jacket pocket. "I thought your twin was dead." The big man looked from Drake to him.

"To quote Mark Twain, 'Reports of my

death were greatly exaggerated,'" Drake drawled, and they both laughed. "I'm going to take your clothes, Smith. You're going to strip down to your boxers, then you're going to go into that room after my brother takes out the phone and you are going to stay in the room. If you come out, I'll kill you." Dixon leveled his gaze at the big man. "Don't think for a moment I won't."

Smithson nodded and started undressing. Dixon winced when the man took off his undershirt. The number of scars littering the skin of the man's back reminded him of Joseph's, but there was an array of dark purple bruises along the man's ribs. Seems Dixon's fists weren't the first ones laid on Smith today.

"What happened?" Drake nodded to the man's back when Smithson looked up.

Smith shrugged and passed his clothes to Drake. "Like I said, they jumped me." Drake handed him his t-shirt and socks after checking them. They secured him in the interior bedroom. He had access to the en suite bathroom and the television. Dixon propped a chair against the door and took an ornate white and gold ceramic vase off a table. He propped it at an angle on the chair. If the chair moved, the vase would fall, and Smithson would be a dead man.

As he turned, he noticed his twin carrying in a large duffle. The familiarity of the bag sent relief through his body and a smile to his face. "Did you bring her?"

"Like I'd leave her at home." Drake opened the duffle and pulled out Dixon's favorite semi automatic forty-five caliber pistol. The thing was old, but she was true. He could shoot a gnat off a toad's ass at a hundred yards with this pistol. His shoulder holster followed, and then Drake got down to business. Dixon examined each of the weapons his brother pulled out, filled his vest with zip-ties, a taser, extra rounds, magazines, a lighter, flashlight, and two pairs of gloves. Drake plunked down three bundles on the couch. Each was designed to attach to his tactical vest. One held blasting caps and det cord, the other enough C4 to level the floor they were currently occupying and the third, well, the third contained a small device that was cushioned in a box. He glanced at the bundle and then at Drake.

"What? I figured it might come in handy. Who knows, right?"

"Thanks." Dixon grabbed the smallest bundle, stripped it of its vest attachment and dropped the box into his pocket. It was always good to have insurance and the duress signal that would bring every Guardian in the tri-state area to their rescue was the best insurance he could ever have.

"Okay, start talking." Drake dropped the empty duffle on the floor by the pristine white couch and leaned back.

A knock at the door startled both of them. Dixon grabbed the vase, put it back on the table and Drake moved the chair before he dashed into the room where Smith was being held. Dixon jogged to the door and cracked it open. "Sorry, it took so long to get back to you, sir. The main desk indicated there was a delivery for you earlier, so I waited for the bellhop to retrieve it from the storage area before I brought the key up."

Dixon took the envelope. The return address told him it was from his office in New York. Paperwork that had been sent before he decided on the last-minute dash to the airport.

He smiled and pulled a fifty out of his money clip. "Thank you. Would you do me another favor? Would you have dinner sent up, service for three? I will be having some associates join me. Steaks and sides. I'll trust your judgment."

"Yes sir, I'll handle that immediately."

Dixon shut the door and palmed the emergency duress button in his pocket. Hopefully, he wouldn't have to use it.

CHAPTER 19

HIS BROTHER WALKED into the room as Dixon stood staring at the floor. He motioned to the chair. Drake slid it under the doorknob and Dixon balanced the vase on the arm again.

"Do you think he'll try to leave?" Drake asked as he sat down on the couch. He pulled his automatic out of his jacket and laid it on the plush, white armrest.

Dixon shrugged. "Beats the fuck out of me. Nothing has gone as planned."

"Hey!"

"Other than you. I know I can always count on you."

"Whatever it takes."

"For as long as it takes." Dixon finished. "I

ordered dinner. I need to bring you up to speed and let you know my thoughts on how to proceed."

Drake leaned back, loosened his tie and unbuttoned the top button of his dress shirt. "Roger that, but how about we start with the fact that this woman is living with you."

"Joy."

Drake nodded.

"Joy is..."

"Essential, I got that, but I need just a little bit more."

Dixon nodded but parried his brother's question with one of his own. "What about the woman you're serious with now? You said there was someone, right? Who is she?"

Drake narrowed his eyes a fraction of an inch. "Tit for tat?"

"Deal." Dixon agreed.

"Dr. Jillian Law."

"Why is that name familiar?" Dixon flashed through the women they'd been with until the connection triggered. "Silly Jilly? Dude, she's Cliff's kid!"

Drake's neck reddened. "She's all grown up now, man."

"No shit?"

"Happens."

"You don't say." Dixon shook his head. Silly Jilly. She was all glasses and knobby knees. Braces too, he definitely remembered Jilly with tinsel teeth.

"So, Joy?" Drake prompted.

"Ah, I told you she was a hired killer who was on a job. That's where we met."

"Yeah, but man, I'm having problems connecting the dots. When did you get together?" Drake leaned forward and grabbed their drinks off the table where they'd abandoned them when Smith had interrupted their conversation.

"Well, we got together that night, like three minutes after we met. We fought and then one thing led to another." It was Dixon's turn to feel a flush start up his neck.

Drake's drink stopped midway to his mouth. "Say what now?"

"There was an immediate attraction." Dixon stared at the drink in his hand. His mind flashed through those first instances and then thought of the last time they'd slept together. The term magical was too prissy and hokey to use, but damned if he didn't think it anyway.

Drake finished the movement of his arm and took a sip of the liquor. "Now it's more?"

"We've connected. It's more." Dixon mimicked his brother's actions and took a small sip of his drink.

"And she's a killer?"

"And we aren't?" Dixon snapped his response.

"Whoa, dude, that *was not* judgment." Drake lifted his hand as if Dixon were a frightened colt. "Sorry for restating the obvious, but I'm still taking in all the information. *You've* lived it all these months, I haven't."

Dixon drew a deep breath and blew it out in a steady stream, relaxing the muscles in his shoulders and back as he did. His brother was right, he needed to chill the fuck out and bring him up to speed. "Sorry."

"No need to apologize, D. Just start at the beginning and fill me in." Drake shifted, stretched out his legs and leaned back.

"Highlight reel." Dixon chuckled at the term they used with each other when filtering bull-shit. "You first."

Drake chuckled and lifted his eyes to the ornate chandelier. "Went to Cliff's after I dropped you off. We didn't know Stratus was hunting us. Jillian had a few really random things happen and Cliff had convinced her she needed someone to look out for her. Enter me. Turns out she's patented a new technology to miniaturize solar arrays while enhancing the efficiency. We, and I use the term 'we' to include Guardian, believed that someone might be after that tech."

"No shit. That could have a ripple effect in the energy community. The OPEC countries would pay to make the tech go away."

"Or make *her* go away."

"Truth."

"We flew to San Jose and picked up the tech. Took a very long road trip ending at what used to be Joseph's cabin in Wyoming."

"Used to be?" Dixon blinked at his brother. "What did you do?"

"Blew the fucker to the moon."

"Holy shit. And Joseph let you live?"

"It would seem."

"Well, fuck me."

"No thanks."

"Wasn't an offer."

"Then don't say it."

Dixon snorted and rolled his fingers, encouraging Drake to continue.

"Before we made a stand, Guardian figured out that Stratus was actually tracking me, Maliki, Chief, and Taty."

"Why not me?"

"Our assumption was Daddy dearest was protecting you."

"Fuck me."

"I'd rather not."

"Ass."

"Jerk."

"Is everyone okay?"

"Solid. Maliki was almost killed. He's in Arizona, laying low."

"The facility in Arizona is up and running?"

"It could have been, but Jason pulled the plug. It is a ghost town except for Maliki and a skeleton staff. Less footprint to attract attention. We don't have the same local shield as we do in Hollister."

Dixon nodded. The town of Hollister, South Dakota had absorbed the Guardians, and the locals refused to talk about anyone who worked at Frank's ranch. It was the tightest lipped community on the planet.

"The big guy said he'd start operations in Arizona once we find a level ground with Stratus. Right now, we don't know or understand the extent of the organization or what they know about us." Drake confirmed what Dixon already knew. Stratus was a virus, and no one knew how much of the world was infected.

Dixon glanced at his brother. "Okay, that's why you're dead."

"Me and Jillian."

Dixon's gut dropped. His mentor would be devastated. "Fuck, what about Cliff..."

"He was told when it was safe. So was her brother. But the rest of the world believes we are dead." Drake drained his drink and pointed at Dixon. "Your turn. Highlight reel."

"Just a minute. Are you going to marry her?"

"Not until your ass gets back to the ranch. She turned me down. Said she wanted me whole again before we got married. She knows us. She understands."

Dixon stared past his brother's shoulder. He was glad Drake had found his woman. He deserved to be happy.

"Your turn."

Drake's reminder pulled him from his thoughts.

"Drove to New York and *against* Jason's wishes, I didn't show up on Daddy dearest's doorstep, but I did make a big blip on his scope. Made him track me down instead of appearing out of the blue. That's how I met Smith." He glanced at the door. "I think our old man wanted to keep me close. I was hoping that the work I did for him would prove my fealty, but I found out I was just doing a puppet on a string dance for him. He didn't trust me." Dixon shook his head. "He gave me a job working for him. I was shaking down pimps, pulling the last dollar from the fist of whores who were strung out on the drugs he sold to them. I hunted down drug dealers who tried to cut into his take, shook down merchants for 'insurance' money, and roughed up the local bookies for skimming the profits. You know, fine, upstanding, work for our fine, upstanding, old man."

Dixon slugged the rest of his drink and handed it to Drake. His brother lifted off the couch and went to the bar. Dixon continued as

Drake refilled the tumblers, "I did that for shit...forever, but it was only for about four...no five months. After that, he pulled me into The Residence."

"The what?" Drake interrupted

"The egomaniac named his fucking house, he called it The Residence. He had a brass nameplate at the front door."

"You're shitting me. You mean like The White House or The Taj Mahal?"

"Exactly, anyway, that is when I realized the bastard was sicker than either of us could conceptualize." He closed his eyes and tried to chase away the image of the people that had died because he hadn't chosen between them. The thought of the sick mothers that he'd extorted a building from, and the list of names he was authorized to take out. The people that circled in his father's infected waters made him sick. Then there was that wall of fucking horror behind the bookshelf. The pictures of him as a child. The memories of what he'd endured and the innocence on the face of his half brother.

"Hey, I'm right here. Breathe." Drake's voice called to him from a distance, only it wasn't a distance, the man was next to him on the couch. He felt the familiar touch of a reassuring hand on his shoulder and glanced over at the exact same eyes that looked back at him from the mirror every morning.

He took a breath and continued, "Joy is my sanity. At first, it was completely physical. We'd fuck. She'd walk. The perfect way to blow off the stress of dealing with him."

Drake snorted, "We've been blowing off a lot of steam, brother. Since the day we figured out sex was a thing."

Dixon chuckled, "Fuck you."

"No thanks."

"Ass."

"Jerk."

He flipped off Drake and continued, "Then she started showing up at my apartment. The woman has no clue what a boundary is or even how to find one." Dixon laughed and felt some of the darkness fall from around him. "She is a dichotomy of personalities rolled up into a sexy as fuck package. I mean one minute she's dressed in haute couture and the next she's wearing cargos, combat boots and slitting throats. She grunts like Frank, swears more than anyone on Alpha Team and then turns around and...brings me a scraggly assed Christmas tree with lights and a star." Dixon thought about their time together on Christmas Eve. The truths she'd told him. When she offered her heart on a platter, exposed and beating, just for him. "Dude, I'm telling you I never, I mean never, know where she's coming from or where she's going for that matter."

"It's been a hell of a ride, though, huh?" Drake elbowed him.

" I think I love her." Dixon said the words and flicked his eyes to his brother.

"Did it hurt?"

"What?"

"Admitting that?"

"Fuck you."

"Again, no thanks." They laughed, and Drake raised his crystal tumbler. "A toast. To the women in our lives who make us sane."

Dixon lifted his glass and drank to the toast. "I'm going after her."

"I didn't doubt it for a second."

"I'm going to need you to help."

Drake nodded. "You'd pay hell keeping me

out of this."

"What do you know about the labor laws of the United States, the World Trade Organization, and the International Labor Organization?"

"Fuck, not much, why?"

"I'm thinking Senator Simmons is going to give his first filibuster."

Drake pointed at himself. "As in me?"

"As in you." Dixon acknowledged.

Drake snorted, "Mr. Simmons goes to Washington?"

"That's the plan."

Drake sighed, "Fuck me."

"No thanks."

"Ass."

"Jerk."

"Where do we start?" Drake pulled the computer from where it sat on the cushion next to him and placed it on the coffee table in front of them.

"We need to get you up to speed on international trade law. You have to delay that vote until I text you and let you know you're clear. The vote was scheduled to be on C-SPAN, so I'm hoping a filibuster will be televised as well. That will keep the eyes that are supposed to be on me, on, well...me...who is you."

"Okay, your vehicle is taken care of. There is a Guardian suburban in the parking garage three blocks over."

"There are six ways to exit this hotel according to what I pulled off the internet. You are going out the front door to the Hill. Five minutes later, I'm going out the employee entrance near the kitchen."

"You're hoping if there are any eyes on you, they will fall on me as I go. Only D, I have no fucking idea where I'm going."

"That isn't a problem. My entourage will be arriving first thing tomorrow morning. All you need to do is look at your phone, act distracted, and they will martial you to where you need to be. The important thing is to get the floor and not to yield it. While you are regaling the world about the lack of progress of the United States labor laws compared to other nations that are less developed, I'll be working my way to Virginia and finding Joy."

"What about him?"

"We are what...five blocks from Guardian

Headquarters?"

Drake blinked and nodded. "I thought we needed to keep any connection to Guardian out of the equation."

"We are. No one will make the connection. He is going to wait here with an overwatch that no one can see."

Drake lifted an eyebrow. "Who is going to do the surveillance?"

Dixon sighed and scrubbed his face. "We'll reach out to Jade. She can assign someone, on the QT."

Drake shook his head. "Ten bucks says he'll call Stratus or disappear."

"The phones go with us." Dixon wasn't worried about the damn phones.

Drake shook his head. "He could blow everything. If he says a word to anyone, our operation is compromised, and your woman is as good as dead. Are you sure you want to risk it?"

"There isn't a risk. Jade will come through for us." Dixon gazed at the bedroom door. "Open that computer."

"I'm trusting you on this because you're in the trenches, but all I smell here, D, is shit."

"Don't worry, you get used to it."

"I don't think that will happen."

Dixon waited as Drake turned on the computer. "Okay, what was the name of that movie?"

"*Paint Your Wagon.*"

Drake tapped the keys and then laughed. "Dude, it's a musical with Clint Eastwood and Lee Marvin."

"Say what now?" Dixon leaned over and looked at the search engine.

"How have we not watched that?" Drake chuckled, "Who knew Clint or Lee could sing?"

"Right?" He nodded to the screen. "Type in the title of the film plus the words, rain and Tess."

He watched as Drake did as he asked. The top three hits on the screen showed a song...*They Call the Wind Maria.*

"Recognize the name, Maria?"

Dixon shook his head. He didn't know anyone by the name of Maria. "Hit play."

Drake did, and after a fucking commercial the world stopped spinning with the first word of the song.

"Moriah. Not Maria." Dixon whispered. The

sound of the man's voice faded into the background. "It can't be. I wasn't supposed to have any help from Guardian." He looked up at his brother.

"You don't know she's actually *that* Moriah." Drake muted the music. "We need to take a breath and listen to the whole damn thing to make sure there isn't something else."

Dixon nodded, and they started the song over.

"Know anyone by the name of Joe?" Drake asked after he hit the button so another song wouldn't queue up.

"You know that isn't what she was trying to tell me." Dixon leaned forward and stared at his shoes.

"Okay, so she's a Shadow? Why would she let you know that?" Drake put the computer on the coffee table and assumed a matching position as his brother.

"I think it's one of two things. Either she is letting me know so I know she can handle what is going on, or she's letting me know so I can inform Guardian she's in trouble." Dixon shook his head. "I don't know that she wasn't asking for help."

"You think she's telling you to leave her, that she's got this?"

Dixon shook his head again. "I don't know."

"You're not leaving her." Drake's statement wasn't a question.

"No shit, but I do have a question for you."

"Yeah, what's that?"

"Gummy Bears or Sour Worms?"

"Shit."

Dixon smirked. His brother, his other half, knew him like no other.

Drake laughed, "Bears, and it's not like I didn't see that twist coming. So much for my filibuster. Dammit, I was looking forward to it, too."

"Liar." Dixon called him on it.

Drake laughed leaned back and inclined his head to the computer. "No seriously I was getting a semi thinking about learning international trade laws." They both laughed and Drake continued, "My one shot at being a senator flushed the second that song played, didn't it?"

"Absolutely." Dixon confirmed.

"Thank God." Drake laughed and stood up. "Better get me two bags of bears."

CHAPTER 20

"Dude, you realize we are not prepared to take out a small army." Drake grumped for at least the tenth time. Dixon ignored him. Again.

"Seriously. I've counted seventeen men, three women and that little fucking rat of a dog."

"Shut up, and they might not hear you." Dixon used the night vision goggles as he focused away from the house and the lights that made the damn things useless. He was thankful for the standard tech in the Guardian Suburban. Speaking of which... "How the hell did you get a Guardian Suburban without telling Jason or Jacob that you were here?"

Dixon pulled the goggles from his eyes and stared at his brother.

"Simple." Drake shrugged. "Jewell." He popped a gummy bear into his mouth and chewed on it.

Dixon gave his brother the stink eye. "What did you tell her?"

"Not a damn thing. Just asked her to have a Suburban standing by at the airport. She did it, and I'm leaving it at that."

"Jason's going to nuke her ass when he finds out." Dixon put the goggles back over his eyes and scanned the outbuildings. There were three guards on the small brick building. He grabbed a gummy bear and popped it into his mouth.

"He won't find out from us, so unless she decides to waltz in and let him know we are up to something..."

"Like that would ever happen." Dixon chortled softly.

"So, she's good." Drake agreed. He glanced over toward the large house. "Seventeen men, three women, and a fucking ankle biter. What's the plan?"

"Right now, I say we take out those three, get Joy and get out."

Drake made a dismissive noise. "So simple. Eloquent even."

"Thank you."

"I was being facetious."

"Really? I never would have known. And facetious? Really? What's wrong with sarcastic? Have you been reading that damn thesaurus again?"

"No, and I can know words, asshole. Besides, the point I am making is what are we going to do after we spring the assassin from the building?"

"Oh." Dixon dropped the goggles. "We go back to D.C., and I vote."

Drake shook his head. "And then they out you as a murderer?"

"Their witness has disappeared. Remember?"

"Their witness is snoring in a soft bed in a great fucking hotel after eating three fucking meals," Drake grumbled as he popped a handful of gummy bears into his mouth. "I should have gotten the Sour Worms."

"Poor baby." Dixon reached into his vest and

pulled out a bag of the sour coated gummy worms. Drake always changed his mind halfway through a mission. He'd learned to be prepared.

"Awesome." Drake used his knife to slice the bag open. He pulled two out and popped them into his mouth before he moaned, "Fucking delicious."

"Does your fiancée know what a fickle bitch you are?" Dixon took a worm from the bag.

"She isn't my fiancée. I told you she turned my ass down." Drake moved the bag away from Dixon. "I had to come rescue you or I'll never get married."

"Damn, that's right." Dixon was amused and hurt for his brother at the same time.

"Last light is out." Drake carefully rolled up the bags of worms and bears and pocketed them.

Dixon handed his brother his set of goggles before he set a hand on his brother's arm. "What do you know about The Fates?"

"You mean the mythical ones?"

"Yup."

"Uhhh...three goddesses. Clotho was the one who did the loom thing and made the thread of human fate or was it life? Lachesis was the one who doled it out and then the third...Atropos was the one that snipped that bitch. Why?"

"Three women you say?" Dixon glanced over at the house.

Drake groaned, "You don't actually think?" Dixon looked back at him and lifted his eyebrows. Drake groaned again, "Fuck me."

"No thanks."

"That wasn't an offer. Seriously. There are fourteen men in that house." He pointed to the manor and then pointed to the squat brick building. "Only three over here. That we can see."

"But three, maybe four or five over here, versus fourteen and three women who may or may not be mythical goddesses."

"Yeah. There is that." Dixon glanced back at the building where he knew Joy was being held.

"Three against fourteen is better odds than two against fourteen." Dixon smiled and swung his eyes from the small outbuilding to the grand colonial mansion sitting on the ridge of the mountain.

Drake sighed, "Don't forget the maybe demigods."

"Couldn't forget them." Dixon acknowledged.

"Seriously, you want to take them on? We could call in some reinforcements."

"And what if they aren't The Fates? We blow your cover, and it sets Guardian back eight months, plus pisses off Archangel. No thank you." Dixon mentally listed the reason they needed to do this shit by themselves, even though he knew his brother was well aware of the reasons.

Drake shifted and glanced at the small building. He looked at Dixon and held up a finger. "*First*, you told me she was roughed up. How much help can she be?"

"She's a Shadow. I've seen her totally fucked up and still plenty spry." She'd be an asset even injured. "You have no idea of the magnitude of badassness packed into that tiny package." Dixon put down his goggles and extended his hand.

Drake sighed and pulled out the gummy worms, handing the bag to him. "*B*, we don't know for a fact she's *that* Moriah or hell if she *is* Moriah and not a Joe or Josephine or Josey."

"*B* does not come after *'first'*. *'Second'* comes after *'first'*, and *'B'* follows *'A'*." Dixon took a worm and handed the bag back to Drake.

"Tomato-Tahmahto," Drake replied before he popped a piece of candy into his mouth and chewed on it.

Dixon rationalized out loud, "If she's injured so badly that she can't fight, we'll leave. But dude, if we are this close to The Fates and we don't try to—*A*, fuck them up—*second*, take one if not all three of them—or *C*, gather any intel we can from that place—Jason would kill us."

"Okay, if I can't mix up the identifiers, neither can you. And you forgot *D*."

Dixon glanced at his brother. "What's *D*?"

"*D* is Jason is going to fucking kill us no matter what we do. I'm not supposed to be in Washington, and you are not supposed to be going on a rescue mission to spring your lover who may or may not be a Shadow. We are so fuckity-fuck-fucked no matter what we do."

"Granted...but how bad could he freak if we bring home a Fate or two with us?"

"Oh..." Drake's head rolled to the mansion. "There is that."

"Right?"

"So..." Drake extended the bag of candy to his brother.

"Whatever it takes, D." Dixon grabbed another worm and watched as his brother's smile grew.

"Fuck yeah, it has been far too long, and if you ever leave my ass again, I'm going to beat the ever-loving fuck out of you." Drake extended his fist and Dixon reached out and bumped it. "As long as it takes, D."

Dixon waited until Drake stowed the candy once again, and they lifted silently from the small knoll where they'd been watching the house. Dixon rolled out to the left, Drake to the right. They'd done this maneuver so many times they could do it in their sleep. Their feet took measured steps, and even though Dixon couldn't see Drake, he knew exactly where his brother would be. They approached the building from different sides. Each would silence the guards as they approached. The men outside the building were tired and cold, and that limited their movement. Dixon sprang up behind the first man. Beyond a grunt, the guard didn't make a sound.

He lowered the man's weight down quietly and pressed forward to the corner of the building. He peeked around the corner. There was only one guard standing at the front of the door. He leaned against the door, and his low voice rumbled as he spoke on the phone. Dixon pressed against the brick of the building and listened. Whoever 'Baby' was, she was making the man happy enough to reach down and grind his hand against his cock. Dixon caught motion at the other end of the building. He stifled a laugh when Drake stuck his finger in his mouth and acted like he was barfing. God, he had missed that man.

Dixon grabbed a rock and tossed it into the trees in front of the man. He didn't even glance in the direction of the sound. Drake stuck his head around the corner. Dixon shrugged. Drake picked up a stone and tossed it with some speed. The thing clanked among the branches. The guy glanced up but dropped his gaze almost immediately. "Yeah, and then what?" The man spoke into the phone. Dixon assumed he was trying to sound sexy, but the guy sounded like he was in pain, and maybe he was because he was bucking into his hand at this point.

Tired of waiting, Dixon stood, and Drake mirrored him. They walked toward the man who did not look up. Not once. Drake cocked his head, and Dixon shook his head. *No, Drake, not now.*

His brother raised his eyebrows up and down quickly. *Fuck.*

Drake stomped up beside the man and leaned against the building. The guy glanced over at him and then back down at his own feet. Dixon stopped and waited. *One Mississippi, two Mississippi, three–* The phone in the man's hand flew from his grasp as he scrambled for his weapon. It took less time for Drake to take the man out than it did for the guard to realize he'd fucked up. Dixon reached out and grabbed the phone. He flashed the screen to Drake. The display read *Hardcore Phone-Sex Hotline.*

Drake grabbed the phone and carefully placed it so it wouldn't disconnect. Dixon shook his head. Drake smiled and shrugged before he nodded to the door.

Dixon raised his hands and signed, *we don't know if there are guards inside. Be careful.*

Drake acknowledged him. They each stood on one side of the door, and Drake reached up to open the door, letting it swing in gently. There was no noise that he could detect. Dixon went low, and Drake went high as they rolled around the door frame and entered the building. The large area was filled with gardening crap–a small lawn tractor, clippers, shovels, rakes, and other assorted items.

They moved down the length of the building, clearing behind and between items that were big enough to conceal a human. At about midway they both dropped and found cover at the sound of a toilet flushing.

Dixon glanced over to where he knew Drake was hunkered down. The door directly in front of him swung open. Dixon reared up, and with everything he could put into it, he kicked it shut. The body behind the door slammed into the jamb. The door ricocheted off the body and flew back at Dixon. He side-stepped the slamming piece of lumber and lunged.

The man's rifle clattered to the ground, and

Dixon let it go, knowing Drake would be there within seconds. He grabbed a handful of shirt and pulled the man down, colliding the man's face with his knee. His arm went around the stunned man's neck. The other hand grabbed his chin, and Dixon applied torque, snapping his spine. He let the guy drop to the floor and swung around, instantly ready to act. Drake's back was to him, his weapon up as his brother scanned the room for any additional threats.

Dixon tapped Drake on the back, and they moved as one person to the last door in the building. They squared up outside the door. Drake on the right, Dixon on the left. Some things never change. Dixon watched as Drake thumbed the deadbolt on the metal door. The deadbolt on the outside wasn't engaged. Drake's eyes flashed to Dixon's.

Dixon nodded, and Drake turned the door handle, pushing it in carefully. The smell of blood and feces hit Dixon. Something or someone was dead. Drake signed *I'll go. If she's gone, you don't need to see it.*

Fuck that. Dixon rolled into the room and came face to face with a long thin knife. "Hello, Quick Draw. What took you so fucking long?"

Joy lowered her hand which held the knife and limped toward the door. "Thank fuck. Fresh air."

SHE KNEW IT WOULDN'T TAKE DIXON LONG TO put the pieces together and find her, or at least she hoped he would. Actually, she thought he'd be here long before now, especially if he called Guardian. She'd left her Guardian issued cell in her car, and the computer geniuses at Guardian could have tracked her in a nanosecond. Even though the thing was turned off. Which it was...wasn't it? Whatever. She needed a bath and fresh air. Especially fresh air. The bastard on the floor had come into the cell they were holding her in with the intent to rape her. He told her his friend would come in after he 'broke her in' and they'd party. The man didn't have time to think about his next sentence before she'd killed him. Hell, she'd have been out of the fucking room if it had a door handle or the hinges had been on the inside, but no such luck. She was waiting for the other one to decide to join the fun when Dixon finally showed up. Just like a fucking senator. Slow to make a decision.

Dixon grabbed her arm. "Are you injured?"

She glanced up at him. The concern on his face made her feel so damn good. Like she mattered. She'd never mattered to anyone before. It was a feeling she could get used to, real fast. Joy reached up and pulled him down for a quick kiss before she answered him, "Other than having a shovel handle broken across my back? I'm fucking fantastic." She rolled her shoulders and nodded to the door. If she let herself think about it, the pain would stop her from moving forward. So, she wasn't going to think about it. But she needed something else. Desperately. "I need fresh air."

He wrapped his arm around her and walked toward the door with her. "You're limping."

She held up the knife, the hilt of which was the heel of her shoe. The knife was ingenious. It was made of tiny steel pieces that folded and bent until the mechanism on her heel was pushed down. That held the steel into place, forging a knife out of the tiny shards. The small pieces that were present when the lever was up made the material malleable and able to fold down into a pocket located in the arch of her shoe. "I'm only limping because I may have broken my heel."

"Damn good thing we brought you a change of clothes then."

"We?"

Drake rolled into the room and she stilled. She cocked her head and glanced from Drake to Dixon. "Huh." Moriah flicked her knife from one to the other. "Yeah, I don't get it."

"What?" Both he and Drake asked at the same time.

"I heard once you guys were impossible to tell apart." She pointed at Drake. "He's dead, so that makes him a ghost."

"You're a Shadow. We should get along well."

Moriah cocked her head before she grunted and limped to the front of the small cell. It fucking stank.

"What did that mean?" the man she'd believed was dead asked.

"The grunt?" There was an amused edge to Dixon's voice, which was directly behind her.

"Yeah."

"Beats the fuck out of me. I told you she

grunts more than Frank." Dixon put a hand on her arm stopping her. He did a quick check of the exterior of the room before he nodded back at them.

Moriah stepped out of the cell and took a deep breath of air. A small knapsack was placed in front of her. She opened it and looked in. Fucking fabulous. She pulled out her worn combat boots with socks stuffed inside, a long sleeve black shirt and her black camo pants. Moriah lifted her dress over her head.

"Whoa, dude!"

Moriah's head snapped around.

"Turn your fucking ass around." Dixon's hand was on his brother's shoulder, and he spun the man.

"But– that's one hell of a bruise." Drake turned his head and tried to see her over his shoulder.

Dixon growled, "I see it, and I'll take care of her. My woman, my view."

She grabbed the shirt and pulled it over her head. A small smile crept across her face. She rather liked that. *His woman*. She played the words in her head while she shoved her legs into her camos. *I'll take care of her*. Well, dammit, she didn't need to be taken care of, obviously, but fuck yeah, she'd let him...every once in a while.

It took less than two minutes to get her clothes on, her boots laced and borrow a real fucking knife from Dixon's brother. The live brother, not a ghost, which was particularly helpful. She hefted the Interceptor 911 in her hand. The hilt was too large, and the blade was a bit big for her tastes, but she was back in business.

"What's next?"

"He thinks The Fates are in the mansion." Drake nodded to Dixon.

"Huh." Moriah's brain slotted the information, and she nodded, stepping out toward the only exit of the building.

"Hey, where are you going?" Drake's voice again.

She stopped, spun and cocked her head at Dixon's brother. *Was he really that thick?* The man was a certified genius, right? Or did she just assume that? Dixon was...*oh, maybe Drake was the slow one of the two.*

She glanced over to Dixon. "He slow?"

Dixon's eyes bugged out before he nodded. "Yes. Extremely."

"Hey!" Drake cuffed his brother.

Moriah put her hands on her hips and waited until they both looked at her. "If there is the slimmest chance that The Fates are up there, we're going hunting. If you want to stay here, keep quiet. If you want to play with the adults, keep quiet and follow me." She spun again, and trusting Dixon to keep his brother in check, she headed out.

"Dude, I'm not sure I like her."

She heard Drake's comment and let it slide off her back. *Like she fucking cared.*

"Like I fucking care." Dixon's response sent a shiver up her spine. "She's perfect for me. You've got your own woman. Deal with it."

"But she's bossy as shit."

"She's used to working alone," Dixon countered.

"I'm used to working in silence." Moriah hissed at them as she waited for the brothers to shut up and join her at the door of the building.

"See. Bossy." Drake took up position on the right of the door, Dixon on the left. They moved in perfect precision. She watched as they put on their game faces and was pretty fucking impressed with the way they moved out of the building, clearing the entrance before both of them ghosted ahead of her into the woods. They moved silently down the exact path she would have taken. The thickets and brambles thinned about twenty-five feet inside the tree line, and that's where they moved forward.

They paused at the back of the house. The woods were closer here and the open space they'd have to travel to reach the house was limited. It was the best way to access the home.

Moriah took a knee along with the men and settled in to watch the home. About every five or ten minutes someone could be seen in the shadows near the house. Obviously, one solitary nighttime guard for the entire structure.

"Amateur hour," Drake whispered. He reached in his pocket and pulled out a plastic bag. Joy's eyes dropped to his hand. *What. The. Fuck.*

Dixon nodded and reached over to pluck some candy from the bag. Drake moved his arm offering the bag to her. Moriah's eyes skipped from one brother to the other. "Seriously?"

"What? It's stakeout food." Drake explained as Dixon grinned at her and winked.

Moriah's eyes swung back to Dixon's brother. "Are you twelve?"

"Nah, I'm legal." The man extended his hand again.

Moriah shook her head. "No, thank you."

Dixon chuckled and took another grab at the confections. "So, full breach of the back door?"

Moriah slowly turned her head toward her lover. She nodded and purred, "I like the sound of that."

"Holy fuck. Things I don't need to know." Drake shoved another piece of candy in his mouth. "I think I need mental bleach."

Dixon cleared his throat and adjusted himself in his pants. Yeah, *he* liked the sound of that too. She smiled and winked at him before she focused on the house again.

"I'll go in first. Give me two minutes before you follow. I want to make sure there aren't motion detectors or an alarm system that will trigger. The guard isn't moving far from the house, and there may be a reason for it. If they see me, they may think I escaped. If they see you, they will go into defense mode."

"That makes sense." Drake nodded and grinned at her.

Moriah cocked her head again and examined Dixon's brother. It was entirely possible that he *was* slow. "Of course, it makes sense. What, exactly, do you do for Guardian?" She kept her focus on the man but could feel Dixon laughing silently beside her.

"I run the training complex with him." A shit eating grin spread across the Drake's face.

Moriah nodded. "Oh, so your brother can keep you from playing with sharp objects. Good to know." She didn't wait for any comebacks and darted forward. Granted she had a smile on her face. She could really enjoy some verbal banter with that guy. He was...interesting. Not breathtaking and required for her peace of mind, like his brother, but amusing nonetheless.

She dashed across the lawn and pushed behind a bush, bracing her back against the house. *Fuck. That. Hurt.* Her bruised muscles screamed when her shoulders made contact. She ground her jaw shut.

The sound of nylon moving against nylon held her in place. The guard that had just walked around the house made another circuit. Her eyes cut to the wood line. She couldn't see either brother. She allowed her breath to escape before she drew another steadying lungful of air. The man walked past her. She timed her move to coincide with his turn at the corner of the house. There were no windows at that location, and it was dark. The lights from the front of the house and at the back door didn't reach the far corner of the home. She drew another breath and pushed up, careful to plant her feet firmly with each bounding step. The guard turned, and she launched. She used his leg as a ramp and grabbed his neck as her legs swung up around the man's shoulders, using all ninety-three pounds of her person to pull him forward and to the ground. They rolled, and she was up, the knife in her hand thrust into the base of the man's skull and through his spine. He stopped moving instantly. She moved away from him and braced against the house again. Her back and shoulders violently objected her every move.

She moved forward slowly. Just a few more feet before she could get to the back door. She slammed back into the wall of the house and slid down the foundation behind a bush when the back door opened. She blinked at the little poof of white hair that bounded out of the house. The dog daintily moved forward before it copped a squat and did its business.

She narrowed her eyes and glared back at the wood line. *That* would have been nice to know. Fucking dogs were a huge problem. The door opened again, and a woman's voice called to the poof. "Sasha, come in here now...fucking dog."

Moriah reached down to the ground. She felt around until she found a rock and tossed it near the poofy thing. The bundle of fur turned and started sniffing where the rock had landed. Moriah shook the bottom branch of the shrub she was hiding behind, and the dog bounded toward her. Perfect!

"Sasha, no. Come here. Dammit, it's cold out here!" the woman whisper-hissed at the dog before she stepped out of the house. She pulled her silk robe around her and clutched the lapels, trying to ward off the cold.

Joy watched as the woman walked down the stairs. She waited until the dog buried its head under the bush she was behind. It growled. Before it could bark, she grabbed it by the scruff of the neck and put her hand over the muzzle. It whined like crazy, and that was what she wanted.

The woman scurried to the bushes. "Sasha, come here!" Her whisper-hiss had all the hallmarks of becoming hysteria. She watched as the brothers ran up behind the woman. Dixon grabbed the woman, his hand covering her mouth. Moriah held the dog. It struggled against her hold, wiggling and trying to go to the aid of its master, but she couldn't let it make any noise. The woman swooned in Dixon's arms, and Drake picked up her feet. The men bolted to the tree line and she followed with the tiny piece of fur in her arms.

When she caught up with them, she nodded. "We take her and get the fuck out."

"Agreed." Dixon and Drake spoke at the same time.

"Well?" Moriah demanded. "Move!"

"See, bossy as hell." Drake grumped as he grabbed the woman and threw her over his shoulder. "Lead the way."

Dixon nodded and took the point. Moriah watched their six and kept the dog quiet. By the time they reached the Suburban the animal was settled in her arms. Drake flopped the woman into the back of the vehicle. Dixon zip-tied her arms and legs. A thin silver blanket covered her from view even though the windows were tinted black. They closed the door and turned to her. "What are you going to do with that?" Dixon pointed to the white puff of fur in her arms.

Joy looked at him and grunted. Damn fool, what did he think she was going to do with the dog? She was going to take it with her and make sure it had a good life. It wasn't like that woman would be able to take care of it anymore.

Drake's laughter was low and still quiet, "Oh my God, you were right. She's Frank in female form."

Dixon chuffed, "I told you."

Dixon held open the door for her, and she climbed into the back seat of the huge Suburban. Thank fuck it had heated seats. She ached, and she needed sleep. Dixon pulled her seatbelt across her and leaned in for a kiss. "I will always come for you." He dropped his lips reverently across hers. Moriah reveled in the tenderness. She sighed as he lifted away. The dog in her arms laid its head down and closed its eyes.

"Looks like you got yourself a pet." Dixon stroked the fur before he lifted his eyes to her.

"You or the doggie, Quick Draw?" She winked at him, and Drake chuckled from the front seat.

"Me. Definitely me. I'll follow you to the ends of the earth." He lowered for a kiss again.

"Yeah, just scratch his ears, and he'll follow anyone. As much as this lovely reunion is sappy sweet and all, we really do need to get going." Drake's words broke through the kiss they shared.

Moriah waited for Dixon to shut her door before she turned her seat warmer up to the highest setting. She leaned her head back and closed her eyes, relaxing for the first time since she'd received Dixon's text to follow Smith.

Her eyes popped open again. "Where's Smith? Did he make it out?"

Dixon twisted in his seat. "He did. He came to me and told me where you were."

"You didn't kill him?" She was impressed.

"He was going to, but I talked some sense into him." Drake chuckled and grabbed the candy bag out of his vest.

"Stakeout food?" She asked.

"Nah. Road trip food." He pulled onto the gravel road and headed to the highway.

She closed her eyes again. "Dixon, your brother is kinda weird."

"I know, baby. I know." His voice was the last thing she heard as sleep overtook her.

CHAPTER 21

"WHAT'S THE PLAN, D?" Drake drove the road that would take them back to D.C. from Virginia.

"We have to get her to Guardian, but you're dead and I'm undercover. If we pulled this shit off, Stratus won't know it was us, and they won't know Guardian has her."

"And if we fucked up and performed an unauthorized operation, killed those men and kidnapped a woman and her dog, we're screwed."

"I think the dog is the least of our worries. Fact, I'm authorized to conduct the undercover operation as I see fit. Guardian has given me the latitude to break the law in order to succeed. I have a coded list of people I can take out."

"I'm fairly positive none of the men we eliminated tonight were on that list," Drake drawled as he popped another gummy bear into his mouth.

"It was an operation where we needed to ensure complete silence. We've done these operations overseas before."

"Overseas and sanctioned through Guardian." Drake reminded him.

"This mission is sanctioned. We're covered. I'm covered, and you were never here."

"Bullshit. I'm not leaving you to take any blame."

"There won't be any blame. We can have Joy, ahh...Moriah take her back. She followed Smith. She figured it out, and she takes the credit for bringing in a Fate."

"But the kills, D. She's a Shadow, and she isn't an authorized agent within the United States."

"Archangel authorized me to do what was necessary to protect Dixon." Moriah's voice floated up from the back seat. "I'm not worried in the slightest about the kills. They were necessary."

"I won't lie to Jason." Drake shook his head before he shot a glare over at Dixon. "I will not go down that road."

"Nor will I. What we need is a face-to-face meeting with Jace." Dixon stared out into the darkness as his brother drove the car. They were at an operational fork in the road. Hell, they had so many avenues they could drive down it was more like the interchanges in D.C. The roundabouts will get you there, but it isn't the most direct route.

"Where do you propose we meet?" Moriah's voice pulled him from his thoughts. He glanced back at her and smiled at the little white piece of fluff. It was out cold with all four legs in the air and pink belly exposed, completely trusting Moriah to take care of it.

"I'm open for suggestions."

"I have an idea." Moriah groaned as she turned back to look at the woman they'd trussed up and dumped in the back. "Did you drug her?" Moriah winced as she turned back. She must have seen something in his look. "I'm fine. Been worse than this too many times to count. Soft tissue damage."

"Doesn't mean I like it." He'd have loved to make sure every one of the fuckers that took a swing at her had paid for it, but he'd settle for those he took out tonight. "And to answer your question, yes, she's drugged."

"Where are we going to meet?" Drake interrupted.

"There is this apartment in D.C. Bengal used to live in it, but it has become a bit of a landing pad for the Shadows as we come and go." Dixon could tell she was tired by the soft inflection and breathiness of her voice. "I'll arrange it. I just need a phone."

"Here." Drake handed his to Dixon who passed it to her. "It's safe." He added glancing over his shoulder to talk to her. "It's a Guardian device."

Moriah hit the numbers and then put the phone on speaker. They could all hear the thing ringing. "Operator Two-seven-four, good morning Alpha-Five."

"Negative. Sunset clearance, zero opera-tive." Joy responded quickly.

"Standby, zero operative." The operator's voice didn't vary an iota.

"She has to be a computer. Always at work. Same operator." Drake looked at Dixon.

"I don't know how anyone could be that level. Definitely artificial intelligence." Dixon agreed.

"Or the same woman with a motherlode of Xanax." Moriah interjected causing them all to laugh.

"What the actual fuck are you doing with Alpha-Five's phone, and what has happened to make you call at the ass-crack of dawn?"

"We need to deliver groceries." Moriah's statement hung in the air. Dixon twisted in his seat to see if the phone was still active. It was.

"When?" Archangel's question rang through the cabin of the Suburban.

Moriah looked at him. Dixon glanced around the area and guessed about an hour maybe a little bit more. He mouthed the response to her.

"Two hours." She replied.

"Your ward?"

She chuckled silently, but answered, "Both are safe."

"This better be good." The anger in the man's voice was crystal clear.

"I wouldn't call you unless it was necessary." Moriah confirmed.

"Archangel out."

Moriah stretched forward to hand him the phone and hissed at the effort. "I'm going to sleep. Wake me when we get to D.C." She adjusted the dog in her lap and carefully laid her head back against the seat.

Dixon handed the phone back to Drake. They rode silently for at least a half hour before Drake spoke again. "Where do you think we'll go from here?"

Dixon gazed at the horizon. The lights of the city glittered before them. "I don't know."

"You not coming home isn't an option." Drake sent a sideways glance at him.

"It might be the only option." His brother wasn't always on the same page as he was.

"Bullshit. We can do a Fury on your ass, too."

"To what end? The Fates will fill the seat with a stooge that will vote their way."

"And what says they won't kill you or another senator and do the exact same thing they did to get you elected?" Drake fired back.

"Nothing." He conceded his brother's point.

"Damn straight nothing. You've done your time. You've closed the doors to your past. It's time to come home. Let this go. Guardian has the resources to take it from here. You don't need to be involved any longer. If that woman is Stratus, the information they can pull from her will be a gold mine. If it turns out she is a Fate, we've got the ammo we need to take them all out." Drake's voice held a shit ton of emotion, emotion that Dixon echoed in the very fiber of his being.

"It will be Guardian's call." Dixon glanced at his brother. "I'm ready to come home, but all of this, it is bigger than either you or me. If it comes down to the safety of this country or my ass being back on South Dakota soil, you know which option will win."

Drake slid his eyes to his brother. They exchanged stares for several seconds before Drake nodded and turned his attention back to the roadway.

CHAPTER 22

"Why the fuck did we stop at a supermarket again?" Drake carried two totes up the stairs as did Dixon.

"Because she is living on a fixed income and she's sweet." Moriah was walking stiffly in front of them. She wanted to carry a tote, but Dixon was damned if he was going to allow the woman to put any additional strain on her back and shoulders. They'd parked the SUV and made sure the dog and the woman were warm, well secured and out of public view before they made their way into the building.

Moriah lifted a hand and pointed to the apartment on the right. "That's where he's waiting." She kept walking and rapped gently on the door in front of her.

They were silent in the hall. The small shuffling sounds on the other side of the door could be easily detected. The door opened with only a small gold chain between them and a tiny old woman. Dixon saw her smile before the door shut, the chain rattled and then it reopened.

"Nancy! What a wonderful surprise! What are you doing here so early?" Dixon watched as 'Nancy' gently hugged the frail older woman.

"Mrs. Henshaw, my friends and I are going to be staying next door for a short while, and we noticed the refrigerator isn't working. Do you think you'll have room to store our groceries?" Moriah waved at the four totes they were carrying.

"But of course, dear. Please, come in! I'll make coffee."

"I will, just for a little bit, but these guys have been traveling all night. They are going to go into the apartment and grab some sleep." Moriah exchanged a set of keys for one of the totes he was carrying. "Just set them by the door, I'll get them." She narrowed her eyes at Dixon, daring him to object.

"Not a problem, *Nancy*." Drake placed a very light emphasis on the name as he leaned forward and placed the totes he carried by the door. Dixon followed suit with the other bag.

Dixon listened to the two women as they slowly made their way down the hall. For some reason, making sure the old lady was okay was a priority for Joy or Nancy or Moriah...he sighed. What he didn't know about the woman could fill a terabyte hard drive. What he *did* know, were the important things. He knew *her*. The name she went by wasn't important. What mattered was all the moments they'd spent together. The times where she was the only sanity in his life when it spiraled out of control. The small secluded seconds when they were completely honest with each other, when they exposed their battered souls and damaged hearts, those were the important times. Those honest glimpses were what mattered. A name, a profession, or even their fucked-up pasts, didn't matter.

Drake cleared his throat, snapping Dixon back to the hall where he stood. He gave his brother a fake smile, dangled the key from his hand and asked, "Ready to face the music?"

"No, not really," Drake responded but moved to the other apartment door anyway.

Dixon inserted the key and opened the door. The short hallway was tiny, and between the two of them, they filled it. Drake slowed for a moment, causing Dixon to bump into him. He gave his brother a shove.

"So, tell me why I'm having this conversation, in person with *both* of you. And you'd better make it good because I'm thinking of throttling you both at the moment." Jason's gravelly voice floated around his brother, who was still blocking his way.

Dixon gave Drake another shove. Jason stood in the small—okay, fucking tiny—front room, wearing blue jeans and a grey sweatshirt with faded blue lettering that read United States Air Force. Beside him sat a person Dixon wasn't expecting. Gabriel sat in the only chair that would hold someone his size.

Drake slid over into the micro kitchen and Dixon followed suit. They may or may not have been using the high counter between them as shelter. Drake gave him a quick look. Yeah, they were using it, and they both knew it.

Dixon leaned forward and placed his elbows on the counter, staring at the two men in front of him. Neither looked happy.

"Talk now and don't leave anything out."

"Shit went downhill the second I stepped foot in New York." He shook his head. "Not one damn thing went according to plan."

"I've heard." Jason's arms crossed over his chest.

"From Moriah?" Dixon countered.

Jason lifted his chin. "She wasn't supposed to reveal herself to you."

"It wouldn't have mattered. She was taken by Stratus, and I was getting her back at any cost." Dixon was laying that fact out there. She was his, and that needed to be known.

"I'll be dead in my grave if I don't show when he calls, " Drake added.

Jason glanced at Gabriel who smiled and held out his hand.

"Fuck." Jason groaned and reached into his back pocket, withdrew his wallet and handed the man a crisp one hundred dollar bill.

Dixon glanced at his brother, who shot him

a look at the exact same time. Dixon swung his attention to the two men in front of him. "The bet was?"

"Not what you'd imagine." Gabriel folded the bill and placed it on the table. "I bet Jason your fucking father wouldn't break you."

Both Dixon and Drake swiveled their attention to Jason. "You bet against me?" Dixon felt like he'd been sucker punched.

"No, I countered his bet because I knew you were stronger than that. I told him you'd complete the mission without dragging your twin into it." Jason chuckled. "I would never bet against my men or my family, and I consider you both."

Well hell, didn't that set a man on his ass?

"Start from the beginning. We need to know everything." Jason pulled out a stool from the other side of the bar and sat down. The thing groaned under his weight.

Dixon leaned back against the refrigerator, but before he could start the door opened, and Moriah walked in. She stood beside him and crossed her arms. There was a tiny flinch. She was hurting. Dixon lifted his arm and dropped it across her shoulder giving her a little tug.

She held firm for all of two seconds before she melted into his side.

"From the beginning." Jason repeated.

Dixon returned his attention to Jason and began, "Well, from the get-go the entire mission took a radical right-hand turn. I got into town and immediately let it be known I was back..."

MAKE IT STOP ALREADY! MORIAH WANTED nothing more than to take a shower and shut the men in the apartment the hell up. They'd beaten the horse. The damn thing was dead. Past skeletal, down to dust and the dust had been blown away. Fucking hell, they could talk.

"Isn't that right?"

She blinked up at Dixon. "What?"

"I said you needed to see a doctor."

She pulled away and bit down on a wince. "I'm fine." Her tone carried all the *don't fuck with me* attitude she could shove into two words.

"Sure, you are." She turned her glare on Dixon's brother. The man had a smart mouth.

"What? I saw the bruise across your back.

I'd be down for the count with an injury like that." Drake shrugged.

Moriah twisted her neck, and it cracked before she spoke. "Then you're a wuss."

All four men laughed. She cocked her head and observed them. Her delivery must have been off. That wasn't meant as a joke.

"Everyone is clear on the way forward?" Gabriel asked. Moriah didn't *not* like the plan. It was...well it was not entirely comfortable, but to be with Dixon, she'd walk barefoot over broken glass.

Dixon glanced at his brother before he looked down at her. She shrugged and regretted it immediately. He saw her wince and nodded. "We'll leave now."

"The woman should be waking up within the next hour or so," Drake interjected as he tossed the keys to Archangel.

"Got it."

"Before you go, Dixon, we need a word," Gabriel said, and Moriah understood she was dismissed. She stepped out of the small apartment and glanced at Mrs. Henshaw's door. She'd call the woman tomorrow and let her know they had to leave suddenly and to please use the groceries so they wouldn't go to waste. Moriah hated the fact that the woman's children didn't check on her. They'd wanted to put her into a nursing home. It would have killed the woman's spirit. Damn good thing Bengal had set up a support system for her. Hell, they'd even started paying her rent. Lycos had made a letter up and sent it to her telling her the rent was being subsidized by a new government program. They'd each contributed to the fund to make sure Mrs. Henshaw didn't have to choose between rent, heat or food.

Drake followed her out and shut the door. "You're good for him."

She glanced at the door across the hall and whispered, "I'm an assassin."

"And?"

"And? How can an assassin be good for anyone?" She crossed her arms and leaned against the wall carefully.

"He doesn't see what you do for a living. He sees who you are as a person."

"A killer is a killer."

"Then we are all damned to hell and should just blow our brains out." The sarcasm dripped off Drake's words.

"Probably, but I'm too damn busy to worry about your dilemmas." She wasn't going to back down to this guy. She loved his brother, but she wasn't so sure she even *liked* this one.

Drake sighed and glanced at the door he'd just closed. "Listen, I don't know you. You don't know me, but we both care for that lug more than just about anything in the world. I know you'd die to protect him and so would I. Why don't we cut through the shit? You hurt him, and I'll hunt your ass down, and I will kill you."

For the first time since she'd planted herself inside that SUV last night, she smiled. This guy had just climbed up ten or twenty rungs on her respect ladder. "You could try." She lifted an eyebrow in challenge.

He stared at her for about thirty seconds before he nodded. Once. *Challenge accepted*. Not that she'd ever give him the opportunity. She'd cut off her arm before she'd hurt Dixon.

"I approve, by the way."

"I don't need your approval," she spat automatically before she cocked her head and glared at him. "What exactly do you approve of?"

He chuckled. "You and him. Together, the

two of you somehow make sense. You're not who I'd choose for him." Drake leaned back against the wall and mimicked her stance. "But then again, this decision is one I am happy I wasn't involved in. He's healing and finally moving forward. With you. That is what I approve of. The fact that he's coming into his own, which is all I ever wanted for him. The relationship we have as twins is unique. The relationship you have with him is one of a kind. Don't hurt him, Moriah."

She stared at Drake. She didn't doubt that he loved his brother. She could see what Dixon meant. The brothers communicated without words or without too many words. She mentally rolled her eyes at the verbal diarrhea she'd heard last night. The brothers were close, and that was a fucking good thing.

This posturing Drake was doing was a testosterone driven mandate he must have felt was necessary. Whatever. She was secure enough in her acceptance of who she was to not give a shit about any other relationship Dixon may have. No matter how close the brothers were. The only dynamics that mattered were what she and Dixon felt for each other. They'd connected. That connection was purely physical at the beginning. Not now. Not since Christmas Eve. Before that, if she was honest.

The door opened, and Dixon walked out. His eyes found her before he looked at his brother. That single action let her know how much she meant to him. He looked for her *before* he looked for his brother. Priorities were easy to understand. Dixon was hers, and she was his.

"Are we ready?" Dixon asked.

"As we'll ever be." Drake spoke up, answering for her. Damn but the man could talk. She moved off the wall, but Drake's voice stopped her again. "You know when I said Jason was going to be pissed?"

"Seem to recall something about it, but I was hyped up on gummy bears at the time, so I wasn't responsible for my actions." Dixon got a fist bump from his brother. Yeah, thirteen-year olds.

"Dude, did you ever think he'd kill you?" Drake laughed and slapped his thigh. Moriah lifted an eyebrow at the duo.

"Figured he might be pissed enough to do it, but..." Dixon shrugged.

Drake lifted a fist and Dixon bumped it again before he said, "Whatever it takes."

"As long as it takes." She parroted the response at the exact same time as Dixon. When the men looked at her, she pointed to the stairs. "Well?"

"See? Bossy as fuck." Drake chuckled and slapped his brother on the shoulder.

CHAPTER 23

DIXON WAS DRAGGING ASS. He watched the comings and goings of various Senate staffers as politicians came into the room. The vote would happen in less than three minutes. He knew the C-SPAN cameras were recording. The digital camera had a red light next to it, and it was a requirement that the light be on when the camera was active. He held his phone in his hand. Waiting.

The clerk started the roll and Dixon glanced around the room. His phone vibrated, and he immediately answered it. "Joy?"

"No." The mechanical voice replied.

"I told you I wanted to talk to her before I voted." Anger laced his response.

"You will vote as we direct, or she dies."

"She could already be dead. If I don't talk to her, you don't get your vote."

"And then you are exposed as a murderer."

Dixon snorted, "And your eyewitness? Where is he?" There was a pause before Dixon continued, "He came to me and told me he worked for you."

"You killed him?"

"You'd be surprised at what I am capable of doing." Dixon lifted his eyes and glanced around again.

"You will regret challenging us. The evidence we have is damaging enough to ensure you are arrested."

"I regret nothing. You, however, will regret the day you decided to take Ms. Nguyen from me. Let me talk to her."

"Perhaps. If you vote our way."

"You know that won't happen unless I talk to her." Dixon looked up as the clerk neared his name.

"Your choice. Vote for us, she lives. Vote against us, she dies," the controlled mechanical voice replied.

Dixon terminated the connection and

answered when his name was called. He stared at the C-SPAN camera while the rest of the roll was called and through the vote. He leaned forward, ignoring his legislative assistant, who'd settled beside him at the start of the vote. "Mr. Simmons, the Senator from New York, how do you vote?" Dixon stared at the camera as he responded. "Nay."

"Mr. Simmons, the Senator from New York votes nay," the clerk droned after his response.

Dixon stood and buttoned his jacket. "Sir?" His aid blinked at him as if he'd grown three heads in the last sixty seconds.

"Stay here and bring me the results of the vote." His directive dropped his aid's ass back into the chair. The man nodded. Dixon glanced at his watch and pushed forward through the crowded hallways and across the massive lobby of the old, distinguished building. He swung into the coat he'd been carrying and stopped just inside the doors. He adjusted the vest underneath his button-down shirt and, after casting a glance around, adjusted the Velcro to close the armor plating. The blood pouch that circled the vest added a couple inches, but not enough that cameras would notice. Dixon slid his gloves on and took a breath before he reached in his coat pocket and pushed the small device that he cupped in his hand. He stood aside to let others out while he counted to sixty as directed.

He took a deep breath and exited. He moved exactly as directed. Straight out of the building. He stopped fifteen feet clear of the door and stood still. Completely still and positioned the large capsule he'd been given between his back molars. Fuck. This waiting was harder than–*Fuck!*

The force of the bullet that hit his chest pushed him back like the kick of a fucking mule. Dixon's body twisted, and he crumpled as he smacked the ground. The echo of a shot couldn't be heard, at least not by him. He'd bitten the capsule when the bullet struck his vest. He gasped. Fucking hell. His chest heaved. He gasped again. A face appeared over him. Fuck, he gasped again. He was never so damn happy to see that fucking eye patch. Dixon tried to reach up, his body jerked, stiffened and then...

"Is he okay?" Jacob watched Adam as he filled a syringe. The ambulance they were in jolted through traffic.

"He'll be fine. Sore as a motherfucker, but all right." Doc answered as he administered the drug.

"Are we ready?" Jacob shouted up to the front of the ambulance.

"Roger, Skipper. You got less than a minute to get strapped in." Chief answered as he drove.

"Get that in him before we hit that ramp, Doc."

"Not helping, Skipper." Doc pulled the cap and injected the medication into Dixon's arm. The needle went into a sharps container, and Doc scrambled for the NASCAR-style seat belt system. He latched the last clasp about two seconds before the ambulance hit the ramp and flew at sixty miles an hour into the open back of a semi. A myriad of ropes and foam stopped them inside the trailer.

Jacob held his eyes closed and concentrated. The wail of the waiting ambulance fired, and the noise echoed away from the overpass. He heard the trailer door close and felt the truck lurch forward before he opened his eyes and reached over to flip on the interior light. "Chief?"

"Good to go, Skipper."

"Doc?"

"Fucking hell, I'm getting too old for this shit."

"Yeah, don't I know it?" Jacob chuckled and palmed his phone. "We made the swap."

"Roger that. How is he?" Jared asked over the phone.

Jacob looked at Doc who'd unstrapped and was feeling for a pulse. Doc nodded and leaned back. "He's okay."

"Now comes the hard part."

"Do we have our doctors waiting?" Jacob asked.

"Yes. It is going to be tricky, but we've covered every base that we can possibly cover." Jared's voice sounded distracted. "Hold on." Jacob could hear a conversation in the background.

"Jason relayed the woman is going to be gold, if not platinum."

Jacob nodded. "Gold fucking works."

"I agree. It's a start." Jared replied.

"Jewell, how long to the airstrip?" Jacob shrugged out of the seat belt system.

"About an hour and a half due to traffic. Drake is waiting to take off." Jewell's voice came across the connection.

That was good. Jacob glanced at Dixon, who looked like death with the blood all over him. "Roger that. Apprise him we are on our way."

"Dude, like that didn't happen the second you were in the ambulance," Jewell chastised.

"Silly me, thinking you'd wait for instructions," Jacob quipped.

"You've met her, right?" Jared joked along.

"Hey! You say that like I'm Jade or something," returned Jewell's indignant response.

"Love you, Button." Jacob laughed as he ended the call.

"You okay here, Doc?"

"No, Skipper, I'm going to cry because I'm afraid of dark, closed-in places." Doc lifted his blue eye up, and Jacob flipped him the finger. Adam busted out with a hearty laugh. "Yeah, I'm just going to make sure Dixon sleeps for a little bit longer. That medication made him seize pretty damn hard. He's going to ache like a motherfucker."

"Sucks to be him."

"It could be worse. He could actually be dead."

"Truth." Jacob put out his fist, and his best friend collided his own against it. He moved to the front of the ambulance and sat his ass down in the area between the two seats so he could talk to Chief. "Where you been, man?"

Chief chuckled and scrubbed his face. "All over Russia. Following rumors and leads."

"Nothing on Taty's sister?"

"Nothing." He glanced at Jacob. "We're back for good. It's killing Taty. Hoping and having that hope crushed. She made the call."

"Fuck, that sucks, man."

"It does. How have you been? Any new kids?" Chief's eyes glittered with humor.

"Fuck you, man." Jacob chuckled as Doc's shout of laughter came from behind him. "Nah, I think we are done on the kid front." Jacob pulled out his phone and slid his finger across the screen, pulling up pictures of his four boys. "They're everything. What about you? You and Taty going to have kids?"

Chief shrugged. "We haven't talked about it." He handed Jacob's phone back to him. They sat in silence for a moment before Adam moved forward and sat on the other side of the opening from Jacob. "Shit sure has changed." Chief mused.

"Isn't that the truth," Jacob replied. "We've been through the grinder."

Adam murmured a soft, "Amen. Time for the young ones to step up to the plate. Unless it's to deter a global threat, a brick of C4 isn't getting my ass off the ranch again." Adam looked up at Jacob. "This is a young man's game."

"I agree," Chief added from the driver's seat. "I want to go home. For good."

"I think I'm still making an impact where I'm at now. Tori likes what she's doing. We'll stay. I can't speak for the Wonder Twins."

"Hell, Drake's got his woman. I don't know where that leaves Dixon, though." Doc glanced back at his charge.

"Fuck, you don't know, do you?" Jacob laughed and looked up at the ceiling of the ambulance. "He's got a woman."

"Who?" Both Chief and Adam asked at the same time.

"Moriah."

"The Shadow? That Moriah? Shut the fuck up," Chief said at the same time as Adam whistled.

"No shit," Jacob confirmed.

"How?"

"When?" Again, Chief and Adam spoke at the same time.

"Fuck if I know. Could be an interesting story."

Adam scratched the side of his face and asked, "Have you ever seen her?"

"Nope. I've heard the code names for hell, maybe five or six Shadows besides Bengal and Anubis. I've heard *her* name maybe a handful of times...if that."

Doc glanced back at Dixon. "He's been through a ton of shit in his life. Not sure he could survive much more."

"Jason said he was doing okay." Jacob glanced back at half of the original Alpha team. "If she's bad for him, she'll have more to deal with than just Drake."

"True," Chief replied. He chuckled. "We're so fucking old."

Jacob threw back his head and laughed. "We aren't though, all things considered."

"Yeah, well tell me this, old man, what time did you go to bed last night?"

"Fuck you." Jacob groaned. He and Tori had fallen into bed exhausted at nine-thirty. Which was a good thing because Jason had awakened him at the ass-crack of dawn instructing him to gather a team. He knew Doc was in town because Keelee and Tori were doing something this weekend with the box he'd had Justin open for her. She steadfastly refused to open it until both she and Keelee were able to spend time together.

Chief appeared three hours after he'd texted. His hair was once again long and fell between his shoulder blades. He looked good. Tired but good. Jacob cleared his throat. "I've been tasked with building new teams. Probably a new Alpha Team too."

That snapped heads his direction. "What? You said it yourself. We're old. This is a young man's job."

"Yeah, but dammit." Chief's words echoed his own thoughts.

"So why are we staffing up?" Adam was perceptive as usual. Chief swung his eyes to Jacob waiting for his answer.

"I'm not able to tell you the reason right now, but we are going to have twenty-six teams. I'm working with Jared and Nic to mix the teams, keeping one domestic law enforcement specialist on each unit. We are blending the responses between the two branches. The shit that is on the horizon is forcing us to streamline and move people around. Not many are happy about that. Breaking up teams was a harsh decision, but the needs of the many."

"You did not just quote *Star Trek* to us did you?" Adam dropped his head back, hitting the exterior wall of the ambulance with a thump.

"He did." Chief lifted his hand and split his middle and ring finger.

Jacob laughed and shook his head at his communications specialist. The man was so much more than that. The team had become his family. He'd never have believed it years ago when Gabriel had given him the helm of Alpha team, but each and every man on the team was a person he'd lay down his life for, and they had proven time and again they'd do the same for him and each other.

"We will be sending them through the complex, getting them up to speed."

"What about the Arizona complex?" Chief's brow furrowed.

"Jason mothballed the opening for a couple more months." He forestalled the questions with a raised hand and a quick, "For reasons I can't go into now." Jacob assumed it would be just a matter of time before that site was up and running.

"Twenty-six teams, plus a domestic branch and a Shadow presence. Damn, did you ever think when we joined Guardian it would ever turn into what it is?"

"What we did laid the groundwork for what Guardian was going to become." Adam's words drifted across the quiet that descended at Chief's question.

"Are you coming to the ranch?" Chief asked both of them. His eyes moved from Jacob to the Adam.

"I'll be back at the weekend. Tori and Keelee have a couple days up in Cape Cod." Adam rolled up to his knees and leaned over Dixon for a moment.

"Do you think we'll ever do this again?" Jacob's eyes were closed when he asked.

"God, I hope not." Doc laughed. "It's time to let this go, to move on, move up, and move the young ones into our old positions."

"It was a good run," Chief added.

"A damn good run," Jacob agreed. It was the end of an era.

CHAPTER 24

DIXON WOKE UP, and he wished like hell he hadn't. He groaned as he rolled to sit up. He knew the vibration under his feet. He glanced around to orient himself. He was aboard Gracie. He'd recognize her bedroom any day of the week. The door opened and Joy...ahh...Moriah slipped into the cabin. He lifted, straightening, and winced at the soreness in his muscles.

"The pirate doctor said you'd want this." She extended her hand, and he blinked to bring two Tylenol into focus. "I saw you stirring so I figured I'd go get it."

Dixon narrowed his eyes at her to keep her in focus. "Pirate?"

"Eyepatch?'"

"Oh, Adam. Wait, you were watching me sleep?"

Moriah grunted and lifted an eyebrow. "Not much else to do at thirty thousand feet above the ground." She lifted her hand again. He took the pills from her and the bottle of water she held out.

Dixon swallowed the tablets and drank half the bottle in one go. He dropped the bottle to ask, "Everything went okay?"

She nodded and sat down beside him. Dixon sighed when her small hand landed on his back, and she started rubbing circles against his aching muscles. They hurt, like a motherfucker, a side effect no one bothered to tell him about, thank you very much. Not that he would have changed his mind.

"Archangel stated there were no cell phone videos posted. A few still pictures, but what they show is the blood. You know gore sells. Guardian was able to manage the crowd at the Hill and also at the hospital, and you died officially at eleven thirty-seven this morning.

"Thank God Asp is a damn good shot." He rolled his shoulders and flinched at the ache in his ribs. He felt like he'd been kicked by a shod horse. "What about you? Did you let Doc take a look at your back?"

She shook her head. "I'm fine. Sore, but I've been there, done that...got about twenty t-shirts, you know?"

"Yeah." Dixon allowed himself to lie back on the bed. Moriah carefully lay beside him and he winced a little as she rolled toward him. "Shit moved fast, huh?"

Moriah's body tightened against his. "What do you mean?" Her words sounded cautious.

He blew out a shallow lungful of air. "Look, when Jason and Gabriel were making this plan, we didn't get much of a say in it. We were kind of swept away because shit had to get done, and it had to be done fast. Do you have a problem with me living at the ranch? I mean, for all intents and purposes, I'm dead. As in a very public, national-level-type, dead. I'm not going to be doing anything but running the complex, and whenever the one in Arizona starts up, I'll be there to help out. That's what Gabriel and Jason wanted to talk to me about. The training centers will be my life. I'm okay with it because the ranch in South Dakota is my home, but I don't want them or me to make decisions for you."

Dixon felt her move. She sat up, folding her legs in front of her and stared down at him, her knees touching his ribs. He lifted his arm and pushed her lush black hair off her shoulder.

"Fuck you."

His hand froze in mid-air. Well, that wasn't the way he saw this conversation going. "Excuse me?"

Her lips pulled tight for a moment before she lashed out, "Fuck you for thinking I wouldn't come with you." She lifted away from him and glared down at him. "Fuck you for thinking I wouldn't want a home or a family, and fuck you for assuming I'd do anything I didn't want to do. I'm fucking *here*, aren't I?"

Dixon sat up. "You are here." He confirmed her words because, seriously, he must still be drugged. What was happening here?

"Then I've made *my* decision. What in our past has led you to believe I'm someone who does shit she doesn't want to do?" She stood and pulled her shirt off revealing an expanse of pale skin and a light pink bra.

Holy hell, she was pissed and stripping.

Dixon's mind blanked for a moment, what had she asked? "Ahh...nothing?"

"Damn straight nothing. I'm my own person." She unbuttoned and unzipped her jeans. They hit the floor.

Fuuuck. Dixon reached out and grabbed the delicate piece of elastic that held up the barely-there pink thong. "Yes, yes, you are." He acknowledged as she leaned forward when he pulled the fabric.

"*I* do what *I* want. Always. Understand?" Her hands ran up his arms, over his biceps and rested on his shoulders.

"I understand completely and if I don't, I'm sure you will help me see the light." He leaned forward the two inches that separated them and kissed the skin above the lace cup of her bra.

"And right now, I want to do you." She applied gentle pressure and pushed him back into the mattress.

"I'm okay with that." Dixon had about two seconds of warning before she unfastened his suit pants and pulled them to his ankles. His boxers went next.

She kneed up onto the bed and straddled

his growing erection. Her hand went to the tie that was loosely knotted around his neck. She lifted it and let it slide through her fingers before she grabbed the shirt tails of his blood soaked, wrinkled white button-down and ripped every button off of it with one massive pull. "That's better." She slid the end of the tie out of the knot and tossed it to the side. Her hands ran down his chest, stopping to tweak his nipples.

Dixon groaned. He ran his hands up the length of her thigh and grabbed the thin material of her thong. She looked down at his fingers and then back at him. "What are you waiting for?"

Dixon jerked it sharply, tearing the material away from her. She laughed and reached behind her, lifting his heavy cock to her core before she lowered onto him. She wasn't wet, and the friction was intense, hot and fucking perfect, but he grabbed her hip. "I don't want to hurt you."

She reached down and removed his hand from her. "You would never hurt me." She lifted and lowered, slowly encasing his cock with her heat.

Dixon pulled her down to him when she finally took him all in. When she settled over him he spoke. "I couldn't. Hurt you. I'm in love with you."

He watched her eyes as they searched his face. There was no outward reaction to his words. Finally, she nodded. "I know." She leaned down and kissed him softly before she whispered, "Don't fuck this up, Quick Draw."

The laughter that bubbled out of him wasn't intentional. The woman never said what he expected her to say. Why would he think she'd tell him that she loved him too? He brought her back down to him and consumed her in a soul-baring kiss. He did love her. The woman. The individual. The assassin. Joy. Moriah, hell even Nancy. Every facet of the woman was a revelation, and he knew he'd only scratched the surface of the countless nuances that formed the person with whom he'd fallen in love.

She lifted and lowered on top of him. The friction and heat were agonizingly perfect. Dixon's hands explored her body, caressing, touching, and holding her the way she would only allow him to do when they were together. He wanted to protect her, to encircle her in his love so no one could ever touch her or hurt her again, but that wasn't who she was, and he knew in order to love her, he needed to accept that fact. He did. He accepted her for who she was. She was his. For some fucked up reason, she had chosen to be his, and he wasn't going to second guess it.

Neither of them broke the kiss for more than the length of time it took to fill their lungs with much needed air. Their connection was too important. When she shattered over him, he held her hips and thrust up into her. The white hot need built and catapulted him into his own orgasm. He lifted his hips and thrust into her before he released. She relaxed on top of him, and he wrapped her in his arms.

The moments like this, where she let herself be vulnerable, were her declarations of love. He understood her in a way he'd never been able to understand another soul. She was his haven, his peace, and his solace when he walked through his hell. He would be her comfort and warmth when her load became too much to bear. It was what they'd built their relationship on, and those foundations were solid and perfect...for them.

CHAPTER 25

JASON KING GLANCED around the table as he entered the conference room. Jacob, Jared, Nic, Jade, Zane, and Gabriel were already seated. He glanced at Zane.

"She's on her way. There was an issue she had to handle." Zane offered the explanation as to why Jewell wasn't in the room.

Jason lowered himself into the seat, and all eyes swiveled to him. "They just touched down. They are home."

A collective sigh from all the people seated at the table sounded. He agreed. This operation had been a gamble, and the stakes were ones that he'd never want to wager again, but Dixon had hit pay dirt. Well, actually Dixon, Drake, and Moriah had hit pay dirt, and he'd like to strangle them all for the rules they broke to find the gold mine, but fuck him if he wasn't impressed. Damn rogue operators, all three of them. Hell, he glanced at the table. There wasn't one member of his inner sanctum that wasn't rogue. That made him one lucky son of a bitch.

The figure of his sister jogging down the hall stole everyone's attention. She skittered through the door, slammed it shut and hit the buttons to frost the glass and soundproof the room. "Sorry I'm late." She dropped three bags of candy on the table and flopped down beside her husband.

"What was so important that you had to make us wait?" Jason had learned his sister's priorities shifted at times.

"Whoa, it was epic. Cassie was here, and we broke the code I found on the darknet. And by we, I mean her. I have no idea how her mind works like that. I would have never thought to–"

"Jewell." Zane's voice stopped her machine gun quick spill of words.

"Huh?"

"Does this pertain to the operation we are working on?" He smiled at her. Jason took in the look of adoration on the assassin's face. Fuck, that man was perfect for his sister. He kept her focused and sane. Which, considering it was Jewell, was a lifelong endeavor of epic proportions.

She sat up straight and blinked at her husband. "Ummm...yeah kinda...well no, but it could."

"Okay." Jason took control of the meeting. "Jewell, we will talk about your code breaking event when we are done here. All right?"

"Sure." Jewell nodded and reached for the nearest bag of candy. She took two pieces, handed one to her husband and tossed the remainder of the bag to Jason. He leaned forward and grabbed the bag. "Jared, bring us up to speed."

Jared nodded and pointed the remote at the screen. Jason read the reports as they'd come in, so seeing the latest from the press was no surprise. The shooting was under investigation. The DNR they'd put in place for Senator Simmons was hotly debated in the media, as were the country's gun control laws.

"So, nothing new." Jared flashed through the headlines, stopping at several salacious ones, and the ones that screamed conspiracy theory. "How did your talks with the Director of the CIA and the FBI go?"

"The FBI and CIA aren't a problem." Guardian had deep ties to the organizations thanks to FBI Agent Cole Davis and Tori's friends at the CIA. Jason leaned forward and swiped his tablet. He started the laundry list of updates he needed to give and receive. "First, after the conclave of alphabet soup this morning, Gabriel and I briefed POTUS and have his blessing to continue to go after Stratus."

Jade's head whipped up at that. "Wait, you mean there was a chance he'd stop us?"

Gabriel chuckled. "Weirder things have happened. Who knows how deep Stratus' reach runs?"

"True." Jason agreed. "Nic, the mansion?"

Nic read off the report. "The estate is actually owned by a little old lady who lives in a retirement home in Boca Raton, Florida. The caretaker was found dead in the tree line. The bodies of the people Dixon, Drake, and Moriah claimed to have killed were not there. The place was professionally sanitized. No finger-prints anywhere."

"They did all that in just a few hours," Zane muttered and glanced at Jason. "Sorry."

"It was my thought, too. No need to apologize." Jason agreed with his brother-in-law.

"The phone call to Dixon's phone today?" Jade asked.

"We were able to trace it to a general location. We got within a five-mile radius." Jewell tapped on her tablet before she sent a picture to the screen taking down Jared's slide. "New York. Manhattan to be exact."

"There is no way to narrow that location down?" Jacob asked that question.

"We don't even know if the caller was actually in New York. Whoever bounced this shit around the globe was good." Jewell chewed on her bottom lip and sent a glance toward Jason.

"And here is where I ask you what you found out with Cassie." He leaned back in his chair and waited.

"Okay, there are several messages on the dark web that I have not been able to break, no matter what computer program I use.

Remember I told you about them when I found them?"

Jason nodded. It was part of the concern that led him to push Dixon into service to find a way into Stratus.

"So, I called in Cassie, last summer, but things went to hell for her if you remember."

"Oh, believe me, I remember." Jason sent her a look that made her drop her eyes.

"Yeah, well she's in a better place now, and she and Van were able to stop by for a couple hours and she's worked with me the last three days. She found the key, and this is what the messages I've found said. She tapped on her tablet, and three sentences flashed up on the screen.

> *Hard drive coding has a glitch*

>*You've finally made progress?*

> *Give me six months. Vista was damn good.*

"Vista?" Jason asked as every eye in the room swung to Jewell.

She nodded. "I don't know what hard drives they have. I know we have Vista's originals, and the information we got off them was shit that could have taken us all down, but..."

"What?" Jared asked before anyone else could.

"Okay, this is just supposition, but what if the woman that Vista was tracking wasn't Jade? We made huge leaps of logic when we determined it was her. There was nothing at the undercover site that would lead us to believe the cult she was with was in bed with the Bratva."

Jewell pulled a pencil out of her hair and chewed on it as her eyes flitted around the table. They finally landed on Jason. "I think we need to pull all the information out again and examine it to make sure we didn't make any errors."

"How long have you been worrying about this?" Gabriel asked.

Jewell's eyes flicked to him and then to Zane. "I just have this gut feeling that we missed something. I can shove it to the back of my mind most days, but it is something I keep spinning around." Jewell shrugged. "This last message was the most recent I found and it was time stamped three and a half months ago. So, if they are holding true to their timeline, we have about two months to go over everything before they have access to what we have."

"Jared, add this to the mountain of questions we'll be asking our newest guest and see if Kowalski knows anything about this," Jason spoke to his brother as he glanced over at Jewell. "How many do you need to work this?"

"Alonzo and probably two others. I just need to make sure we didn't miss something. We'd pretty much set out an answer and worked to that conclusion. We assumed it was one of us. What if it wasn't?"

"Let's go with that assumption. Assume it wasn't Jade and work from there." Zane nodded his head. "Use a clean slate. That will reduce your stress and make it easier to find pieces that fit rather than forcing them."

"All right. That's settled. Jewell, make it happen." Jason turned back to the rest of the group. "Jared, the woman?"

"Ah yes, she's...pleasant." He chuckled and shook his head. "Like a rattlesnake. She has no citizenship in any country that we can find. Her fingerprints and DNA do not match anyone in known databases, and she'd rather kill us than talk to us. We've processed her, and we are letting her chill out before we start our sessions. I'll have to go to Kowalski or bring him back. I believe he's in Mossad's possession at the moment. He might cooperate more if we bring him back to the States."

"No need, Jade and I can go to him. We wouldn't want Kowalski to get anything he wants." Nic offered, glancing up the table to Jason for approval. The ex-Guardian member who'd worked for the Bratva wasn't the most loved man on the planet.

"Do it. I need to know what he knows about the hacker and what safeguards he had, if any." Jason glanced at Jewell again. "Get me a specific list of questions you want to be answered. I'll farm them out to Jared and Nic."

"Roger that." Both Jewell and Zane answered at the same time.

"Awww...fuck, that's cute," Jade sniggered, and Jewell threw a piece of chocolate at her.

Jacob leaned forward and pulled the candy bag away from Jewell before he spoke, "Anyway, back to business. Dixon and Drake are out of circulation. Both are dead to the world, and both are okay with it. Chief and Taty are calling it quits, too. Adam has tapped out. It's time to make the call and appoint the people we want at the top of Alpha team."

Gabriel leaned forward. "It was one hell of a run, but I agree with the decisions of your team. They will continue to provide us with valuable support, but they are no longer the ones we need in the field. We have a system in place now that we didn't have when I pulled you in to run Alpha team. We have expanded, and we need to change our organizational structure again."

He glanced at Jason. Well it was time, wasn't it? He nodded back at his mentor, boss, and friend. Gabriel continued, "We are going to take Stratus down. In order to do that we will need dedicated teams who focus on nothing but Stratus. Jacob, due to your experience with overseas operations I'm making you the lead on the teams dedicated to eradicating those bastards. I want ten of the best teams you can form. Use any Guardian from any branch, including Shadows if necessary. I want the best of the best."

Jacob shook his head. "Okay, but I have about a million questions. First and foremost are these ten teams in addition to the twenty-six we are forming?"

"Yes. We have enough seasoned team members that we can give most their own team. Training will have to be ramped up, and assignments will be held back until we know they are operationally ready, but Guardian will continue, full force in addition to going after Stratus. We will work all this restructuring over the course of the next couple of months. We're open for suggestions and input, but with the mandate from POTUS this morning, Guardian will be the lead in tracking down all things related to Stratus."

Gabriel focused his attention on Jared. "When this gets set up, Nic will be taking your place on Dom Ops, along with Jade. He leveled a stare at Jade as he spoke. "Don't act surprised. You're damn good at this management shit, whether or not you'll admit it."

Jade's eyes opened wide, and she nodded. Jason wanted to chuckle. It was the first time he'd seen his sister speechless.

"Jared, you will work with Jacob. You will coordinate with all agencies and organizations needed to facilitate the teams, and you will be in charge of the interrogation of any witnesses or suspects. Pull your best from the field and bring them up to speed. You and Jacob will run the new branches of Guardian together."

Jared slowly leaned back in his chair. "I, too, have many questions."

"Noted. As I said before we will work them." Gabriel leaned back in his chair and smiled like a Cheshire cat. "I'll be in charge of both of you."

Jason did laugh at the expressions on his family's faces before he spoke, "Which means I'll be left with the normal day-to-day Guardian operations. Thank fuck, because the pace has been killing me."

"Anna approved this?" Jacob's question set off a round of laughter.

"She was the one who suggested it. It seems my retirement wasn't very enjoyable for her." Gabriel laughed along with everyone else.

Jason waited for the good-natured ribbing to fall to a natural end. "We have our mandates. Jared, information from Lady Rattlesnake is essential. I'd rather not use drugs, but..."

Jared nodded. "Understood."

"Jewell, you let me know the second you find anything that we've overlooked."

"Will do." She moved to stand up.

"Wait." He held out a hand stopping her. "I said if you find anything *we've* overlooked. If you find anything, this isn't on you or your section. We are a unit here. You and your team aren't the end all be all here. The buck stops with me. Not with you. Do you understand?" Jewell's eyes misted, and she blinked hard a couple times before she nodded. "Good. Now everyone get the hell out of here. My wife is craving rice crispy treats, and I have to go buy marshmallows." Jason stood, ending the meeting. He looked up and caught his brother's attention. "Jacob, a minute."

He waited for everyone else to file out and closed the door behind them. "We've been tasked to support the Department of Homeland Security. Your contact's name is Silas Branson. If he ever calls, give him what he needs."

Jacob sighed and nodded. "Roger that. Do I dare ask what the fuck is going on?"

"I don't know, and honestly we have enough on our plate without worrying about what the DHS is doing. Just support the man when, or if, he calls. Got it?"

"Noted." Jacob opened the door and waited for Jason to grab his tablet. "Marshmallows?"

"Yeah. Didn't Tori have any weird cravings?" They headed down the hall toward Jason's office.

"Oh, hell yeah. Fresh strawberries and dill pickles." Jacob slapped him on the shoulder. "The fun is just beginning, Daddy."

Jason watched his younger brother stroll down the hall toward his office. So many things *were* changing. He glanced down at his tablet. Most of the changes were for the good of the organization. Others? Well, he'd fight those battles when they made it to that particular war zone.

CHAPTER 26

MORIAH HUDDLED inside the long down coat that Dixon had purchased for her at the local feed store. She snorted and shook her head. *The. Local. Feed. Store.* My God, she *was* in fucking Kansas, Toto. Check that. She was in South Dakota. One of those fly-over states. You flew over them. You didn't live in them. But here she was a week after her lover had been "killed", watching him ride across the frozen field. He and his brother had ridden out to the solar array to fix or modify something. Moriah was sure if she tried, she could remember what they were supposed to be doing, but about thirty seconds into the conversation between Dixon, Drake and Drake's woman, Jillian, her eyes had rolled into her brain, and she'd lost interest. So she'd wandered over to the Shadow facility and made herself a sandwich before she plopped her ass down in front of the massive television. Dixon had found her there a couple hours later. She smiled at the memory.

"Sorry about that." He draped his arm behind her on the couch.

She leaned into him. "What are you sorry about?" She aimed the remote at the television and muted the show she'd been watching.

Dixon shrugged. "I shouldn't have ignored you."

Moriah slid back against the couch cushion and narrowed her eyes at Dixon, laying an exaggerated squint on him. "Don't do that."

His eyes flashed to her and he blinked. "Don't do what?"

"Don't act like you need to babysit me. This is your life. I get it." She did understand that. In the last week she'd witnessed Dixon, Drake, and the man they called Chief, work through a mountain of administrative shit that had suddenly flooded them from Guardian Headquarters. Some sort of training ramp up. So be it. She'd find something to do. The place was fucking big enough, there had to be something she could do...right?

Dixon twisted on the sofa. "No, this is our life. Both of ours." *He took both of her hands in his.* "You understand that, right? I want you here permanently." *He cleared his throat and slid down to his knees from the couch. He moved so he was between her legs.* "I want to ask you to marry me. I want to do this right, so it would help if I knew what your real name is." *He dropped his eyes and shook his head.* "I'd pictured wining and dining you, maybe a big romantic gesture." *He threw his head back and gave a self-deprecating laugh.* "Fuck, I've been carrying this around since Jacob flew it in." *He pushed his hand into his front pocket and pulled out something flashy and bright.*

Moriah sat up straight. Wait, what in the hell was happening here? *"Holy fuck, you're actually proposing to me?"*

"Well, yeah, I was trying to, but I think I'm fu.... Umph."

She pushed her lips against his, shutting him up. Damn the man could ruin a sure thing with all his fucking words. She pulled back and held up a finger. "First, shut up." *His eyes widened, and he nodded.* "Second, my name is Moriah and has been since I left that horrible place, but people here know me as Joy. I can deal with that name because you know that old saying, 'Joy cometh in the morning.'" She waggled her eyes at him.

Dixon's shoulders moved as he tried to suppress the laughter that ripped through him. "I can guarantee that wasn't the intended meaning of that verse." He tried hard, she'd give him that, but his laughter almost obliterated his response.

"Huh. Well, Joy is what you've called me. I'm happy with that name. The person I was before I joined Guardian is dead. Kinda like you and your brother." She stopped him when he started to speak by pressing two fingers against his mouth. "Third, I have conditions to this marriage gig."

"Can I talk now?" The words came out from behind her fingers and held a heavy lisp but she understood them.

"I don't know. I kinda like it when I do the talking." She drew a deep breath and gave a dramatic sigh. "If you must."

"What are your conditions?" He lifted the ring to her left hand and pushed it onto the fingertip of her ring finger before he looked up at her.

She refused to look at the ring. She wasn't going to get sucked into the fairy tale. Not yet. "Condition number one, I get to have a job. There has got to be something I can do around this place. I'm going to go batshit crazy and flip my wig if I don't find something to keep me busy, so you need to find me something."

"You'll be in charge of training close-quarter fighting. We have a full slate of training for the next year, with only two weeks off in July and two weeks off for Christmas and the New Year." He held the ring in place with one hand and reached into his pocket and pulled out a sheet of paper. "Five classes a week, plus you'll be the alternate for physical training when Drake and I have to go to Arizona to assist in the set-up of that complex."

She glanced down at the paper. It was an official job offer, signed by Jacob King. Well hell, she could do that.

"What other conditions do you have?" Dixon slid the ring up her finger to the first knuckle.

"Condition number two, if we get married, we are having kids. Maybe not this year or even the year after that, but I want a family. A normal family where the mom and dad are home every night and there is dinner on the table, stories at bedtime and love. Lots of fucking love, because I only do permanent marriage-type shit, and it won't work if you don't love me enough."

He leaned forward and dropped a tender kiss on

her lips. "I love you so fucking much, and I'll give you a reason to fall deeper in love with me every day."

He dropped for another kiss, but she moved, slipping away from him. She held up three fingers. "Hold on there, cowboy. Two more conditions."

"Okaaay..."He stretched out the response.

She could see the laughter in his eyes. Whatever, the next condition was a deal breaker. "I will never, ever, have to get on a horse. For any reason. Ever. That is nonnegotiable."

His entire body shook with laughter, but she kept a straight face. "Horses are fucking huge and smelly, and I'm not going to ride one. Ever. Period. No matter what. Not happening."

He leaned forward, his head resting on her shoulder as he laughed. Somewhere between the guffaws and bouts of uncontrollable laughter, she got a semblance of agreement. She wrapped her arms around him and pulled him in to her. "Fourth and final condition."

He lifted away and swiped the heel of his hand at the tears that had formed while he was laughing like a fucking loon. "Anything."

"Good. I need you to eventually achieve that ten, Quick Draw—so practice is a must." She smiled at him and held up her hand to admire her ring. The diamond looked huge. She was sure it was some kind of super special cut because of the way it sparkled, but it could have been a rock he'd found outside, and she would have loved it just as much.

"So let me see if I remember your conditions. In order for you to agree to marry me, you need a job, won't ride a horse, demand I love you and our kids forever and fuck your brains out—especially in the morning?"

"Yeah, I don't think that was the order I said them, but that's the gist of the conditions. Wait! I have one more."

"Really? What would that be?"

"I don't want the big wedding thing. Justice of the Peace. You, me, Drake and Jillian and as soon as possible."

"You have a deal."

"Excellent. Then I suggest we start practicing on your 'ten'."

THE MEN WERE TALKING AND LAUGHING AS THEY approached, their horses content to walk side-by-side. She glanced to the right at the sound of snow crunching under boots and saw Jillian trudging through the snow.

"Hey, Joy." Jillian leaned up against the boards of the corral fence where Moriah waited.

She glanced over and smiled. She liked Jillian. The woman was a straight shooter and didn't have any of those backstabbing, bullshit tendencies that beautiful women in the city put out there. Hell, none of the women she'd met on the ranch seemed fake, which was hella refreshing. She tried to return the favor, but being herself was hard because sometimes she wasn't too sure who that person was anymore. But here on the ranch, she was Joy and she liked that. She was happy with who she was becoming. She usually didn't play nice with other women. It was just the way things were, but hey, she liked not to have to pretend to enjoy someone's company.

"Are we still going to Rapid tomorrow?" Jillian leaned against the top board and gazed over the fence. Of course, Joy was standing on the bottom board to do the same thing. Just about everyone on the ranch was taller than she was. Except Lizzy and Kadey. Those little girls were sweet and amazing, and Joy loved watching them play together. It reminded her of the good memories she had of her sister.

"That's the plan." Joy glanced back to the men who were now identifiable. Dixon was riding the reddish-brown horse he usually rode, and Drake was riding one with color blotches all over it. Frank had told her Dixon's horse was a sorrel and Drake's was a paint...and that was as much as she ever wanted to know about the animals.

"Are you spending the night in the city?"

Joy snorted. "City?"

"Well, it's as close to a city as South Dakota has." Jillian chuckled and then got quiet. "Do you like it here?" The question was softly spoken, almost as if Jillian wasn't sure she wanted to know the answer.

Joy stepped down off the board and turned to face the other woman. "It is different here. I'm not exactly comfortable in my surroundings yet, but I do like the solitude. I think the people here are solid, and the things happening on the other side of that big ranch house are important. Mostly though, I am happy because I'm here with Dixon. What has happened to get us here is in the past, and now I'm free to love him." She shoved her hands in her pocket. "I never thought I'd have that."

Jillian let out a lungful of air. "Oh, thank God!" She lurched forward.

Joy jumped out of Jillian's reach and crouched low, ready to fight.

"Whoa...okay, so now I don't need to ask what you did for Guardian, seems like you are one of the people Drake trains." Jillian laughed and held up her hands stepping back.

Joy straightened and shoved her hands back in her pockets. "Sorry." The heat of a blush flamed on her face.

"Don't be. I was just going to hug you, but next time I'll warn you first."

Jillian was still chuckling. That was cool. It probably meant Joy hadn't freaked the woman out too badly.

"Yeah that's probably advisable for a while. Why were you going to hug me?" Joy stepped up on the board again to put some distance between them. Being the greeter at Hugs 'R' Us was not in her future. Besides, she liked being able to watch Dixon ride in. Something about a man on a horse. The silver-belly Stetson didn't hurt either. The men's voices were louder now and almost discernable.

"Well that is a long story, but in a nutshell, Drake asked me to marry him. I told him I wouldn't until Dixon was home, and by home I meant that he was back and was whole. We weren't sure he was going to make it through this mission."

Joy didn't look at her companion. There were times when she wondered if Dixon was going to make it too. Her mind flashed to that horrible day in the gym. "He made it."

"Yeah and I think you had more than just a little bit to do with that."

Joy's head snapped around toward Jillian.

The woman raised a hand. "I haven't heard a word about what actually happened, just call it gut instinct."

Joy shrugged. "He made it. That's what's important."

"That and he's happy." Jillian nodded and turned toward the field the men were riding through. "I was so excited because now I can tell Drake I'll marry him."

"Yeah?" Joy smiled at Jillian. "That's awesome. Congratulations."

"Thanks, but I do have one hell of a favor to ask of you." Jillian glanced at the men and leaned in toward Joy.

Joy's eyes flitted to the men. There was no way they'd be able to hear if they talked low, but what the fuck, she could do conspiratorial.

CHAPTER 27

"IT'S good to have you home."

Dixon chuckled. "For the twentieth time in the last twenty-four hours, it is really good to be home." Crown, his horse, blew out a snort of air. Drake would take that as an agreement.

"How did the meeting go with Jason this morning?" Drake reined his horse around a rock outcropping.

Dixon sighed. "He's got Smith in protective custody, which pretty much means he's only allowed to be in the small apartment where we'd met Jason and Gabriel. He is allowed to visit Mrs. Henshaw, but his ankle bracelet will alert Guardian if he strays any further. They're working through Smith's involvement with our father and Stratus. Jason isn't going to let that slip past him. I gave Guardian a copy of the video. The fifteen-year-old girl turned out to be twenty-three with a rap sheet as long as your arm."

"That sucks for him. He didn't seem like a bad guy." Drake shook his head. "I hope the whole thing with Stratus can be cleared up. Just like our sperm donor to use a mind fuck to keep him in line."

Dixon concentrated on the horizon as he spoke, "I told Jason I'd take Smithson here at the ranch. Don't know if he'll allow it because of Smithson's past, but he could do well out here away from all that shit."

Drake made a noise of agreement and they rode in silence for a while.

"How did Joy take the four-legged surprise you flew in yesterday?" Drake chuckled at the face Dixon made. "Man, did you know that little dog could yap like that?"

"Better question, who knew you were a cat man?" Dixon laughed and glanced toward the ranch house.

Joy was up there with the piece of fluff white dog that he'd had Jacob send on the last transport to the ranch. The piece of fur had charmed the crew and had free roam of the aircraft. It was a spoiled mutt. No, not a mutt, a pomapoo. A Pomeranian-poodle cross breed. Five pounds of fluffy white fur with black eyes and a black nose. It had been staying at Jacob's while Dixon and Joy got situated at the ranch. Tori had taken the pup to get clipped, and it now looked like an Ewok and damned if Dixon didn't think the little bear-like thing was awesome.

Unfortunately, Drake's cat wasn't impressed. The dog chased the cat for about thirty seconds until the cat slapped the dog. That ended the initial chase. Then the evil cat would lie in wait for the dog and jump out at it, scaring the hell out of the pup, only to have the dog tear after the cat and start the process over again.

"You excited about tomorrow?"

Dixon glanced at his brother. Since he'd been home, Drake hadn't mentioned anything about him and Jillian getting hitched. It sucked for his brother. Drake was head over heels in love with Silly Jilly. The woman had indeed grown up. He could see why his brother was gone over her. She was beautiful, but she wasn't Joy. His Moriah. He lifted his face into the wind and let the words of the song he'd listened to over and over again roll through his mind. "Yeah man, I'm excited. Nervous, too. You know we didn't have the best role models growing up."

Drake nodded before he chuckled. "Yeah but look at who we have now."

Dixon lifted a finger. "The Skipper".

"Joseph," Drake interjected. "Wait, that's probably not a good example."

They busted out laughing. "Nah, that man worships Em." Dixon could only wish to be that good of a husband.

"Adam. Justin." Drake added.

"Fuck, we could be here all day," Dixon conceded.

"True that," Drake agreed.

"If I can be half the man Frank is with Miss Amanda, I'll be happy." Frank was their father. The one they'd chosen.

"Amen, brother." Drake reached out with a closed fist and Dixon bumped it.

"Has Jillian said anything?" Dixon stared at

his brother, but Drake only shook his head. "Dammit man, you need to ask again."

"Fuck, you don't think I haven't thought about it every day since you've been back?" Drake snapped. "Sorry. I'm sorry. It's just, if she said no again...I think I'd fucking die."

"She'll say yes." At least Dixon hoped so, they seemed to be in love. He hadn't been around for them falling in love or dealing with the consequences of their own deaths, so...yeah, he had no fucking idea, but he'd be damned if he wouldn't encourage his brother.

"You can't know that." Drake shook his head. "No, I'm happy. She's happy, or at least I think she is."

"You should take her with you to Arizona next month. You guys have been cooped up on the ranch for months," Dixon offered.

"It's not the ranch, man. We both love it here." Drake shrugged. "I'm just going to leave it alone. She'll tell me when she's ready."

Dixon reached out and tapped his brother's arm, pointing to the barn. "Ain't that a pretty sight?" Joy was standing on the fence and Jillian was beside her.

"Yeah, who'd have thought we'd have found ourselves women."

"Separate women." Dixon glanced at his brother. "I don't think I've ever told you that I'm sorry."

Drake fixed a surprised stare on Dixon. "For what?"

"For making you share, for sucking you into my life and almost obliterating yours." He needed to make sure Drake knew that he was aware of what he'd done.

"Fuck, man. It sounds like shit to say it out loud, but the women didn't mean anything to me. As much as you think you sucked me into your life, I can guarantee I wanted to be there. I dove in head first because I needed to be there for you and, you need to listen to this, I needed to be there for *me*." Drake pulled his horse to a stop. Dixon followed suit. They were close to the barn. They needed to have this conversation in private.

"But you found Jillian as soon as I was out of your life."

"And you found Joy. It wasn't because we weren't in each other's lives. It was because it was the right time for us. Separately or together, I have to believe we are adult enough to know that these women are special. We would have recognized it. I know it." Drake leaned forward and adjusted his cowboy hat.

Dixon let his brother's words sink deep into his soul. Yeah, they would have recognized it. He glanced at Drake. The look they exchanged carried more meaning than any words. They were solid. He smiled and nodded toward where the women stood talking. "Joy thinks our emotional development stopped at thirteen years old." Dixon laughed. "She believes it."

"Not like Jillian hasn't mentioned my juvenile tendencies." Drake added.

"Hell, there has to be a common denominator there," Dixon said as he nudged Crown, giving him permission to head to the barn.

"Yup," Drake said before they looked at each other. "The women," they said at the same time and laughed.

"Fuck, it's so good to have you home." Drake held out his fist and Dixon bumped it for the twenty-first time in the last twenty-four hours. It *was* fucking good to be home.

CHAPTER 28

"Over here." Joy pointed to the public bathroom just outside the county clerk's office. "We'll be right back." She tugged Jillian into the bathroom, leaving two identical men blinking and standing in the hallway.

"Where are they?" Joy hissed as Jillian's fingers flew across her phone. Her soon-to-be sister-in-law looked up and shook her head. "There was an accident on the highway that snarled traffic. They'll be here in fifteen minutes."

"Shit. Okay. We need to stall." Joy glanced around the small bathroom.

"Can't we just stay in here until they arrive?" Jillian slipped her phone into her purse.

"Ah, and leave those two alone in the hall? I'm not willing to bet they won't decide to 'speed' things along and go do the paperwork without us." Joy tapped the toe of her boot against the floor. "What can we do to..." She glanced at Jillian. "Go out there and tell Dixon to come in here. You keep Drake out there."

"What? You want me to tell Dixon to come in here? It's a ladies room."

Jillian actually looked scandalized, and that shit was so funny Joy threw back her head and laughed. "It's a one hole with a lock. Go, keep your man distracted. I'll keep mine occupied if you get my drift." Joy lifted her eyebrows suggestively.

"Oh, damn...okay...um..." Jillian muttered as she opened the door. Joy leaned against the wall and waited. One...two...

"Joy?" The door flew open and Dixon rushed in. "Are you okay? Jillian said..." He watched as she pushed the door shut and flipped the lock. "Ummm...whatcha doing there?"

"I think you need to relieve some stress, Quick Draw." She reached toward his belt buckle that was about the size of a salad plate.

She liked the cowboy couture he was rocking. Those jeans fit him perfectly. They'd decided to be casual and comfortable for their union. They both wore jeans. Her five-inch heeled boots weren't cowboy as much as they were Rodeo Drive, but hey, she was in the neighborhood of western...kind of.

His hands snaked out and grabbed hers. "Babe, you can't be serious. We have to get married."

"We have time. At least fifteen minutes or so." She slapped his hands away from hers and unfastened his jeans. "Now shut up, and let me suck you."

"Fuck, that's the hottest thing you've said to me today," Dixon's voice was all low and growly. It sent a shiver across her body. The man was deliciously possessive, and because it was Dixon, that implied ownership thrilled her.

His zipper dropped a split second before his jeans and boxers. Joy dropped to her knees and consumed him. His cock plumped in her mouth and fuck, it was delicious. Perfectly delicious. She lifted the heavy length and licked to his balls, giving each the attention Dixon loved. Her hand stroked his shaft. She moved back to his cock head and sucked him in, rolling her tongue around his crown. His hands snaked into her hair and his hips rolled. *That's it babe, get lost and give it to me.* Dixon groaned and his hips stuttered with small cautious thrusts. She grabbed his hips and pulled him toward her, encouraging him to let go. And let go he did. She sucked hard, putting intense pressure on his wide mushroom head. Her hand slid quickly up and down his shaft while her other hand reached his balls and tugged them. Dixon slapped his hand against the tile wall. The sound echoed in the small space. The tangy, salty release of pre-cum coated her tongue. Joy doubled her efforts and drove her man crazy. Both of Dixon's hands found the back of her head, and he held her as he took over, thrusting into her mouth. His breathing was harsh and loud. His breathless grunt when he came was music to her ears. She sucked and licked him clean before gracefully rising from her knees. She reached up and he lowered, joining her lips with his. Fuck, she would never get enough of this man. Never.

"I think you sucked all the stress right out of

me." Dixon slumped against the wall when she stepped away.

"Good." She winked at him and opened her bag before she turned to the mirror. Her hair needed a brush run through it. Her lips were swollen and darker than usual.

She pulled out her brush, closed her eyes and ran it through her hair. Dixon liked her hair. His hands were always playing with it. She heard Dixon zip up and felt him move behind her. His hands landed on her shoulders and his lips hovered near her ear. "Am I going to find out what caused this impromptu blow job?"

"Sure you are, Quick Draw. Someday." She glanced at her watch. Perfect. Hopefully there were no further delays, although she could spend some time with her legs wrapped around her personal cowboy. She laughed and twisted to kiss him. "Are you ready to get married?"

"I thought I was before, but now, bring it on. Right now, an earthquake couldn't stress me out."

She heard voices in the hall and smiled. "Right. That's a good thing, Quick Draw, because I only do stress free weddings." Joy flipped the lock and opened the door. She recognized most of the people in the hall, some in more intimate detail than others. Her eyes flicked to the handsome one in the three piece suit and his husband. Yep, endurance. She let her eyes flit over the rest of the group. So much for a small wedding.

"Holy Shit!" Dixon's face lit up with a huge smile. "Skipper? Jared? Jason? Oh fuck, is everyone here?" Dixon fell into hardy hugs and back slaps.

Joy slid out the door and moved away from the crowd. The twins and Jillian were engulfed in men and women. Dixon's head swung this way and that, searching for her. He found her and beckoned her to him. She shook her head and winked. She didn't "people" well. This was his thing, not hers.

"Thank you." Frank Marshall's voice didn't surprise her. She'd seen Miss Amanda and Frank sauntering down the hall when they'd escaped the bathroom.

Her brow furrowed when she looked at him. "For what?"

"For letting Jillian and Drake hijack your

wedding plans," Amanda said as she rejoined her husband after hugging Dixon, Drake and Jillian. Thank God she didn't try to hug Joy. That would have been awkward.

Joy nodded and regarded the laughing mass of humanity huddled in the small hall.

"Does he know yet?" Frank asked.

"No, he thinks everyone is here for Dixon, and so does everyone else." Amanda chuckled and beamed a huge smile at her. "When is Jillian supposed to drop the hint?"

"We have to go to the clerk's office. She said she'd do it there. They can get the license today just like Dixon and I are, and the judge has time to do the double ceremony."

"What about the fact that they don't..." Amanda's words drifted away.

"Jason has provided new identification that they will be using." Joy didn't care what name was on the license, she just wanted to know she was married.

"Oh. I guess that will work. For now." Frank nodded his head.

Joy slid her eyes in his direction. "For now?"

Frank grunted and nodded toward the group. A smile split Dixon's face as he pushed through the crowd. He bent down and kissed Joy soundly on the lips before he hugged Amanda and then did the same to Frank.

He grabbed her hand. "Are you ready?" Joy nodded and Dixon let out a whistle, stopping all conversation. "We need our witnesses."

Joy watched as Drake and Jillian made their way through the crowd. They all filed into the clerk's office. Dixon smiled at the woman behind the counter. She seemed to be over-whelmed as she watched all the people trail through the door. "Can I help you?"

"Yes. We need to get our license. Then we have an appointment with Judge Carsten." Dixon pulled Joy to him. Which wasn't awkward at all. She snorted at that thought which earned her some sniggers from the peanut gallery. Dixon provided the clerk their false identity. Again, Joy wondered if marrying a person with a fake ID made the marriage null and void? Even if the participants were in fact assuming the names as their permanent personas? Whatever. She was marrying the man she loved, and fuck what anyone else thought.

"Here you go, sir. Judge Carsten's chambers

are out the door, to the right, up the flight of stairs, take another right and it is the second office on the right."

As Dixon picked up their license and handed Joy back her fake identification, Jillian cleared her throat. "Ma'am, we'll need ours as well." She laid out her driver's license and forty dollars.

The room went silent. Drake glanced around and lowered his voice as he spoke to Jillian. Joy assumed he was trying to keep the conversation private. She hadn't been around this inner circle of people for long, but one thing she did know was that not much was done in a vacuum. Well, sex was private, unless someone was waiting in a closet to rifle through her employer's desk. She glanced at the two men and a sly smile crossed her face. Stamina. Yep. In spades.

She tuned back in to the event happening beside her. "... do this? Are you sure?" Joy's eyes popped to Dixon's brother. Oh, fuck her standing. Were those tears? The man's hands were shaking. She glanced at the rest of the macho men around him expecting a few sneers, but not one person looked anything but happy.

"I'm sure. He's home and you're both happy and whole again. I love you." Jillian whispered and everyone in the fucking room cheered. Well, except the clerk and Joy. Joy shrugged at the poor little mouse of a clerk. The woman rolled her eyes and pulled Jillian's identification toward her and started typing again.

Joy was swallowed up in a hug. Dixon surrounded her and lifted her off her feet, carrying her to the corner of the room. "Are you okay with this?"

Joy put her hands on her hips and stared at him. "I'm here, aren't I? Jillian asked me if it was okay. She thought it would be important to both of you if we did a double wedding ceremony."

"And all the family?"

"Well, yah, that was her idea. Not mine." Joy leaned over and peeked at the crowd before she righted again and returned her gaze to her soon-to-be husband. "You know I don't 'people' well."

"We can ask them to wait outside the judge's chamber." Dixon pushed her hair back from her face as she stared up at him.

"Now that's just rude." She crossed her arms. "I thought you liked these people."

Dixon gave her a quizzical look. "They are my family. Of course I like them."

"Then it would be rude, and you're not that kind of person." She lifted a finger. "I am, but I'm not a selfish bitch, so I'll just go with the flow today. That cool with you?"

He dropped his forehead to hers. "Have I told you today how much I love you?"

"Huh, no, but I get it, Quick Draw." She pushed him up and nodded toward the suddenly silent room. "Lead the way. I think these people are here to see you and your brother get married."

Dixon smiled down at her. "Take my hand, Moriah. I promise I'll always lead the way."

She snorted and shook her head. "Bullshit, Quick Draw. You'll lead when it's your turn."

"Oh fuck, I think I'm in love with this woman." The man she knew as Jacob King crowed as they walked back to the group.

"Too bad, big guy. She's mine." Dixon laughed and elbowed his way through the throng of people in front of him.

EPILOGUE

"DID THEY EVEN TALK?" Drake pushed his heel against the wooden slats of the porch that circled his and Dixon's house and snuggled closer to Jillian on the porch swing. The heaters they'd installed in the ceiling of the porch kept the outdoor area warm even in the middle of winter.

"Not really. I mean, Frank'd say something, and Joy'd grunt, and then fifteen or twenty minutes later she'd say something, and he'd grunt." Jillian laid her head on his shoulder and laughed. "They didn't need any conversation. Did not need it. I mean, they were perfectly content to just...be."

"I'm happy Dixon found her. He loves her."

Drake dropped a kiss on top of Jillian's head.

"They are perfect for each other." Jillian laughed and craned her head back so Drake could see her smile. "I'm not the only one who doesn't like horses!"

"What are the odds that we'd both end up with women who were afraid of those gentle giants."

"I'm not afraid of horses." Drake and Jillian both jumped at Joy's words. She exited the house with Dixon behind her. Sasha, the white poof of fur, barked and tried to jump up on the chair where Cat was perched. Cat glowered down at the offending canine and dropped off her perch. She scampered into the house after swatting at the dog. Sasha barked happily and damn near levitated into the house following Cat. They played like that all day long. Dixon was fighting a smile at the uproar, which didn't help Drake's laughter.

"You *are* afraid of horses." Drake returned to the conversation because he loved taunting Joy. For an assassin, she was easy to rile up. Joy shot him a death glare, but that only egged him on. He chuckled, "Go for a ride with me if you're not afraid. I double dog dare you."

Dixon put his arm over her shoulder and pulled her into a hug. The woman was pocket sized. Tiny, but from what Anubis had told him, she was one deadly asset. He'd seen what she'd done to the man in the cell and the guard outside the mansion, but her diminutive size made it difficult to believe.

"Leave her alone, Drake," Jillian admonished with a laughed reprimand.

"I can fight my own battles." Joy's muffled response shot back. She glanced at Jillian and winked. "But thank you for handling my light work."

Jill smiled at her. "I know you don't need the assist, but I got your back, girlfriend." She slapped Drake on the leg. "Come on, Frank will have a fit if we're late."

Drake lifted out of the swing and helped Jillian up. They switched off the heater on the way down the steps.

"Why a middle of the week dinner?" Jillian asked as they walked two-by- two up to the main house.

Dixon turned back and answered her. "He said he had something to tell us. Don't know what."

They fell into silence as they walked. Huge snowflakes fluttered down from the heavens like feathers. Joy lifted a hand, and they all watched as a large flake landed on her finger and melted away. Her wedding band caught Drake's eye. They were both married. It was a miracle and a blessing. They both were afforded a life they never thought they'd have.

"It is so beautiful and peaceful here." Joy glanced back quickly as if she was embarrassed to have said the words.

"That's why this is home," Jillian sighed. "It has always felt like that to me." She glanced up at Drake and smiled.

Joy shot them a quick look before she gazed up into Dixon's eyes and a wide smile spread across her face. "It feels like home to me, too."

Drake had watched Dixon kiss a multitude of women, but tonight, what he saw was different. It was reverent. He recognized the emotion. It was the way *he* looked at Jillian, as if the world wasn't complete without her—because it wasn't. He gazed down at Jillian, who turned from watching Dixon kiss Joy and met his eyes with a loving smile.

"We are complete now."

Drake shot a glance at his brother and then nodded. He brushed a snowflake out of Jillian's hair. "We are, and I love you." He lowered for a kiss and was smacked in the back of the head with a snowball. Ice water melted down his neck.

"Asshole!" Drake shouted as Jillian laughed and shrieked, ducking another snowball heading their way. They both dipped down and gathered handfuls of snow. Drake laughed as he lobbed many poorly formed snowballs at his brother. They dashed up the trail, hiding behind their wives and laughing when the ladies verbally shredded them for being giant wusses. He finally threw his arm around his brother. "Fuck, I'm glad you're home, man."

Dixon smiled back at him, pushed a handful of snow in his face, and darted away as he yelled over his shoulder. "Me, too!"

FRANK WATCHED THE FOURSOME. THEIR TRIP TO the house was a circus of laughter and antics. He rocked Amanda back and forth on the outdoor swing with the heaters blazing. He was happy to have his boys back. He'd talked with Chief and Taty earlier in the day. He knew his boys, and he knew Chief would have difficulties accepting his offer in front of people, so he'd chosen to speak with him earlier. Although Mike was private by nature, he was family, and Frank wanted him to know that. The conversation was emotional, but it was good.

"Have a seat." Frank nodded to the new swing and rocking chairs they'd added to the porch. Dixon and Joy took the chairs and Drake and Jillian dropped into the swing.

"Been doing some thinking." Frank glanced at Amanda who smiled at him and patted his leg with her hand, giving him the encouragement to do what he felt he needed to do. "It comes to mind that the two of you"—he wagged a finger between the two men— "have recently become orphans."

Dixon snorted, and Drake's eyes flashed when they slanted over to meet his. "I'm going to rectify that. I know I ain't the best at explaining things, but I'd be damn honored if you'd both become Marshalls."

"What?" Dixon and Drake spoke at the exact same time.

"I thought you two were geniuses? I'm saying I want to adopt you into the family." He lifted a hand stilling the comments he knew were coming. "I understand there might be some technical complications seeing as you're both legally dead, but according to Gabriel, we can make it work. He's going to get your identities changed legally. You'll be my sons. You'll be Marshalls, and I can write you into my will and legal papers."

Drake and Dixon exchanged looks for a moment. "What about the girls?" Dixon asked. "Are they okay with this?"

"Keelee knows the ranch is too big for her to run by herself, and she and Adam are set. I'm proposing we split the ranch five ways when the day comes that Amanda and I pass on."

"What?" That was Drake.

"You, him, Tori, Keelee and Chief." Frank shrugged. "That's five, right?"

He looked at Amanda who laughed. "Last time I counted, yes."

"Why would you do that?" Drake asked. He was squeezing Jillian's hand tightly. The woman's eyes bugged out, and she tugged at the connection, but the boy didn't seem to notice.

"Son, let go of your woman's hand." Frank watched as Drake realized what he'd been doing.

"Shit, babe, I'm sorry." He rubbed her hand, and his eyes filled with concern.

"I'm fine." She pointed back to Frank. "Finish your talk."

"The reason I'm doing it is because you boys mean the world to me. You two, Chief, and Keelee are the future of this ranch. Tori will always have a part of the land, even though she's decided to become a city mouse. The rest of the family are squared away and will always have a place here on the ranch, but they aren't ranchers." Frank pushed the swing and glanced from one shell-shocked face to another.

"Is that a yes or a no?"

"Yes!"

"Hell, yes!" The twins spoke over each other.

"All right then. It's settled." He stood and was immediately hugged by two men. He gave as good as he got. The boys were family, and family was everything. He swallowed hard and slapped *his* boys on the back. "Come on now, dinner time. Don't make me wait."

He watched as his boys collected their women and headed inside. He helped Amanda out of the swing and pulled her into him.

"You didn't tell them."

"No need. There will be a time and a place to talk about things of that nature. Tonight isn't one of them. They are happy. Let that settle in their bones for a while before we face other things."

He lifted her chin and saw the tears in her eyes.

"Hey, now. None of that. We have time, we have hope, and we have a wonderful family if both of those things run short."

"I love you, Frank. You can't leave me." She whispered into his collar.

"I love you, too." He dropped a kiss on her forehead and sighed. This time, the future wasn't for them to decide.

To read the next in the Kings of Guardian Series, Passages, click here!

The End

ALSO BY KRIS MICHAELS

Kings of the Guardian Series

Jacob: Kings of the Guardian Book 1

Joseph: Kings of the Guardian Book 2

Adam: Kings of the Guardian Book 3

Jason: Kings of the Guardian Book 4

Jared: Kings of the Guardian Book 5

Jasmine: Kings of the Guardian Book 6

Chief: The Kings of Guardian Book 7

Jewell: Kings of the Guardian Book 8

Jade: Kings of the Guardian Book 9

Justin: Kings of the Guardian Book 10

Christmas with the Kings

Drake: Kings of the Guardian Book 11

Dixon: Kings of the Guardian Book 12

Passages: The Kings of Guardian Book 13

Promises: The Kings of Guardian Book 14

A Backwater Blessing: A Kings of Guardian
Crossover Novella

Montana Guardian: A Kings of Guardian Novella

Guardian Defenders Series

Gabriel

Maliki

John

Jeremiah

Guardian Security Shadow World

Anubis (Guardian Shadow World Book 1)

Asp (Guardian Shadow World Book 2)

Lycos (Guardian Shadow World Book 3)

Thanatos (Guardian Shadow World Book 4)

Tempest (Guardian Shadow World Book 5)

Smoke (Guardian Shadow World Book 6)

Reaper (Guardian Shadow World Book 7)

Hope City

Hope City - Brock

HOPE CITY - Brody- Book 3

Hope City - Ryker - Book 5

Hope City - Killian - Book 8

STAND ALONE NOVELS

SEAL Forever - Silver SEALs

A Heart's Desire - Stand Alone

Hot SEAL, Single Malt (SEALs in Paradise)

Hot SEAL, Savannah Nights (SEALs in Paradise)

ABOUT THE AUTHOR

USA Today and Amazon Bestselling Author, Kris Michaels is the alter ego of a happily married wife and mother. She writes romance, usually with characters from military and law enforcement backgrounds.

Made in the USA
Las Vegas, NV
03 November 2021